coming home

Coming Home

This book is a work of fiction. Names, characters, places, and incidents are the product of the author's imagination or are used fictitiously. Any resemblance to actual events, locales, or persons, living or dead, is coincidental.

coming home

MELISSA GRACE

Author's Note

Dear Reader,

Coming Home contains sensitive topics such as depression, suicidal ideation, loss by suicide, anxiety, and mentions of substance abuse and parental neglect. This story is intended for audiences 18 years and older, and its contents might be triggering for some readers.

As someone who struggles heavily with depression and anxiety, I want to encourage you to protect your mental health. If that means taking a step away from this book, that's okay. It'll still be here if and when you're ready. ♥

If you or someone you know is in crisis, you can dial 988 to reach the Suicide & Crisis Lifeline.

Love Always,
    Melissa Grace

*This one belongs to the hearts who wonder if they'll always
feel broken.
You are worthy.
You are enough.
But above all, you are loved.*

"We cannot direct the wind, but we can adjust the sails."
—Dolly Parton

ONE

McKenzie

"MY HATRED FOR YOU KNOWS NO BOUNDS," MY FRIEND, KIA, muttered through gritted teeth, holding her hand up like a shield to hide her face from the other patrons.

A handful of servers at Applebee's approached her with a giant piece of chocolate cake, singing an enthusiastic rendition of "Happy Birthday."

"You love me. Besides, you're the one who said you wanted cake." I popped a fry into my mouth and grinned as the rest of our table sang the last bars of the song at an obnoxiously loud volume. A few people nearby clapped before returning to their jumbo-sized margaritas, and our waiter unceremoniously plunked the plate in front of Kia with four forks before disappearing.

I reached for one, but Kia swatted my hand and shook her head, the beads in her braids swaying like a crystal chandelier.

"You're out of your damn mind," Kia said. "I earned this shit."

"Can it be my pretend birthday next time?" Jen asked as

Kia took a bite, closing her eyes and letting out a satisfied moan.

Ravi's eyebrows shot up to his hairline. "What exactly is in that cake?"

"Pure ecstasy," Kia garbled around a mouthful of chocolate. "That right there is better than sex."

I jutted out my chin. "See. You can't be *that* mad at me."

"Oh, I can," Kia teased, sliding a fork over to me. "But go ahead and have a bite. God knows you aren't getting anything resembling ecstasy any other way."

I elbowed her hard in the ribs. "I hate you."

"Love you," she sang as Ravi and Jen grabbed the remaining silverware. "Dig in, knuckleheads."

"So how old are you on this pretend birthday, anyway?" Ravi winked. "Twenty-nine and holding?"

"Fuck that shit." Kia narrowed her dark eyes, framed by oversized teal glasses. "I've earned every single one of my years. I'm fifty-nine and looking mighty fine, if I do say so myself."

Kia's deep brown skin shimmered gold against her hot-pink suit. She owned a trendy boutique in East Nashville, and her impeccable fashion sense regularly made people assume she was at least a decade younger.

"Fuck yeah, you are." Jen dug her fork into the cake.

"So, where is it you're going after this?" Kia asked, poking me with a long almond-shaped nail.

"Oooh, do you have a date?" Ravi asked.

I snorted. "No. My friend Katie's hosting a game night."

Jen tucked her sleek blonde bob behind her ears. "That's the owner of the restaurant where you work, right?"

"Yep," I answered. "She's been having them once a month since spring."

Kia dug in her purse for her lipstick. "That sounds fun."

It had taken some prodding on Katie's part to get me to go, but I'd actually ended up having a good time.

"And are you coming to group next month?" Ravi asked, his chestnut eyes peering at me cautiously.

I tensed and dropped my gaze to my lap. "I don't know. Work's been crazy. It's hard for me to make it out there."

"Liar," Kia said. Despite the quip, her voice was soft and not the least bit accusatory.

"It's hard." Jen gave me a sad, knowing smile. "We get it."

Ravi cleared his throat. "How many years will it be?"

"Fifteen," I managed through the lump in my throat, picking at a loose string on the rip of my jeans. That was also how old I was when I lost him. Knowing that the days without him would soon outnumber the ones I got to love him suffocated me. I couldn't think about it without my hands getting clammy.

"You should come," Kia urged. "It'll be good for you."

"Or if you don't want to come, maybe we could all skip out and do something together," Ravi suggested. "Just the four of us."

My chest tightened. Ravi and Jen hadn't missed a single group meeting in three years. It had been a lifeline for them after losing their fifteen-year-old son. And I understood because for a long time, it had been the same for me. But the closer I got to this anniversary, the more weathered the threads holding me together became. One small gust of wind could scatter all the pieces of my heart I'd spent years trying to reassemble.

I was supposed to be making progress—not going backward.

"I think that's a great idea," Kia said. "It can be your birthday next time."

The walls of the restaurant pushed in on me like two pieces of bread, and I was the peanut butter in the middle oozing out.

"Or we can all come over," Ravi suggested. "Bring cake and tequila."

"And movies," Jen added. "We can watch your favorite."

"I thought you hated *Speed*," I said.

"I do," Jen replied. "But I love you."

Kia arched a brow. "And Keanu."

"I guess he's okay," Jen said with a wave of her hand.

I laughed, and the walls retreated.

"I'll think about it," I agreed before tugging on my jacket. "I better get going. I'm supposed to be at Katie's by seven thirty, and I told her I'd pick up some beer on the way."

"Is the taillight on your truck still working okay?" Ravi asked as I got to my feet.

"It is." I smiled. "Thanks to you."

"See you next month?" Kia asked.

"It's your turn to pick." Jen's nose was already scrunched with preemptive disappointment, knowing exactly what restaurant I would select.

I pretended to consider my options. "Olive Garden it is, then."

Jen faked a gag, and I tossed a wave over my shoulder as I headed out.

It was late September, which was code for *still summer* in Nashville. But the nights had turned cooler with the promise of golden autumn sunsets, horror movies, and decaying leaves. My brain wanted to love fall, but my heart never let me forget why I couldn't. It sensed the chill in the air long before the temperatures dropped. It was the kind of bone-deep cold no amount of blankets or heat could ever remedy.

The kind that came from losing the one person who was supposed to be by my side through every season of my life.

———

"You made it!" Katie beamed while welcoming me inside through the back door, her honey-colored ponytail bobbing. Voices from her living room filtered into the small kitchen, and my breath quickened. Even though I'd been to these game nights before, I still got nervous every single time.

"Got the last two they had." I held up the six-packs of Lovebird beer I'd gotten from Jackalope Brewing Company because I knew it was Katie's favorite.

"McKenzie!" Her boyfriend Dallas pulled me into his tattoo-covered arms for a bear hug as though we hadn't all seen each other hours before at work. "You brought brewskis!"

I wrinkled my nose and made no effort to return his embrace. "No-ski. I brought beer. Because I'm not an over-grown frat boy." My mouth quirked as I turned to Katie. "Literally, how do you put up with him?"

"You love me," Dallas said, going back to putting the finishing touches on the charcuterie boards they'd made.

"I love you like I love tequila, Tommy Lee," I quipped, using the nickname I'd bestowed on him because he was a former drummer. "In small doses." That wasn't entirely true. I had come to enjoy working with Dallas almost as much as I loved working with Katie. He got on my damn nerves most of the time, but he had an almost brotherly quality to him that I liked. The thought sent an icy chill down my spine, and I took a step back.

I cleared my throat. "So, is everyone else already here?"

"Yeah," Katie answered, pulling her phone from her back pocket and tapping across the screen. "Everyone but Luca."

If I hadn't seen the guy who was Dallas' former bandmate with my own two eyes at our friend Ella's wedding last year, I would seriously question if Katie had made him up. They'd invited him to every single game night, but as far as I knew, he hadn't so much as sent a text to say he couldn't come. What an asshole. Even I had more manners than that.

Dallas tugged on her shirtsleeve. "You left him a message earlier, Butter Bean. That's all you can do."

"Maybe I'll just try one more time. It can't hurt, right?" Katie brought the phone to her ear, her hazel eyes glittering with hope for mere seconds before disappointment cast a shadow over them.

Her shoulders sagged as she dropped her hands to her sides. "His voicemail box is full."

"Hey. It's okay." I reached out and squeezed her arm, annoyed with this jackass for daring to hurt the sweetest person I'd ever known. "We're still gonna have fun."

She nodded. "I know. I'm just worried. It's been forever since any of us have heard from him."

"Like, how long?" I asked.

"Since the grand opening of the restaurant," she said. "Remember he sent those flowers? I sent him a text to say thank you, and he told me then he was doing some traveling. We haven't heard from him since. He didn't even come see Ella last month after…you know…"

She trailed off, and I jerked my head back. "*Seriously?* Shit. Is the guy dead or something?"

Katie flinched, and I immediately wished I could shove the words back in my mouth.

"This is just how Luca is," Dallas explained. "He won't be found unless he wants to be. There's a reason he's the only member of Midnight in Dallas who didn't move here. He likes his space."

"Even still," I said, "it's kind of shitty not to let *anyone* know he's okay. He has to realize you guys are worried."

Dallas shrugged. "This isn't the first time he's disappeared, though it is the longest. After the band's first tour, he skipped out of the country to Amsterdam for a month and nobody heard a peep from him. And he's definitely ignored our calls plenty of times. He'll come around eventually. He always does."

"Are you guys coming or what?" Katie's loudmouthed friend Caesar hollered from the living room, and I rolled my eyes.

"No," I shouted back.

"Is that McKenzie James?" His shout was tinged with a smile.

"No," I said again. "It's your worst nightmare."

A chorus of laughter followed before he said, "It *is* McKenzie!"

I tugged on Katie's arm. "Come on. Let's go kick Caesar's ass at Pictionary."

She gave me a tight smile. "Okay."

Dallas lifted his brows and pointed at me. "But you can't just draw dicks for everything this time."

I held my hands up like a criminal caught in the act. "I make no promises."

TWO

Luca
———

I HAD NO IDEA WHAT TIME IT WAS. BASED ON THE CHEESY infomercial for some commercial-grade blender flickering on the television, I suspected it was late.

Why did these things always play in the middle of the night, anyway? Did people often wake up at 2 a.m. to take a piss with the irrepressible urge to buy kitchen appliances possessing the horsepower of a small lawn mower? The woman on the screen was wearing a hideous orange jumpsuit and was way too fucking happy about pulverizing a bunch of green vegetables to a pulp. Anyone buying a Vitamix at two thirty in the morning wouldn't be making a smoothie that didn't contain body parts, and there was nothing anyone could say to convince me otherwise.

I sat up on the couch and pushed my fingers through my hair, thick with grease, studying the woman with the severe ponytail and too-white teeth. Locked inside my sixty-five inch television in her prison-issued ensemble, I imagined her as my cellmate.

"Isn't this amazing?" she shouted over the power drill

8

sound of the blender. "In a pinch, I like to use this bad boy to shred the meat for my world-famous chili. It's *that* good. It'll tear your chicken up in no time."

Chicken. I snorted. *More like the testicles of some asshole named Ted. This blender can beat* any *meat, guaranteed.*

I fished for the remote, finding it wedged between the cushions, and clicked the Off button.

Sorry, lady. I prefer solitary confinement.

My apartment was dark without the glow of the television, but that wasn't saying much. The blackout curtains I'd installed in the spring had been closed for months. What little light that did manage to sneak inside came only when I opened the door to grab my grocery delivery or takeout on the rare occasion I actually felt like eating.

I hadn't seen another human in weeks. Not since I'd ordered Chinese and the Uber Eats guy had forgotten to bring up my spring rolls. He jumped as though he'd seen a ghost when I answered the door, nearly dropping the Styrofoam container. I couldn't entirely blame him as I snatched the food from him. I'd been avoiding my reflection, but in that stranger's wide stare, I'd seen enough to know I didn't want to see myself at all.

I padded through the minefield of take-out boxes, plates, and half-empty cups of coffee that littered the floor on my way back to the bedroom. The only light guiding my path came from the modem in the corner of the living room that I hadn't bothered to conceal even after years of living here.

The bedroom was submerged in darkness except for the angry-looking red numbers on the digital clock resting on the nightstand next to my phone, letting me know it was just after 3 a.m. I flopped on the mattress, cloaking myself in the cool, dirty sheets. The short trek from one room to the next had been enough to put me out of breath.

I reached for my phone as a reflex, but the screen remained black. I'd turned it off days ago and hadn't made an effort to turn it back on. There were dozens of unopened messages and voicemails that had been accumulating since I'd been "traveling," but I hadn't been able to bring myself to listen to them. Not that it would matter if I did. At this point, everyone that had tried to contact me probably either hated me or had forgotten about me. As they should.

My throat was thick as I shoved the phone beneath my pillow and closed my eyes, waiting to be welcomed into the black void of a dreamless sleep.

Buzz… Buzz… Buzz…

I pried one eye open, attempting to orient myself in the darkness, and the buzzing continued.

Was there a fucking fly in my ear? How was that even possible? I had the place locked down tighter than Folsom Prison. How had a goddamn fly managed to get in my home, let alone in my fucking ear?

I lifted my head off the pillow, and the sound became muffled.

"What the…" I shoved my hand under the puffy cotton beneath me and grabbed my phone. The light from the screen made my head hurt as an unknown number flashed across the screen. Hadn't the damned thing been off the night before? How was this fucking possible? I went to swipe my finger over the Decline button, but my hand slipped, causing me to hit Accept instead.

"Shit. Hello?" I answered, my voice gritty like gravel.

There was a pause and a beep followed by a chipper baritone. "Hello! I'm looking for Luca Sterling, please."

I grunted. "Uh…"

He took that as a green light to keep going. "This is John from USA Auto Services, and we've been trying to reach you about your car's extended warranty. Could I—"

I ended the call and face-planted into the pillow with a groan, my phone still clutched in my hand. The damn thing hadn't been on in days, and when I somehow managed to power it on in my sleep, a fucking scammer named John is the one calling me. I would've been willing to bet he and his buddies were the ones clogging up my voicemail too.

I rolled onto my back and scrubbed my hand down my face before illuminating my phone screen again. I had to type in my passcode because even the facial recognition software couldn't discern who I was anymore.

There were five hundred forty-three unread text messages. I didn't check to see who they were from, opting to look at my full voicemail box instead. My finger hovered over the screen, prepared to mass delete John's shady attempts to scam me out of money. But I stopped when I found the names of my friends and former bandmates stacked one on top of the other, sometimes alternating, sometimes back-to-back: Katie, Derek, Dallas, Dallas, Jo, Liv, Katie, Antoni, Derek, Ella, Ella, Jax, Grace, Cash, Cash…and the list went on. There were only three unknown numbers wedged randomly between their names.

I scrolled all the way back to the first message on May 27, put it on speaker, and let it play.

"Hey, Luca! It's Katie." I pictured her bright grin as her voice continued. *"So, Dallas and I are starting this new thing.*

We're hosting monthly game nights. Our first one is next Saturday night, and we were hoping that if you're back in town, maybe you'd come by. If not, hopefully you can come next time. Okay, that's all. Talk to you later."

One from Dallas came in only days after.

"Hey. Are you coming Saturday or what? Call us back, dude. Where are you?"

A message from Derek left in mid-June came next.

"Hey, man. It's me. Just checking in. Jo and I are in town this weekend so we can go see Jax and Liv at CMA Fest, and we were wondering if you were going. We'd love if you could come over for lunch beforehand. Little Addie's getting so big. You've got to see her. Let me know if you're back, and we'll grill out. Oh, yeah. That's a thing I do now."

"Hey, Luca. It's Liv. Jax and I are playing at CMA Fest, and we were hoping you could come. We're all getting together for lunch at Derek and Jo's beforehand. Well, not all of us. Ella and Cash and Grace and baby Betty are still in LA. Antoni and Nate will be in town, though. Anyway, we'd love to see you. Jonathan and Chloe miss their Uncle Luca, and we miss you too. The adoption will be official next month. Isn't that crazy? Anyway, call me when you can. Bye."

God, it *had* been a long time since I saw the kids. Months were practically years in kid time. They probably looked so different now. Children had never been my thing, but I enjoyed seeing my friends' kids. It never occurred to me that they liked seeing me too.

I moved my finger down and selected one of the unknown numbers.

"Hi, this is John from—"

"Fuck you, John." I skipped down the list and played a message Jo had left just after the Fourth of July.

"Luca! Where the heck are you? Did you get the pictures I sent of Addie watching the fireworks? Seriously, where are you that doesn't have a cell signal, mister? Katie and Dallas are having another game night next weekend. Please say you'll come."

"Hey, Luca. It's Cash. I was just calling to see how you're doing. Haven't heard from you in a while. You know if you need anything, I'm just a phone call away, all right? Hope to talk to you soon. Bye."

"Excuse me, Mr. Sterling. Hi. This is your friend Antoni. Remember me? You know, the one you haven't spoken to in months. *If you'd kindly let me know where you are so I can fly my gorgeous behind there and kick your ass, I'd greatly appreciate it. Listen, I know you like your space and shit, but this is getting a little ridiculous. Call me back. I'm worried about you. We all are. So, call me."*

The next message I listened to came from Grace and kicked off with an earsplitting shriek.

"Luca, it's Grace, and I just called to tell you I'm engaged!" I swallowed hard as her voice cut off midscream. I'd known Grace before she even started dating her British superstar boyfriend. She was still in high school when I met her, and now she was getting *married?*

Her mom Ella came next.

"Luca, where the fuck are you? It's August first. Fucking August, and no one has heard hide nor hair of you. We miss you. We're worried about you. Just freaking call me or someone and let us know if you're alive or shacked up on a yacht with a supermodel named after a fruit. And my oldest daughter is engaged. Engaged, Luca. AARP won't stop sending me shit in the mail, and I still have a baby girl at

home. Is this the kind of irony Alanis Morissette was singing about?"

"Luca, it's Cash. Listen, we got some bad news. Ella's mom passed away this morning." My breath caught in my throat. *"She and Grace are devastated. We're about to board a plane home to Nashville now. The funeral is gonna be on Wednesday at Harpeth Hills Memory Gardens, and we're all coming back to the old house after. It would mean the world to Ella if you came. It would mean a lot to me too. Call me, okay?"*

"Luca, it's Jax. Dude, where are you? I know you don't want us in your business, but come on, man. Missing Ella's mom's funeral? This isn't like you. I get that you're traveling, but seriously? You couldn't come back for that? What's going on?"

With a trembling finger, I tapped the last message Ella left, fully expecting a tongue-lashing from hell because it's what I deserved. Instead, her voice broke, and it was obvious she was speaking through tears.

"Luca, please call us. Please. I'm worried. It sucked that you didn't even come to my mom's funeral. It fucking sucked, but I'll get over it, okay? I'm just really concerned about you. Call me. I'm begging you."

Every message was a needle digging deeper beneath my skin, trying to reach a splinter embedded so deep it had become part of me. I'd missed so much. And *they'd* missed *me*. I didn't think they would. I didn't think I mattered. I'd always been the outsider of the group. The disappointment. I blinked furiously, sending salty liquid spilling over my lids, tracing invisible lines down to my ears. I wasn't like them. They were better than me. But they still missed me?

The last message came from Katie the evening before,

asking me to go to their game night and letting me know they missed me. Her normally peppy voice was heavy with sadness. I'd let her down. I'd let them all down.

Even still, they hadn't forgotten me. I'd ghosted them. I'd completely shut them out, but they hadn't turned their backs on me. I was the one who'd walked away. I told them I was traveling because it was easier than telling them the truth. It was easier than telling them everything fucking hurt and that sometimes I wished it would just stop. That *I* could just stop. I wanted to shut my eyes and disappear. I wanted a second to fucking breathe without this imaginary fist around my neck, choking the life out of me.

My entire body shook, cold and hot at the same time. Every breath came in ragged sobs that made me feel like I'd jumped into the deep end of the pool when I couldn't swim.

I missed my friends. I used to try to piss them off just for fun—always testing the waters to see who would abandon me first. I picked fights and gave them shit, but it wasn't because I didn't care. I did. I just couldn't tell them I fucking loved them. I didn't know how. How could I ever be good enough to love them? Would I ever be good enough to be loved *by* them?

Even when I didn't deserve them, they never gave up on me. *I* had given up on me.

But they were still there. I could go back. I could try.

With a trembling hand, I reached over to the nightstand and turned the light on.

"Are you sure you don't want to sit?" The counselor, who couldn't have been older than I was, peered up at me from the armchair she was sitting in.

I shook my head and shoved my hands in my pockets. I did *not* want to sit. In fact, I wanted to make a fucking break for it. Coming here was a mistake.

Lacey Milburn was the first person who could see me out of the numerous counseling centers I'd called. I'd left messages well outside of business hours, probably because part of me hoped nobody would return my call, which would mean I wouldn't actually have to come.

But Lacey did. She called the next afternoon and offered me her last appointment of the day at 8 p.m. She'd greeted me at the door herself Wednesday night and locked it behind us, not at all unlike a serial killer. I followed her to the small office. It was homey and filled with colorful paintings on the wall, and it smelled like freshly brewed coffee.

This chick was prissy, blonde, and squeaky fucking clean. She wouldn't know misery if it jumped up and bit her in the—

Lacey cleared her throat. "Why don't you tell me a little about why you're here today, Luca?"

"Do you know who I am?" I asked. Not in the pompous way celebrities attempted to throw their clout around like confetti, but in a way that said *I hope you don't.*

She glanced at the leatherbound notepad poised in her lap. "You're Luca Sterling."

"You know what the fuck I meant," I said, narrowing my eyes. "Do you?"

Lacey paused a moment, tucking a loose sliver of her hair behind her ear, and nodded.

I ran my tongue along my teeth, attempting to remove the acidity from my mouth. But it was pointless because that bitterness was coming from my very core. The bitterness was me.

"Then *you* tell *me* why I'm here, Lacey," I said. "I'm sure you already have your theories, so let's hear 'em."

"I really don't. That's not how I work. That's not how *this* works." She shifted uncomfortably in her chair, tugging the sleeves of her pale pink cardigan over her hands.

"I don't know why the fuck I'm here," I admitted. "I'm sure no sooner than I walk out your door, it'll be on fucking TMZ."

"It won't. I can promise you that."

"I don't believe you."

"Well, do or don't, that's up to you," she said, her voice even as a set of parallel lines. "The only way someone will ever know you were here is if you told them yourself or if they followed you, and I tried to prevent *that* by seeing you at a later hour."

I squinted at her. "You mean you don't normally see patients at 8 p.m.?"

She shot me a look that called me a dumbass in thirteen different languages.

"Why the fuck would you do that for me? Because I'm famous? Did you want a front row seat to the shit show?" I fired off my tirade of questions one right after the other and waited for a reaction, but she was immovable. "Oh. Let me guess. Because you fucking 'care'?" I curved my fingers around the invisible word, hugging it. It was the closest I'd been to anything resembling a hug in months.

"Yes. I do care." Lacey gave me a faint smile and shrugged as she leaned forward, resting her hands on her lap. When she did, the sleeve of her sweater slid up her wrist an inch, revealing a swipe of black ink I couldn't quite make out.

Little Miss Priss has a fucking tattoo?

"I didn't take you for the tattoo type," I said. "What is it? A fucking butterfly? No, wait. A sparrow. Chicks fucking love bird tats."

She pulled her sleeve up farther and turned her arm so I could see. "It's a semicolon."

I snorted. "What? Why? You big into grammar or something?"

She chuckled and tugged her cardigan back down. "No, nothing like that. Though I do have strong feelings about people who don't know the difference between *your* and *you're*." Her gaze dropped to the floor for a second before returning to me. "To me, the semicolon represents a sentence not yet finished. It means there's more left to say."

"You couldn't have come up with something better than punctuation?"

Her jaw tightened, letting me know I'd successfully made a chink in her armor.

Fuck. What am I doing? This lady worked me into her schedule when she didn't have to, and I'm being a prick.

"I…" I swallowed hard, heat rising to my cheeks. "Shit. Sorry. I'm wasting your time."

"It's okay." She raised her brows, the corner of her mouth tugging upward. "You're paying me by the hour."

Something shifted inside my chest, as though her witty comeback had made an impact and cracked across my sternum. Maybe it wasn't *her* armor that was breaking down.

"Fuck. I don't know why I'm such a goddamn dick all the time," I said, sinking onto the leather couch across from her and digging the heels of my palms into my eyes. "What the fuck is wrong with me?"

"You're hurting." She said it so simply, as though I'd

asked her for the time or a weather report or if she liked weird grammar tattoos. "And hurt people will hurt other people sometimes. Luca, everyone is fighting battles we can't see."

I scrubbed my hands down my face and blew out a breath. "I still don't trust you."

"I don't expect you to. Trust is earned. And I've got the time if you do."

"Because I'm paying you by the hour."

"Exactly." She grinned. "And since you haven't sprinted for the door, I'm guessing you're not in a hurry to leave just yet. So, how about we begin by you telling me a little bit about yourself?"

My mind was screaming at me to bolt, but my legs were heavy and weary. I was exhausted of fucking running, and if I was being honest, running hadn't fixed a damn thing. Maybe it was time to try something new.

I finally answered with a single nod. "Okay."

———

"Have you had any thoughts of harming yourself or others?" Lacey asked.

I somehow felt even more depleted than when I'd arrived at Lacey Milburn's office fifty minutes earlier. But it was a different kind of emptiness than I'd come in with.

Once I started giving voice to the monsters under my proverbial bed, they all started lining up, impatiently awaiting their turn to introduce themselves. After making their presence known, they exited my body and scattered across the room, staining Lacey's colorful walls gray.

I was aimless. Without the demons filling every square inch of my soul, I felt strangely alone. Even demons started to feel like friends when they were the only company you had. They eyeballed me from where they loomed in the corners, a silent agreement that this separation was only temporary, and that they'd be coming home with me.

"Luca," she said again, "have you had any thoughts of harming yourself or others?"

"God, no. I would never hurt someone," I said. "I mean, yeah, I've gotten into a few bar fights in my day, but that was because I was being a fucking dick. I would never set out to hurt anyone."

"Good." She paused, tilting her head. "Now, what about you? Have you considered hurting yourself?"

"No." I hesitated. "It's not that. I just…Sometimes I wonder what it would be like to not feel anymore. To not be miserable all the fucking time."

"But you don't have a plan to harm yourself?"

I shook my head. "No. I don't."

She nodded. "While I don't think you're a risk to yourself or others, I do think it would be beneficial for you to be around people you trust. Do you have anyone like that nearby?"

I shook my head. "Not here. My friends…my *family* lives in Nashville."

"Would you be able to go visit them? Or perhaps they'd come to you?"

"I could go there," I said. "But that would make it hard for me to come back here for therapy."

She crossed her boot-clad feet at the ankle. "How would you feel about virtual appointments?"

I shrugged. "Okay, I guess."

"I want to make sure you're getting everything you need, Luca. So here's my suggestion," she said. "You go to Nashville and spend some time with your family. While you're there, I want to meet with you virtually a couple times a week to start. But if at *any* point you start to have thoughts of harming yourself, I want you to go straight to the hospital, okay? And of course, I'll only be a phone call away."

"Okay."

She gave me a small smile. "Let's get you scheduled."

A couple of moments later, Lacey walked me toward the door and unlocked it.

"All right, Luca, I'll talk to you in a couple of—"

"Is this fucking normal?" I blurted out, cutting her off. There was a large lump in my throat as though I'd swallowed a Magic 8 Ball with the screen stuck on *Outlook not so good.* "I have everything. Well, not literally, but pretty fucking close. I was successful. I have enough money that I don't have to worry about shit for a really long time. If I can have all that and *still* not be happy…" I trailed off, leaving the unspoken question hanging in the air. *Will I ever be?*

Lacey placed a hand on my arm, and I nearly flinched. It was the first time anyone had touched me in…well, a really long time. It felt foreign, like the burn of a new tattoo or like I'd grown an extra appendage.

"I can't promise you happiness," she said, and for the first time, I caught the hint of a southern lilt in her voice. "I wish I could, but I think happiness is a lot like rest stops. Life is the road we travel, the hardships we face, and the rest stops are those happy moments in between all the life we're living."

"So then, what am I doing this for if I might not ever be happy? Isn't that kind of the point?"

"You ever ride with the windows down, music blaring, screaming your favorite song at the top of your lungs?"

I nodded.

"All that matters in that moment is your tires against the pavement and the wind on your face. It feels good, doesn't it?"

"Yeah, I guess it does." Until my appointment with Lacey, I hadn't been behind the wheel in months.

"The right tunes can completely change the experience," she said. "Therapy and working on yourself is a lot like that. It doesn't always change the road you're on, but it can change the ride."

Her words followed me through the darkness as I got into my car. It was a short drive home, but I made it with the windows down and the music up as loud as it would go.

THREE

McKenzie

"WHAT ABOUT THIS ONE?" MY MOM WORE A WIDE GRIN AND high ponytail, a plastic hanger looped over her finger with a faded red tee attached.

I squinted to read the text printed across the front. "The Sun is Always Shining Down on Beaver Town." My nose wrinkled involuntarily. "Gross. Put it in the cart."

She laughed, and we continued flipping through the racks of The Thrift Stop. It had been our Thursday evening tradition for as long as I could remember. First we'd consume a ridiculous amount of tacos from the truck down the street, and then we'd spend a couple hours hunting for T-shirts with funny sayings.

"Right next to Guitar Man Tony," she said, tossing the fabric next to a gray tee with the name spelled out in license plate letters.

I slid garment after garment down the rack, the sound of metal scraping metal producing a sharp, steady rhythm.

"So," Mom said, tucking a loose strand of brown hair peppered with silver behind her ear. "How are you feeling?"

I didn't look up from my T-shirt treasure hunt. "Fine. Work is busy, but I love it. I forgot to tell you about the mulled cider donuts I made this week. Katie wants to add them to the menu."

"That's great, honey. You'll have to bring me one next week."

"Of course."

"And how have things been otherwise? I know it's…well, it's a hard time of year for the both of us." Her voice was soft and timid. "Have you been going to your group?"

"Mom, I'm fine. I went to group last month," I lied.

I didn't need any reminders to know *that day* was approaching. I'd stopped keeping track because when I allowed myself to soak in that claw-foot tub of sadness, it became harder to get out. So, I was left with two choices—wring myself dry from the memories or drown in them instead.

Still, every year as the breeze turned chilly and the leaves began their descent, crashing to the earth, I did too. I didn't need a calendar to remember a time my body could never forget.

"I'm glad you have people in your life who understand and that you're making new friends," she said. "It's important."

My eyes lifted to meet hers. "You're the only person I need, Mom."

The lines on her forehead appeared more pronounced as her mouth turned downward.

"Kenz," she said. "You know you need—"

"More friends," I finished for her. "A lot of mothers would be thrilled their daughter wanted to hang out with them all the time, you know." My eyes darted back to the row of clothes.

"And it's not like I don't have anyone. I have the people from the grief group and Katie. I've even been going to her monthly game nights, and I've been becoming friends with some of her friends."

She raised her brows in surprise. "Any potential suitors on the horizon?"

I opened my mouth to answer, but she cut me off.

"Your cats don't count."

"I don't know what you're talking about," I said as we moved to another rack. "Binx and Earl Grey are distinguished gentlemen."

"They are, but you do have to shovel their shit."

I shrugged. "Better to put up with their shit than some overgrown man-child's."

"Touché, kid."

We went back to silently shuffling through the racks for a moment.

"There's actually something I wanted to talk to you about." Trepidation frosted my mother's voice like icing on a cake.

"Ok*aaaay*," I said, drawing out the word, an unspoken question lingering in my tone. My stomach tied itself into a knot. Maybe her fibromyalgia was beginning to flare up again. God, I hated seeing her hurting, and I knew that pain also meant she wouldn't be able to do the things she wanted or needed to. What if she lost her job? She'd been working for a well-to-do dermatologist doing medical billing from home for the last ten years, and her boss always seemed understanding, but maybe there'd been budget cuts. Whatever—I'd get two more jobs to help take care of her if I had to.

"And before you get all worried, I promise it's nothing bad," she said, but something was off. I detected the slightest tremble in her voice. "In fact, it…I think it could be a good thing."

I stopped browsing, giving her my full attention. "Well, out with it, then."

"Dr. Rossi is taking some time off next month," she began. "She's going back home to Italy for a few weeks."

"Does this mean you're going to have some time off?" I asked. "I'll see if I can get away from work. Maybe we could go somewhere. Oh, maybe a road trip would be fun."

"Well, that's the thing, Kenz. Dr. Rossi has offered for her senior staff to go with her as a bonus," she said, excitement creeping over her face. "It'll just be me and two others, and Dr. Rossi, of course. We'd be staying at her family's summer home. It's just…it's a once-in-a-lifetime opportunity. I've never been out of the country before, and this is the kind of trip I could never afford. She'd be paying for our airfare and most of our food, all while still receiving our paychecks."

"Wow. That's awesome, Mom. Of course, you should go," I said. "That's incredibly generous of her."

"It is, isn't it? There's just one thing." She paused and took a breath. "It would mean I wouldn't be here on…on the anniversary."

"Oh. Right." My heart sank until it felt like it was circling a drain, only seconds from being squeezed through the pipes of grief until there was nothing left but a few grimy streaks letting me know something had existed there before.

She came around the rack to where I was standing and placed her hands on my arms. "I know we've always spent that day together, and I don't want to leave you here if—"

"You should go," I insisted, forcing a smile.

"But—"

I grabbed hold of her shoulders. "No buts. Brennan would want you to, and *I* want you to. You deserve this."

"What will you do, though?" she asked, blinking back the glossy film that coated her eyes.

"Actually, some friends mentioned the possibility of getting together that day, so really, it works out," I said, though I had no intention of seeing anyone or even crawling out of bed. "Don't worry about me." She seemed unsure, so I forced a smile again. "The only thing you need to worry about is getting some good luggage. Now come on."

I grabbed the cart and steered it toward the back of the store, forcing the lump in my throat down as far as it would go.

FOUR

Luca

THE DEMONS LACEY HAD COAXED OUT OF ME THE NIGHT before had made the voyage home with me, but instead of letting them linger in the shadows, I turned on all the lights and set about doing laundry so I'd have clean clothes to pack. I even changed the sheets and started picking up. With every coffee-stained mug I placed in the dishwasher, I felt a sense of pride.

Most people probably loaded their dishwasher without even thinking about it, but over the past few months, every task had become heavy, weighted with expectation. When I'd told Lacey about this, she'd suggested I start with a single cup. If I felt like doing another, I could. If not, it was okay to stop. But once I started, I *couldn't* stop. Cleaning my space was the only thing keeping me from losing my shit.

With the place mostly cleaned and some clothes washed, I finally settled into bed a little after 3 a.m. Part of me wanted to drive straight to Nashville, but I didn't want to show up at such an early hour and freak anyone out. Calling didn't feel right either. I owed people an explanation, and they deserved one given in person. I'd gotten a lot wrong in the past, but this was one thing I was determined not to fuck up.

Lacey had told me about a couple of podcasts she liked, so I put one of them on. The lady's voice was so monotone that it eventually put me to sleep. When I woke twelve hours later, I was still exhausted, leaving me wondering if the demons had been throwing a fucking rave all night.

I filled my suitcases in a daze and set out a little after 5 p.m. before I had the chance to lose my nerve. A quick stop for gas and a shitty cappuccino that nearly made me see noises, and I was on my way.

With "Welcome to the Black Parade" by My Chemical Romance playing on repeat, I drove down I-65 south without knowing my exact destination. The closer I got to the city my friends called home, the more I realized nowhere really felt like mine. Not my apartment. Not Nashville or even the roads I'd spent the majority of my twenties watching pass by from the window of the tour bus. My own body didn't even feel like home.

As I got closer, an instinct I couldn't identify took over. The wheels of my car were pulled toward an exit I vaguely remembered. Turns I hadn't made that often before suddenly felt familiar. Shame slithered up my neck and settled into my cheeks as I turned onto the tree-lined street. I should have been here more.

I pulled into the driveway and cut the engine a little after eight, white-knuckling the steering wheel for a moment. What would they think about me just showing up like this? Being mere feet from the door made me realize that maybe a phone call wouldn't have been the worst fucking idea.

"Just get out of the fucking car," I muttered to myself. "One cup at a time."

Pocketing my keys inside my jacket, I got out and grabbed my bags. With every step, the monsters clawed at my feet, tugging me back toward the car. Each stride forward was met with resistance. But I kicked away the gnarled fingers clinging to my jeans as I climbed the stoop. I might not have been home, but I was somewhere I felt safe. And that was close enough.

I knocked on the door three times in rapid succession, my heart pounding with my fist.

The muffled sounds of the television muted, and I heard a faint, "Be right there!"

Dull footfalls got closer until they were accompanied by the click of a lock, the creak of a door, and then a gasp of surprise.

"Luca." Katie bounced outside and her arms were around me in a quarter of a second. "Oh my God. I can't believe you're here. Do you know how worried I've been? How worried we've *all* been? You better have a good explanation, mister. You better have dropped your phone into a toilet in Amsterdam and lost your passport or been detained by the embassy or something because—"

I don't know who was more stunned by the emotion that started fucking leaking from my eyes—me or her. But I didn't have the energy to care. Every bit of strength I had left was clinging to my friend like she was the last thread holding me to the earth.

She said my name again, this time more softly. "I…I didn't mean it. I'm not upset. I was just giving you a hard time. Luca, you're scaring me. Please talk to me."

"Hey, Butter Bean, is everything okay?" Dallas froze when he stepped into view, his eyes growing wide before narrowing with concern. "Luca? Are you okay?"

I shook my head, unable to string together any words that made sense.

He stepped onto the stoop and reached for my shoulder. I only broke my embrace with Katie to grasp onto Dallas who wrapped me in a bear hug so tight it might've suffocated me if I could have caught my breath.

Katie stepped aside but kept a hand on my arm. Her features were blurred, but even through the rainstorm that clouded my vision I could see the alarm on her face.

"We've got you," Dallas said in my ear. "You hear me, brother?"

It took everything I had to whisper, "I'm sorry."

"You have nothing to be sorry for." Dallas pulled his head back, his hands on either side of my face. "We've always got you."

"Come on," Katie said, squeezing my shoulder. "Let's get you inside."

⸻

I WOKE TO THE WHISPERS OF HUSHED VOICES AND THE SMELL of freshly brewed coffee. I shot up, a colorful afghan falling off my chest, revealing yesterday's clothes. It took a few seconds to remember I wasn't alone anymore and that the sounds coming from the next room weren't from the demons that haunted me; they were from my friends, and I happened to be on their couch.

Their geriatric dog, Emilia, was curled up at my feet. I'd actually been the one to find her—or more accurately, she'd found me when her owner left her, diaper and all, at my place after a one-night stand, never to return. She was prissy and tiny enough to be carried around in a bag, but she was also mostly blind. I wasn't exactly in a position to take care of myself, let alone anyone else, but it fucking bothered me the way this chick had discarded the pup like she was trash. I felt sorry for the dog. I knew what it was like to be rejected for things beyond my control.

"Hey, girl," I murmured, reaching to stroke the top of her head. She opened her eyes, but I wasn't sure she could really see me, so I let her sniff my fingers. That elicited a soft wag of her tail. "It's good to see you too."

My head throbbed, and my throat burned like a cut doused in alcohol. It was like a hangover, except I hadn't had a fucking drop to drink in over a year. I dropped my head back onto the pillow I was fairly certain wasn't there the night before and pulled the blanket tighter around me. Emilia twirled in a circle, pawed at the blanket, and flopped back down to resume her slumber.

"Hey," Katie said, appearing in the doorway. "You're up. Want some coffee?"

"Coffee would be good," I said.

"Black, right?" she asked.

I made a half-hearted attempt at a smile. "Like my soul."

When she returned with a mug a couple of moments later, I sat up, keeping the blanket over my lap. I turned the blue ceramic in my hands, reading the phrase printed across the middle.

One day at a time.

One cup at a time.

I couldn't help but feel Katie had selected that mug just for me.

"Thanks," I said, taking a sip of the dark liquid as she sank into the armchair across from me with her own cup cradled in her hands.

"You sleep okay?" Dallas asked as he entered the room, sitting on the arm of Katie's overstuffed chair.

"We were going to set you up in Jo's old room," Katie said, "but by the time we came back in here, you were already out. You looked so peaceful, I didn't want to disturb you. And Emilia refused to settle until we let her lie down with you."

Watery images of the night before flashed through my mind. Me, trying to no avail to piece together sentences about why I was there, but unable to do so. Katie and Dallas, wide-eyed and helpless as they did what they could to comfort me. Hoarse whispers as my head was gently lifted off the cushion of the sofa and placed on a cloud. The gentle weight of something being draped over my body. A soft lump resting on my feet.

"I'm sorry about last night." My voice came out gritty, like sandpaper, and I cleared my throat. "I didn't mean to show up like a fucking wreck."

"You have nothing to apologize for," Dallas said. "That's the thing about family. You can show up any way you need to."

"That's right," Katie agreed. "And we're going to be here for you. *All* of us."

My ears snagged on the last part of what she said. "Who else knows I'm here?"

"I told Liv and Jo," Katie answered, which meant that by now, everyone knew. "Luca, we've all been worried about you. They know the most important part—that you're safe. I didn't tell them anything about how you showed up, just that you did."

I released a slow breath and nodded.

"How are you feeling?" Katie asked.

"Empty." It was the first word that came to mind. "Like I could sleep forever and it wouldn't be enough."

"We've got the guest room all ready for you if you want to lie back down for a while," Dallas said.

Katie leaned forward, her elbows on her pajama-clad knees. "But how about we get you something to eat first? We can talk more over breakfast, or we don't have to talk at all. Whatever you need."

"You guys don't need to rearrange your lives for me," I said, pushing my hand through the mess that was my hair. "I know you've got work."

"We're going to take a couple days off," Dallas said. "Perk of shacking up with the boss." He tossed Katie a wink.

"I don't need babysitters," I snapped and immediately regretted it. "I'm…I'm sorry."

"We just want to be here," Katie replied, unfazed. "Besides, my staff can take care of things when I'm not there. I went through this whole thing after my MS diagnosis where I had to learn how to delegate and trust my employees." She paused for a beat and swallowed hard. "Anyway, when you're feeling up to it, you've got to come in and check out the place. I think you'll be proud."

My chest tightened as Dallas rose to his feet. "I'm making breakfast. How about some pancakes? Maybe some bacon and eggs too?"

I didn't want to eat anything, but my stomach growled in protest, so I agreed.

"Coming right up," he said before leaving the room.

A moment passed, and I brought my eyes up to Katie.

"I *am* proud of you," I said. "And I'm so sorry I wasn't here to tell you that." It wasn't enough. It would never be enough, but it was all I had to give at that moment.

"You're here now," she said. "That's what matters."

I nodded once and took another sip of coffee. We sat in silence, listening to Dallas clatter around the kitchen. It made me think of the time I hung out with Katie when she was sick. Her best friend Jo was living with her at the time and was putting on a big charity event. She didn't want to leave Katie, and with everyone else we knew going to the event, Jo asked me to stay with her. I'd never been the nurturing type, so I knew I was probably a last resort, but it still made me feel good that I'd been considered at all. We watched terrible movies and did these ridiculous face masks and laughed, but mostly we just existed in each other's company. For a long time, Katie had primarily been the friend of my other friends. But that night, she became mine too. After that, our friendship grew, and she became like a sister to me. For someone who had no real family to speak of, that meant a lot.

After Dallas poked his head in to announce that breakfast was ready, I took a seat at the table as he served our plates. Katie placed Emilia in front of her food bowl before topping off our coffees and joining us.

"I started therapy. A couple days ago," I finally said, staring down at the steam swirling over my mug. "I wasn't traveling. That whole time I acted like I was out on some big fucking adventure, I was actually rotting in my apartment, wishing I could disappear."

Katie brought her hands in front of her mouth almost as though she was praying, and Dallas set his fork aside.

"In fact, I was fairly certain your lives, everyone's lives, would be better if I did."

"Luca." Katie's voice was almost inaudible. "That couldn't be further from the truth. You have to know that."

"I do now," I admitted. "I reached...a scary point. My

thoughts had become so dark they distorted my reality. When I hit my lowest point, something happened. My phone, which had been dead for who knows how long, powered on. I expected nothing but telemarketers and wrong numbers, but what I found was all of you. I listened to your messages that had collected over the last several months. And that's when I realized that even if I didn't deserve it, you guys were still here for me."

Dallas drew his brows together. "Didn't deserve it? Of course, you deserve it. We fucking love you, dude."

Katie sniffed and reached across the table to touch my arm. "Yes, we do."

"I know we haven't always seen eye to eye," Dallas continued. "And I know my stubborn ass hasn't always been good about showing it, but you're like a brother to me. And that means even when I don't like you, I still fucking love you. I will never turn you away. You hear me? Not ever."

My throat worked to swallow down the lump in my throat. "I shouldn't have lied to you, but I didn't know how to tell you guys the truth either. That I was fucking falling apart for no goddamn reason. That the pressure of simply fucking existing over the past few years had become too much."

"I'm so sorry we weren't there for you." Katie gave my hand a squeeze. "We should have been there."

I shook my head. "I lied about where I was because I didn't *want* to be found. Even if you'd shown up, I don't think I would've opened the door."

Her face fell. "I understand."

"But the door is open now," I said. "Look, I don't know what the fuck I'm doing, but I do know that I don't want to do it alone anymore."

"And you won't," Dallas said. "We're going to support you."

"You can let us in as much or as little as you want," Katie added. "Just please don't completely shut us out again." Her voice broke on the last word, her bottom lip trembling. "And don't…don't disappear, okay?"

This time, I was the one to reach for her hand. "I won't."

"All right then." Her shoulders loosened a little, but I couldn't help but notice the tears pooling at the corners of her eyes. She surveyed the table before rising to her feet, tossing her napkin on the table. "That syrup is almost empty. I'll just go grab some more out of the pantry."

Dallas glanced up when her voice cracked slightly, concern flashing across his face, then returned his focus to the plate in front of him.

"These are some good pancakes if I do say so myself," he said, attempting to sound chipper. "Eat as much as you want. I can always make another batch if you're still hungry."

I sliced through one of the fluffy pancakes with my fork, my gaze lingering on the doorway Katie retreated through.

When she returned with the bottle, her eyes were dry, but her smile didn't reach her eyes. I knew my actions had hurt her. They'd hurt *all* of my friends. But witnessing that heartache in person as Katie tried to hide the tears I'd caused cut me far deeper.

The pain reminded me that if I ever felt myself longing to disappear someday in the future, I couldn't give in. I couldn't allow myself to fade away again.

FIVE

McKenzie

A WEEK PASSED, BRINGING OCTOBER WITH IT. I THREW myself into work, doing anything I could to avoid thinking about the fact that in five days, my mom would be leaving the country. And for the first time, I'd be alone on the anniversary of the worst day of my life.

Luckily, things at Katie's Kitchen had been so busy I'd barely had time to breathe. Katie had been out of the restaurant almost entirely for the past seven days, popping in only a couple of times, which was unusual for her, and Dallas hadn't been in at all. She hadn't given any sort of explanation for either of their whereabouts. Not that she owed me one, but it was unlike her not to tell me what was going on. We were friends, but I was also her second-in-command.

So, when she strolled into the kitchen from the front of the store late Thursday morning, I pounced.

"Katie, what's going on?" I asked, dropping my spatula onto the island that held the salted caramel layer cake I was working on.

"Nothing much," she said, flipping through the overstuffed order notebook we kept by the phone in the back. "Have you seen the slip for the Altman wedding? I got an email that their guest count changed *again*."

"It's in there," I said, leaning against the cabinet beside her. "Are you feeling okay? Is your MS flaring up again?"

"I'm feeling pretty good, actually. I have my days, but overall, it's been a lot better," she answered, continuing to leaf through the pages. "Where did that damn thing go?"

"You'd tell me, right?" I asked. "Because something seems…off."

"Off?" she repeated, plucking a sheet from the binder. "There it is."

I grabbed her by the arms and turned her to face me. "Is something up with you and Dallas? Because if he's being an idiot again, I will hack off his man bun and glue it to his ass."

She laughed and shook her head. "Dallas is great. Seriously. He's fine. I'm fine. Everything's—"

"Fine," I finished for her. "Does this mean you're taking time off for *fun*?"

There was a flash of something in her eyes before she fixed her mouth into a smile.

"Is that so crazy?" she asked.

"It wouldn't be if that was a thing you did without being sick, hurt, or otherwise coerced."

She rolled her eyes and returned her attention to the notebook, making a notation on the Altman order form. "Actually, Dallas is out front right now grabbing a few things to take to Derek and Jo's."

As if on cue, Dallas poked his head in the door. "We've got the goods." He nodded in my direction. "Hey, McKenzie."

"Tommy Lee," I said. "Referring to yourself as *we* now? Did your ego get too big for one person to handle?"

"No." He came all the way into the kitchen, clutching a lilac pastry box, and the most beautiful man I'd ever seen followed behind him.

Luca. I'd met him briefly once before—at Cash and Ella's wedding—right after Ella's boob popped out of her dress like some sort of perverse Whac-A-Mole. He was a friend of Dallas and Katie, and he was on my shit list, regardless of how chiseled his jaw was or how blue his eyes were. His shaggy dark hair, alabaster skin, and all-black clothes made my inner emo-girl heart flutter. Nevertheless, he'd been an asshole to my friends—especially Katie. I'd seen how heart-broken she was at game night and even as far back as last spring when he was a no-show for the opening of the restaurant.

"Luca's in town," Dallas said, as though this jerk hadn't been MIA for *months.* "We're going to hang out with Jo and Derek and see little Addison."

The perfect specimen of a man standing at his side nodded at me in acknowledgment, but I ignored him.

"Oh, nice," I said, returning my attention to the cake I'd been working on. "So, I can expect neither of you will have your hearing when you return."

"Addie's got a set of pipes on her," Katie explained to Luca, snapping the binder shut.

Jo and Derek popped in often when they weren't out of town for work, and of course, they brought their daughter with them. She was cute and all, but I much preferred the silent version that came via the hundreds of photos Katie carried on her phone of her goddaughter making ninety-nine variations of the same exact face.

"She'll be fronting a Midnight in Dallas revival band one

day with lungs like that," Dallas said, while Luca shifted uncomfortably, shoving his hands in his pockets.

"Can't wait," I said in a voice that let him know I most certainly *could* wait.

I got a kick out of teasing him because I didn't know much about Midnight in Dallas before Katie. His celebrity status and the band as a whole didn't mean much to me, but after getting to know Dallas, and after him pestering me to listen to his former band's music, I decided to give them a try. I told Dallas it was cool knowing a guy in a boy band, which shut him up permanently. But truth be told, I liked what I heard.

The door opened, and Sydney, one of my coworkers, peeked her head in. "McKenzie, someone out front is interested in booking a catering gig. Can you come talk to them?"

"I can do it," Katie offered. She knew the customer interactions were the part of this job I liked the least. I could fake it when I absolutely had to, but I was not what one would call a people person.

"Thanks, Katie," I said as she exited through the door Sydney held open.

"And Dallas, would you mind changing the light bulb in the men's room while you're here?" Sydney asked, pressing her palms together in front of her chest. "It went out this morning, and I hate getting on that stepladder."

The hair on the back of my neck stood up. If Sydney and Dallas left the room, I'd be here with Luca. Alone.

"You don't have to do that," I spoke up. "I can take care of it."

"No need," Dallas said, placing the pastry box on the counter. "You're busy, and well, you're also kinda short. I don't even need the stepladder. The hardest part will be remembering where we put the light bulbs. I'll be right back."

He left the room with Sydney on his heels, and suddenly the room was painfully quiet.

I tried to focus on the sound of my playlist and the swirl of my spatula as I worked the buttercream over the cake. It took every ounce of restraint I possessed not to steal a glance at Luca.

"Did we meet before?" he asked, his voice piercing through the silence. "We did, right? At Ella and Cash's wedding?"

I shrugged, not meeting his eyes. *I can't believe he remembers me.*

"That cake, uh, looks good."

"Yep."

"Sorry," he said, and I looked up in time to see him push his hand through his perfect mess of hair. "It's probably distracting to have someone talk to you while you're trying to work."

I snorted, returning my focus to the cake. "It's not. I could do this in my sleep."

"Oh," he said. "Right."

A beat of silence passed between us, and I felt his eyes on me, burning into the side of my face like a hot poker.

"You trying to stare a hole through my head?" I asked.

"No…I, uh, sorry."

"Just so we're clear, I don't like you very much," I said, continuing to swirl the frosting onto the cake as though being caught in this man's gaze wasn't setting me on fire. "I think it's shitty what you did to all your friends, but especially Katie. She's so kind and caring, and you ghosting her like that really hurt her feelings."

He didn't say anything for a moment, and I wondered if he'd heard me at all.

"I don't like me very much either," he finally said. "And it *was* shitty." His voice was so low I had to strain to hear him, even in such a small space.

I chanced a glance at him, and that's when I noticed the deep purple circles that framed his eyes. His razor-sharp cheekbones looked more pronounced than they did the last time I saw him, and his lips were a little dry. Even still, he was insanely gorgeous, and that annoyed me even more.

He sniffled, and his nose twitched before he cleared his throat.

"Oh shit, dude. I'm sorry," I said, dropping the spatula with a clatter. "You're not gonna cry, are you?"

He shook his head, a faint smile gliding over his mouth. "Not right now."

His face and choice of words landed heavy on my heart. "Are you…are you good?"

"Not even a little," he answered. "But it's not because of you."

Fuck. I knew I could be a bitch sometimes, but this was a whole new level for me. The man looked like his damn dog died, and I chose *that moment* to tell him he was an asshole. *I* was the one being an asshole.

"I'm not so good either," I admitted. Partly because it was true, and partly because I had a nagging feeling I needed to let him know he wasn't alone. "And that's also not because of you."

His lips quirked.

"I'm sorry I was such a dick," I said. "I'd say that's out of character for me, but it's not."

He folded his arms over his chest. "Actually, your honesty

is kind of refreshing. Everybody's been walking on eggshells around me for the past few days. So, thank you for keeping me in check."

"Glad I could be of service." I gave him a mock salute. "If you ever find yourself in need of another verbal kick in the ass, I'm your girl."

"You know, I might take you up on that sometime," he said as Katie opened the door to the kitchen and leaned inside.

"Are you ready to go?" she asked Luca. "Dal is making a coffee and then we can head out."

"Yeah, let's do it," he answered, picking up the box of pastries Dallas had left.

"I'll be back tomorrow," Katie said. "Call me if you need anything."

"Call you?" I asked as though that was a foreign concept. "Why would I do that when I could let this place descend into madness?"

"Very funny," she called over her shoulder as she disappeared.

Luca followed behind her, pausing with his back against the door.

"It was good seeing you again, McKenzie," he said.

My stomach flipped, and I hoped my face wasn't giving away how good it felt to hear him say my name.

"You too," I said.

"And I'll keep your offer in mind."

I winced. "Sorry about that."

"I'm not."

His mouth curved into the first genuine smile I'd seen on him, and without another word, he was gone.

SIX

Luca

"Really, I can cancel game night. It's not a big deal," Katie said in the kitchen Sunday morning while Dallas made omelets with Emilia circling his feet. "I just wasn't thinking."

"You don't need to cancel it because of me," I told her, pouring myself a cup of coffee.

She leaned against the worn cabinets, a mug cradled in her hands. "But I know you're not up for anything like that, and I don't want you to be uncomfortable."

"Don't worry about it," I insisted. "I can hang out in the bedroom. I don't want you guys rearranging your lives for me any more than you already have."

"Okay." Her brows threaded together with uncertainty. "But we'll keep this one shorter. I can say I'm not feeling well."

"Seriously, Katie." I moved beside her and nudged her arm with my elbow. "Don't do anything you wouldn't normally do. I may not feel up to joining in, but I'm feeling better than I was a few days ago."

Better was a bit of a stretch, but there had been improvement. Being around friends helped. On Friday I had my first virtual session with Lacey, and she set up an appointment for me to see a psychiatrist in Nashville early the following week. She thought I might benefit from starting medication, and at this point, I was willing to try anything to dig myself out of the dark hole I was in. One shovel at a time; one cup at a time.

"Besides, if we cancel, Caesar will be devastated," Dallas said, sarcasm dripping from his voice. "He gets cranky if he doesn't get his regular dose of McKenzie."

My ears perked. "McKenzie from the restaurant?" I asked, and she nodded. "Is Caesar her boyfriend or something?"

Katie snorted. "Absolutely not."

"Caesar wishes," Dallas said, expertly flipping the eggs.

Katie took a sip of her coffee. "That crush goes one-way only."

"McKenzie mostly just tolerates him," Dallas added. "To be fair, I think she mostly just tolerates everyone. She's not exactly a cuddly teddy bear."

"Dallas," Katie chided him.

"Okay, maybe a teddy bear made out of barbed wire and thorns," he teased.

Katie swatted his arm.

"You know I love McKenzie. She was the only person who could help me pull my head out of my own ass back when I was being an idiot," he said, recoiling. "But I'm not saying anything she wouldn't say herself. The girl isn't known for her warm personality."

I stifled a laugh, thinking back on our brief conversation Thursday. That certainly was a way to describe her, but there was something else buried beneath her prickly exterior. When she thought she might've hurt my feelings, she seemed concerned. And when I told her I wasn't okay, she'd said she wasn't either. There'd been a lost look in her eyes, a sadness that resembled the one in my own.

"She's plenty warm, Dal," Katie said, her lips quirking. "She just likes giving you shit, and I can't really blame her for that."

"She seems cool," I said, keeping my tone casual.

She also happened to be beautiful. Not the type of girl I normally would have gone for or taken home for the night, only to forget her name by morning. Then again, McKenzie didn't strike me as a going-home-for-the-night kind of woman. While I normally preferred girls with long hair, hers was short, barely touching her shoulders. I'd also been known for choosing my conquests by the size of their tits or how short their dresses were. And whereas other women might have fallen over themselves trying to get my attention, she didn't give a flying fuck.

Those other women were gorgeous. Works of art, painted to perfection, that could have been on magazine covers or fashion runways. So glamorous they almost didn't feel real, and it occurred to me in that moment that maybe there was a reason I'd sought them out. If I felt they couldn't possibly be real, then nothing we had could be either.

"She can come across a little standoffish at first," Katie said. "But she's so kind and caring once you get to know her. Truly, I don't know what I'd do without her. She's become such a good friend. I think you'd like her."

There was something about McKenzie that intrigued me. She was beautiful in an unassuming way, like how an autumn sunset streaked the sky with all its magnificent colors without any pomp or circumstance. But there was more to it than that. Maybe it was her brusque attitude. Maybe it was the fact that she seemed like the type of person who was so impossibly themselves it was almost jarring. Like seeing a polar bear traipsing down I-65 south. We read about them and knew they existed, but it's not like we saw them in the flesh, let alone just existing in the world like they weren't some rare, miraculous creature.

"Yeah." I gave a noncommittal nod. "Maybe."

"Okay," Katie said. "Well, if we're doing this thing tonight, I should make a Trader Joe's run after breakfast for some snacks. But you're absolutely sure you're okay with this?" She turned to me. "Because really, we can cancel it and order some Chinese."

"I'm sure," I said. "Promise."

She and Dallas started listing off the things they would need for the evening, but I found my mind drifting back to McKenzie. Maybe I'd find a reason to come out of my room tonight after all, even if just for a minute.

I MUST'VE FALLEN ASLEEP TO ANOTHER ONE OF LACEY'S meditation podcasts sometime after lunch, because when I woke up, my room was dark. Raucous laughter seeped through the slivers of space around the door, letting me know game night had begun.

Despite the minor improvements I'd had, one thing that remained was my exhaustion, particularly during the days right after my therapy appointments. My body reacted to the unearthing of buried feelings as if I were physically digging my way out of a grave—a tomb created by my own mind to hold me prisoner. I clawed my way, one handful of dirt at a time until I was spent.

I released a long breath, scrubbing my hands down my

face before glancing at the digital clock on the nightstand. It was a little after eight, which meant I'd slept the day away and that Dallas and Katie's game night was well under way.

My stomach growled, reminding me I hadn't eaten since late morning. I needed to sneak out to the kitchen and grab something to eat, so I reached across the mattress, pulling the dainty chain that turned the bedside lamp on.

The heels of my palms rubbed the sleep from my eyes, and I stood, trudging across the room to the door. I started to twist the knob, but stopped short when I remembered who might be out there. I probably wouldn't run into McKenzie in the kitchen, but on the off chance that I *did,* I didn't want to look like I'd just rolled out of bed.

I appraised my reflection in the full-length mirror to the right of the door. My wavy hair had flattened in the center but the sides formed points that resembled horns.

"Fuck," I muttered, using my fingers as a comb until I'd managed to make the raven strands look somewhat presentable. I shoved my feet into my Converse because absolutely nobody needed to see my feet.

Satisfied, I left the room and padded down the hall to the kitchen. My heart lurched as I stepped into the doorway. McKenzie was there with her back facing me. I recognized the way her light brown hair skimmed her shoulders. She wore a long sleeve shirt, dark jeans, and motorcycle boots with a green and black flannel tied around her waist. One hand rested on her hip while the other squirted whipped cream into her mouth.

"Everything okay in there, McKenzie?" Katie's voice called.

"Yep," she shouted back. "Be right there. Just grabbing another beer."

Her head dropped back with a heavy sigh.

"Fuck my life," she muttered before taking another pull off the Reddi-Wip.

I choked on a laugh, and she yelped, spinning around to find out where the sound had come from.

"Shit," she said around a mouthful of foamy cream, a dribble spilling down her chin. "What the fuck, dude?"

"Sorry," I said, stepping closer to her. "I didn't mean to scare you. I was just coming in here to grab a snack."

Her cheeks flushed, and she swiped at the corners of her mouth with the sleeve of her shirt.

I cleared my throat. "You missed a spot." Before I could stop myself, I reached out to brush away the white dot clinging to her skin, but she pulled back.

"Thanks, but I can do it," she mumbled, dragging her palm over her face. "Did I get it?"

"Yep," I said.

She held the can of whipped cream toward me. "You want some? I have no idea why, but they keep tons of this shit in the house."

I shrugged and took a squirt before handing it back to her.

"You're staying here?" she asked.

I nodded.

She narrowed her eyes. "And how did you manage to avoid getting roped into game night?"

"Weren't you getting a beer?" I asked, lifting one brow.

She lowered her voice. "What I was actually doing was avoiding Caesar. I always get stuck on his team when we play Pictionary."

A grin tugged at my mouth. "Is he just really bad at it?"

"Yes," she answered. "But he also tries to flirt with me,

which he's equally bad at. He's a nice guy and all, but I'm just not interested. Not in him, not in anyone. Not ever."

"So you're saying there's a chance?" I teased.

"Okay, I told you why I'm in here," McKenzie said, opening the fridge and swapping the can in her hands with a beer. "Now it's your turn."

I caught the cold white door. "For a snack."

"I mean why are you staying here?"

I reached in and grabbed a bottle of water, twisting the top off before pushing the door closed with my hip. I didn't want to tell her the truth because that would take all night. But also because it felt too raw, like pouring hot water on freshly burned skin. Yet there was something about the way she regarded me, her curious green pupils following me without an ounce of judgment. Her head was tilted in concern. Or maybe it was empathy.

"It's…complicated," I began, running my hand along the back of my neck, eyes glued to the floor. "I've been having a…a hard time. And it got to a point that it was better to not be alone for a while."

"Oh," she said, and when I brought my gaze back to hers, I recognized the look of sadness I'd seen there before.

"I'm sorry to hear that," she continued, leaning against the counter, folding her arms over her chest. "I hate when people say that because it sounds ridiculous. So apathetic. But I really am sorry."

"Thanks," I said.

She raked her hands down her face. "If I'm being totally honest, I'm having a tough time too. I'm hanging on by a thread right now and having to deal with Caesar might be what causes it to snap."

I moved to stand beside her. "I'm sorry to hear that."

A ghost of a smile appeared on her lips. "Thanks."

"And if both our lives are shit, we might as well be shitty together," I said. "I'll be on your Pictionary team. If you want me to, of course."

"Seriously?" she asked. "You'd do that?"

I held out my hands. "It's not like I've got a lot else on my schedule."

"Okay, then," she said. "But have you met Caesar? Because that dude is a *lot*."

My lips quirked. "So am I."

She shrugged. "You know what? I'll take what I can get. You want a beer or anything?"

I shook my head. "Nah, I'm good."

"Maybe some pregame Advil? A lobotomy?" she asked, backing away toward the direction of the living room.

I trailed behind her. "How annoying *is* this guy?"

She twisted the cap off her beer and took a swig. "You have no idea."

SEVEN

McKenzie

CAESAR'S FACE WAS PRICELESS WHEN I SAUNTERED BACK INTO the living room with Luca. His eyes went wide as though I'd performed a magic trick, making a hot guy appear out of thin air. When it came time to split into teams, Caesar quickly volunteered for Katie's with Dallas and Sydney, giving Luca a wide berth all evening as though he might bite.

My team consisted of me, Luca, and Katie's friend Margot whom I liked a lot. She had pink hair, a pixie-like frame, and a potty mouth. Between the three of us, we crushed it. Well, Luca and I did. Margot mostly provided colorful commentary, but Luca and I were on the same wavelength. It was almost like there was an invisible telephone line connecting our brains. He understood my crude drawings, sometimes even before I'd finished them. We played three full games and won them all.

"I still don't know how you got that last one," Dallas told Luca after everyone else had left.

"I don't know how you *didn't*," Luca said with a laugh.

"Seriously," I added with an eye roll, pointing to the masterpiece I'd sketched. "There's a dick. There's a chain."

"Dick Cheney," Luca said, holding out his hand to give me a high five.

When his skin touched mine, a shiver coursed from my palm, up my arm, and through the back of my neck. He was so beautiful it was almost painful. Like that time I found a black onyx ring I loved at this vintage jewelry store and then saw the price. It was stunning, one of a kind. But it would never belong to me.

"You two make a good pair," Katie said, stacking the last of the now empty dishes on top of each other to take to the kitchen. "You know, we'd love for you to join us again next month if you decide to stick around Nashville, Luca. I hope you do. Promise you'll come if you're still here?"

If you're still here.

My heart sank. He *was* just visiting, after all. The thought shouldn't have bothered me as much as it did. It wasn't like I was looking for a relationship. Even if I was, I was certain I wouldn't be Luca's type. Curiosity had gotten the better of me after seeing him at the restaurant, and I'd tripped and fallen down a Google rabbit hole that showed him with women on his arm that could make the Victoria's Secret Angels cry.

I didn't normally care much about my looks, but even I knew when I was outmatched. Those girls were elevens, but I was sitting maybe at a seven and a half on a good day.

"I think I could be persuaded," Luca said, his blue eyes like shards of stained glass cutting right into me.

I cocked my head to the side. "Oh, I don't do that."

"Do what?" he asked.

"Persuade. Beg. Plead," I answered, scooping my cross-body bag off the floor and slinging it around me. "If you don't come next time, I'm fine with it being just me and Margot."

"Margot, who thought the hair on the dick's balls was glitter?" Luca countered.

My hands popped onto my hips. "I didn't say we'd *win*."

"Well, *I* will beg," Dallas said. "Caesar was awfully quiet with you here, Luca, and that's good enough for me."

"It was definitely a perk," I added with a chuckle as we all started toward the kitchen. Katie and Dallas carried what was left of the food and dishes, and Luca trailed behind me.

"Well, I'm going to head out," I said, inching closer to the back door. "I'll see you guys later."

Katie plunked the dishes in the sink and wiped her hands on her jeans before giving me a hug.

"I'm glad you came," she said, returning to her tidying. "We'll be back to our normal schedule at the restaurant next week. Thanks for holding down the fort."

"Yeah, no problem." I lingered in the doorway for a second as she and Dallas worked around each other in the way people do when they're totally in sync. He bumped her hip with his, and her lashes fluttered up at him. Why were couples so nauseating?

"I'll walk you out," Luca offered, slipping his arm behind me to open the door.

"Oh. Uh. Okay," I said. "You really don't need to do that, though."

He lifted his shoulders. "It's nice out. I thought I'd get some air."

"Good night," I called over my shoulder as I stepped onto the porch and started down the steps. Once the door clicked shut, the only sounds left were that of my heart pounding in my ears and a moth engaged in battle with the motion light.

"Hey," Luca said when I reached the bottom.

I turned, and there he was, his forearms resting on the railing. For a moment we were in some reverse Romeo and Juliet situation, and I had the urge to climb back up and take one last look at him in case I didn't get to see him again. As hot as his online images were, nothing came close to the real thing.

"Yeah?" I asked, digging my keys out of my bag.

"Tonight was fun," he said.

"Thanks again for saving me from Caesar."

He nodded, dragging his teeth over his bottom lip. "So, next month, then?"

"I'll be here," I said, backing away toward my truck.

I thought I saw him smile in the flicker of the porch light. "Then so will I."

"Look at that. I didn't even have to beg."

My cheeks burned against the chilly night air, and I bit back a smile as I climbed into my truck. All of a sudden, I was a *lot* more interested in game night.

It was Thursday, but it wasn't just any Thursday. I hadn't changed the calendar on my fridge since last month in a weak attempt to avoid this very date. October tenth. Every year I longed to sleep through it and the days after marked the beginning of a series of firsts—my first meal without him, the first holiday in his absence. But the worst was that first time I needed to call him but couldn't. Knowing his voice would never be waiting on the other end of the line or anywhere at all weighed on me like a backpack full of bricks. One trip down memory lane could send me wading into the ocean with the weight of the person who was my world on my shoulders.

Mom called me early that morning, though for her it was a little after three in the afternoon. Her voice was less chipper than it had been in the previous days I'd spoken to her.

"I'm sorry I'm not there today, Kenz," she'd said.

I forced a smile that wasn't there into my voice. "Don't be. He'd be so happy for you, Mom. You deserve this. I don't want you worrying about me, okay? I'm working and then a couple of friends from group are staying over, so I won't be alone."

My lie seemed to satisfy her because by the time we said goodbye, she sounded like she was in better spirits.

It wasn't a complete lie. I *did* have work, and I *was* planning to see Kia, Jen, and Ravi. I really was. But when Kia sent me a text that afternoon to confirm our dinner at Olive Garden, I told her I had to cancel—that I'd caught a stomach bug. I was pretty sure she didn't believe me, but she didn't push. Instead, she told me to feel better and she'd check on me tomorrow.

I stayed at work as late as I could but ran out of things to do a little after seven. We were only open till five, primarily serving the breakfast and lunch crowds. But there was often still plenty to do between daily prep work and catering gigs. It just so happened that in my efforts to avoid real life, I'd managed to finish everything a lot sooner than I would've liked.

With the restaurant locked up, I trudged out into the rainy night and climbed in my truck. I couldn't bring myself to go home. All I wanted to do was drown my sorrows in carbs and hard liquor. Perhaps I'd find some relief at the bottom of a bottle of whiskey. Or at least maybe I'd find some sleep. Immediately, I knew where to go.

There was a dive bar I loved with amazing cheeseburgers

and a jukebox about ten minutes from my place called The Piccadilly Deli. Apparently, it was the name of the restaurant that occupied the building before they shut down, and the owners of the bar were too lazy to change it. The floors were sticky and it smelled like wet socks, yet somehow they still had a ninety-nine health score, so I didn't ask questions.

I parked my truck in the nearly empty lot and ran inside, pulling my hoodie tighter around me. The bartender waved from where he was wiping down the scarred wood bar. He was bald with a soft stomach and sleeves of tattoos that reminded me of Dallas. We weren't on a first name basis or anything, but I came in often enough that he recognized me.

"Hey," he greeted me. "Shitty weather, huh? You getting something to go?"

"No," I answered with a faint smile. "Gonna be doing some drinking tonight."

"Right on," he said. "You can sit anywhere you want."

I nodded and found a small booth in the back near the jukebox and sat facing the door.

"So, what can I get you to start?" he asked, approaching the table. "Do you need to see a menu?"

I shook my head. "Cheeseburger and fries with pickles on the side and a Bushwacker." I could already taste the frosty chocolate cocktail on my tongue.

"Want any chips and salsa while you wait?"

"No, but I *would* love a shot of Jack. Actually, make that two."

"Oh, so you've had a *day*," he said with a chuckle. "You got it. Coming right up."

I studied a scratch in the wood, running my finger along the deep gash while I waited for my first round.

When the bartender returned, he did so with three shots, a glass of water, and some chips.

"Third one's on the house. You look like you could use the extra. Plus, I'm superstitious about even numbers," he said. "And you don't have to eat the chips, but if you're gonna be drinkin', you should probably make sure you're eating plenty too."

"Thanks," I said. "You didn't have to do that."

"I'll have that burger right out for you." He tapped his knuckles against the tabletop before venturing back behind the bar.

I picked up one of the shot glasses between my fingers, tipping it toward the empty space across from me.

"This one's for you, Brennan," I whispered before slinging it back, relishing the way it burned as it slid down my throat. Soon that fire would spread to all of my memories, and with any luck, it would consume them, making them disappear, even if it was just for the night.

EIGHT

Luca

I'D BEEN ON MY NEW ANTIDEPRESSANT FOR THREE DAYS BY the time I had my virtual session with Lacey the Thursday following game night. It was too early to tell if they were helping, but one thing I *did* notice was that my sleep had felt more restful the last couple of nights. Even Lacey commented that I looked a bit brighter.

Of course, by the end of the appointment I was drained again. I wasn't used to putting a spotlight on my pain and handing it a microphone. My instinct was still to pull the curtain down.

Lacey must have sensed this because she presented me with a homework assignment.

"I want you to go out and get a journal," she'd said. "And I want you to spend ten minutes a day writing down how you're feeling."

I'd scoffed. "You want me to keep a diary?"

"It doesn't have to be anything that formal," she'd insisted. "Think of it more like you're dumping these thoughts and feelings out of your brain. You're not worried about making sense here or even forming complete sentences. You can do it for longer than ten minutes, of course, but I find that amount of time either first thing in the morning or right before bed is helpful."

"And am I supposed to read what I write at our next appointment?"

She shook her head. "Nope. This is just to help you get more comfortable giving voice to your emotions."

"So, you won't know if I don't do it?" It was kind of a joke, but also, the idea of writing in a fucking diary made me nauseous.

Her lips had quirked into a grin. "I didn't say that."

Later that evening I lay propped up in bed with a black moleskin notebook opened across my lap, staring at a blank page. My fingers gripped a pen, the tip hovering over that first line, unable to write anything down. But it wasn't annoyance or rebellion keeping me from doing it. It was fear.

What was holding me back? What was I so afraid of?

"Luca?" Katie whispered from the other side of the closed bedroom door.

I shoved the book under my pillow. "Hey, I'm awake."

She opened the door with Emilia tucked in one arm. "We were thinking we might order in tonight. Work was nuts, and neither of us feels like cooking. What sounds good to you?"

Getting out of this bed and out of the house, far fucking away from that damn journal.

"Actually, I think I might go out," I said, planting my feet on the floor. My stomach growled in agreement. All the staring I'd been doing at blank pages had caused me to work up quite the appetite.

"Oh, okay." Katie yawned. "We can do that."

"I can go on my own," I said, making my way over to her.

"Seriously, you guys are amazing, but you haven't had a moment for just the two of you since I've been here."

"Are you sure? We don't mind. I can rally."

I scratched the top of Emilia's head. "I can do this. I think I *need* to do this. Even if I just drive around for a while, I think it'll be good for me to get out."

"You know if you need anything—"

I touched her arm. "I know."

She nodded, a soft smile on her lips. "All right." She turned to leave the room, but I called her name before she could make it down the hall.

"Where's a good place to get a cheeseburger around here?" I asked as she reappeared in the doorway.

"Hmm," she said, her head tilted to one side. "There's some place McKenzie's always raving about. Piccadilly something." She paused, leaning out into the hall. "Hey, Dal? What's the name of that burger joint McKenzie told us about?"

"Piccadilly Deli," he called back over the television.

"Ah, that's it," she said. "I remember her saying it's kind of a dive, but she loves it."

I would've been intrigued even if I didn't want a cheeseburger just because McKenzie was the one who loved it. She didn't seem to dole out her affections easily, so this place must've been special.

"Maybe I'll check it out then," I said, knowing full well that was exactly what I intended to do.

I WANDERED OUT OF THE RAIN AND INTO THE PICCADILLY Deli just before 8 p.m., beads of water rolling off my leather jacket. As Katie had said, it was a total dive, but it was the kind of place I felt comfortable in. There weren't a lot of expectations in a place like that.

My wet boots squeaked against the sticky floor, and the air was stale, smelling faintly of mildew and fried cheese. The walls were black and wallpapered in old, yellowing flyers—everything from concerts to yard sales and lost cats. Only three stools were taken with no bartender in sight. There were a few tables and booths off to the side, but only two were occupied. One was filled with a few guys wearing flannel shirts and ball caps with a construction company logo stitched across the front. But it was the booth in the back that caught my eye.

McKenzie sat near the jukebox, facing the door, the remnants of a burger and a couple fries on a platter in front of her. Two guys who appeared to belong with the construction crew stood next to her table, attempting to engage her in conversation. She seemed thoroughly uninterested in anything but the frosty milkshake-looking concoction she had in front of her.

I moved closer, listening as one of the guys spoke.

"Why don't you let us get you another round?" he asked.

"I'm good," she answered, not looking up from her glass.

"Aw, come on," he pressed. "We don't bite."

"You're too pretty to drink alone," the other guy added, as though that was the pickup line of the fucking century.

"Good thing she's not alone," I said once I reached them, my tone commanding and not at all friendly.

I don't know who was more surprised by my presence—McKenzie or Tweedle Dickhead and Tweedle Dumbass.

McKenzie blinked up at me, swiping a strand of toffee-colored hair off her face.

One of the Tweedle brothers elbowed the other, and they had a full conversation with their eyes. It was one I'd seen play out before.

I had a weird relationship with my fame, but sometimes, it came in handy.

The men scattered like roaches in the light, leaving me and McKenzie to ourselves.

I gestured toward the side of the booth opposite of her. "Is this seat taken?"

"What?" she asked, her cheeks flushed. "I mean, no. Go ahead."

I slid in across from her. "So, what are you doing out on this rainy Thursday night?"

She held up her nearly empty glass. "Drinking. What about you?"

I shrugged. "I heard this place has good cheeseburgers."

"Oh, they do," she said, slurping down the remnants of her drink. "And Bushwackers."

I nodded toward her glass. "Is that what that was?"

"Yep. You should try one."

"I think I'll stick to the burger."

"Not much of a drinker?" she asked, glancing toward the bar, likely in search of the missing bartender.

"Not anymore. I stopped a little over a year ago," I answered. "I didn't like the person I became when I drank."

She shifted her attention back to me. "Who did you become?"

"An asshole."

"And you think that's *different* from who you are now?" The corners of her mouth quirked into a grin.

I lifted my brows in amusement. "You might find this hard to believe, but I was a lot worse back then."

"You couldn't have been that bad or else Katie wouldn't have put up with you." She twirled her straw in her empty glass.

Being my friend was like catching a grenade with your bare hands. I was self-destructing and exploding all over everyone that got close.

A puff of air escaped my lips. "I don't know how anyone dealt with me."

It was the most honest thing I'd said to anyone besides Lacey. I wasn't sure why I said it, but there was something about the look in McKenzie's eyes that reflected my own and made me feel safe.

"I had a bad habit of numbing my emotions with booze… sometimes drugs, and it only ever made me feel worse," I admitted. There were also a lot of women, but I didn't voice that part out loud. "I realized I had to quit that shit if I didn't want to end up in a body bag before I hit forty."

She tugged the sleeves of her hoodie over her hands, studying me. "How's that working out?"

"Well," I said, holding out my hands. "I'm here. I guess that's something."

An expression I couldn't read passed over her face like a storm cloud. A subtle shimmer glittered in her eyes, almost like there were tears hovering just above her lashes.

Her voice was soft when she spoke. "That *is* something."

"My therapist gave me some homework today," I said. "Because that's a thing I do now. Therapy, I mean. She wants me to write my feelings in a journal."

"Oooh, did you pick out a pretty new diary with a lock on it?"

"They make ones with locks on them?"

"You've never been a thirteen-year-old girl before, and it

shows," she teased.

"I guess I don't really need a lock on it, anyway," I said, running my hand along the back of my neck. "Because I can't even bring myself to write anything down."

"What? Why not?"

"I'm not sure, actually," I answered. "It feels like a lot of…pressure."

"Hmm," she said, lips pursed in thought. "Maybe you just need to change how you're looking at it."

"How so?" I asked, leaning closer.

"When I think of a journal or diary, I think of these detailed accounts or letters," she said, moving her hands as she talked. "And that can be heavy. Especially if you're working through something. It can be a lot to relive it. But you're a creative guy. You've got that whole mysterious, brooding musician thing going on."

"Brooding and mysterious, huh?" I couldn't help the satisfied grin that tugged at the corners of my mouth.

"Not the point," she said, rolling her eyes. "The point is, maybe you shouldn't look at it as some elaborate record of your life. Think about it like writing a song."

Why hadn't I considered that? Probably because when Midnight in Dallas broke up, I'd broken too. That band had been my entire fucking world. It was the only thing about me that ever made sense. But it never occurred to me to write anything on my own because I guess I never saw myself separate from the group.

"Songs tell stories differently to different people, right?" she continued. "You could write something that has a very specific meaning to you, but I could read the same words and they represent something else entirely to me. Without context, lyrics are just words. People are what give them meaning. The only thing that matters about your words is that they mean something to *you*."

I nodded, the gears of my mind clicking into place. "That's a good idea. I'll try that."

"Sorry about that. Kitchen got backed up because there's only two of us working tonight," a bald guy whom I assumed was the bartender said as he approached the table. "You've got a friend joining you. What can I..." He trailed off, his eyes nearly bugging out of his head. "Holy shit, dude. You're Luca Sterling. From fucking Midnight in Dallas. It's nice to meet you, bro. I'm Freddy."

I shook his outstretched hand. "Thanks, man. But tonight I'm just any other guy."

"Oh, yeah, of course," Freddy said, lowering his voice. "What can I get you? You seem like a tequila guy."

"Actually, I'd just like a cheeseburger," I said. "I've heard good things."

"You are going to have the best cheeseburger of your life." He tapped his fingers on the table, turning to McKenzie. "You want another Bushwacker?"

"Yes, please," she answered with a smile.

"How about some more chips?" he asked her, arching one brow.

"If you insist," she answered, and he nodded, disappearing into the back.

I chuckled, folding my arms over my chest. "You really *are* doing some drinking tonight."

"I never half-ass anything," she said.

"So, you use your whole ass?"

"Always," she said, sliding out of the booth. "And now, if you'll excuse me, I'm going to find us some tunes to listen to while we wait."

She pulled her sweatshirt over her head and dropped it in the booth. I watched as she made the few short steps to the jukebox and could confirm she did indeed use her whole ass. She pressed one hand over the machine, the other navigating the keypad. With squinted eyes, she leaned forward to see the titles, causing her black T-shirt to ride up, revealing a sliver of her olive skin. I noticed, and one of the creeps in the flannel shirts did too, as he slinked past her toward the sign for the bathrooms.

I wasn't sure what exactly had driven McKenzie to drink, but I wouldn't leave her side until she was home safe. Before she could look up from her song selections, I pulled my phone out of my jacket pocket and tapped out a quick text to Katie.

Ran into McKenzie at the burger place. She's drinking by herself, so I'm gonna hang with her until she's done and make sure she gets home okay.

Katie's reply came fast.

OMG! Is she okay? She seemed a little down at work today, but when I asked she said she was fine.

I'm not sure. She doesn't look like she'll be going anywhere for a while though, so don't wait up. I've got my key.

The dots appeared almost instantly.

Okay. :) Thanks for looking out for her. What about you? Are you good?

I glanced up at McKenzie whose hips were swaying to whatever song was playing. She had no idea how captivating she was just by being herself. And somehow, she *got* me. She knew I needed to put my thoughts into something I under-stood, and that thing was music. It was something so simple, but it took her saying it to make me see it.

I'm glad I came here. This place is great.

But the company I'd found myself in was even better.

NINE

McKenzie

AFTER CHOOSING MY SONG, I DISAPPEARED TO THE BATHROOM and caught a glimpse of my reflection in the cracked glass as I washed my hands. What would Brennan think if he could see me now—if he could *know* me? No longer the gangly teenager who wore her heart on her sleeve but a woman whose soul had been shattered, the pieces forming a mosaic of misery.

I splashed some cold water on my face and blotted it dry with a wad of paper towels before prying my tinted ChapStick from my pocket and swiping it over my lips. My skin looked a bit ashen, so I dabbed the plum color on my cheeks, blending it with my fingers in an effort to bring some life back to my complexion.

It was dangerous to wander the streets of Brennan after dark. Too many shadows lingered there in dim alleyways, waiting to rob me of the few happy memories that hadn't yet been tainted by grief.

I forced my focus to Luca who had shown up looking devastatingly handsome in a leather jacket with his unruly hair. God, I wanted to tame those strands, gripping them between my fingers while he buried his face in—

Whoa. My thoughts screeched to a halt. He was Katie's friend—Katie's very *hot* friend. But still. It was a bad idea. He wouldn't be sticking around Nashville forever, and even if he was, his reputation was that of the love 'em and leave 'em variety.

Even so, the image floated back into my mind like a cloud. It was the alcohol. The shots and the Bushwackers had gone straight to my head. At least, that's what I told myself. Because why else would I be entertaining such absurd thoughts? He was a rock star. Well, a *former* rock star, but fame like his didn't disappear overnight, if ever. I was just some girl, a friend of a friend. I'd seen enough during my internet searches to know I wasn't his type.

And yet…

The devil on my shoulder protested with more tantalizing visions, each one more delicious than the last. During those late-night googling sessions, I'd noticed a very distinct through line. He was never photographed with the same woman twice. Gossip columns and fan discussion boards had much to say when it came to Luca Sterling's abundant extracurricular activities. Maybe it wouldn't matter if I was his type. Perhaps he wasn't that discerning when it came to the women who fell into his bed.

It was a terrible idea. But I longed for a balm to numb my pain, even if only for the night or for a moment. All I wanted was to forget.

Armed with a new mission, I strutted back to the table where my Bushwacker was already waiting for me.

Luca took a bite out of his burger, and I couldn't help but imagine him taking a bite out of me. I leaned forward, wrapping my lips around the straw in the frosty cocktail in front of me. He could whack my bush anytime.

Oh God. Did I shave?!

"Are you feeling okay?" he asked, taking a sip of his soda.

"What? Yeah, of course. Why?"

He nodded toward me. "Your face just got really red."

"It's just the alcohol," I lied.

He dipped a fry in ketchup. "Is this your song?"

Caught up in my own daydreams, I hadn't even realized it had started to play.

"It is," I said, the first verse of "Welcome to the Black Parade" by My Chemical Romance filling my ears.

A genuine smile spread over his face. "This is one of the best albums of all time. They're my favorite band."

"Mine too."

They had also been my brother's. After Brennan died, I clung to anything he loved as a way of keeping a part of him with me.

"There's this My Chem cover band that plays around town sometimes," I said. "Helena's Sweet Revenge. You ever heard of them?"

He shook his head. "No, but that sounds cool. Are they any good?"

"They're amazing," I answered. "I never got to see the actual band, but I feel like these guys sound pretty close. It's been a while since they've been here. I wonder if they're playing anytime soon."

I grabbed my phone off the table and opened up a browser to see what I could find out.

"If they are, maybe we could go," he said, his tone casual as though he'd just told me it was raining outside.

I was sure he didn't mean anything by it, but my body

reacted anyway, my heart fluttering like a wounded butterfly. Even with the odds stacked against me, there was hope.

The Helena's Sweet Revenge website loaded, and I scrolled through their tour updates. My pulse thudded in my ears when I landed on the current date.

What the fuck.

I'd looked only a couple of months ago to see if they'd be in town anytime soon, but the closest venue had been somewhere in Alabama.

"I can't believe this," I said. "They're in Nashville tonight."

"No way." He paused with his burger in front of his perfect mouth. "Really? Where? What time?"

"At The Basement in East Nashville. Doors are at nine."

"We could make that," he said. "If you want to go."

It felt like a sign from the universe or Brennan or *something.*

"I do," I blurted. "But you don't have to if it's not your scene. I know you were probably just being nice."

He snorted, dropping his burger on his plate. "That's the first time anyone has ever accused me of doing *anything* to be nice. I want to go. It sounds like fun."

He signaled the bartender and pulled his wallet out of his pocket.

"Hey, man," he said as Freddy approached. "Can I go ahead and pay our tab?"

"Wait, I've got mine," I insisted, digging in my pocket for my card.

"It's on me." Luca pinned me with a look that told me there would be no arguing, and I was too flustered to try. "This is the second time you've gotten me to do something fun, so I kind of owe you."

"Oh. Well, thanks," I managed, averting my eyes to my drink to keep from staring at his profile and chiseled jaw as he chatted with Freddy.

I slurped down my cocktail, and Luca finished his burger while Freddy told him about his cousin's glam rock band. When we were finished, Freddy moved on to another table, and I rose to my feet, snatching my hoodie off the seat as my brain splashed around in a pool of alcohol.

Guess I'll be leaving my truck here.

"I'll get us an Uber," I offered.

"No need," he said as he stood. "I'll drive."

My emotions swirled in technicolor, and my mouth went dry. "Okay. Sure."

He placed his hand on the small of my back as he guided me toward the door. My eyes found his as we stepped out into the cool, rainy night air, causing me to miss the step down from the sidewalk. He caught my arm, his touch sending a ricochet of electricity through my veins.

His lips quirked, and for half a second I wondered if he felt it too. Then I remembered who he was—but more importantly, who I *wasn't*.

My attention followed him as he jogged ahead to get the car door for me. Maybe it didn't matter if I ended up just another notch on his leather belt as long as he used said belt to bind my wrists together before—

"Hop in," he said, interrupting the X-rated movie playing in my head.

Don't mind if I do.

"Are you cold?" Luca asked over the sound of the radio and the splatter of rain on the windshield of his Tesla. We'd driven the first five minutes or so in silence, with the exception of the GPS interjecting with directions.

"No," I answered. Quite the opposite, in fact. The feeling of Luca's hand on my arm had ignited a fire in my belly that could've taken out entire continents.

"You sure?" He nodded toward my lap where my fingers were stuffed under my thighs to prevent myself from pawing him like a tigress in heat.

I placed my hands on top of my hoodie that was laid across my legs and fiddled with the drawstring.

"So, a Tesla, huh?" I asked, snark coating my words. "I thought only assholes drove those."

"Well, if memory serves, you *did* say I was an asshole." A grin formed along his mouth in the faint glow of oncoming headlights.

"To be fair, I never actually *said* that," I replied. "But I did think it a few times."

"You still think I'm a dick?" He glanced over at me, his eyes shimmering with mischief.

"Hmm," I said, pretending to consider it. "The jury's still out, but I'll get back to you."

"You do that," he said as he entered the on-ramp of the interstate. "So, tell me what else I need to know about you, McKenzie. Besides the fact that you have good taste in music and an iron liver."

"Who says you need to know anything about me?" I asked, my tone coy and flirtatious.

"Maybe I don't need to," he said as the car picked up speed. "But I want to."

My cheeks flamed. "What do you want to know?"

"Where did you grow up?"

"Right here."

"Weird," he said. "I don't remember a cute chick with a smart mouth coming with my car. Were you in the glove compartment?"

"I meant Nashville, you ass." I kept my focus forward, pretending I wasn't reeling from the fact that he'd just called me cute. "I went to school over in West Nashville. My mom still lives there in the house I grew up in."

"Do you have any other family around?"

My chest tightened. "Just her. What about you?"

"You already know everyone I consider family."

I sensed there was more to the story, but it didn't feel right to ask.

"What do you like to do when you're not baking at the restaurant or drinking all of our buddy Freddy's liquor?" he teased.

"This isn't a regular occurrence," I said.

"Celebrating something?" he asked, and when I didn't immediately answer, he added, "Or maybe trying to distract yourself from something?"

"Or maybe I just needed to let some steam out of the kettle, you know? Let loose a little." My tone was far more defensive than I'd have liked. "Is that okay with you, detective?"

"Of course." He held up a hand. "Hey, I'm not judging. I'm the last person on earth who gets to judge anyone."

I pressed my lips together. "I like to thrift."

"Thrift?"

"You asked what else I like to do. I go to secondhand stores and hunt for treasures," I said. "Oh wait. You're a rock star with a Tesla. Do you even know what Goodwill is?"

He scoffed. "I wasn't always a rock star."

"Really? I thought maybe you came out of the womb like that." I swirled my finger in his direction.

"Like what?" he asked.

"A Calvin Klein model with a douchebag car."

His brows raised in amusement. "Are you saying you think I'm hot?"

"Once again, I didn't actually say those words."

"But do you?"

I snorted. "What difference does it make what I think?"

He shrugged. "I just get the feeling you don't impress easily. So, if you think I'm hot, then I must be doing something right."

"You don't need me to confirm anything. I doubt confidence is something you've ever lacked in your lifetime."

"You'd be surprised." His fingers flexed over the steering wheel, and when I looked at his face, the lightness that had been present throughout the evening had been replaced with a pensive expression.

"What about you? What do *you* like to do?" I asked. "Besides meeting girls in dive bars and cutting glass with your chiseled jaw?"

That playful glint returned to his eyes. "I'm working on cutting other things besides glass."

"Oh yeah?" I asked. "Like what? Wooden planks? A pot roast?"

He feigned disgust as he changed lanes at the direction of our GPS guide. "You don't think this jawline is at least worthy of a filet mignon?"

I scrunched my nose. "A New York strip, maybe. Or a sirloin."

"A sirloin?" he repeated with a chuckle. "Now, I'm

offended. Don't make me pull this douche wagon over and kick you out."

"Would you look at that—the jury is back in session," I said. "And they're saying you're an asshole."

He laughed, glancing in his rearview before taking the next exit.

"On a serious note, I guess I don't really know what I like to do anymore. Though right now, meeting girls in dive bars certainly tops the list," he said, flashing me a wink.

Heat rushed up my neck and into my cheeks. "How could you not know what you like to do?"

"It's just been a long time since I did something purely for the enjoyment of it," he explained. "I made music because I liked it, but at the end of the day, it was my job. I went to all those A-list parties because I wanted people to think I was someone I'm not. Back when I used to drink, it was to get drunk and forget all of my problems. I never did anything for the fun of it."

"Sounds like tonight is exactly what you need, then." What we *both* need, I added silently.

"I'm glad I ran into you. Even if you do think I'm an asshole." He smirked at me as we inched closer to our destination ahead on the right.

My lips quirked into a grin. "At least you're a hot asshole."

He started to speak but I cut him off.

"And I reserve the right to change my opinion if you let it go to your head," I said. "So I'd think long and hard about the next words that come out of your mouth."

His mouth twitched. "Long and hard, huh?"

I swatted his arm as he pulled into a parking spot on a nearby side street.

"Hey! Ow!" He recoiled, cutting the engine. "Those were your words, not mine."

It was true. My mind had been in the gutter all evening. And who could blame me for wondering what secrets were contained in those dark jeans he wore?

I ignored him, flipping down the mirror over the passenger seat to check my reflection. I wiped away a stray eyelash before sweeping my ChapStick over my lips.

With every move, I could feel his eyes on me.

"What?" I asked, turning to him and then back to the mirror. "Is there something on my face?"

"Huh?" He cleared his throat, running his hand along the back of his neck. "Uh, no. You look good."

Warmth spread through my limbs as I climbed out of the car, smoothing my T-shirt over my waist. Luca joined me on the crowded sidewalk, and we started toward The Basement. A few faces flickered with recognition, including a blonde in a barely-there halter top and miniskirt who didn't even try to hide her stare.

Seriously? I'm right here.

Not that he was *with* me, but we *were* there together. How did she know we weren't on a date? I had half a mind to tell that girl to take a picture—that it would last longer—but before I could, Luca's hand found the small of my back again, inadvertently letting her know that at least for tonight, he *was* with me.

I flashed the girl a smug smile as we pushed past her. I didn't know if he was doing it so he wouldn't lose me in the crowd or because he was afraid my tipsy ass might face-plant onto the dirty concrete, but I didn't care.

Tonight was all about escaping reality.

TEN

Luca

My hand ended up on the small of McKenzie's back as I guided her toward the entrance of The Basement East. It was the second time my fingers had been drawn to the spot that evening.

I'd noticed a blonde as we were walking up the sidewalk, or more accurately, she'd noticed me. She was exactly the type of girl I normally would have gravitated toward.

But that was before. Before my entire existence had become an open wound, my emotions an exposed nerve. When I didn't care about myself or anyone else. But now, I *did* care, and that shifted my perspective and everything I wanted. It changed *me*.

There was also a part of me that felt protective of McKenzie. Like when I'd seen those creeps leering at her at The Piccadilly Deli. And when I caught the blonde sizing her up in a way that made any beauty the chick possessed evaporate into thin air. I wanted to send a signal to her and anyone else who happened to be watching exactly who I was with.

"This place is packed," McKenzie said over the noise of

the crowd once we were inside. She drew her arms in close to her sides, making herself as small as possible.

"Are you good?" I asked as people squeezed past us.

"I just…" She trailed off and blew out a breath. "I need a drink, and then I'll be fine."

She bounded off in the direction of the bar, and I followed.

"Excuse me," she said, wedging herself between two guys at the end.

At the sound of her voice, one of the guys looked down at her, his thin lips stretching into a smile.

"Get on in here, gorgeous," he said. "Let's get you a drink."

She opened her mouth to speak, but I stepped in.

"Actually, I've got it," I said, McKenzie's back pressing against my chest as I threw my card down on the bar. "But thanks, man." I clapped him on the back.

The guy's jaw nearly disconnected as it fell open.

"Holy shit," he muttered, elbowing his friend, who quickly turned around.

"Is that Luca Sterling?" the dude's buddy whispered loud enough that I still heard him.

"What'll you have?" the bartender asked McKenzie as she poured cheap tequila for another customer.

"I'm getting my own," McKenzie started to argue, digging for her card, but I put a hand on her arm.

"I owe you, remember?"

"A shot of Jack and a whiskey sour," she said, before tipping her head up to me. "And thanks."

When the bartender returned with her drinks, McKenzie pounded the shot and grabbed her cocktail.

"Much better," she said. "I didn't want that perfectly good buzz I had going to waste."

"Where do you want to stand?" I asked, gesturing toward the mob of fans hugging the front of the stage.

"How about over there?" She pointed to the back wall where there were only a few people lingering among a handful of high-top tables.

I nodded. "Yeah, that's good."

"That'll keep us out of the crowd and give us plenty of room to dance."

"Dance?" I asked. My brow furrowed as I followed her, my hand hovering at the top of her jeans. "I don't dance."

"Ah, so all that crap about wanting to have fun was bullshit, then?" she asked over her shoulder before taking a swig of her drink. "Whatever. It'll give *me* plenty of room to dance."

I studied her as we settled in the back of the club until she glanced up and caught my eye.

"What?" she asked.

"Nothing." I smirked, stuffing my hands in my pockets. "Just looking forward to seeing your moves."

She brought her glass to her lips and took a big gulp. "It's a very rare occurrence that I'm drunk enough to dance in public. Or at all." Another swallow and all that remained was ice.

"So tonight is a particularly special occasion?"

"Something like that." Shadows darkened the corners of her eyes. "I'm going to go to the bathroom and grab another drink before the show starts."

She sauntered off before I could say anything, but I kept watch from a distance, so I could step in should any other losers try to talk to her. Luckily this time, nobody bothered her at the bar as she pounded another shot before starting back in my direction with a drink clutched in each fist.

It *did* seem like she was drinking a lot, but she'd said she needed to let loose. All alcohol ever did was make me even more miserable than I already was. If it helped her relax and it wasn't something she did all the time, who was I to say anything? Besides, I was there to keep her safe.

The house lights went out, and the room erupted as a single spotlight illuminated the stage.

"Right on time," she said, a hazy grin spread over her berry-stained lips.

The opening guitar licks to "I'm Not Okay (I Promise)" began to play and four regular-looking dudes stepped into the light. My expectations were low when I saw the lead singer was wearing a collared shirt and khakis, looking like he'd gotten lost on the way to a PTA meeting. But then he opened his mouth, and I was transported to a My Chemical Romance concert.

"Holy shit," I shouted over the music.

"They're good, right?" McKenzie asked, tipping back her drink. She threw her hands in the air, nearly spilling her liquor, and cheered.

"Hell yeah, they are." I bobbed my head to the beat, and my fingers itched to pick up a guitar for the first time in months. They were fucking amazing.

McKenzie bounced in place like a rubber ball, singing along to the lyrics. When the song finished, the audience came undone.

That's when the lead singer finally spoke. "We're Helena's Sweet Revenge. This next one's called 'Welcome to the Black Parade.' Scream it if you know it."

McKenzie gasped and gripped my arm. "This is my favorite."

"Mine too," I said, and I watched as the melody transformed her. She swayed next to me like a wildflower in the wind. Her eyes closed, and she dropped her head back onto her shoulders, face turned up at the ceiling as though it was the sun.

It was the most beautiful fucking thing I'd ever seen. I envied her because I longed to feel that way. Liberated. Uncaged. No longer held captive by my own mind.

The tempo picked up, and she reached for me in the darkness, threading her fingers through mine.

"Come on," she shouted, knocking back the rest of her drink and slamming the empty plastic cup on one of the tables nearby. "You're dancing with me."

"Oh, I…" She wasn't even trying to hear me as she grabbed my other hand. "I really don't know what I'm doing."

I nodded my head to the beat, suddenly self-conscious.

"You don't have to know," she said. "You just have to feel."

Slowly, I began to follow her lead, moving in time with her like we were riding the wind of the same breeze. I twirled her and pulled her into me, our laughter lost in the noise of the crowd. The liquor had given her the courage to let go, but she was my shot of whiskey.

Somewhere along the way, I stopped thinking. The chatter in my head was overtaken by the music, the sweet scent of buttercream on McKenzie's hair, and the warmth of her body in my arms. We swayed together, two wildflowers in a field of weeds, and in that moment, I was free.

"Easy there, Miss Independent," I said, cutting the engine of my car in the gravel drive of McKenzie's house. "Let me help you."

"I don't need help." She'd already thrown open the door and was attempting to exit the vehicle with her seat belt still on. Luckily, the rain had relented or else the inside of my car would have been soaked.

"Right," I said, clicking the button to free her from the strap.

"Hey, I had that," she argued as her head lolled back against the headrest.

"Of course, you did." I got out and hurried to her side where she was dangling from the seat, her legs buckling beneath her like pool noodles.

"I did," she sang, before bursting into an adorable stream of giggles. *"Not."*

"Put your arms around my neck," I told her. "And I'm going to pull you up. Ready?"

She answered with a snort that made my shoulders shake with laughter, but I still managed to get her to her feet.

"This is nice," she said, her voice taking on a slow, dreamy cadence. She planted herself face-first against my chest as I shut the door with my hip. "How do you still smell this good? I smell like the floor at The Basement."

"Well, I did have to peel you off it," I said with a chuckle, securing my arm around her waist. As the night had worn on, the liquor had taken its toll on her. By the end of the concert, she was struggling to keep herself upright.

"Excuse me, mister." She twirled a clumsy finger around my face. "Are you judging me?"

"Nope. I've been the one on the floor *many* times," I said, surveying the sidewalk and the front porch, which thankfully, only had three stairs. "You have a nice place."

"Oh, the house?" she asked. "That's not mine."

"*What?* Whose house is this?"

She exploded into laughter, and my eyes darted around, certain we were both about to get arrested.

"We should go back to the car," I said, but she swatted my arm.

"No, I live here," she explained. "But I don't live in the house. I'm in the apartment. Up there."

My eyes followed her finger that was pointing to a slim iron staircase.

"You don't have to get me up there," she insisted. "I can do it. You can go home."

She attempted to step away from me and stumbled, but I caught her.

"Nice try," I said, wrapping my arms around her. We made it to the base of the stairs that was nearly obscured by beds of shrubs. "All right, we're going to take this nice and slow."

She faced me, her arms circling around my neck, and my heart leapt into my throat. God, she was beautiful. But she was also really, *really* drunk.

"You're pretty," she said. "Like, unnaturally pretty. Are you an alien?"

I laughed. "I don't think so?"

She moved closer, so we were almost nose to nose, and heat rushed up my neck despite the chill of the night air.

"Were you sent here to suck my blood?" she asked.

"I think you've got your aliens and vampires mixed up."

A piece of hair fell in her face as she studied me, and without thinking, I reached to tuck it behind her ear.

She held my gaze, and the moment swelled until all I could see was her.

Her soft hands found my face, and my lids drifted closed, but my heart was split wide open. When I opened my eyes again, she was leaning in with parted lips.

"McKenzie," I whispered. "No."

My body was *screaming* yes, but I couldn't. Not anymore.

"You know I think you're hot," she said, her words slurring together impatiently. "Isn't this what you do? Isn't this, like, *your thing*?"

The blood drained from my face. "What do you mean?"

She huffed out a breath. "I hear you've got a lot of notches on your belt, dude. So, what's another one?"

My jaw clenched. "That's not…That's not who I am anymore."

"Oh. I see." Her voice was cloaked in bitterness. "I'm not notch-worthy. Not hot enough for the rock star."

"That's not it," I said. "At *all*. You're…gorgeous. It's just…I've changed. I don't want to be that guy."

"What guy?" she asked, not meeting my gaze.

"The one who takes advantage of a situation."

"You're not taking advantage of me when I'm throwing myself at you." She slid her hands down my chest. "I don't get it. Why don't you want me?"

I *did* want her. But not like this.

"I…I can't, McKenzie."

Her pretty face fell, and she hung her head. "All I wanted was to forget."

"Forget?" *Forget what?*

She buried her face in her hands. "Why don't you just tell me I'm not good enough to fuck and put me out of my misery?"

"Because that's not the truth," I said.

She rolled her eyes. "Whatever."

"It's not."

"Then what *is*?"

I gripped her chin with my fingers, holding it so she was forced to look at me.

"The truth is, McKenzie, when I fuck you, I want you to be able to remember every perfect fucking minute of it."

Her throat worked to swallow, and her eyes went wide. She opened her mouth to speak, but whether it was to agree or tell me to fuck all the way off, I'll never know because she wrenched herself from my grasp, releasing a geyser of puke into the bushes.

The universe was humbling me.

"Oh my God," she moaned, dropping to her knees.

I gathered her hair in my hands to keep it out of her face.

"Please go, Luca," she pleaded. "Let me die in peace."

"Not a chance."

Once I was fairly sure she'd emptied the contents of her stomach, I picked her up as gently as I could, hoisted her over my shoulder, and carried her up the stairs. We got inside, and she pointed me in the direction of the bathroom where she tried to push me away again while simultaneously hugging the toilet.

Instead, I opened the closet door, found a washcloth, and soaked it in cold water before wringing it out. I gathered her hair into an elastic band I found on the sink and then pressed the cold compress to the back of her neck as I lightly rubbed her back.

"I'm gonna die," she croaked, her insides deciding they had more fight left in them after all. "Can you let Katie know I'm calling out of work dead for the rest of my life?"

I bit back a laugh.

"Hey, Luca?"

"Yeah?"

"I'm gonna need you to leave."

"I already told you I'm not—" I started, but she cut me off.

"Please," she begged. "I've humiliated myself enough for one night."

I narrowed my eyes in a glare that told her to save it.

"Fine," she whined. "You don't have to *leave* leave, but I have to pee, and I'd really like to keep some shred of my dignity."

"Okay," I agreed. "I'll go get you some water and maybe a snack to help soak up some of this alcohol."

She groaned. "Please don't say snack."

"Scratch the—"

"Don't say it!"

I eased her to her feet before leaving the room, shutting the door behind me. Finally, I was able to take in McKenzie's apartment. Lit only by the soft glow of a couple of funky-looking lamps, it was the very definition of cozy. There was a plush green sofa in the living area with an afghan draped across it. Framed art prints and photographs lined the wall that led to the small kitchen with a black refrigerator covered in magnets.

I felt along the wall for the light switch so I could see as I searched the cabinets.

"Glasses," I muttered to myself. "Where are the glasses?"

Once I found them, I pulled one down, returning to the fridge for some ice and water.

As I was filling the glass, a pair of glowing yellow eyes pierced through me.

"What the fuck?" I yelped, stumbling backward and into

the counter. A black cat leaped to the floor in front of me. It peered at me through slits, probably trying to decide whether I was there to rob the joint and how much of a fight it was willing to put up if I was.

Apparently, I wasn't worth the effort, because the cat began cleaning itself, revealing the tiniest white patch on its chest.

McKenzie has a black cat. Of course she does.

With the water in hand, I started back toward the couch, taking in the pictures on the wall. There was some quirky pop art of cats, including one that was dressed like Dolly Parton. There was McKenzie with Katie and Dallas outside Katie's Kitchen, and a few photos of her with more people I assumed were friends. Then there were some photos of what looked like a young McKenzie with a woman who had her nose and her eyes, and a slightly older boy who shared her smile.

He appeared in many of the memories along the wall, but my gaze snagged on one picture in particular. It was of McKenzie and that same boy, both of whom appeared to be teenagers at the time. He wore a My Chemical Romance shirt, and she was grinning up at him like he was her whole world.

The door to the bathroom flung open, and McKenzie stepped out on wobbly legs.

"How you doing?" I asked, rushing to her side.

"I've definitely been better," she said, gratefully taking the water and chugging it down.

"I met your cat, by the way."

"Which one?"

"There's more than one?" I asked. "The one I saw was black."

"That's Binx," she said. "I've always had a thing for *Hocus Pocus*. Creative, I know."

"Where's the other one?"

She snorted. "Probably hiding under the bed because there's a stranger in the house. If you see a round raccoon-looking cat on stick legs running around here, his name is Earl Grey."

"I'll make sure to introduce myself," I joked. "How about we get you in bed and let you sleep this off?"

She nodded, and I followed her to her room, hovering in the doorway.

"How are you feeling? Should I bring a trash can in here just in case?" I asked.

"Actually, that might not be the worst idea." She gave me a weak smile.

"You have some ibuprofen? I could bring you some and refill your water while I'm at it."

"Yeah," she answered. "It's in the medicine cabinet."

"I'll go get that while you get changed. Just open the door when you're done."

I didn't run into any other cats as I took her glass and set about getting what I needed, and it wasn't long before I heard the click of the door opening. When I entered, I found McKenzie in an oversized sweatshirt that nearly went to her knees and nothing else. I didn't know how it was possible for someone to be that fucking adorable.

"Thanks," she said, taking the water and pills from my hand, and knocking them back as I placed the bathroom trash can beside the bed.

I peeled the covers back, and she climbed inside.

"How's that?" I asked.

"A lot better than the bushes, where I'd probably still be if it wasn't for you."

I grinned. "Glad I could help. Are you sure I can't get you something to—"

"God no," she groaned. "I can't even think about food. Actually, I'm kinda hoping this bed swallows me up, and I can disappear into the abyss."

I shook my head and chuckled. "All right. Well, I'll just be in the living room if you need anything."

"Luca, seriously. I appreciate you helping me. But please go. In fact, if we could just pretend none of this ever happened, that'd be great."

My throat tightened. "I don't want to do that."

"God, I can't imagine why," she said, raking her hands down her face. "Especially after I literally turned into a volcano of vomit."

"Maybe I'm into that sort of thing," I joked. "You never know."

That elicited a weak smile from her, and I wondered how much of this she'd remember in the morning. I wasn't even sure how much I *wanted* her to remember. Not because I hadn't meant what I said. But because I did with every fiber of my being. And that scared the shit out of me.

She looked up at me with her green eyes. The lightness from the concert had been replaced by a penetrating sadness. Even with all of the pain I'd been feeling, I'd have taken on the heaviness of whatever was weighing her down in a heartbeat.

She rolled over on her side, and I ran my fingers along her back and stroked her hair. The only noise came from the soft whir of the ceiling fan overhead.

Finally, she whispered into the darkness. "Thank you."

The next thing I heard was the sound of her slowed breaths that turned into soft snores as she drifted into sleep.

ELEVEN

McKenzie

LUCA'S BREATH TICKLED MY NECK BEFORE HE SANK HIS TEETH into my tender flesh with just the right amount of pressure. His palms slid under my T-shirt, smooth against my back as his fingers expertly found the clasp of my bra.

I let out a little gasp as he freed my breasts, my hands gripping fistfuls of his luscious dark hair.

"The truth is, McKenzie, when I fuck you, I want you to be able to remember every perfect fucking minute of it." His voice was a low growl against my ear that caused my core to tighten. "Can you do that for me?"

"Yes." The word came out in a ragged whisper.

"I want you to memorize the way I fuck you," he said, his thumbs rolling over my nipples. "God, I can't wait to taste you."

His name was a prayer on my lips as I begged him to take me. "Please, Luca."

"You rang?"

I shot up like a lightning bolt, nearly falling off the bed, to find Luca in jeans, a T-shirt, and no shoes standing in the shadows of the doorway to my bedroom.

"Luca!" I scrambled to cover my bare legs with the blanket. Binx glared at me from his spot beside me on the mattress.

"Uh, yeah." He blinked. "Were you expecting someone else?"

"No...I...of course not."

My head pounded, and the inside of my mouth felt like a hayfield on fire in the middle of a drought.

"I brought you some water," he said, nodding toward the nightstand.

"Thanks." I grabbed the full glass of water, chugging it down despite the protests from my churning stomach.

"I was just about to come get you, actually. I ordered in some coffee, breakfast sandwiches, and a couple pastries." He stretched and the ripple of his bicep nearly made me drool.

I cleared my throat. "Oh wow. You didn't have to do that."

"Thought you might be ready for some food after all that alcohol." A grin crept across his face. "I figured last night made you work up an appetite."

Oh.

Oh my God.

Did I? Did we?

The color drained from my face. Images from the night before flashed through my mind in blurry snapshots. The Piccadilly Deli. Burgers and Bushwackers. Trying to forget. Shots—*soooo* many shots. Helena's Sweet Revenge at The Basement. Luca.

"Right," I said, my already hot cheeks smoldering as I recalled the way he'd shown up at my table looking like a daydream. The way he'd placed his hand on the small of my back like it belonged there. Talking together in the car. His warm hands in mine as we danced.

But that was when things turned fuzzy. How had I gotten into my apartment? Those stairs were steep on a good day, let alone when I was hammered.

"You want me to bring your breakfast to you?" he asked, like this was just our normal Friday morning routine.

"No, no," I answered too fast. "I'll be there in just a sec."

He raised his brows. "Are you okay?"

"Yeah," I said. "Just a little woozy is all. I probably need to eat."

"All right," he said, shoving his hands in his pockets. "Well, it's ready when you are."

He disappeared from view, and I flopped back like a dead fish. My hair stuck to my neck, damp with sweat, and the scent of whiskey emanated from my pores. I squeezed my eyes shut, pressing the heels of my palms into my sockets as I tried to conjure up more memories. They trickled in, one by one. Being folded into the passenger side of Luca's Tesla. Luca's arms around me as he all but carried me up the damp pathway.

My brain was a browser with too many tabs open, the cursor spinning. All I knew was I'd give anything to control-alt-delete my way out of this and start over.

I tossed the covers aside and slid out of bed, tiptoeing toward the door. Binx judged me through slanted eyes as I made my way outside the room with my back against the wall and peeked into the kitchen.

Luca was facing away from me as he unpacked a brown paper sack, pausing to take a sip of coffee. He seemed relaxed as Earl Grey studied him from the floor, hoping for a crumb. His locks were disheveled, but whose hair wasn't a mess after they'd just woken up? It didn't mean we'd had sex.

It was just a dream, right?

I took another step closer, the floorboards creaking beneath my feet.

He turned and smiled when he heard me. "There's a bacon, egg, and cheese situation over here or sausage if you'd rather have that."

Was his inflection weird when he said 'sausage'? Gah. Shut up, McKenzie.

"Sausage sounds great," I said, padding over to the counter.

Seriously? "Bacon," I blurted out. "I mean bacon."

He handed me a foil-wrapped sandwich and a large take-out coffee cup.

"I wasn't sure how you took your coffee, so I got a pour over," he said.

I took a drink, the caffeine going straight to my addled brain.

He turned back to the bag and plucked out some sort of jumbo muffin. "I love these things, but really, they're just breakfast cupcakes."

"Fuck," I cursed, slamming my breakfast on the counter. My eyes darted to the clock on the microwave. It was just after 10 a.m. I was late for work. And not just a little. "Oh my God. Katie's going to fire me."

"I'm sure she won't."

"Damn it," I wailed as I ran back to the bedroom and began a mad search for my phone.

Binx jumped off the bed, officially over my shit.

Same, buddy. Same.

"Looking for this?" Luca asked with a playful smile,

leaning against the doorframe with my phone in his hand. "It must've fallen out of your pocket when you took off your pants last night. I found it on the floor this morning."

I took off my pants?! Fuck me. I mentally slapped a palm to my head. *He probably already did, and I just don't remember it.*

I didn't have time to think about that. I had to text Katie, so I snatched the device out of his grip and opened the message app.

There were several unread texts already waiting for me, but only one from Katie. I held my breath as I swiped to open the message.

Good morning, sunshine! You've been killing it lately and you stepped up big time recently when I needed you. Dal and I are in this weekend, and we have a full staff, so I want you to take today and tomorrow off. Enjoy a (paid) long weekend. Thanks for being amazing!

I reread the text three more times before lifting my gaze to Luca. "You didn't…Luca. Please tell me you didn't tell Katie we…that you didn't tell Katie anything."

He tilted his perfectly shaped head. "What are you talking about?"

I turned the phone so the screen faced him. "She gave me today *and* tomorrow off. For literally no reason. Sounds fishy to me."

"Or lucky, depending on how you look at it."

"I haven't had enough coffee for this." I pushed past him and stormed back into the kitchen, taking a swig from my cup.

"You're overthinking this," Luca said, joining me, and picking up his muffin. "It sounds like Katie just wanted to do something nice for you as a way of saying thanks for all the shit you've been doing while they've been away helping me get..." He paused and cleared his throat. "While I've started working to get my shit together."

I studied him for a moment. He'd never said why he was visiting beyond mentioning he'd been having a hard time and needed to not be alone. I hadn't pressed because it didn't feel like my place, but I *did* wonder. He dropped his gaze to his feet, which indicated it might still not be the right time to ask. So, instead, I shifted my focus to the fact-finding mission at hand.

What had actually happened last night?

"On a scale from one to ten, how much did I embarrass myself last night?" I asked, taking another pull from my coffee. "Like, twenty-three?"

"Nah." He grinned. "Only like a six. Seven, tops."

I scrubbed my hands down my face. "Great."

He laughed. "I'm kidding. It wasn't that bad."

"How bad is not that bad?"

"You don't remember?" he asked, his top teeth scraping over his lower lip.

Had I kissed that perfect mouth last night? It seems like something that would be engraved into my memory forever like a secret message in a locket. One meant for me and only me.

"I gotta be honest," I said, "after leaving The Basement, I don't remember much."

He nodded, leaning against the counter beside me. "Well, by the time we got here, you were pretty far gone." An amused smirk spread over his face. "In fact, I did have to carry you up those steps."

"Oh God."

"But that was after you, um, puked in the bushes," he said

with a wince, as though that somehow made this knowledge less embarrassing.

"Fuck," I cried, my cheeks burning hot. "I'm sorry you had to see that. Shit, why didn't you just leave me out there to rot with the worms? This is so embarrassing."

"Trust me," he said. "I've seen much worse. I've *been* worse."

"Is that supposed to make me feel better? Because it doesn't." I took a ginormous bite of my bagel sandwich, grease dripping down my chin. *Whatever. It's not like he hasn't seen worse.*

"You were fine," he assured me. "I got you upstairs, you…chilled in the bathroom for a bit, then went to bed. I slept on the couch."

So, we hadn't had sex. *Whew. It was all a dream.* One I wished was real, but I'd rather be able to remember it, so I could replay it like a movie for the rest of my life. Not that I'd ever get the chance to make it a reality. Especially after what he'd witnessed the night before.

"Actually, Earl Grey kept me company."

"Wow, really?" I asked. "He's usually a little weird about strangers." Visitors were allowed in my apartment so infrequently that both of my cats were generally put off by any sort of unexpected company. I was sure my cats were also pretty displeased with me. First, I'd brought home a stranger, and then I'd interrupted our usual nightly routine of me singing made-up songs to them while I washed my face before our bedtime snuggles.

"Well, we must have met in a past life then, because I woke up with him sleeping on top of my head," he said. "I've never been a big animal person, but I think that cat could bring me over to the dark side."

"Speaking of, I better feed these guys before they decide to pack up and go home with you." I grabbed their bowls from the spot by the fridge and padded over to the small pantry, scooping some food into each of their bowls. They happily received it, Binx letting out one of his signature chirps, and Earl Grey purring like a boat motor.

And just like that, I was back in their good graces. Animals were so much easier than people.

"You did say something last night that I wanted to ask you about, though," Luca said, pinching off a bite of his muffin and tossing it into his mouth.

Oh no. I'd thought the potential for more embarrassment had already passed. What the hell could I have said? Glimmers of my dream returned to me, and my palms started to sweat.

"What was that?" I asked, trying to play it cool as I returned to my coffee.

"You said something about wanting to forget."

I nodded and closed my eyes. The reason for my drunken display of idiocy burned through me like the whiskey down my throat. I'd made it through the night, but there Brennan was, waiting for me the next day. I never forgot for long—not that I wanted to. But sometimes, I *did* think about how much easier life would have been if I could've forgotten. Maybe I wouldn't be so fucking scared of letting people in, constantly afraid of the singular moment that would rip them from my life forever.

"What were you trying to forget?" he asked.

I froze, placing my coffee cup down. Outside of my mother and my friends from group, no one else knew. Not even Katie, despite how close we'd become. But Luca had watched me spiral out of control the night before, and he hadn't left. He'd stuck by my side and taken care of me. I owed him some honesty.

"Come here," I said, walking over to the wall that held all of my thrifted art finds and beloved pictures.

"This is my brother, Brennan." I pointed to my favorite of me and Brennan when we were teenagers. "He passed away fifteen years ago yesterday."

"McKenzie, I'm sorry," he said softly. "How old was he?"

"Seventeen," I answered. "He had his whole life ahead of him. He never even got to see his favorite band play a show. Never got to have his own apartment. He used to play guitar. He was good too. I swear, he could have been in a band one day if he'd wanted to."

"How did he…I mean, what happened?" he asked with a shake of his head. "If that's not too personal to ask."

I reached out, touching my finger to the distressed wood frame. The photo was taken over Labor Day weekend, a little more than a month before I lost him. Brennan, Mom, and I were never big outdoorsy people, so we'd stayed in, playing games and watching old movies. I don't even remember what was happening when our mother took the photo of us. Brennan, who was wearing his favorite My Chemical Romance shirt, was looking directly at her. But my eyes were on him, my lips stretched in a cheesy grin. I'd probably caught him cheating at Monopoly again or maybe he'd just told us one of his ridiculous one-liners that could put all dad jokes to shame. He was the only person who ever made me smile like that.

I turned to Luca, hot tears filling my eyes. "He took his own life. I was the one who found…" I trailed off and drew in a breath, moisture sliding down my cheeks.

He swallowed hard. "Were the two of you close?"

I nodded. "I had no idea he was so depressed—that he felt

like that. He was my best friend. He knew me better than anyone. Aside from our mom, he was the only person who made me feel safe enough to be myself. But I...I couldn't keep *him* safe, and I lost him."

Luca didn't say a word. He simply pulled me into his arms, his chin resting on top of my head. I sank into him, letting him hold me as I wailed into his chest. Maybe it was the raging hangover I had or the fact that in less than twenty-four hours, Luca had seen me at my absolute worst. Or maybe it was because there was something about him that made me think he might understand the darkest shadows of my heart because he lived in darkness too.

Only when my sobs quieted did he pull away, and even then, it was so he could look into my eyes.

"I need you to hear me when I say this, McKenzie," he said. "I didn't know your brother, but I can tell you his death was not your fault. When someone makes up their mind about something like that...He didn't tell you because he didn't want you to know."

"But I should have seen the signs."

"You're not hearing me. He didn't give you any because he never wanted to hurt you. He loved you too much to do that. When people feel like that, they aren't thinking about the pain it will cause anyone else. They just want *their* pain to end. They want to stop feeling like a fucking burden. They're not trying to be selfish because they think the most selfless thing they could possibly do is to remove their broken fucking pieces from the picture."

His face disappeared behind a wall of my tears. "I don't believe you. I could have done something. I *should* have done something."

He placed his hands on both sides of my face, pressing his forehead to mine.

"I'm telling you there's nothing you or anyone else could have done," he whispered, his words full of anguish. "Because there was nothing anyone could have done for me."

"What do you mean?" I asked, my voice hoarse.

"My friends had left every door open for me, but it didn't matter. I pushed them away. I didn't want to *be* here anymore." His eyes turned glassy. "Existing in this mind, this body, that tried to sabotage me at every turn. That's why I disappeared. You know how hard Katie and Dallas tried to reach me, but I lied to them. I told them I was traveling when I was really rotting away at home."

I blinked, unsure what to say.

"I didn't speak to anyone for months because I didn't want to. People can try to help, but *we* have to be able to receive it." His thumbs stroked the tender skin beneath my eyes. "I'm so sorry you lost your brother. I can't imagine the grief you've felt all these years. But his death wasn't your fault."

It wasn't until I heard him say it that I began to wonder if it was true. Luca seemed to understand Brennan in a way I'd never been able to. He'd felt that way before.

"You really think so?" I asked.

"I know so," he answered, pulling me back into his arms.

I leaned into him, allowing his embrace to carry the weight of my pain, while I also made space for his. I didn't know how long we stayed like that, holding each other's broken hearts together. When I finally looked back up at him, I made a silent vow to myself.

There may have been nothing I could have done to save my brother, but I'd do everything in my power to keep Luca from ever feeling that way again.

TWELVE

Luca

———

It wasn't like I hadn't imagined it since I started this whole fucking healing journey—what it would've been like if I'd actually made the choice to leave this world for whatever came next. How it would have affected my friends. But imagining it and facing it were two entirely different things. McKenzie's grief for her brother was still an open cut, even fifteen years later. In my head, I imagined that agony faded with time. But maybe it merely scabbed over, scratched open with every milestone that passed without them or with every birthday or holiday missed.

I rubbed my hands along the tops of her shoulders. "Thank you for sharing that with me. I know it had to have been hard. I wish I'd known last night. Maybe there was something I could have done to help."

"Honestly, you just being there was…really great," she said. "And you kept me from doing anything stupid. Well, anything more stupid than getting wasted and puking in the bushes."

"Do you normally spend the anniversary alone?" I asked.

She shook her head. "I'm usually with my mom, but she had the opportunity to go on the trip of a lifetime to Italy, and I told her she needed to take it. I wanted her to, and Brennan would have wanted that too. Then I made plans with some friends, but I don't know…my mind started going to some dark places, so I canceled. Then I ended up at The Piccadilly Deli, and you know the rest."

"I'm glad I ran into you." For so many reasons. So that I could keep her safe. Because I enjoyed her company. Because she saw the darkest parts of me in a way many couldn't, and it didn't seem to scare her.

"Me too. And I'm sorry I broke down on you like that," McKenzie said, pulling out of my grasp and dabbing her fingers beneath her lashes. "This isn't like me. I don't do this."

"Do what?" I asked.

"Talk about shit," she said with a nervous laugh. "You know. *Feelings.* I'm more of the suffer in silence type. Or on rare occasions, get blackout drunk."

"I can relate to that," I admitted. "But all that managed to do was send me to therapy, so maybe it's good to talk about shit sometimes."

"Maybe," she said with a faint smile.

I reached out, swiping away the lingering dampness on her cheeks with my thumbs. Her gaze snagged on mine. My eyes were drawn to her mouth like a bee to a flower. I swear, her bottom lip quivered slightly. Did she feel it too? Could she see the effect she had on me?

This wasn't like *me*. None of it. I didn't take care of people. Hell, I barely took care of myself until recently. I didn't do the *feelings* shit either, and I *definitely* didn't do relationships. I was into more…*casual* connections, but there was nothing casual about what I felt forming between McKenzie and me.

She let out a small shudder of a breath. "But I think that's enough feeling for one morning."

My chest tightened, and I pushed my hand through my hair to keep myself from touching her. I'd wondered if she'd remember the rest of what happened the night before. I'd almost hoped she would, but she didn't. It was what I'd been afraid of, what I'd wanted to avoid. I hadn't wanted her to hook up with me in a moment of drunken delusion and regret it. The old me would have been far less discerning or too drunk myself to make the right call, but now…things were different. Though, I'd kind of hoped her drunken desires might reflect her sober ones.

"Yeah," I said. "How about we finish breakfast and then go pick up your truck?"

"That would be great," she said. "And a shower. I smell like a whiskey sour."

I shot her a playful grin. "I wasn't going to say anything, but yeah…"

She swatted my arm and rolled her eyes, heading back to the counter. We finished our food and coffee, chatting while the cats wove between our feet. Then I waited while she took a quick shower, trying to keep my mind from wandering to the space behind the closed bathroom door.

"Ready?" she asked when she emerged with damp hair and wearing a black sweat suit. How was she so fucking cute in sweats?

I shrugged on my jacket and reached inside the pocket for my keys. "Ready."

Suddenly, I itched to get my journal back in my hands. Finally, I had something to say.

I RETURNED TO DALLAS AND KATIE'S AFTER TAKING McKenzie back to her truck and immediately opened the moleskin journal. With McKenzie's advice to think of it like writing a song at the forefront of my mind, I found that the words came easier. They weren't cohesive or even *good,* but they were mine.

After pouring over the blank pages for a couple of hours, scratching through lines, and adding new ones, I began hearing melodies in my mind. Of course, when I'd come back to Nashville, I hadn't thought to bring my guitar. Music had been the last thing on my mind. So, I took Emilia for a quick field trip to pick up a coffee and a pup cup before heading to Guitar Center.

"If you tell anyone about this, I will deny it," I said to Emilia as she licked the whipped cream from the tiny cup I held for her in my lap. Not that the geriatric dog could hear me anyway. "Who even am I?"

When we got to the store, I tucked Emilia under one arm and went inside. There were a few other customers, some being helped by employees wearing black button-downs with the Guitar Center logo.

"Hey, man, can I help you?" a tall young-looking guy asked as he approached. His eyes widened as he leaned a little closer. "Holy shit, dude. You're Luca Sterling. Big fan."

"I need a guitar," I said by way of a greeting.

"I can definitely help you with that," he said eagerly, clasping his hands together. "Follow me. I'm Quentin, by the way."

I nodded, too focused on the mission at hand for pleasantries, and trailed behind him.

"Cute dog," he said over his shoulder.

"Thanks."

Quentin came to a stop in front of a wall filled with electric guitars and started rambling about the different models they had available.

"You can't go wrong with a Fender Strat," he said, tapping his fingers along a seafoam green version propped against a stand. "But I'm a Schecter guy myself. The necks are slimmer, and they're just a bit more versatile depending on what your needs are. I play in a Metallica cover band, and my C-1 FR shreds like a fucking dream."

That was *not* what I needed. I wasn't envisioning soaring guitar solos or anything like that. I wanted something a bit… softer.

"Actually, I think I'd like to check out your acoustics," I said, gesturing down the wall with my thumb.

Once again, Quentin launched into more specifics about each of the various brands that I didn't really care about. I had enough talent in my left fuck-you finger to make any guitar sound good. What I really needed was something that felt right.

I was drawn to the Gibson Hummingbird hanging in front of me.

"Here," I said, pressing Emilia into Quentin's chest. "Hold her."

"Oh, uh, sure." He hesitantly scratched the pup's ear. "I never had a dog growing up. I did have a ferret once named Nikki Sixx. I used to take him to school in the pocket of my hoodie. One day he chewed a hole through it and stuck his head out of my stomach like in that movie *Alien*."

"Believe I would've kept that one in the vault, Quentin," I said, sitting on a nearby stool with the Hummingbird propped on my leg. The neck fit in my hand like it was made for me. I started strumming the melody that had been in my head all day as Quentin yammered on about his old ferret, and Emilia let out an annoyed huff.

"…and one day he got out of his cage, and the little fucker got into a hole in the drywall," Quentin said with a heavy sigh. "Never saw him again after that."

I stopped playing and stood, snatching Emilia from Quentin's grasp, and handed him the guitar. "I'll take this one."

Emilia and I returned home with the brand-new guitar, and she snacked in the kitchen while I went back to the bedroom. I opened the notebook and began to play, the gravel in my voice filling the silence.

"The only way I can win is to fix the game so everybody loses
Pay to play, drop your guard
Won't know what hit you, but you'll feel the ache of my bruises
Because when you get high, I go low
Pull back, don't get too close
Or I'll go
So it goes"

I dropped my pick to the pen-scrawled page with a smile and nodded. It was far from perfect, but it was a start. But more importantly, it felt fucking good.

It was as though I'd taken a sledgehammer to the wall I'd built between me and my emotions. Once I gave voice to one feeling, another would raise its hand and demand to be heard. By the time I heard Dallas and Katie's car pull in the driveway that evening, I'd filled half the notebook with lines upon lines of my thoughts and incomplete songs.

I was glad I'd been able to find an outlet, but I wasn't sure I wanted anyone to actually *hear* what I'd written, so I put it away for the night. I went into the living room and thanked Katie for sending McKenzie the text earlier that morning, giving her the day off.

"Of course. I was happy to do it," she said. "How was she today?"

"Okay, I think," I answered. I wasn't sure if Katie knew about McKenzie's brother, and if she didn't, it wasn't my place to tell her. "She didn't say a lot about what was bothering her last night, but she did seem to be feeling better when I dropped her off at her truck."

Katie gave a solemn nod. "Thanks for looking out for her."

She and Dallas told me about their day while I kept quiet about mine. Then Dallas mentioned they were going to watch a show before they made dinner and asked if I wanted to join them, but I opted to lie down for a few minutes.

I was physically exhausted, but my mind was wide awake. About half an hour later, I realized staring at the ceiling wasn't doing me any favors, so I decided to get up and do some laundry. When I'd first started staying there, Katie insisted on doing every little thing for me, including throwing my wash in with theirs. But once I started to regain my footing, I'd gotten into the routine of heading down to the musty basement in the morning after they'd left for work to wash a load so I wasn't tying up the water in the old house while one of them was in the shower.

With my earbuds in, I turned on some music and piled my

heap of dirty clothes into a basket. I carried it through the hall and into the kitchen, opening the door that led to the basement. Balancing on the rickety steps, I pulled it shut behind me in case Emilia wandered in and got curious. I descended the stairs, an old Blink-182 song playing in my ears. When I got to the bottom and turned toward the machines, a shriek pierced through the music, and I nearly tumbled backward.

There was Dallas, sitting buck naked on top of the washer with his legs spread and Katie—thankfully, still in a bra and some shorts—standing between them. Unfortunately, that wasn't enough to keep me from seeing Dallas' whipped cream-covered dick *or* the patches of white stuck to Katie's chin.

So that's *why they keep all that shit in the house!*

"Fuck," I shouted, dropping my basket to the concrete floor, sending my clothes scattering as I covered my eyes with one hand and plucked my earbuds out with the other.

"I'm sorry. I didn't know you guys were down here."

"We thought you were resting," Dallas cried.

"I was," I said with a shudder, squeezing my eyes shut. But it was too late. The vision of Dallas and his banana split dick was already burned into my retinas. I'd never be able to listen to "All the Small Things" ever again. "I couldn't sleep, so I thought I'd do laundry. How was I supposed to know you'd be down here receiving mouth to south resuscitation?"

"Oh my God," Katie muttered. "Kill me now."

"You couldn't have put a sock on the door or something?" I asked. "Maybe a Tide Pod? I mean, you *are* in the laundry room."

"You can open your eyes now," Dallas said.

"I'd rather not." I'd never get that image out of my head as long as I lived.

"We're covered," Katie said, but I opened my lids slowly, just in case. Sure enough, they'd both managed to get their clothes back on.

Katie's cheeks were flaming red, and Dallas' face was partially obscured by his hand.

"Sorry, guys," I said, piling my clothes back into the basket. "I'm gonna…go be anywhere but here."

"You don't have to leave," Katie said, tugging at the hem of her shirt. "You can use the machine."

"I think I'm gonna pass on that." I nodded toward the stuff in my hands. "In fact, I might just burn these and start over."

Dallas shot me an annoyed glare. "Really? You *do* remember we all had to hear you have sex in the bathroom that one time at Sunday dinner, right?"

"Not my proudest moment," I said with a wince. "Listen, I'm gonna go out and grab something to eat if I can find my appetite again. Maybe I'll go for a drive. At any rate, I won't be back for a few hours."

Katie tucked a piece of hair behind her ear. "Seriously, you don't have to go anywhere."

"Oh, I do," I said, backing away toward the stairs. "Because I've got to go buy some bleach to wash Dallas' whipped cream wiener out of my head."

Dallas grabbed the aerosol can and popped the top, pointing it at me. "You better watch it."

I scrunched my nose. "Again, I'd really rather not."

He threw a towel at me, but I dodged it, ran up the stairs, and was in my car in less than ninety seconds. I headed to a local pizza joint and picked up a pie. But I didn't open the box right away. Instead, I found myself driving down the same roads I'd been on the night before until they led me back to the house with the upstairs apartment and a truck parked outside. Before I could stop to ask myself why I was there, I was climbing the iron staircase, pizza in hand.

I tapped out three rapid knocks on the door, and only *then* did my mind pause long enough to wonder what the fuck I was doing showing up at McKenzie's unannounced—or at all. But I didn't have long to consider it because she appeared, wearing an oversized fuzzy sweatshirt, leggings, and no shoes.

"Luca," she said, blinking as though I was some sort of apparition. "What are you doing here?"

What *was* I doing there? I couldn't tell her the truth. Not the part about Dallas and Katie because I couldn't bring myself to relive *that* ever again. But I also couldn't tell her that when I got in my car with nowhere to be, she was where I wanted to go. She was my somewhere.

I swallowed hard, holding out the pizza box. "Um, I thought maybe you could use some dinner?"

She studied me for a moment with narrowed eyes, but finally stepped aside, her lips curling into a half smile. "Well, you thought right."

THIRTEEN

McKenzie

Luca was in my kitchen. He'd shown up unannounced and uninvited *with dinner*. This time he wasn't here out of some misplaced obligation to keep watch over the drunk girl.

Why is he here?

"What do you want to drink?" I asked, naming the different sodas I had on hand while I pulled a couple of plates down from the cabinet. When I turned back to the counter, I saw he'd already opened the fridge.

"I was just about to ask you that." I'd almost forgotten he'd familiarized himself with my kitchen only hours ago.

I bit back a grin. "Coke Zero."

He wrinkled his nose, grabbing my drink and a regular Coke for himself, placing them on the counter. My cats blinked at me, equal parts annoyed and curious about the deviation from our normal routine before sauntering off to the bedroom.

"How do you drink that shit?" Luca asked. "Don't you miss the real sugar?"

"There will be no Coke Zero slander in my house. *That shit* is the nectar of the gods." I reached for a piece of pizza in the open box at the same time he did, and our hands collided in a spark of electricity that made my stomach flip.

"Oh, sorry," I said, feeling a rush of warmth climb up my cheeks.

He pulled his hand back and shoved it through his dark hair. "No, you go ahead."

I grabbed a couple of slices, plopping them onto my plate, and he did the same.

"You want to watch a movie or something?" I asked, nodding toward the couch.

"Sure," he answered, following me to the sofa where my television was on the Netflix home screen.

"What do you want to watch?" I asked, clearing my throat to mask the hint of nervousness clinging to my voice.

He squinted at the screen. "So, you're into true crime?"

"Huh?"

He pointed to my recently watched queue. "There's a whole lot of serial killers right there. Should I be worried?"

I snorted. "That's called being a woman."

"What? Being obsessed with psychopaths?"

I barked out a laugh, setting my drink on the small wooden coffee table. "Being prepared, in case you end up on a date with a murderer or if you tell the wrong guy 'no.'"

"Shit. Seriously?"

"Uh, *yeah*," I said. "Dudes are freaks."

He raised his brows at me. "What if I'm a closet psycho killer?"

"Then you're a stupid one, because you already had the perfect opportunity to cut my face off and wear it for Halloween, but you chose not to take it."

He gave me a casual shrug, taking a sip of his Coke.

"*Or*," he began, "maybe I just wanted to wait until you were sober to show my freaky side."

My center tightened as I remembered the dream I'd had the night before.

Dream Luca's words had started a forest fire in my belly. *The truth is, McKenzie, when I fuck you, I want you to be able to remember every perfect fucking minute of it.* Unfortunately, though, it had all been a dream.

"That should be fun," I quipped. "Gives me a chance to test out my taser."

"Your *what*?" he asked around a bite of pizza.

"My mom got it for me last year off QVC or something," I explained. "It looks like a tube of lipstick, but it's actually a mini taser."

"I'm intrigued."

"You want me to use it on you?"

"Um, kind of," he said with a smirk. "Okay, so what else do you like to watch besides true crime?"

"Well, I also have a fascination with cults."

"Anything that doesn't involve coercion, manipulation, or murder?"

"Ah, so nothing fun," I teased. "I like a lot of stuff. Horror movies, rom-coms from the eighties and nineties."

"Rom-coms?"

"You know," I said, reaching for my soda. "Romantic comedies."

"I know what they are," he said with a chuckle. "I'm just surprised. You don't strike me as the mushy type."

"I'm not, but Meg Ryan is. And I happen to enjoy watching her find love in hopeless places."

"If Meg Ryan can do it, why can't you?" he asked.

"Because she isn't real," I explained. "I mean, Meg is, but the characters she plays aren't. That's why it's fun. There's no danger of getting hurt. Unless, of course, you watch the one where she gets with Nicholas Cage, in which case, prepare to cry."

"So, you're saying real people cause pain and heartbreak?"

"Duh."

"Why do you think that?"

"Have you *met* people?" I asked.

A strand of hair fell into his eyes as he looked over at me. "What about Dallas and Katie? They seem to be doing pretty okay for a couple of real people."

"For now," I said before I could stop myself. "It's just…I mean, you never know. People leave." I paused, clearing my throat. "What about you? Do you believe in all that?"

He chewed his pizza, forehead creased, deep in thought.

"I don't know," he said finally. "I used to think that love stuff was all made up. Something people used as an excuse to justify their unhinged behavior over a silly crush or for some deep-seated desire to get married and start a family so they won't be alone."

I nearly choked on my pizza. "And what do you think now?"

"Marriage is still questionable, and kids are a definite no."

"I know, right? Gross."

"But maybe that whole love thing is real." His eyes bore into mine, clear and infinite like tiny crystal balls. I worried that if I stared too long, I'd start to see my future within their depths. "I've seen all my friends find it."

"Or maybe they're just delusional."

"Maybe," Luca said. "But they're happy."

"Isn't that kind of the same thing?" I joked.

He grinned. "But it sounds nice sometimes, you know?"

I did know. But there was no delusion, no love worth the weight I'd carry if I lost it.

"Sounds like you're the one watching too many Meg Ryan movies," I said, chomping into my slice.

"I've never seen one," he admitted.

I reached for the remote. "Guess we know what we're watching then."

"Let's watch the one you were talking about earlier," he said. "The one with Nicholas Cage."

"You're out of your mind," I said, flipping through the movie options. "That one is not beginner friendly."

He blew a puff of air through his luscious lips. "I can handle it."

"The hell you can."

"I can," he insisted. "Movies don't make me emotional."

"Probably because you're watching fucking *Die Hard*."

"What's wrong with *Die Hard*?"

"Nothing," I said. "But it's not exactly the tug on your heartstrings kind of film."

"I can handle it," he said again. The corner of his mouth drew up into a playful half smile, and I couldn't help but wonder what those lips tasted like.

"Fine," I said, returning my attention to the television and scrolled until I found *City of Angels*. "Guess we'll find out soon enough."

THE CREDITS ROLLED, AND I SNUCK A GLANCE AT LUCA WHO stared straight ahead, a pained expression on his face. His cheeks shined, and his hands rested on his knees, gripping them so hard his knuckles had turned translucent. Binx and Earl Grey, who had nestled themselves between us, were unbothered.

"So," I said, discreetly swiping my fingers beneath my lashes to collect my tears before they could spill over. "What did you think?"

He blinked in silence, unmoving. Just when I thought that maybe he hadn't heard me, he finally spoke.

"That *was* an act of violence," he said, facing me.

I choked on a laugh. "One that *you* asked for."

"For fuck's sake." He tugged at the collar of his shirt, using it to soak up the moisture on his skin. "You could have warned me."

"I did," I said, scratching Binx behind one ear. "*You* said you could handle it. Amateur."

He scoffed. "Don't think I didn't hear your cute little sniffles over there."

Cute? Warmth spread up my neck and over my cheeks. I bit back a grin. "I don't know what you're talking about."

"Like hell you don't," he teased before turning his shimmering blue eyes into the most adorable puppy dog face I'd ever seen. He drew his lips together in a quivering pout and sniffed. "That was you for the last third of the movie, even though you knew what trauma awaited us."

"Was not," I argued.

"You thought you were being sneaky wiping away those tears, but I *saw* you."

"What do you expect?" I asked. "I'm not a monster. At least not when it comes to fictional characters. I reserve my contempt for real people."

"I call bullshit," he declared, leaning back with his elbow propped against the sofa.

"Funny, because I call bullshit on you too, *Mr. I-can-handle-it*," I fired back. "Maybe you're not the emotionally aloof guy you've led people to believe you are, either."

"Emotionally aloof, huh?" he asked. "I thought I was an asshole."

I shrugged and flashed him an amused smirk. "Same thing."

"Seems there's more to me than you thought."

"I *guess*," I said with an exaggerated eye roll.

His tongue flicked over his lips before they stretched into a smile. "Maybe next time we can pick something less depressing. *Top Gun* or *The Fast and the Furious*."

Next time? My stomach did a backflip.

I scrunched my nose. "I've got to draw the line there. Nobody moves me to tears like Vin Diesel."

"Oh, really?"

"Those muscles," I said, wiping away an imaginary tear. "They're works of art."

"So, that's what it takes to win you over," he said. "Biceps as big as your head."

Actually, I prefer pale dudes with eyes that see right into your soul, who know how to use their fingers on a fretboard, and also, probably on a woman.

But I couldn't say any of that out loud, so instead, I said, "That, or like, vampires. More Lestat or Louis than Edward Cullen. I prefer my vampires to be more charming than sparkly."

"Sparkly?" he asked. "Is that a thing? Do they dress in sequins or something?"

"Never mind," I mumbled. I'd already disturbed the man

enough for one night without detailing the entire *Twilight Saga* for him. Maybe I'd save that for next time.

He ran his long fingers along Earl Grey's back. "It's getting late. I should probably get going."

"Oh, yeah." I rose to my feet with him. "I'll walk you out."

"This was fun," we both said as we moved toward the door.

A nervous laugh crept out of my throat. "Thanks again for dinner. That was…unexpected."

"But not unwelcome?" he asked, his hand hovering over the knob.

I shook my head. "Not unwelcome at all."

He dragged his fingers through his hair and fixed his gaze on me, taking a step closer. It took all the strength in my body to not close my eyes as I breathed him in, the scent of coffee and the quiet calm after a storm drawing me in.

"Would you maybe want to hang out again tomorrow?" he asked. "If you're not busy, of course. I know you have the day off, and you probably already have plans."

"I don't," I said, probably a little too quickly.

"It's just that…I think I've decided I'm going to rent a place here. At least short-term while I figure out what's next."

"Oh, really?" I tried to temper the excitement in my voice.

"Dallas and Katie have been great to let me stay with them, but I think I need a space of my own," he said. "And I could use someone who knows the area well to help me find something."

I attempted to keep my tone as casual as possible. "I could do that."

"Okay." He grinned. "Pick you up tomorrow at eleven?"

"Perfect."

He started to twist the door handle but stopped midturn. "I should probably get your number. You know," —he paused, digging his phone out of his jacket pocket— "in case something comes up and you need to cancel."

"Yeah, of course." I punched my number into his device before handing it back. His fingers danced across the screen, and within seconds, my own phone chimed from the kitchen counter.

"And now you have mine too."

My heart jumped and kicked its heels. "Great."

"Then I guess I'll see you tomorrow," he said, "unless something comes up."

With one last smile, he opened the door.

"Sounds good," I said. "If anything changes, I'll let you know."

But of course, nothing would. There wasn't anything that could keep me from spending another day with Luca.

"Good night," he called over his shoulder as he started down the stairs.

"Night," I replied, watching him cross the yard before locking the door behind him.

I squealed and ran back to the sofa, scooping up Earl Grey like a small child and twirling with him in my arms.

"Early Bird," I sang his nickname off-key as Binx made a beeline for the bedroom to get the hell out of Dodge. "The most distinguished kitty-man I ever did see. Can you believe? Luca wants to hang out with me…"

<hr>

A LOUD KNOCK ON MY DOOR SATURDAY MORNING JOLTED ME out of the cozy cocoon that was my bed. *Shit. Is that Luca?*

Did I oversleep? I snatched my phone from the nightstand to find it was only a little after eight thirty.

Binx and Earl Grey regarded me through slits, probably wondering who I was and what I'd done with their antisocial mother.

There was another knock, and I threw a sweatshirt over my loose T-shirt and shorts.

"Coming," I shouted, padding to the living room.

I flung open the door to find Kia with a drink carrier in her hands containing two coffees.

"I thought I was going to have to send out a search party," she said, a you've-got-some-explaining-to-do expression on her face.

I winced. "Sorry."

"I've got to be at work by ten, so you better get talking," she said, pushing past me.

"Wait a second," I said. "You've never been here before. How did you even know where I live?"

She placed the drinks on the coffee table and settled onto my sofa. "It's not that hard to find people these days. Even if they don't want to be found."

"But—"

"If you must know, I showed up at the restaurant this morning looking for you," she explained. "The girl working told me you were off today, and I said I must've gotten confused on where we were meeting. Then I said I'd misplaced your address and couldn't get you on the phone, so she got it out of your file for me."

I folded my arms over my chest and joined her on the couch. "I'm pretty sure it's illegal to be giving out employee information like that."

She pursed her fuchsia lips. "Maybe. But I did tell her I

was serving you court documents, so maybe just let that one slide."

"Kia!" I swatted her arm. "How the hell am I supposed to explain that?"

"That sounds like a *you* problem," she said with a laugh. "Should've answered your phone. Now, drink your coffee and tell me what the hell is going on."

"Nothing," I insisted, but she pinned me with a glare. "Fine." I took a deep breath and gave her the abridged version of the chain of events, beginning with me going to The Piccadilly Deli and ending with Luca asking me to help him find a place after he brought over dinner the night before. But when I got to the part about the morning when I told him about Brennan, I couldn't skip over what Luca had confessed about his own struggles, though I asked her to keep it between us. If anyone could understand someone trying to heal, it would be Kia. After what we'd been through, how could she not?

She studied me with her elbows perched on her knees, nodding slowly. "Hmm."

"Hmm?" I questioned. "What do you mean 'hmm'?"

Her oxblood nails tapped against the coffee cup cradled in her hands.

"It's just…Is this really a good idea?" she asked, a hint of trepidation in her voice.

"What do you mean?"

"Under any other circumstances, I'd be thrilled that you met someone you seem to like," she said. "But with your history…after Brennan…do you think it's wise to get close to someone like that?"

I narrowed my eyes. "Someone like what?"

"A guy dealing with the kind of shit he is." Her voice was

soft, understanding. "That could be very triggering for you. It could also put a lot of undue pressure on the relationship."

"First of all, we're just friends. It's not that serious."

She cocked her head like she wasn't buying what I was selling. "I don't think you've seen the way your face lights up when you mention his name."

The burn of my cheeks was giving me away. "Okay, well, whatever. Even if I *did* like him, so what? He's been through some serious shit, but who hasn't. I mean, look at us and Ravi and Jen. *We're* friends."

She shook her head. "That's not the same thing."

"Yes, it is," I argued.

"No," she said, the word sharp and final. "It isn't. We" — she twirled her slender finger in a circle between us— "are connected because we lost people we loved. It sounds like Luca almost decided to *be* lost."

"And?" I asked. "So what? He doesn't deserve a friend?"

"Of course, he does," she said. "All I'm saying is you might not be the right person to fill that role for him."

"I think I'm exactly the right person," I said. "I understand him in a way nobody else does because I know what loss feels like. Maybe I can keep him from...I could stop it from happening again and—"

She held out her hand and cut me off. "And *that* is what I'm talking about."

"What?"

Her brown eyes bore into mine. "You can't save him, McKenzie. That's too much responsibility for one person to take on. And even if you could, it's not going to bring Brennan back."

"I know that," I snapped. "Don't you think I know that?" She moved to place her hand on my arm, but I pulled away. "Did you come here to check on me or to lecture me?"

"I'm not trying to lecture you, but I *am* worried about you."

"Just because you've apparently decided to live the rest of your life alone doesn't mean I—" Her eyes went wide, and I clapped my hands over my mouth.

She swiped her tongue over her teeth. "I'm going to give you five seconds to reel that back in."

"Kia, I'm sorry," I said. "I didn't mean that."

She arched her brows.

"I didn't," I promised. "It's just...I don't know. I feel protective over him."

"And *I* am protective of you," she said. "I'm sure Luca's a great guy, but he's not my friend. *You* are. I don't want to see you get hurt."

"He's not going to hurt me," I stated with a lot more conviction than I felt.

"Maybe not on purpose," she said. "Just...be careful. That's all I'm saying."

I dropped my gaze to the cup in my hands.

"Look, I've said my piece," she said. "I'll let it go."

"I like him," I confessed.

"I can tell."

"Please be happy for me," I said, eyes pleading. "I haven't felt like this in...well, *ever*. I want to be excited. And I want you to be excited with me."

"On one condition," she said.

"What?"

"No more disappearing acts." She gave me an accusatory stare. "He needs a support system, but so do you."

"Promise."

She rose to her feet. "Come on, then."

"Where are we going?" I asked.

"I've got ten more minutes before I have to go," she said with a grin. "And if you think I'm leaving you to your own devices to pick out an outfit, you're out of your mind."

FOURTEEN

Luca

"So, where should we start?" McKenzie asked from the passenger seat of my Tesla. She looked especially cute in tight black jeans, boots, and a button-up sweater that dipped in the center. The cardigan had slipped off her shoulder, revealing a lace strap, making me wonder what was hidden beneath the heavy fabric.

I cleared my throat, refocusing my attention on the road. "Actually, Dallas called the realtor he used when he moved here, so we're meeting with her at eleven thirty over in Midtown."

"Realtor?" she asked. "I figured you'd just be looking to rent for now."

"I am, but apparently, she deals with fully furnished rentals too," I explained. "She has a lot of…clients like me."

"Ah," she said as though it all made sense. "High profile people. Celebrities. Rock stars."

I grimaced. "Former rock stars."

"Pretty sure it doesn't work like that," she said, smiling

over at me, her eyes obscured by a pair of aviators. "Once you're in the club, you don't get to leave."

"Someone's been watching too many cult documentaries," I said with a smirk.

"Is it a club you even want to leave?" she asked, gazing out the window.

"What do you mean?"

"Did you want the band to break up?"

"There wasn't exactly a band to continue with after Derek and Jax decided to leave."

She pinned me with a pointed stare. "That's not what I asked."

I flexed my hand against the steering wheel. "No, I didn't."

"I'm sorry," she said softly.

"What for?" I asked, changing lanes. "It was bound to happen someday. Honestly, we're lucky to have stayed together as long as we did."

"So? That doesn't make it any less shitty for you," she said. "Have you considered joining another band?"

I released a heavy sigh. "Not really. I don't think it would feel right. Midnight in Dallas worked because we had such a solid foundation as friends. The idea of starting over...I just don't think I can do it."

"Fair enough," she said, and after a few beats, she asked, "Do you think you'd ever move here? You know, on a more long-term basis? Or do you have family elsewhere you might want to live close to?"

I shook my head. "All of my family's here."

"Really?" she asked. Her tone was content and casual, as though we were discussing the weather. "Did you grow up here or did your folks move here?"

"No, I mean the guys *are* my family," I said. "I…I don't have anyone else."

She frowned. "Oh. I'm sorry. I didn't realize."

"It's okay," I added. "You couldn't have known."

"Are they…" she trailed off, her eyes resting on me. "Are your parents still alive?"

I sighed. "I don't know."

She continued studying me, waiting for me to speak again.

"I went into state custody in Kentucky when I was ten. My father went to prison when I was about seven, and I guess it was too much for my mother to handle because she wasn't sober for another minute of her life after that. I tried to hide it and take care of her, but eventually, one of my teachers caught on," I said, focusing intently on the traffic in front of me as the GPS spat out directions.

"Luca…"

"I grew up in a group home until I eventually aged out of the system."

"Fuck," she said. "I'm sorry."

I shrugged. "It wasn't an ideal upbringing, but the people that worked for the home helped me learn to be independent from an early age. By the time I graduated and found a job, I at least felt prepared to be on my own. While some kids were going on vacations with their families or playing sports, the house manager, Mr. Fink, was teaching me and the other kids about budgets and how to do things for ourselves."

"He sounds pretty great."

"He was," I said with a nod. "He's the one that got me into playing the guitar."

"Did he teach you?"

"He taught me some," I answered. "But once I mastered the basics, he said I needed a real professional. When I was thirteen, he introduced me to his aunt Gladys." I couldn't help but smile at the memory.

"Gladys?" she asked. "Did Gladys have a last name or was she like Prince?"

I chuckled. "It was Hibbert, but she was one of those people whose energy was so big she didn't need a last name."

"A legend," McKenzie said.

"In her own right. She was a retired music teacher," I said. "She was pushing sixty at the time, and she chain-smoked cigarettes like she was single-handedly keeping big tobacco in business, but the woman could rock out like Hendrix."

She laughed then, and I glanced over, catching the way her nose crinkled when she smiled.

"That might be the coolest thing I've ever heard," she said.

"She was the best," I said. "She taught me everything. Don't get me wrong, she was also a hard-ass and made me practice seven days a week. If we were working on a piece and I messed up, she made me start from the beginning over and over again until I got it right."

McKenzie's eyes widened.

"It's not as bad as it sounds," I assured her. "She taught me discipline. I may not have agreed at the time, but looking back, it was definitely something I needed help with. Especially once I discovered girls." I flashed her a mischievous grin.

She snorted. "Those pesky girls. So, what happened to Gladys? Did you keep in touch with her?"

I turned into the parking lot of the condo complex where we were meeting the realtor.

"I did," I said. "At least, for a while. I lost track of her not long after the band made it big. I tried to get in touch with Mr.

Fink, but the number I had for him wasn't good anymore. Wherever they are, I hope they're happy. They deserve all the good things in life."

"So do you, you know." There was a softness in McKenzie's eyes when they met mine as I put the car in park. "Do you ever think about trying to find your parents?"

"I did when I was younger, but not anymore," I answered. "Even if they tried to reach out to me, I wouldn't respond. Too much time has passed. I don't wish them any ill will, but I don't wish them well either."

"But what if we could find Gladys?" she asked as we climbed out of the car and onto the sidewalk.

"I think it's better I don't," I said, letting out a long, slow breath. "At this point, the woman would be in her eighties, if she's even alive at all. She might not even remember me."

McKenzie's lips quirked as I held open the door to the lobby.

"What?" I asked.

"Nothing."

"What's that face for?"

She nudged me with her elbow. "I don't think you could be so easily forgotten."

"Sugar, I think I've shown you just about everything I've got." Darcey Dubois drummed her dagger-like nails against the granite countertop in the fifth unit she'd displayed. We'd traversed the city with her showing us different high-rise apartments and penthouses, but they all felt sterile. Each one was filled with white walls and sleek lines, void of anything that resembled a home.

I scrubbed my hands down my face before exchanging glances with McKenzie.

"Surely you've got something else," McKenzie said, pressing her palms against the bar.

"I thought that penthouse over in Germantown was lovely," Darcey said, lightly touching her teased red hair, ensuring there wasn't a single strand out of place. "The square footage was amazing for the price."

"It was," I said. "It was just…kind of bland."

"But you'd be within walking distance of everything. All the restaurants and shopping, not that you do your own," Darcey said, her heels clicking against the checkered tile.

"I don't mind driving," I said.

"Do you have anything that's not smack-dab in the middle of the city?" McKenzie asked.

Darcey clicked her tongue, digging her phone out of her handbag. She pursed her crimson lips, swiping her finger over the screen.

"Well, there is one place," she said finally. "But it might as well be in another country."

"How far is it?" McKenzie asked.

Darcey grimaced. "About thirty minutes. It's in Leipers Fork. It belongs to an artist who's been living abroad for a few months. The place looks like it belongs to a bunch of hobbits."

McKenzie snorted. "Do you have any pictures?"

Darcey nodded, handing her the phone.

I stepped behind McKenzie so I could look over her shoulder. My chest touched her back, and I caught a whiff of flowers on her hair.

"These are some wealthy hobbits," McKenzie said, stifling a laugh.

The place was decidedly *not* a home for hobbits and looked more like a cottage out of a storybook. Ivy lined the stone walls outside, and it was surrounded by a wrought-iron fence and a garden filled with greenery. The inside was cozy, well-lit, and full of personality from its blue-painted front door to the sunroom that overlooked the backyard. It looked smaller than the other places Darcey had shown us, but the charming outdoor space more than made up for that.

"What do you think?" I asked McKenzie.

"It's beautiful," she said, scrolling through the photos. "Look at that magnolia tree out back. You could put a hammock there and probably enjoy it all the way through the first part of December with the way the weather is here. It would be the perfect place to read." She smiled back at me. "Or write."

A vision flashed through my mind of McKenzie resting her head against my shoulder as we swayed in a hammock surrounded by falling autumn leaves, an open notebook perched on my lap. I blinked it away.

"And there's a claw-foot tub," she practically purred. "I've always been fascinated by those."

Another image of McKenzie appeared behind my eyes, only this one was a lot less G-rated.

I cleared my throat. "Have you ever used one?"

She shook her head. "No, but don't they look kind of magical? How could anyone be sad in a claw-foot tub?"

"You'd be losing about a thousand square feet," Darcey interrupted, "and the gas fireplace like the units I've shown you. It has a woodburning—"

"I'll take it," I said, cutting her off.

McKenzie turned to me with wide eyes. "Really?"

"Don't you want to see it first?" Darcey asked.

"She has a point," McKenzie said. "It might be worth checking out. Just to make sure there aren't any hobbits hiding in the attic."

"If there are, they can help with the rent," I joked.

"Afraid not, honey," Darcey drawled. "Unless you can get them to cosign the lease."

"That's okay," I said. "They can keep me company."

"If you're sure, I can call over to the office and have them start the paperwork," Darcey said.

I placed my hands on McKenzie's shoulders and squeezed. "Let's do it."

"So, how does it feel to officially have your own place in Nashville?" McKenzie asked later that evening. After finishing with Darcey, we'd ended up tucked into the back corner of a hole-in-the-wall tavern polishing off a dinner comprised of every appetizer they had on the menu.

"Technically, it's not mine," I reminded her over the screech of someone singing off-key karaoke to an old Hank Williams track.

"It is for at least the next six months," she said, popping a fried pickle into her mouth. "With an option to extend for three more months after that."

"Thanks for thinking of that, by the way," I said, dipping one of the batter-covered slices into a cup of ranch dressing.

She shrugged. "I just figured it was worth having the choice. You never know. You might find a reason to stay."

What if I've already found one? The thought snuck up on me like a thief in a dark alley. McKenzie didn't seem to realize the weight of her words or the effect they'd had on me.

She was too busy scooping as many toppings as she could onto a chip from our plate of nachos.

"And that garden out back will be the perfect place for you to write," she continued, finally popping the chip into her mouth. "But you do need a hammock."

"Definitely," I said, wiping my fingers over the napkin in my lap. "Actually, there's probably a few things I'll need to get settled in. Maybe you could, uh, help me?"

Her eyes met mine, and I swiftly added, "Because your place is just so cozy, you know? I want that too."

A dazzling smile spread over her lips, so big it nearly made her eyes disappear.

"What?" I asked.

"Don't you know what this means?"

"A trip to Restoration Hardware?"

"No!" She balled up the wrapper of her straw and threw it at me. "I get to take you thrifting."

I couldn't help the grin that stretched across my own face. Her excitement was contagious.

"I'd like that."

Her happiness spilled over like a bubbly soda that had been poured too fast. I drank her in as she detailed all of the stores we would visit and some of the best finds she'd discovered at each one.

We continued to talk long after the bill had been paid and our plates had been cleared. The bar had become packed, and karaoke had been replaced with a live band singing covers of songs from the late 90s and early 2000s.

"They're pretty good," McKenzie said, nodding toward the small stage.

"Yeah, they are," I replied. The group was made up of four guys who barely looked old enough to drink. The lead guitarist was pale and lanky and reminded me a little of myself way back when. Talented enough to be sure of himself, but too overcome with insecurity to allow room for such confidence. He hid it behind an aloof exterior, but when he thought no one was looking, he scanned the faces of the crowd for their approval.

Everyone erupted into cheers as the band finished their version of a classic Aerosmith tune. Seconds later, they played the opening notes of a My Chemical Romance song I'd have recognized anywhere.

McKenzie gasped and grabbed my hand.

"Come on," she said, jumping to her feet. "We're dancing. And hey, I'm not even drinking, so the chances that I'll end up puking are slim to none."

"Oh, I—" I began, trying to find a reason not to, but she stopped me in my tracks.

"They're playing our song."

She tossed a flirtatious smile at me, and I allowed her to pull me from the booth, unable to resist the siren call of her hips as they began to sway. She dragged me a few feet from our table toward the back of the room and laced her fingers through mine. I spun her around, and she threw her head back with laughter as I matched her energy, bounce for bounce.

How had she bloomed so beautifully in the weeds life had sown around her? I longed to pick that wildflower and keep her all to myself, but what if I did and my own shortcomings caused her to wilt?

What if she never grew back?

The song transitioned into something with a slower beat, and she slid her hands up my chest, resting them behind my neck while my own curled around her waist. God, I wanted to kiss her, but what if that scared her away? On her own, she was strong and resilient. But what I felt between us was delicate—formed from a connection of shadows and a mutual understanding of what lurked there.

She leaned in closer. "Luca, I—"

But before she could finish that sentence, a tall hipster-looking guy loomed over us, wearing jeans so tight I was surprised he could breathe.

"Shit," he said, knocking into my shoulder, pushing me apart from McKenzie. "You're Luca fucking Sterling."

I nodded at him in a greeting. "Good to see you." I hoped it would be enough to satisfy him, so I could return my focus to McKenzie, who was shooting eye daggers at the guy.

"I'm such a big fan, dude," he continued. "What are you doing here? This place is a shithole."

I tightened a protective arm around McKenzie. "Just hanging out."

Surely, that would give him the hint.

"I'm buying you shots," he said, his voice rising. McKenzie's eyes darted around, clearly worried about the same thing I was: if he got any louder, he'd draw attention to me, and any hope for a peaceful evening would fly out the window.

"I'm good, actually," I said. "But I appreciate it."

"Aw, come on," he pressed. "Have a drink with me."

He started to wave over a couple of his buddies who were carbon copies of him. One of them already had their phone out.

"No, thank you," I said a bit more firmly this time.

But he would not be deterred. Instead, he plucked his phone out of his pocket.

"I want to take a picture with you," he slurred, and McKenzie flashed me a worried glance. "My girlfriend's never gonna believe I met you."

I held out my hand to stop him. "Not tonight, man. I'm just here trying to have a good time."

He recoiled like he'd been slapped. "Seriously, dude? It's just a fucking picture. What—are you too good to talk to your fans now?"

"That's not it," I began, but McKenzie squared up to the hipster dipshit, and I tightened my grip on her.

"He said *no*," McKenzie spat through gritted teeth.

His gaze shifted to her for a second too long, and I thought I was about to get into my first sober bar fight. But then he brought his stony face back to me, glaring as though he was sizing me up.

"Whatever," the guy said, leaning close enough that I could smell the gin on his breath. "Everybody knows Jax was the real talent. You're nothing but a fucking drunk and—"

His tirade was interrupted when McKenzie's fist connected with his mouth in a resounding thud that told me both he and McKenzie would be hurting in the morning.

"He. Said. No," she barked, not backing down. "Leave him alone."

The guy swiped his hand over his bleeding lip. "You little bitch."

He took a step closer to her, and that was all it took for me to break. With fistfuls of his shirt clutched in my hands, I slammed him into the nearest wall.

"Touch her and fucking die," I snapped. "Do you understand me?"

Suddenly, he was out of words.

"Say it," I seethed.

"I understand," he said without looking at me.

McKenzie tugged on my arm. "Luca, we have to go."

The bouncer stalked toward us, and I released the asshole with one last shove.

As security got closer, he found his voice again. "You're a piece of shit, you know that? You'll fucking regret this."

I didn't turn around as we headed for the door. With one arm around McKenzie's shoulders, I held my other high enough that he would see it and gave him my middle finger.

FIFTEEN

McKenzie

"Are you okay?" Luca asked as we stumbled into the chilly night.

I clutched my throbbing fingers. "I'm fine," I choked out.

"Let me see," he said, taking my right hand in his, inspecting the tender flesh. "Can you move it?"

"Fuck." I winced, squeezing my eyes shut. "That hurts."

"Okay, well the good news is, I don't think it's broken."

"And what's the bad news?" I asked through clenched teeth.

He tilted his head, scrunching up his face in a way that said he regretted the news he was about to deliver.

"It's gonna hurt like a son of a bitch for a couple days."

I rolled my eyes. "Thanks, doc, for your astute assessment."

"You didn't tell me you were a street fighter," he teased, stroking my palm with his thumb. "Do you have any frozen peas at home?"

"What?" I asked, my brow furrowed in confusion. "Um, no, I don't think so."

"Come on, let's get you some for that lethal weapon you've got there." He hooked his arm around my shoulders and led me to the car.

"Peas?" I asked. "Why peas?"

"Works better than ice," he said, starting the ignition. "Because they're small, which makes it easier to wrap around your hand."

I buckled my seat belt with my left hand. "Sounds like you've done this before."

"I've been in my share of bar fights," he said with a sly smile. "None quite as epic as this, though. What were you thinking?"

"Honestly, I don't even know," I admitted with a laugh. "I think my rage caused me to blackout."

He started in the direction of the supermarket just down the street. "That guy was like, three times your size. You could have gotten yourself killed."

I pinned him with an accusatory stare. "Oh yeah? What about your touch-her-and-die move?"

He bit back a grin. "*We* were a bit more evenly matched."

"Whatever," I said. "I just couldn't let that asshole talk to you like that. Those awful things he was saying…"

"To be fair, they were true," he said, his voice growing soft.

"First of all," I began, "you're not a drunk. You don't even drink."

"I did."

"Well, you don't anymore, and that guy was a dick for judging you, anyway. Fuck him."

"And Jax always was the favorite," he said. "Being the lead singer and all."

"So?" I said. "That band wouldn't have been the same without you, and you know it."

He was quiet for a moment before he spoke again. "It means a lot that you stood up for me. But please don't risk your life for me again."

"Hmm," I said, pretending to think. "No deal."

"McKenzie," he warned.

"What if we get mugged and I need to use my taser to ward off a burglar?" I asked. "Or you get kidnapped, and I'm the only person who knows, forcing me to use my particular set of skills to save you."

He snorted. "Thanks, Liam Neeson, but I've got it handled."

I pursed my lips as he pulled the car into the lot and parked. "Fine. But only if you promise me the same. No more throwing guys against walls at bars."

"I can't promise that."

"Why not?" I countered.

"Because I can't be responsible for what I'll do if someone threatens you," he said, gripping the steering wheel. "When I saw that fucker step up to you, something inside me snapped."

Butterflies wearing boxing gloves fluttered around my stomach. "Really?"

Luca's Adam's apple bobbed as he worked to swallow. "Don't act so surprised. I care about you." A weighted silence fell over us, our eyes locked. There'd been a palpable energy between us when we'd been dancing back at the tavern. A current so strong, I could almost see it with my naked eye. Had he felt it too?

After another second that felt like a lifetime, he cleared his throat. "I mean, we're friends. Obviously, I care."

My heart sank, but I forced a defiant smile over my mouth. "Then it looks like we're at a stalemate, buddy. Because I'm never just going to stand by while someone treats you like that."

He heaved a defeated sigh as I flung open the door. With his arm around my shoulders, he guided me inside and bought a ninety-nine cent bag of diced frozen carrots because they were out of peas. As we headed back outside, he carefully wrapped the icy vegetables around my injured hand, standing there on the sidewalk.

"Thanks," I said.

"Now, hold that there," he said before leading me back to the car.

I allowed him to open the passenger door for me.

"We better get you home before you join a fight club," he said once he was behind the wheel.

"Do you think it's that easy to join?" My lips quirked into a grin. "Is there a yearly membership fee? Like Costco? Or do you think it's more of a month-to-month thing? I wonder if there's any perks."

He shook his head and stifled a laugh. I stole glances at him as we chatted during the short drive back to my place. When we got there, he insisted on walking me to my door.

"Really, I can manage on my own," I insisted, bounding up the stairs.

"But what if a bear's up there waiting to maul you to death?" he joked.

"If there's a bear on my doorstep in the middle of Nashville, we have bigger problems," I said once we reached the front stoop. "Besides, would you really be dumb enough to fight an actual wild animal for me? They're a little more dangerous than drunk hipsters harassing people in bars."

"Yes," he answered without hesitation. "I'd kick that bear's ass."

I giggled. "Looks like we need to watch some Discovery Channel because I'm pretty sure that's not how it would go."

He snickered with me, the porch light illuminating the tiny creases at the corners of his eyes.

"Then I guess I'd be eaten by Smokey Bear," he said, stepping closer.

"Seems more likely." Our laughter slowed until the only sounds remaining were that of the crickets and the drum of my heartbeat slamming in my ears.

"Thanks again for coming with me today," he said.

Thanks for being such a great pal. He didn't say those exact words. In fact, I was fairly certain he'd never so much as uttered the word *pal* in his life. But it didn't matter because the sentiment was still the same. This had been nothing more than two friends hanging out.

I gave a lighthearted shrug. "Yeah, it was fun. And now you have your own little hobbit house."

"Thrifting this week?"

"If you still want to."

"I do," he said quickly. "I need you to come work your magic. Make the place more homey."

The corners of my mouth stretched upward. "Okay. Well, um—"

Whatever words I was about to say left my mind when he pulled me into his arms. I melted into him like butter on warm bread, my body greedily filling up every empty space between us. I drank in his warmth, desperate to memorize how it felt to be held by him: somehow safe and dangerous all at once.

With Luca around, no one could ever hurt me—no one but him.

"I'll text you?" he asked, releasing me with a squeeze to my shoulder.

"Sounds good."

He nodded, starting down the steps, and I leaned against the railing, watching as he went.

"G'night, Fight Club," he called over his shoulder.

"Night," I replied, scrubbing my hands down my face.

I was in over my head. The silly fantasies I'd had about Luca had given way to something more. Something deeper. I didn't know how to stop it. Even knowing he'd probably never feel the same, I wasn't sure I wanted to.

***

THE NEXT WEEKEND, ON SUNDAY, I WENT TO LUCA'S NEW place to help him get settled in with some of our thrift finds from our shopping excursion, including a few I'd discovered on my own later in the week.

"That Buried Treasures place was a hell of a find," he said, unpacking some of the records we'd selected for the old player in the living room. We spread everything out on the dining table while we figured out where it should all go. "I can't believe they had this album by The Civil Wars. Do you know how rare this is? It's been impossible to find since they broke up."

"I didn't, but what's even more shocking to me is that you'd want it," I said with a laugh, pulling a Muse record from the bag.

"What do you mean?" he asked.

I shrugged. "It's just that they're known more for their sad, emotional love songs than their amazing guitar riffs."

"You think I can't be sad and emotional?" He lifted his brows. "Or in love?"

"I don't know," I answered, keeping my voice even. "Based on our previous conversations, I just assumed you'd never been in love."

"If it feels like this…" His gaze dropped to the album in his hand, and he held it out in front of him. "I guess I haven't. Have you?"

I snorted. "Absolutely not." I didn't want to attempt to elaborate and risk tripping over my words or saying something that might allude to the feelings I may or may not have been developing for Luca, so I moved to the other side of the table and started unpacking one of the other bags.

"By the way," I said. "Look what I got you." I extracted the ceramic squirrel from my bag of goodies.

A grin tugged at the corners of his mouth. "And what is that, exactly?"

I ignored his obvious question and continued. "His name is Randy McNutt."

He barked out a laugh as he came around to where I stood. "And he has a name?"

"I thought he'd fit perfectly in your hobbit hole."

"That sounds vaguely dirty."

"Listen, what you do with your hobbit hole is none of my business," I deadpanned, placing it on the table and fishing out the next item, which he gaped at like it was a foreign object.

"What the hell is that?" he asked through squinted eyes.

"It's an egg separator." I rolled my eyes, handing him the tiny plastic device designed to look like a small chicken.

He turned it over in his fingers. "And what am I supposed to do with it?"

"Seriously? You use it to separate eggs. Like, if you're making an omelet or baking something that only calls for a yolk."

He bit back a laugh. "I don't cook."

I snatched the little chick out of his hand and set it in the sink to be washed.

"Well, I do," I said, my stomach dropping when I realized the implications of what I'd said.

His smile made my heart want to leap out of my chest and into his arms.

"Are you going to cook for me?" he asked with a hint of amusement.

"Probably not," I said as coolly as I could manage. "But now you have it, in case I'm ever feeling generous."

"What else is in that bag, Mary Poppins?" he asked.

"I'm not sure if I'm going to show you," I said, folding my arms over my chest.

"Why not?" His crystal eyes pierced through me, doing nothing to help me get over the crush I'd developed.

"Because first, you defiled Randy McNutt, and then, you made fun of my egg separator."

"I thought it was *my* egg separator?" he quipped.

I cocked my head to the side. "The egg separator I got for you."

He grinned as I returned to my bag. "How much stuff is in that bag?"

"Only a couple more things," I said, digging out a small framed print of a bunch of raccoons playing poker. "I thought this would look good on the mantel."

His mouth twitched. "That thing is hideous."

"Isn't it?"

"It's perfect," he said, taking it from my hands and heading into the living room.

I followed, smiling when he placed the ridiculous picture front and center above the fireplace.

"It's as though it always belonged here," I said, sitting on the overstuffed sofa. "And who knows—maybe the owner of this joint donated it, and here I am bringing it back where it belongs."

"You didn't have to do this." Luca sat beside me, so close our knees almost touched. "Bring me all these things."

"Didn't have to or you preferred I wouldn't?" I teased.

"I love it all. Even Randy McNutt," he said. "No one's ever done anything like this for me before."

"Bought you weird shit from a thrift store?"

He shook his head, his voice growing soft. "Been so thoughtful."

His words were like the strike of a match, lighting my cheeks on fire. My heart simultaneously fluttered and sank, its battered wings desperately trying to keep it afloat. The feelings I had for him were only growing, and I had to remind myself he only saw me as a friend.

I cleared my throat as I caught a glimpse of his guitar case in the corner of the room.

"Acoustic?" I asked, gesturing toward the case. "I never would have guessed that."

He shrugged, letting out a low chuckle. "Yeah, I'm trying something different. My other guitars are back home in Kentucky, but after what you said about trying to get my words out like I was writing a song, I went and got a guitar. I thought an acoustic might be a better fit."

I couldn't help the smile that crept over my face. "And how's that going?"

"I've been writing a lot," he admitted. "Once I started looking at it like I was creating music, it's like the floodgates opened up."

"I'm glad. Maybe I can get you to play something for me sometime," I said, before quickly adding, "you know…if you want."

"Actually, there's something I've been working on this week." He rubbed his hand along the back of his neck. "Can I…can I play it for you? See what you think?"

I blinked in surprise before nodding. "Of course."

Luca brought his guitar back over to the sofa and sat, accidentally dropping the pick on the floor. He almost looked nervous.

"Okay, just know this isn't completed yet, so I'll probably change some things," he said. "It's just a verse, but…I think I like where it's going. And I—"

"Luca, you don't have to explain it," I said, giving him a small encouraging nod. "Just play it for me."

He raked a hand through his hair. "Right. Sorry. I guess I'm a little rusty."

I tried to hide my smile as he began to play the most bittersweet melody. It felt like a hand around my heart. And then he began to sing.

"Locked inside the confines of my own mind
A cage built by my own hands is still a prison
How long must I cry alone in the dark
Until shame becomes my true religion
Knees down at the altar
Jump then falter
I wish I were someone else"

His voice was the kind that reeled you in—the kind that stopped you midstep, forcing you to hang on every word. It was warm and filled with emotion that caused my throat to tighten.

When he stopped playing, he looked at me, trying to gauge my reaction. I must've stared at him a little too long with my jaw slack, because he finally spoke.

"Oh wow, okay," he said, setting the instrument down and propping it against the couch. "That bad, huh?"

"What? No," I insisted, touching his arm. "It was that *good*. I just…That was amazing, Luca."

His eyes widened. "Seriously?"

It was the kind of song that deserved to be heard by the masses.

"You…uh…never mind." I stopped myself before I could finish the sentence. Luca had been dealing with a lot. Telling him he should consider putting his work out there for public consumption was probably not the best idea.

"Tell me," he said.

"Oh no, it was nothing," I said in the *least* convincing tone possible.

"Tell me," he repeated, more forcefully this time. "Or else I'll assume you really hated it."

I held up my hands to stop that train of thought before he could even go there.

"No, that's not it," I said, hesitating. "I was thinking that's the start of the type of song people would listen to over and over again. Those are the kind of lyrics that make people feel seen."

He looked taken aback. "Really?"

"Yes. That was incredible. And your voice is…well, it's beautiful." Just like him.

A slow smile spread over his lips, and even in the soft glow of the lamplight, I could have sworn I saw the hint of a flush kiss his cheeks.

"I have a few more lines in my notebook that I think might fit into the next verse," he said. "Maybe…I could show you?"

"I'd like that."

My heart hammered in my chest as he left the room to retrieve his journal. I was determined to soak up any pieces of Luca he was willing to share.

SIXTEEN

Luca

"And how are the meds working?" Lacey, my therapist, asked through the speaker of my laptop that was placed in the center of my coffee table. It was near the end of our virtual session on the Thursday after McKenzie came to help me get settled in.

"So far, so good," I answered. "I had a follow-up yesterday, and we're gonna keep my dosage where it is for now."

"This is great progress, Luca," she said, a hopeful lilt woven into her voice. "And you even got your own house close to Nashville."

I shrugged with a grin. "At least for a while."

"I think that's good for you," she said. "You're close to your friends, and I think the change of scenery will be helpful."

"Yeah, I'm really enjoying it." I glanced around the cozy, eclectic living room of what McKenzie referred to as "the hobbit house." "It's a nice place."

"And you've been writing," she said as though I'd done something much greater than putting pen to paper.

"It's not a big deal. Besides, I'm not even sure how good any of it is." That wasn't entirely true. McKenzie had told me it was something special, and I knew she was speaking the truth.

"It doesn't matter if it's good," Lacey reminded me. "It matters that you're being vulnerable—that you're stepping out of your comfort zone and finding ways to cope. Neither of those are easy tasks. You're doing great."

I gave her a sheepish smile. "Thank you."

"It sounds like this new girl you're seeing has been a good influence on you," she said. "She sounds supportive."

"Oh, uh, McKenzie?" I asked, heat rushing to my cheeks. "We're just friends."

Lacey arched a brow, then nodded. "Okay."

"What was that face for?"

"There was no face," she insisted.

"There was, in fact, a face."

She tilted her head, and even through the laptop, I could feel her eyes burning into me.

"The way you described McKenzie made it sound like there was a bit more going on," she explained. "You seem to really care about her."

My stomach twisted. Damn, I knew she was a therapist, but was I really that transparent?

"Well, of course I do," I said. "We're friends."

Lacey studied me through thousands of tiny pixels. "Is it possible that's what you're calling it because you're afraid to admit you feel something more for her?"

I cleared my throat, rubbing my thumb along my jaw. There was no denying I had feelings for McKenzie. But it was so foreign, so completely different from anything I'd ever experienced that it scared the shit out of me.

"It's okay to be scared," Lacey added. "This is uncharted territory. You're not used to letting people in, and there's a big difference in allowing someone into your orbit as a friend and potentially seeing them as something more."

"What do you mean?" I asked.

"If you open yourself to something more than friendship, you run a greater risk of getting your heart broken," she said gently, her kind gaze fixed on me through the screen. "Of being abandoned."

Her words were a punch to my gut. It wasn't a fear I'd given voice to yet, but it was there, bubbling beneath the surface. Lacey knew a lot about my childhood and how much of my life I'd spent feeling unwanted. My friends now had become like family but those friendships had formed over many years. I'd only really known McKenzie for a few weeks, but I'd met her in the middle of one of the darkest times in my life. Despite that, she'd shined her light on me and helped me find my way.

"I'm not even sure she feels the same," I said. It was the closest I was willing to come to an admission.

"Have you told her that you see her as more than a friend?" she asked.

I snorted. "No."

"Do you want to tell her?" she countered.

I slid my tongue over my teeth, considering what she said. Yes and no. I did, but I was fucking terrified.

"I'm not going to pressure you one way or another," Lacey continued. "Only you'll know when and if you're ready for something like that. But there could be an opportunity for you two to share something special."

My heart jumped into my throat. "What if she doesn't feel the same way?

"That's certainly a risk," she said. "And only you will know when you're ready to take that chance. Life is full of uncertainty. Sometimes you end up going through parts of it alone, but there's also a possibility you'll find someone who will take your hand and walk beside you."

I chewed on her words for a moment. "That scares the shit out of me."

"Which part?"

"All of it," I answered. "Telling her how I feel and having her reject me. Or worse, I let her in and she rejects me later."

"There's a chance it could go either way," she said. "However, there's also the possibility you could form a lasting relationship. One you'll never have if you don't try. When you're ready to take that leap, you'll know. And I'm always here to talk you through it if you need me."

I tried to visualize what McKenzie would do if I told her how I felt…what she would say. But it was hard for my own desires not to take over, imagining taking her beautiful face in my hands and kissing her like I'd wanted to since that first night I took her home from The Basement East. I'd envisioned the moment our lips would finally meet, both of us perfectly sober and aware of every touch. I'd wanted to do it that night at the tavern after I signed the lease for the hobbit house before that jackass had interrupted us. There had been a shift in the energy between us, so subtle that if I'd blinked I might have missed it. Had it all been one-sided or was she feeling it too?

"It's just something to consider," Lacey said. "Maybe you should write about it. Explore those emotions swirling in your head."

"Yeah," I said. "Maybe."

"Okay, well, I've got you booked for next week, but if you need anything between now and then, you know where I am."

I nodded. "Thanks, Lacey."

We said goodbye, and I snapped my laptop shut. My head flopped against the couch cushion, Lacey's words still settling into the crevices of my mind. Just then, my phone pinged with a text. I glanced down, a smile spreading across my lips as I read the text McKenzie had just sent:

Just checking in on you and Randy McNutt. Tell him I said hi. 🙂

THE NEXT NIGHT WAS GAME NIGHT AT DALLAS AND KATIE'S, but because it was just me, McKenzie, Derek, and Jo in attendance, the evening quickly devolved into us sitting around and chatting. It was rare that Jo and Derek were both in town *and* had a sitter, so they were taking full advantage.

"So, you're gone for two weeks, right?" McKenzie asked Katie from where she sat beside her on the couch. Katie and Dallas had just informed us about a spur-of-the-moment trip they were taking.

"Leaving Sunday?" I added, making sure I understood since Emilia would be coming to stay with me down at the hobbit house for the duration of their trip.

"That's right," Dallas said, rubbing his palms together. "Italy, here we come!"

"Willam Deveraux is opening a new restaurant in Florence, and he wants us to be there for the opening," Katie explained, turning to me. "He's been something of a mentor to Dallas and me. When I forgot to hire the servers for our first big catering gig, it was Willam and his staff that stepped in to help.”

“Oh wow,” I said, shocked. There was still so much I didn’t know, so many things I’d missed in the months I’d been gone.

“He’s kind of a big deal,” McKenzie added.

“What else are you two doing while you’re there?” Jo asked.

I couldn’t help but catch the shift in Katie’s demeanor. Her eyes fell to the glass of wine in her lap, and she picked at invisible lint on her jeans.

“Just seeing the sights,” she said. “We figured it would be nice to extend the trip since we’ll already be there. You know I’ve always wanted to go to Italy.”

“Well, yeah,” Jo said, twisting her auburn hair off her shoulders. “That’s where you always wanted to take your honeymoon.”

Katie’s cheeks flushed as she and Dallas exchanged a glance. Neither of them had ever been particularly good at keeping secrets.

A veil of silence fell over the room.

“Wait...” The wheels in Jo’s mind started spinning at warp speed as Derek did the mental gymnastics to catch up.

McKenzie’s eyes widened. “Shut up.”

“What?” Katie asked, taking a sip of her wine, her cheeks turning scarlet as Dallas concealed his mouth with his hand.

“Oh boy,” Dallas muttered, rubbing his finger along his upper lip.

“Don’t *what* me,” McKenzie said, sitting up straight, pinning Katie with her eyes.

“And you darn sure better not *what* me,” Jo countered, and I couldn’t help but smirk. Despite going from being an uptight news reporter to the slightly less uptight woman of Derek's dreams, she still found it hard to utter certain four-letter words.

"I'm not exactly the most observant guy, but even I can tell you two are up to something," I said, staring them down from the armchair where I sat with Emilia curled up on the cushion beside me.

Katie started to turn to Dallas, but McKenzie swatted her with a pillow. "Don't look at him. Look at me."

"And me," Jo demanded, narrowing her eyes at Katie.

Katie sighed, and a sheepish smile crept over her face. "We were going to tell you when we got back."

"Holy shit," Derek said, his eyes widening.

"Oh my God," Jo shrieked, her voice a high-pitched dog whistle in my ear. "You're getting married?"

Dallas held up his hands like he'd been caught stealing from the cookie jar. "We got the marriage license yesterday."

"You sneaky bitches," McKenzie said through a wide grin.

"Actually," Katie began, swallowing hard. "We got married yesterday."

"On your lunch break?" McKenzie asked, her mouth dropping open. "Geez, that only took an hour? They really need to make that more difficult."

Jo's face froze in horror.

"We decided we wanted to do it for the trip," Katie explained. "It's next to impossible to find times where everyone can be in town, and this trip came up last minute. We wanted to jump on the opportunity."

Jo opened her mouth to speak, but no words came out.

"I think you broke her," McKenzie said, gesturing toward Jo with her thumb.

"Please don't be mad," Katie pleaded. "We were going to

tell you as soon as we got back. We thought we'd plan a reception later this year so we can give plenty of lead time for everyone to clear their schedules."

"Why didn't you call me?" Jo squeaked. "I would have been at the courthouse."

"You guys didn't get back in town till today," Katie reminded her before turning toward McKenzie. "And you had to hold down the fort at work."

"And I'm chopped liver," I teased as she shook her head and rolled her eyes. "But really, congratulations, you two. That's—"

"I don't accept this," Jo said, rising to her feet.

Dallas scratched his temple. "It's too late for—"

"I said I don't accept." Jo crossed her arms. "No. Did you write your own vows and say them at the courthouse?"

"No," Katie said. "We were just so excited and living in the moment—"

"Katie, you always wanted that," Jo said, cutting her off. "To write your own vows, have a champagne toast, and wear a pretty dress."

"Yeah, but I also wanted the Italian honeymoon, and I don't know…When this trip came up, it felt like a sign," Katie said. "Then yesterday, I looked at Dallas and realized I didn't want to spend another day not married to him."

Dallas gazed at her, his eyes warm with emotion. "So, I asked her to make an honest man out of me, and she said yes."

"The timeline just got jumbled a little," Katie said with a soft laugh.

Jo's lips pressed into a firm line. "I'm going to give you a wedding tomorrow. *We* are."

"What?" Katie's brow furrowed. "You can't do that, Jo. I appreciate the gesture, but there's not enough time. Liv and

Jax are on the road. There's no way Ella and Cash or Grace can get here that fast. Or Antoni."

"They'll be here for the reception," Jo said, already pacing the living room. "But you deserve to have a wedding, Katie. We're here, and we want to celebrate you."

She looked to McKenzie for backup, but McKenzie just shrugged. "I do, but I'm a lot less pushy about it."

"Even if we wanted to, we have so much to do before we leave Sunday," Dallas said. "We don't have time to plan a wedding."

"You don't need to," Jo said, lifting her chin. "Because we've got it handled."

"We?" I finally spoke up. "I'm not exactly a professional wedding planner."

"Yes, *we*," Jo said, focusing her eyes on me. "I am volun-telling you."

McKenzie stifled a laugh, and I bit back a grin.

Derek sat back in his chair and chuckled. "Uh-oh."

"Please, Katie." Jo dropped to her knees in front of her best friend. "Let me do this for you."

"Aw, look, Tommy Lee," McKenzie said to Dallas, a sickly-sweet smile plastered on her face. "Jo's proposal is gonna be better than yours."

Dallas tossed a pillow at her over Katie's head.

"Come on, Katie," Jo begged. "Will you let me do this for you?"

Katie's face softened, and she looked to Dallas, a question burning in her eyes.

He held up his hands. "I want what you want. You know that."

Katie nodded, a smile growing on her face as she turned back toward Jo, who waited impatiently for her answer.

"Okay, then," Katie said. "Yes, you can plan a wedding for us. But only on three conditions."

"Anything," Jo said.

"The only people who will be there, besides whatever officiant you find, are in this room. It can't be over-the-top, and it must be after 8 p.m. because I'm busy till then."

Jo was silent for a moment, and I thought those stipulations were going to be enough for her to call the whole thing off.

But finally, she spoke. "You have my word."

"Then I guess we're getting married tomorrow," Katie said, her face glowing as Dallas watched her with a matching expression, his hand reaching to squeeze her thigh.

Jo threw her arms around Katie and hugged her before bouncing to her feet. "I have to go. I have so much work to do."

"So much self-inflicted work," McKenzie muttered, but Jo was too busy listing off the tasks she needed to accomplish to notice.

"Luca, McKenzie, I'll be in touch tomorrow with everything I need you to do," Jo said, talking to herself as she left the room and walked out the back door, which snapped shut behind her.

Derek nodded slowly and sighed. "How long do you think it'll take her to realize I have the keys?"

It was only a matter of seconds before we heard the creak of the wood followed by Jo shouting. "Derek!"

"Guess that's my cue," he said, standing. "Congratulations, guys. Seriously, this is amazing. And I know whatever she manages to cook up for tomorrow will be perfect."

"Blink twice if you need help, Derek," McKenzie joked as he trailed after Jo.

Once they were both gone, McKenzie shifted her attention to Katie. "Are you sure this is what you want? If it isn't, I'll find a way to reel in Bridezilla."

"Is she Bridezilla if she isn't the one getting married?" I asked.

"Wedding planner-zilla doesn't have quite the same ring," she quipped, turning back to Katie.

"Actually, this is perfect," Katie said, looking like she meant it. She reached for Dallas' hand, and he held her in his gaze like nothing else in the world mattered as long as she was by his side. I knew him well enough to know he didn't need whatever Jo had up her sleeve, but because it was important to Katie, it was important to him.

Lacey's words echoed in the back of my mind as I watched my friends look at each other with pure love and adoration.

Some risks are worth taking.

McKenzie caught my eye, her head tilted in a question. She'd clearly caught me battling my own thoughts on the front lines of my brain. But I just shook my head. I wasn't ready to throw down my weapons just yet.

SEVENTEEN

McKenzie

"ON A SCALE FROM ONE TO IRATE, HOW MAD IS JO GONNA BE when she finds out you turned Emilia into the bouquet?" Luca asked as I wove artificial orange roses into the elderly pup's collar. I'd already glued some of the blossoms to her diaper, and I'd found a small froufrou dress at the pet store and glued dozens of flowers to it. Once she had it on, she'd be the cutest, fluffiest bouquet on the planet. Luca was already watching her for Dallas and Katie since they'd be busy preparing for their trip, so he brought her to my place, allowing me to work my magic without being under the watchful and mildly terrifying eye of Jo.

"She told me to get creative," I said with a shrug. "So that's on her."

Jo had put me in charge of the flowers and cake. Luca had offered up the garden of the hobbit house as the location, which was especially generous since that meant Jo had commandeered his space since around noon. He'd been all too happy to bring Emilia over that evening so I could enact my plan. I'd gathered all my supplies, and together we sat on the floor with Emilia tucked between us, while my cats gave us the stink eye from a safe distance.

Luca smirked. "And by the time she realizes what we did, it'll be too late for her to do anything about it."

"What *we* did?" I asked.

He stroked the top of Emilia's head as she sat before me, soaking up the attention with her cloudy eyes half closed.

"Well, yeah," Luca said. "You don't think I'm gonna let you take the fall by yourself, do you?"

I couldn't hide my grin as my eyes snagged on his mischievous baby blues.

"You know, you told me you weren't much of an animal person," I said as I continued to work. "But I beg to differ. You like my cats, and you clearly like her." I scratched Emilia behind the ears and booped her freckled nose.

He chuckled. "Emilia doesn't count. She's like a sweet old lady. You can't hate an old woman."

I pretended to cover her ears, my mouth wide with feigned shock. "You never discuss a lady's age, especially not if you're going to call her old."

"I don't think she can hear me, anyway," he said with a laugh. "I'm pretty sure those ears are just for show now."

"You hear that, Emilia? Uncle Luca doesn't want to admit he's a big ole softie." I picked up the tiny dog, holding her in front of my nose, which she kissed, giving me a faint wag of her tail.

"Am not," he protested, his lips quirking at the corners.

"Don't you listen to him," I cooed at the pup before carefully putting the small outfit I'd crafted on her and turning her to face Luca. "Whatcha think?"

He gave me a hearty laugh as he took her from my hands. "I think she might be the cutest thing I've ever seen."

The corners of his eyes crinkled with his smile as Emilia licked his chin, causing my heart to flutter like a hummingbird's wings. He seemed so much softer than I'd given him credit for before I'd gotten to know him.

"So, Dallas and Katie…getting married," I said, sitting back, resting my weight on my hands. "Should you object so we can save them from themselves or should I?" I teased.

"Afraid it's too late for that," he said with a laugh that slowed to a contented smile. "And I'm pretty sure they know what they're getting into. They seem happy."

"Yeah, they do," I agreed with a sigh. "It just seems like such a life-altering decision."

"Getting married?"

"Well, yes. But even just committing to someone without the formality of a piece of paper—that's a big deal."

"So you think they're crazy?" he asked, stretching his long legs out in front of him and crossing them at the ankle.

I sighed and pressed my lips together as I considered his question. If someone had asked me a few weeks before, I would've said yes. Outside of my affinity for Meg Ryan movies, I wasn't one for romance or the idea that one person could come along and change your heart on a cellular level.

But then Luca came into my life. Even if this crush of mine would never become anything more, it had shown me, despite my numerous protests to the contrary, that maybe I *did* want somebody to love.

"I don't, actually," I finally admitted. "I might even go so far as to say it's sweet."

"Hmm…" Luca said, a smile forming on his lips.

"What?"

Those adorable wrinkles appeared at the corners of his

eyes again, making me want to throw every ounce of caution I'd ever had to the wind.

"Guess I'm not the only one who's gone soft," he said, his voice low.

He held my gaze for a moment, and I could feel my pulse thundering in my ears. His lips were parted slightly, and he looked like he was on the verge of saying something—the kind of something that could split my life in two, into a definitive before and after.

"McKenzie," he began, and my breath hitched in my throat.

"Yeah?" I asked, almost inaudibly.

Before he could get any further, his phone pinged. He squeezed his eyes shut for a second, then retrieved his cell from his back pocket.

"It's Jo," he said with an exasperated breath. "I should get back. She and Derek probably need help setting up."

And just like that, the moment was gone.

"I guess I'll see you in a bit?" he asked, and I nodded.

"Yeah. I've got to get ready and swing by the restaurant to pick up the cake."

We both rose to our feet, and he scooped Emilia into his arms. I followed him out onto the front stoop and watched him leave, like I had too many times already.

Too many times without him knowing he's the only person I never wanted to walk away.

I SQUARED MY SHOULDERS, LETTING OUT A NERVOUS BREATH as I stepped out of my truck at Luca's house around 9 p.m. The temperature was a chilly sixty degrees, and the night sky was clear. The small cake I made was nestled safely on the floorboard of my passenger seat. I was about to retrieve it when Jo came running out to meet me in a flowy rust-colored dress, and I prepared for her to read me the riot act about turning the dog into a bouquet.

"Everything is set up," she said with one of her signature high-pitched squeals. "Dallas is waiting out back with Derek and Luca, but I've got Katie in one of the bedrooms with Emilia—who looks adorable, by the way. That was so creative. But anyway, Katie hasn't been outside yet. I want her to be surprised." She paused, regarding me with a tilt of her head. "You look amazing. Wow. You're…you're, like, *hot.*"

I rolled my eyes. "I'm going to pretend you don't sound so surprised."

But she was right. I *did* look hot. I'd taken extra time on my hair and makeup before sliding on a slinky black dress and a shimmery shawl I'd found at the thrift store ages ago that I'd been holding onto for some future special occasion that had never happened. But I figured the wedding of one of my closest friends was a good enough reason, along with the blind hope that the moment Luca and I shared earlier hadn't been all in my head.

Jo watched as I carefully extracted the cake, and she shut the passenger door for me before we started toward the house under the glow of the outside lamps.

"So, you were able to find an officiant?"

"Yep," she said with the enthusiasm of five shots of espresso. "And a string quartet."

"*What?*" I asked.

She gave me a shrug as though it was normal to just pull a four-piece ensemble out of one's ass.

"Working in television has its advantages," she said as we walked. "So, there are some outdoor heaters to keep everyone nice and toasty. Oh, and I didn't do a ton of food. I hired someone to make a little grazing board, and of course, we have the cake you made. I figured they wouldn't be able to stay too late, and we have to be home by midnight so the sitter can leave."

"You really thought of everything," I said, genuinely impressed.

Jo raised her eyebrows, repeating my own words back to me. "I'm going to pretend you don't sound so surprised." She grabbed the front door for me and followed as I placed the cake at the center of the rustic dining table that held the graze board, champagne in ice buckets, and a variety of autumnal flowers.

"Come on," she said, grabbing my arm. "You've got to see Katie."

I hung my shawl on the back of one of the chairs before she led me to the spare bedroom she'd turned into a makeshift bride's room, and when she turned the knob, I caught my first glimpse of Katie.

I brought my hands in front of my mouth. "You are stunning."

She had on the perfect cream-colored lace gown with bohemian sleeves that draped elegantly over her lithe arms. Her hair fell in soft waves around her face, and she wore a flower crown made of cream and orange roses. Emilia slept on a pillow nearby.

"This was all Jo," Katie said.

"But your beauty is all you." Jo reached for her best friend's hands, giving them a squeeze.

"Are you excited?" I asked.

"Actually, I'm kind of nervous," Katie admitted. "I know we're technically already married now, but this feels… different."

"Well, if you've changed your mind, I can pull the truck around. You can just hop in the back," I said with a grin.

She and Jo laughed.

"I don't think I need a getaway car," Katie said.

My own emotions clouded my eyes. I couldn't even come up with a snappy comment or a single Tommy Lee and Pamela joke.

I nodded. "I know. You really love him."

"I do," she said, her eyes glittering as Jo fanned her own face.

"Save it for the ceremony," Jo insisted, pulling Katie into a hug as the faint sound of string music filled the air. "It's time."

I knelt to scoop up Emilia, handing her to Katie. "Don't forget your flowers," I said with a grin.

Jo led the way, and I looped my arm through Katie's as we trailed behind her.

"I'm happy for you," I said. "Thank you for letting me be a part of this."

"Are you kidding me?" she asked, covering my hand with hers. "I couldn't do this without you. Jo may be my matron of honor, but you're my maid of honor."

I scrunched my nose, unable to resist teasing her. "Can you call me something else? I'm afraid that might ruin my street cred."

She leaned into me. "How about we call you one of my best friends?"

We stopped just inside the back entrance, and I wrapped her in a hug. "I think that's perfect."

Jo was pressed against the wooden door, her eyes lit with excitement. "Ready?"

Katie nodded. "Ready."

Jo opened the door, and I audibly gasped when I saw what she'd done. She'd transformed the backyard of the hobbit house into a magical candlelit dreamworld. Near the back of the garden was the quartet, giving us the most beautiful soundtrack. Dallas looked dapper in his suit as he stood waiting beneath a floral archway lined with fairy lights, the preacher and Derek at his side.

And then there was Luca.

My heart lurched when my gaze landed on him, the chilly breeze tousling his hair. He wore gray slacks and a simple black button down with the sleeves rolled up. I'd never seen anyone more perfect.

I took a breath to ground myself as Jo started down the back stairs and up the glowing path that led to Dallas. She took her spot on the other side of the archway, and I began my descent down the stairs. I swallowed the lump in my throat as Luca caught my eye, his hand raking over his mouth, an unreadable expression on his face. Jo smiled at me as I took my position behind her.

Then we turned our attention to Katie. She looked like an angel as she floated toward us, her eyes glittering. But most of all she looked happy, in love, and unafraid. She reached Dallas' waiting hands, and I had the perfect view of his face as he looked at his bride.

My throat tightened when I saw the tears slip down his cheeks. But his smile said it all. He'd waited his whole life for her, long before he even knew her name. Back when she was nothing but a distant dream, a someday maybe, a wish he didn't know would ever be granted.

I never allowed myself to hope that big before, because it felt too impossible. Too rare and precious, like witnessing a star shooting across the sky. Even if I could be lucky enough to spot one, would it last?

There, under a late October sky, as Dallas took Katie in his arms, I started to believe. Maybe it *was* possible for me.

EIGHTEEN

Luca

From the second McKenzie emerged from the back door in a silky black backless dress, I was mesmerized. It felt like my heart was leaping through my chest to get to her, though my feet stood still. I only looked away long enough to see Katie start down the aisle, but then my focus was drawn back to McKenzie. She radiated beauty and love and something else I couldn't quite put my finger on. The way she watched Dallas and Katie with misty eyes made her look vulnerable and open in a way I hadn't seen before.

It was different from that morning she'd told me about Brennan—when she'd looked as if she was the one lone soldier left on a watchtower, unwilling to abandon her post. Now, she was unguarded, the gate to her heart left unlocked, the wrought-iron bars swinging in the autumn breeze.

The preacher started the ceremony, but I kept finding myself looking at her as she swiped tears from beneath her lashes. Then Katie began to say her vows.

"Dallas, from the moment we first met, I knew you were special," she said, her voice wavering. "At the time, I only knew you as the drummer of one of my favorite bands, but it wasn't long before I saw everything that makes you who you are…the man I love. Your quiet confidence. The way you can take my bad days and turn them good with a single smile or one of your silly jokes."

Katie paused, smiling through her tears. "You take the ordinary and make it extraordinary, just by being you. I promise to care for you and support you, to fight with you and for you, and to never go to bed without kissing you goodnight. You are the center of my universe, the golden sun that casts light on all the darkest parts of me. And I vow to always share every part of myself with you, even my shadows. Dallas Stone, I promise to grow old with you and love you, all the days of our life."

I heard Dallas' soft laughter before he spoke. "The first time I saw you, I think, deep down, I knew you were the one I was meant to be with. My heart recognized something in yours. Something that felt like home. You make me better, Katie. With your gentleness, your understanding, and with the kindness you show everyone lucky enough to be in your orbit. If I'm your sun, then you are my whole world. You're the air I breathe. You are what keeps me going when it feels like everything is falling apart."

My eyes searched for McKenzie's, and I found myself blinking away tears when she gazed back at me. *She* was who had kept me going these last few weeks. I didn't need to put on an act with her or pretend to be okay. She saw me as I was and accepted me all the same. McKenzie made me better.

Dallas' voice broke, and he took a moment before continuing. "I promise to protect you and hold you when you ask me to and even when you don't. As long as I live, you'll never have to face anything alone. You're my best friend and the love of my life, Butter Bean. And I'll spend every day of forever loving you, cherishing you, and choosing you. Always."

Choosing you. I swallowed hard, trying to rein in my emotions, but they would not be silenced. Maybe I'd been looking at this love thing all wrong. It was terrifying, yes. I knew, because as afraid as I was to admit it, I'd been falling for McKenzie since the night I ran into her at that dive bar. What made it scary was the lack of certainty, the fact that so many things could change. I could end up being too much or not enough and risk losing everything.

But maybe real love was never just about feeling. Maybe it was about choosing. Making the choice to stick it out for better or worse, through heaven and hell. Choosing to stand by someone in their not-enough-ness until they could find their way home again. After all, wasn't that what my friends had done for me over the years? No matter how hard I pushed away, they always pulled me back.

I was lost in my own thoughts until I heard the preacher declare Dallas and Katie husband and wife, and they shared their first kiss post-ceremony. We all cheered for them as the quartet began to play. I found McKenzie once again, tears free-falling down her beautiful face as she clapped.

"Congrats, you two," I said, making my way to the happy couple first and pulling them into a hug as Derek snapped a few pictures.

"I love you, brother," Dallas said, clapping me on the back before leaning into my ear. "I'm glad you're here." The look in his eyes when he pulled away told me he meant more than just for the wedding.

"Thank you," I said. "For everything."

"You make a lovely bride, Katie," I said to her, and she

pulled me in for another hug with Emilia tucked under one arm.

McKenzie stepped closer to me, and I felt my pulse vibrating throughout my entire body.

Just like Dallas' heart had recognized Katie's from the very beginning, there was something about McKenzie's that called to mine. Without ever realizing it, I'd chosen her. I didn't know what that meant for the future. All I knew was, I wanted to find out. I had to.

"McKenzie," I started to say, but then Katie spoke up.

"Okay, ladies," she said, holding up Emilia in her flower outfit. "Who wants to catch the bouquet?"

McKenzie laughed. "Normally, I'd say *ew, gross*, but this puppy bouquet is too cute to pass up. Besides, I don't think it counts since it's not a real bouquet. Gimme."

She reached for the pup, and Emilia responded by licking her chin as she took her in her hands.

"This was perfect, Jo," Katie said, throwing her arms around her best friend. "Thank you all for doing this for us. And thank you, Luca, for letting us use your place."

"Seriously, this house is gorgeous," Dallas added.

Derek nudged my arm. "I knew we'd get you to move here eventually."

"It's only temporary," I said. "It's a short lease."

I could have sworn I saw McKenzie's face start to fall at that, but she turned her attention to watch the quartet.

Jo grinned. "I guess that means we've got a little more time to persuade you to make it permanent, then."

"You know what?" I said, my eyes lingering on McKenzie's back. "I think I could be convinced."

"This was the most perfect day," Katie said, leaning into Dallas' side as they sat on one of the outdoor benches. The preacher and the string quartet had long since left, the cake had been eaten, and we'd FaceTimed our friends who couldn't be there with the good news. Afterward, we all ended up back outside, basking in the soft glow of the candles and twinkle lights as the outdoor heaters warded off the evening chill. Emilia was tucked away safely inside, snoozing on a pillow.

"Yes, it was," Dallas agreed, kissing the top of his bride's head. "Thank you all again for everything you did to make it happen."

"I'll never forget this as long as I live," Katie said.

"And now you get to honeymoon in Italy." Jo grinned as Derek hooked his arm over her shoulders where they stood nearby. "Thanks for trusting me with your special day."

Derek shook his head, his eyes wide with awe. "How did this happen? How did we get here?"

"What do you mean?" I asked.

McKenzie nodded her head toward Jo. "Well, your lady is kind of a miracle worker slash uptight control freak, so I'd say that had something to do with it."

"Hey," Jo said, with mock indignation.

"I didn't say those weren't some of your best qualities." McKenzie held up her hands like a shield where she sat at Katie's other side.

Derek chuckled. "That's not what I meant. I just…It seems like yesterday we were kids playing in your garage, dreaming of the big lives we wanted to live someday," he said, looking at Dallas before turning to me. "Then meeting you and finally becoming a band and traveling the world.

Everything is so different now. Now we have marriages, love, families...entirely new careers. How did it happen?"

Dallas' mouth curled into a smile, and he shrugged. "We grew up."

"It's pretty weird, isn't it?" I asked. "In so many ways, things are the same." Like us. Somehow I knew that no matter where life took us, we'd always have each other.

"But things are different too," Derek said, reaching over and giving my shoulder a squeeze. "*We're* different."

I shoved my hands in my pockets and smirked. "I don't know. Sometimes I don't think I've changed at all."

"You have," Dallas assured me, the words heavy with pride.

He gave me a knowing glance, the kind that said everything without him saying a word. The kind of look born from a lifetime of friendship.

I cleared my throat. "Thanks, Dal."

"We better get going," Jo said. "We've got to get back to relieve the sitter."

Katie rose to her feet, holding her hand out to Dallas. "Yeah, we need to get home too. Our flight leaves bright and early tomorrow."

Dallas pressed a kiss to her temple. "We'll sleep on the plane."

Together, we blew out all of the candles and turned off the heaters before heading inside so everyone could grab their things.

"I'll come back tomorrow and help clean up," Jo said, starting toward the front door.

"Don't worry about it," I said. "I'll take care of it."

"Are you sure?" Jo asked. "I don't mind."

I nodded. "Really, it's fine. It's not like I have anything going on anyway."

We walked outside together, stopping at the bottom of the porch steps.

"Thanks again for keeping Emilia," Katie said to me.

"Glad to do it," I replied.

McKenzie and I exchanged hugs with our friends before they drove away, leaving just the two of us standing side by side beneath the glow of the moon.

She ran her hands over her bare arms to ward off the chill. "Are you sure you don't want help cleaning up?" she asked, tilting her face up to me. "I can stay."

My breath caught in my throat as I gazed down at her. God, I wanted to kiss her. I wanted to tell her all the things I'd been dying to say for weeks. She was right there. All I had to do was…

"That's okay," I said, immediately kicking my own ass inside my head.

Her eyes seemed to search mine for something far deeper than wondering if I needed help throwing away a few party plates.

"You sure?" she asked softly.

What the fuck are you doing, Luca? Tell her how you feel. Kiss her. Do something.

"Nah, I've got it," I said instead.

McKenzie nodded, glancing down. "Okay. Well, I guess I'll talk to you later?"

"Yeah," I said. "Yeah, of course."

She hesitated a moment before starting down the path to her truck.

"Good night," she called over her shoulder before climbing in, the ignition roaring to life.

"Night," I said, shoving my hand through my hair as I went back inside and shut the door.

I blew out a breath as I walked into the kitchen, frustrated with myself for being such a fucking coward. What was I so afraid of? Why couldn't I just tell her how I felt?

Then, I saw it hanging on the back of the chair she'd been sitting at: McKenzie's shawl. Before I could talk myself out of it, I snatched it up with my fist and jogged back to the door, flinging it open.

My chest tightened when I found McKenzie already standing there.

"Hey," I said, barely above a whisper.

"Hi."

"You forgot this." I held the fabric out to her, and she reached for it.

"Thanks."

My heart raced, thundering in my ears. This was it. I just had to put fucking words together.

She gave me a wistful smile and started to turn away, but I grabbed her by the wrist, spinning her around to face me.

A soft gasp escaped her perfect fucking mouth as I closed the distance between us, slipping one hand around her waist, while the other snaked up her neck, my thumb running along the soft skin of her jawline.

"Luca," she whispered, leaning into my touch. "What—"

I swallowed the rest of her words as I crushed my lips to hers, setting off a Fourth of July fireworks show behind my eyes. She let out a whimper of surprise before tossing the shawl to the floor, sliding her hands up my chest and into my hair, taking fistfuls of it between her fingers. My tongue entered her mouth, and she tasted sweet like vanilla buttercream. I pulled her tighter against me, longing to savor every inch of her.

She eventually broke our kiss, leaving me breathless, desperate to reclaim her warmth. Her chest rose and fell with shallow pants, and for a second, I thought she was going to ask me what the hell I was doing. But then she gave me a sultry smile that nearly brought me to my knees as she leapt into my arms, wrapping her legs around me.

Her hands cupped my face as she whispered against my mouth. "Fucking finally."

NINETEEN

McKenzie

HE KICKED THE FRONT DOOR SHUT BEFORE PROPPING ME
against it, his hands under my ass. His lips against my neck
were like a white-hot branding iron, claiming me. I tightened
my legs around him, feeling the outline of him through the
thin fabric of his slacks as he pressed his hips against mine.

"Bed," I managed between kisses, twining his thick,
luscious hair around my fingers. It was every bit as soft as I
imagined it would be, while the rest of him was as hard as I'd
dreamed.

He stumbled through the house with me in his arms,
pausing only to lean me against the wall once to get his bear-
ings, his tongue taking the opportunity to taste my collarbone.

"Now," I pleaded, and he carried me the rest of the way to
his bedroom where he finally allowed my feet to touch the
ground. The room was dark except for the watery ripples of
light from the moon through the window.

It was finally fucking happening.

"McKenzie," he said as I kicked off my shoes, my hands
desperately working the buttons on his shirt. I nearly sighed in

relief when I got to run my fingers over his smooth bare chest. It was firm and taut and warm against my skin.

"Yes." My reply came as I turned my back to him and guided him toward the zipper of my dress.

He trailed kisses across my shoulders as he slid the spaghetti straps down one by one. His fingertips grazed the bare skin of my back before finally coming to rest just above my hips.

"Are you sure?" he asked, tugging on the zipper, his mouth on my neck.

"Yes," I cried again, tilting my head to give him better access.

The silky fabric of my dress gave way, and it crumpled to the floor, leaving me wearing nothing but a pair of black lacy panties that made my butt look amazing. I may or may not have coordinated my undergarments based on my sheer delusional hope that a moment like this would occur.

His hands slid down my sides and cupped my ass, his fingers digging into my soft flesh.

"McKenzie," Luca practically growled my name. "I need to hear you say it. Are you sure?"

My heart nearly stopped. My mind traveled back to the dream I'd had about him the night I'd gotten hammered and woken up with him in my house. It was a fantasy I'd revisited often since that night, though there were different variations of it. But no matter how I found myself falling into his arms, he always said *"The truth is, McKenzie, when I fuck you, I want you to be able to remember every perfect fucking minute of it."*

This wasn't a dream, and I was damn sure going to remember every single second.

"Yes." I faced him then, and his eyes traveled down my bare chest like a viper about to strike. "I want you."

"But—" he began to say when I cut him off, already fumbling with his belt.

"Do you want to have a conversation right now, or do you want to fuck me?" I asked. "Because I know which one I want."

His eyes darkened in a way I hadn't seen before, setting my core on fire. He helped me finish removing his belt, chucking it to the side.

"I know what I want," Luca murmured, sliding one hand around my neck, his lips crushing against mine while his other hand took care of the button and fly on his pants. I hooked my greedy fingers through his belt loops and shoved them down.

"Are you sure?" I asked, tossing his own words back at him, taking him in my hand through the cotton of his boxer briefs.

He groaned and bucked against my hand but didn't once drop my gaze.

"I know *exactly* what I want." His voice was husky and low and deep, stirring parts of me I didn't know existed. He was so close he could have owned my mouth, but he didn't. He waited. Instead, he grinned against me, the warmth of his breath making my skin tingle. One hand gripped my jaw while the other found my breast, rolling his thumb over my nipple as I whimpered against his mouth.

I'd never wanted anyone more.

"Then take it." I was practically begging. "Take *me*."

In one fluid movement, Luca lifted me off the hardwood floor and placed me on the bed. He nudged my legs open, taking one of my feet in his hand. He trailed wet kisses from my ankle, up my calf, and to my thigh. The closer he got to my fiery center, the more I craved his touch.

He crouched at my core, releasing a hot breath over the fabric of my panties.

"Luca," I said, his name a pleading whisper on my lips.

With a devilish smile, he hooked his fingers over the lace and dragged them down my legs slowly before tossing them aside.

He drank me in as I laid there, exposed and vulnerable.

"God, you're beautiful," he rasped.

Even through the darkness, I could see there was something more than lust in his eyes. Something soft, something gentle. I'd seen glimmers of it before; that night at The Piccadilly Deli, then in that cozy tavern after he'd signed the lease on the house. It had even been there earlier that day when he was at my place with Emilia. He'd been on the verge of saying *something*. I just never imagined it would end up like this, with me having him the way I craved him.

"You're not so bad yourself, you know," I said, my voice catching at the end. I sat up, my hands traveling the length of his body until they reached the last piece of clothing separating us. My fingers grazed his skin just above the elastic, teasing him before I slid it down, revealing every last inch of him.

"Fuck," he moaned as I took him in my hand, moving in slow, languid strokes. "God, that feels good."

I tightened my grip, making his eyes roll back. "You have no idea how good *I* can feel."

"Goddamn it, McKenzie." He grunted, reaching over to the nightstand to wrench open the drawer, nearly causing it to fall to the floor. His fingers groped inside until he found his wallet, which he pulled out and dug through for what he was *really* looking for: a condom.

My breath hitched in my throat. Every nerve in my body was raw, yearning for him. I couldn't wait any longer. I snatched the wrapper from him, ripping it open with my teeth before I took the thin latex and rolled it over him.

He pushed me back and brought himself down until he hovered over me, his strong arms caging me to the mattress.

"Now," I said, nipping at his bottom lip. "I want you."

I reached between us, guiding him to my entrance, and he buried himself in me with one thrust. He hooked my leg against his side, allowing him to push deeper inside me.

My neck arched into the pillow, my eyes fluttering closed from the overwhelming feeling of pleasure of having him fill me. But his voice brought me back.

"Eyes on me," he murmured, an intoxicating mix of commanding and tender. "I want to see you when I make you come apart."

Jesus Christ.

I gave a feverish nod, my hands wandering, desperately seeking to know every inch of him. He brought his lips to mine in a soul-stirring kiss as he moved in and out of me. I writhed beneath him, meeting each pulse of his hips with my own.

He continued to move with slow motions, gliding his pelvic bone over my clit in an agonizing way.

"You feel like heaven," he whispered.

"More," I begged between pants. "Faster. Please."

He obliged, and my body worked with his, frantic for every ounce of friction it could get.

"Tell me what you want, McKenzie," he said, his gaze growing hazy, his tempo quickening.

My answer came as easy as my own breath.

"You."

And it was true. I wanted him in any and every way he'd give himself to me. Whether it was one night or the rest of my life, I wanted—I *needed*—him.

"I need you." The confession escaped my mouth without permission, and I shuddered a breath.

Those three words ignited a fire in Luca, and he took my body and made it his. He rocked against me—his body the bow, mine the violin. He played me expertly, paying attention to every single note. Every thrust drove me closer and closer to the brink until I was standing right on the edge.

My eyes threatened to drift closed as my release beckoned me closer, but his hand captured my face, causing them to snap open again, his calloused fingertips imprinting on my flesh.

"Uh-uh," he said, shaking his head. "Eyes on me, remember?"

A breathy whimper escaped my lips as he plunged into me, grinding against my most sensitive spot. Every nerve in my body was screaming for more, and he gave it willingly.

"Fuck," he said with a groan. "I'm so close."

"Oh God," I murmured, the weight of his words pushing me even further.

"Let go, McKenzie," he whispered. "Let go with me."

And I did. My muscles tensed and my walls collapsed around him, sending him crashing with me. He shattered against me as he threaded his fingers through mine, pressing a kiss to my lips that swallowed our cries of pleasure as we rode out our aftershocks together.

Luca sagged against me, burying his face in my neck as I

pulled him closer. He responded, his arms tightening around me.

My breathing slowed, but my heart didn't. Now that I'd had him, all I wanted was more.

"Holy shit." I flopped back against the mattress, my head sinking into the pillow. "That was…"

Luca's chest rose and fell with every shallow breath as he settled next to me, resting his head on his hand. "Incredible?" he asked, his eyes shining in the glow of the moonlight that danced through the room.

Perfect. Mind blowing. A damn near religious experience. Somehow, no words came close to touching how good sex was with Luca. While he recharged, he'd taken it upon himself to turn my limbs to liquid using only his tongue. I didn't know my body was even capable of experiencing that many orgasms within such a short time period. And just when I thought for sure I would combust from pleasure, he was ready for round two.

"I might never walk normally again," I said with a laugh, pulling the sheet tighter around me.

He chuckled. "Good. I can't have you forgetting about me too quickly."

"Hmm…" I sighed and tried to feign an air of nonchalance before flashing him a wink. "I'm sure I'll at least remember you for the next two to three business days."

He slipped his arm around me, pulling me against him. "Only two or three, huh?"

"Well. Give or take."

That couldn't have been further from the truth. There was

no chance I could forget him, *ever.* Now that I knew what it felt like to be with him—the way he moaned when he lost control and the way he looked at me as though I was the most magical fucking creature he'd ever laid eyes on—I couldn't get enough. I was addicted.

"You'd better be joking." His voice was a low rumble as he grinned against my cheek.

I raised my brows. "Or what?"

His smile faded to something more heartfelt and serious as he brought his head up to look at me, tucking a piece of hair behind my ear.

"McKenzie," he said, his voice barely above a whisper. "I hope you know I don't want this to be some one-time thing."

I smiled softly. "Really?"

He shook his head and leaned closer, pressing a kiss to my forehead. "No."

I trailed my fingers over his bare arm. "I gotta be honest, I wasn't sure how you felt about me."

"What do you mean?"

"Obviously, I knew we were friends, but…" My gaze dropped. "It seemed like anytime I thought we might be getting closer, you kind of pulled away."

He tilted my chin, forcing me to look at him. "That's because this is different for me. This is uncharted territory."

I gave him an I-don't-believe-you smirk. "Respectfully, your mastery of the female anatomy would suggest otherwise."

"*That* is not what I mean," he said. "Sex for the sake of sex is easy. But doing it with someone you care about? That's something else entirely."

My stomach did a somersault.

"This," he said, gesturing between us. "This connection,

liking someone, caring if they like me back…that's all new for me."

I placed my palm against his cheek, and he turned to kiss it. "I like you too, you know," I said.

He covered my hand with his. "You truly didn't know how I felt about you?"

I shrugged. "I mean, I hoped. But I didn't know."

"You really don't remember what happened the night I took you home after the My Chem cover band show, do you?"

"No, and I don't want to." I groaned. "You told me enough for me to know I embarrassed myself."

He paused and took in a breath. "I didn't tell you everything."

The bottom fell out of my stomach. "What do you mean?"

He hesitated a moment, and I swatted his chest.

"What didn't you tell me?" I asked.

"Before you got sick that night, you tried to kiss me. Actually, you kind of wanted to do more than that."

Heat burned up my neck and into my cheeks.

"Oh God." I buried my face in the pillow. "*Tried* to? Does that mean I attempted and failed?"

"It means I stopped you," he confessed. "But—"

"Are you trying to kill me?" I cut him off, my voice muffled by the memory foam. "Why are you telling me this?"

He chuckled softly. "Look at me."

"Sorry, I can't. I'm busy trying to melt through this bed and into the floor."

He laid his head next to mine, pushing my hair out of my face.

"Look at me," he said again, and I did.

"I told you no, but it wasn't that I didn't want you," he began. "Because believe me, I did. In fact, I specifically said that I did, but that when we finally had sex, I wanted you to be able to remember it."

"Wait." I raised up on my elbows, my mouth falling open. "You said that?"

He bit his lip. "I probably shouldn't have said it out loud but—"

"I remember that." I gasped. "But I was so fucking toasted, I thought I *dreamed* it."

He propped himself up so his lips were only inches from mine.

"So, *that's* why you looked all hot and bothered the next morning." He raised his brows at me. "I'm pretty sure you woke up moaning my name."

I punched him in the shoulder. "And *I'm* pretty sure I've watched enough true crime to kill you and make it look like an accident."

He laughed and pulled me into his arms. "Come here."

"You could've let me continue to live in ignorance, you know," I whispered against his neck. "That would've been the polite thing to do."

"But then you wouldn't know how long I've wanted you," he said, his tone sincere, tender. "Or that you had me so hot for you that I had to um…take matters into my own hands in your bathroom while you were asleep."

My eyes went wide as I sat up to look at him, my lips curling into a grin. "You did *what* now?" I asked.

He winced. "Yeeeah. I probably shouldn't have admitted that. But I needed you to know…I've wanted you this whole time."

"Hold up," I said, attempting to piece together the order of events. "This was…this was even *after* you saw me puke my guts up? I was disgusting."

He touched my nose with his finger. "Even when you're gross, you're beautiful."

"That is weirdly romantic." I laid down with my head on his shoulder.

"So, how was I in your dream?" he asked with a smug lilt. "Was I good?"

"Did you think about me while you were playing the five knuckle shuffle in my bathroom with Palmela Handerson?" I shot back, dissolving into a fit of giggles.

"Fuck yeah, I did," he said, his shoulders shaking.

When our laughter slowed, he tightened his arms around me and kissed the top of my head.

"You're better than any fantasy I've ever had," he whispered against my hair. "I never dared to dream as big as you."

My breath caught in my throat. His words made it sound like he was referring to something much bigger than the amazing sex we'd had. Part of me wanted to ask what he meant, but I didn't want to jinx it, so instead, I nestled closer, listening to the sound of his heartbeat. This was a dream I never wanted to wake up from.

TWENTY

Luca

THE SUN FILTERED IN AROUND THE EDGES OF THE BLINDS, kissing the freckled skin of McKenzie's shoulder. Her back was facing me, the faint rasp of her breath and birds singing outside the window the only sounds in the room.

Her hair shimmered, the light casting a golden halo over her head.

I traced slow circles over her back, allowing my fingers to move gingerly over her skin.

She sighed and let out a low moan.

"Hi," I whispered, squeezing her hip.

"Good morning." Her voice was still thick with sleep and couldn't have sounded sexier if she tried. "You know, if you keep doing that, I may never leave this bed."

"In that case…" I slid closer to her and brushed my hand through her hair, placing a kiss in the crook of her neck.

I allowed my lips to trail up toward her ear, stopping when I spotted a tiny tattoo tucked behind her earlobe. Though I hadn't noticed it before, I instantly recognized the symbol because I'd seen it before on Lacey's wrist at our first appointment. I recalled what she'd said when I'd noticed it. *The semicolon represents a sentence not yet finished. It means there's more left to say.*

"You have a tattoo," I said.

"What? Really?" she asked with an exaggerated gasp. "How'd that get there?"

I laughed as she rolled over to look at me.

"Smart-ass," I said, my thumb grazing her cheek. "How long have you had it?"

Her face softened. "About fourteen years."

I nodded, tucking a piece of hair behind her ear. "What does it mean to you?"

She sighed and rolled her lips inward. "It's kind of a heavy story. You sure you're up for that this early in the morning?"

I gave her a faint smile. "I'm up for anything that has to do with learning about you."

She glanced down a moment before bringing her eyes up to mine. "I got it just before the one year anniversary of Brennan's death."

"Did you get it for him?"

She shook her head. "I got it for me." Her gaze dropped, and she chewed the inside of her cheek for a moment. "After Brennan died...I lost myself. He was my best friend. Without him...life changed. It was like all the color drained from the earth, leaving me in this endless gray. It became...too much."

I touched her chin, tilting her head back to me as I waited for her to continue.

"I was just going through the motions of life rather than living," she explained. "On the outside, I was functioning— for a while, anyway. I went to school and did just enough to make people think I was fine. But on the inside, every breath was like a knife twisting in my back. Everything reminded me of Brennan. He was gone…yet he was *everywhere*."

"I'm so sorry," I murmured as her eyes turned glossy.

She cleared her throat. "It got to a point where I couldn't do it anymore. The mask I'd tried so hard to keep up started to slip. I could hardly get out of bed in the mornings until eventually, I stopped. I just…I didn't want to do it anymore, you know? I didn't want to…"

I brushed a tear off her cheek and nodded.

"Live," I finished for her. I understood that feeling all too well.

"At first, it was just this feeling of not wanting to shoulder this loss anymore, but it became something more. Something deeper. It went from being a distant thought to me thinking of how I'd do it. My own mind became a terrifying place to be."

I swallowed hard, forcing down the lump in my throat. "McKenzie."

"So, I told my mom. I confessed everything I was feeling, and she did everything she could to bring me back," she said. "She got me into therapy. She took time off work to be with me. We went on little weekend trips so we could spend time together. She did what she could to make life worth living again, even though she was dying inside. She was so afraid of losing me too."

My chest tightened as I listened to her, realizing how hopeless she'd felt after losing her brother—and how incredibly close I came to not having the privilege of meeting her.

"Right before the anniversary of his death, my mom and I went to this tattoo place," she said. "I'd always wanted a tattoo, but of course, she'd never allowed me to get one. And I wasn't eighteen yet, so I couldn't have done it without her permission. But she took me and said we were getting one together."

"What made you decide on a semicolon?" I asked.

"Because they represent a pause. A break in a sentence, a before and an after. They're there to remind us that even though Brennan's story is over, we still have more to say."

I studied her, this beautiful, perfect woman who'd altered the course of my life by simply existing. I was so grateful she'd gotten the help she needed back then and that I was able to wake up next to her now. I must've been quiet for a moment too long because she spoke, reaching out to touch my face.

"What are you thinking?" she asked.

I took a deep breath. "I was just thinking how thankful I am that you stayed. You…" I trailed off, my eyes searching hers. "I know we haven't known each other long, but you've…you've changed me. You've made me lighter. Better. You make me want to *be* better."

She tried to look away, but I stopped her, taking her face gently in my hands.

"You do," I said.

Her eyes lingered on mine for a moment before she leaned in and kissed me. It was nothing like our first kiss from the night before. There was nothing hurried or frenzied about it. It was slow, deep, tender. The feeling of her soft lips against mine was the only thing tethering me to the earth as my heart soared.

She pulled back so she could see me and said three words that made me feel like I could do anything as long as she believed in me.

"So do you. You make me want to be better too."

Her lips drew me in again, beckoning me closer. I'd spent

a lot of my life feeling like I didn't quite fit anywhere. But with her, in her arms, I finally belonged.

We sipped coffee in bed and ate leftover cake for breakfast, talking about everything and nothing at all as Emilia snuggled between us. McKenzie threw on one of my T-shirts, and even with yesterday's eyeliner smudged beneath her eyes, she was the most gorgeous woman I'd ever seen. I started to imagine more days like this, spent just being together.

"Have you worked any more on the song you played me the last time I was here?" she asked.

"Actually, I finished it," I answered. "I was so inspired by your feedback that I wrote the rest of it the next day."

"Play it for me," she said, pressing a kiss to my lips.

"You really want me to?" I was nervous to share it, but I also trusted her completely. It was because of her I'd even started writing music to begin with.

"Please."

"Okay," I agreed.

I brought the guitar into the bedroom, sat at the foot of the mattress, and began to strum the chords. She lay on her side as she listened, and I kept my eyes closed as I sang the words.

I poured my soul into every single syllable, giving her everything I had. It was vulnerable and terrifying, but it made me feel alive—simultaneously lost and found.

My voice faded to a whisper as I finished, the sound of her sniffling bringing me back to the moment.

"Luca," she said, swiping her fingertips beneath her lashes. "That was beautiful. It was…everything."

I placed the guitar on the bed and shifted closer to her. "Really?"

She nodded. "I know you started writing just for you, but I think you have something here. Your words could...they could help people."

The prospect made me both nervous and excited. I hadn't written with the intention of sharing my songs with anyone. But maybe. Maybe I could. Maybe I *should*.

"You think so?" I asked.

"I know so."

I moved so I was lying beside her and Emilia, stroking the tips of the pup's ears as I contemplated what she'd said.

"Maybe I could show Jax and Liv what I've been working on," I said. "Maybe they would want to record my stuff."

"You could." She tilted her head as she gazed at me. "But I think what makes your words so special is that you're the one singing them."

I raised my brows. "You're saying you think I should perform? By myself?"

"There's no better person to tell your story than you."

I pressed my lips together, mulling the idea over in my mind. I'd never wanted to or even considered going solo.

"I don't know," I said, shaking my head. "I've only ever been part of a band. Jax...he was the talent. The lyricist, the singer."

"But I think *you* were the heart." She paused and placed a hand on my arm, giving it a squeeze.

I blinked in disbelief. *The heart of the band? Me?*

"And you are just as talented," she continued. "Even more so, if you ask me. And your voice...Luca, you don't even realize how good you are. You made me feel every word you sang."

It wasn't that I thought of myself as *un*talented, but as the lead guitarist, I'd felt more like an entertaining sideshow than the main event. Jax had been the one with the songwriting chops. He'd been the one with the voice that had been the highlight of our glowing reviews. Sure, we'd won several awards over the years, but part of me had always looked at those as his.

We all pitched in here and there when writing songs for the band, but every idea had started and ended with Jax. I'd been content to go along for the ride, giving only what was asked of me, never offering too much of myself.

"It would be weird to get on a stage again without them," I said.

"It would," she agreed. "But I imagine it felt a little strange when you started writing your own songs without them too."

"It did."

"But it was worth it, right?" she asked. "It felt good after you did it?"

"Yeah," I admitted. "It did."

"I know it's scary, but I think it could be good for you too. You've spent years helping to tell stories that weren't yours and letting people make up their own narratives about you. I know the press hasn't exactly been kind to you."

"They're going to spin the story how they want to anyway, so I just never really saw a point."

"You—your truth—matters," she said, touching my chest. "Other people don't get to tell you who you are. Only you get to decide that."

"You really believe I can do this?" I threaded my fingers through hers and turned her hand over so I could kiss her knuckles.

"I do," she said. "But what do *you* think?"

The seed she'd planted in me grew then, faith and confidence taking root in my mind. Her belief in me watered the soil that had once been dried up with doubt.

I gave her a single resolute nod. "I think you're right."

And I knew just the person to call to help me make it happen.

I SENT CASH A TEXT AS SOON AS MCKENZIE LEFT ON Sunday, asking if he had time to speak with me over Zoom the next day. He agreed, and we set up the call for noon on Monday.

When my friend and former manager's face came over the screen, it was like no time had passed since I'd seen him, even though it had been several months. I asked how he was, then quickly shifted the topic to his wife Ella.

"Is she around? Can I talk to her?" It killed me that I hadn't been there when her mom had passed away. I'd been so wrapped up in my own pain that I'd shut out the rest of the world. I still remembered how much it hurt when I heard the news on my voicemail in the middle of the night, the night before I visited Lacey's office for the first time.

"She's at a doctor's appointment with Betty," he said. "It's just a regular checkup. Our little girl is growing like a weed."

I nodded. "How is Ella?"

"It's a day to day thing," he answered, his gaze falling. "Her mom had Alzheimer's for so long that Ella felt like she lost her over and over again. I think what hurt her the most was when she really slipped away there toward the end and Ella knew she'd never see her mom as *her* again."

"I'm so sorry." I released a shuddering breath. "I should've been there."

"It's okay," he tried to assure me. "It's—"

"It's not," I interrupted. "And I'll always regret it, but I just…I wasn't in a good place, Cash. I was—"

This time, *he* cut *me* off. "It's okay. You were fighting your own battles, man. I just wish you would have told us what was going on. We would have been there for you in a heartbeat."

"I know," I said. "But that's just it. I don't think I was ready for help. I had to get to a place where I could even be open to the idea. It took me a while, but…I feel like the clouds are lifting."

He studied me for a moment through the camera of his laptop. "Well, you look good," he said in that earnest, brotherly way he had about him. "And you're feeling better?"

"I am," I answered. "I feel like I'm making progress."

"I'm proud of you. What you're doing…it's not easy. It's…" He trailed off, scrubbing his hand over his mouth. "God, I went through a dark period after Carrie died. You and the guys knew I was struggling, but you didn't know the full extent. I threw myself into my work, and it helped that Midnight in Dallas really took off during that time. It gave me something to put every ounce of my energy into. But when I was home during the tour breaks…that's when it would hit me the hardest."

"Jesus, Cash," I said. "I wish we'd known how bad it was." Losing his first wife had been devastating for him, but he'd carried it so well we must've missed just how much the loss had affected him. It had been hard for us all. She'd become an unofficial part of our team.

"I wish I'd told you instead of trying to deal with it

alone." He gave me a sad smile. "We need each other, Luca. People need their people."

"Yeah." My throat tightened. "They do."

"And…I want you to know I'm sorry," he said, his voice growing thick.

"What for?"

"I should've seen it," he said. "I should have realized…I wasn't always fair to you. I wasn't as understanding as I could've been."

I shook my head. "You have nothing to apologize for. If you'd have tried to be there for me, I would've pushed you away. I wouldn't have listened."

"But I should've tried." He paused for a moment before speaking again. "I love you, brother. I haven't told you that enough, but it doesn't make it any less true."

"I love you too."

He cleared his throat, dabbing at the dampness on his cheeks.

"Fatherhood is really doing a number on you, huh?" I teased.

"You have no idea," he said with a laugh. "So, you said you had something you wanted to tell me. What's going on?"

"Well," I began, "I've been doing some journaling as part of my therapy. At first, it was like pulling teeth, but someone much smarter than me suggested I look at it like writing a song. So, I did, and I'd…I'd like to share something I've been working on."

"Really?" His eyes widened. "I'd be honored."

I performed the song I'd played for McKenzie, attempting to channel the same energy I'd had the day before. Once again, it felt good to sing, and I got lost in the music. Every word felt like a step in the right direction, taking me a little closer to who I was supposed to be.

When I finished, Cash sat in silence so long I thought the app had frozen.

"Cash?" I said. "Are you there?"

"Yeah, sorry," he said, leaning closer to the camera. "I'm here. I'm just…*Wow*, Luca. That was incredible. I'm a little speechless right now."

I chuckled. "I hope that's not a bad thing."

"Definitely not," he said. "But are you sharing this with me for the reason I think you are? Are you considering putting some solo stuff out there?"

I sucked in a breath. "Yeah. I am. If you think it's good."

"I think it's brilliant. Have you worked on anything else?"

"I've got a couple others that are just about finished and a notebook full of shit I'm trying to make sense of."

"How soon do you think you could have enough material to cut an EP?" he asked, rubbing his thumb along his jaw. "Five songs max."

My stomach did a flip. "I think I could be ready in a couple weeks. Three, tops."

He tapped his fingers on the desk, lost in thought. "And how would you feel about doing a couple of small showcases? Maybe even playing The Bluebird?"

"Are you serious? You think I'm good enough for that?" I asked, my heart skipping a beat. I'd never actually played the historic venue before. It wasn't even something I'd let myself fantasize about because that was the stage for storytellers. So many of the greats had played there over the years, people whose names were synonymous with extraordinary songs, the kinds that stuck with you for a lifetime.

He didn't hesitate. "Absolutely."

I sat back in my chair, running my hand along the back of my neck. "Then yeah. Yes. I'd love to."

"Look," he said. "I would come out there myself and help you get ready for this, but it's a tough time for me to leave Ella and Betty, and I've got some work going on here in LA. However, I can send someone in my place." A soft smile played over his face. "I trained her myself, and she's been needing a solo project to work on to really get her feet wet. I'll be available to assist from out here in any way I can, but I trust her to take the reins if you do."

I grinned, knowing exactly where his line of thought was leading. "Let's do it."

"Great," he said. "I'll have Grace in Nashville by the end of the week. In the meantime, you keep working on those songs, okay?"

"That sounds good." I smiled, unable and unwilling to hide my excitement.

I couldn't wait to tell McKenzie. I wasn't sure what felt better—Cash being on board or knowing I had McKenzie to share the news with.

TWENTY-ONE

McKenzie

"I LOVED IT, BUT I WAS DEFINITELY READY TO COME HOME," my mom said as we perused the nearly empty aisles of The Thrift Stop the following Thursday evening. "I missed you." She'd just finished telling me about her trip and all the delicious wine and food she'd consumed.

"I missed you too." I smiled at her as I slid hangers down a rack filled with shirts. I plucked one off the rack and held it up for her. It was blue with a picture of a Rosie-the-Riveter-looking character printed on it.

My mom squinted as she read the words. "'Strollin' for Kelsey's Colon.' Well, that one has to come with us." She took it and put it in the cart she was pushing.

"Kelsey's friend did her dirty sending this one to the donation pile," I said.

"I don't know who Kelsey is, but I hope she and her colon are doing well."

I laughed as I pawed through the clothes. My phone pinged with a text from my back pocket, and when I checked the screen, I couldn't stop the smile that spread across my face.

Luca: *Randy McNutt told me to tell you he misses you.*

My fingers flew quickly across the keyboard as I typed my response: *I miss him too. But I'll see him again Saturday.*

Bubbles appeared and then another text.

Luca: *Do I really have to wait that long?*

My lips pressed together as I tapped out another message: *I thought we were talking about Randy?*

Luca: *What if it's really me who misses you? Do I still have to wait till Saturday?*

"Earth to McKenzie," my mom said, nudging me with the cart.

I shoved my phone back in my jeans. "Sorry."

She cocked her head. "And who was that?"

"A friend," I answered, not looking at her as I continued to swipe through the shirts.

"Uh-huh," she said in a way that made it clear she didn't believe me one bit.

"What?"

"If that was a friend, then why do you look like the cat that swallowed the canary?"

"I never understood that saying. How big is this cat if it's swallowing a whole-ass bird?" I asked.

She folded her arms over her chest. "And now you're changing the subject."

"I'm just saying," I began, feigning far more interest in the clothes in front of me than I felt. "Could a house cat— even one the size of Earl Grey—consume a bird in one gulp like a boa constrictor? Seems unlikely."

"You're blushing." Her tone was more amused than accusatory.

"And you're delusional." I rolled my eyes, but the heat in my cheeks gave me away.

"Who's the guy? Where'd you meet him? Is he cute?" She fired off her barrage of questions in rapid succession. "What am I even saying? Of course, he's cute if he caught your attention."

"Do I need to remind you that I'll be the singular person in charge of your care one day?" I teased. "Are you trying to end up in a home?"

"It's worth it if I get to hear about this *handsome suitor*." Her eyes lit up as she made a poor attempt at a British accent.

"Suitor? This isn't *Bridgerton*." I heaved a dramatic sigh. "And he's far from the proper type."

My mother squealed like she was my best girlfriend—which, really, she always had been.

"What's his name? What's he like?" she asked.

I hesitated, enjoying leaving her hanging a little too much.

"Come on," she insisted. "Humor an old woman. I haven't had any action since—"

I plugged my ears. "LA LA LA. I can't hear you."

"If you don't tell me who this guy is, I'll tell you about the time me and Blaze Henderson—"

"Ew. Whose name is unironically Blaze?" I wrinkled my nose in distaste. "Fine. His name is Luca. Luca Sterling."

She tilted her head, tapping her fingers on the handle of our cart. "Why does that name sound familiar? Is he a friend of yours from group? I swear you've mentioned him before."

"I haven't. But you might have heard of him." I dropped my voice low so only she could hear. "Because he's kind of, sort of famous."

She blinked, her mouth hanging open. "I'm sorry. What?"

"You know that band Dallas from work was a part of?"

She nodded. "I love them. I listen to them all the time now."

"Seriously?"

"What?" she asked, pretending this wasn't woefully weird. "They're good. That friend of yours, Katie, she's a lucky girl. I've always had a thing for guys with tattoos."

"I'm gonna try really hard to scrub that from my brain, thankyouverymuch."

She leaned against the cart. "Hey, I said I'm old, but I'm *not* dead. In my head, I'm not a day over thirty-five."

"Still weird," I sang, moving down the rack.

"So, wait. Which one's Luca?"

"He was the guitar player," I answered. "Fair skin, dark hair, piercing blue eyes."

She got quiet, and I turned around to find her studying her phone.

I dropped my head back onto my shoulders. "Don't tell me you're googling him."

She didn't bother lifting her eyes from the screen. "Okay. I won't tell you."

I snatched the phone out of her hands, but her face was already filled with concern.

"Kenz…" Her brows drew together as she frowned. "He's very handsome, but those first headlines that popped up…Is all of that true? Because if it is—"

"It's not," I said, cutting her off. "Or at least, it isn't anymore. He's…kind and understanding and—"

"Not a womanizer?" she asked softly.

I shook my head emphatically. "He isn't. I swear. I know what you're thinking."

"And can you blame me?"

I sighed. "No. I can't."

"Sweetheart, your dad was charming and sweet and beautiful once upon a time too. Before he started drinking and sleeping with every woman he could convince to get into bed with him." Her face fell as she looked at me. "Before he left me with two children and no way to contact him."

"You know I'd never get involved with someone like him."

She narrowed her eyes at me. "You think I thought your father was like that when we got together?"

She took her phone back and enlarged one of the articles she'd found before handing it back to me. The headline read: *Loaded Luca Sterling Gets Tossed Out of Bar After Late Night Brawl.*

"Mom, I'm telling you." I pointed to the date on the piece. "This is from three years ago. He's not like that anymore. He's sober. Don't judge him before you even know anything about him." My words came out sharper and more defensive than I intended. "I…Sorry…"

"No, it's okay. You're right." She took a breath as she tucked her phone back in her purse. "Tell me about him."

I sighed, a faint smile pulling at the corners of my mouth. There was only one thing I needed to tell her in order to make her understand.

"He was there for me the night of the…*anniversary*," I explained. "I was at a bar drinking alone, with every intention of getting drunk. I just wanted to…not feel anything anymore."

Her face fell, and she pressed her hand to her chest. "Oh, honey. I'm so sorry. I shouldn't have left you here all alone."

"I'm not sorry," I said with a shrug. "Because you

deserved the break. And also because Luca found me. He didn't know at first what was going on. All he knew was that he wasn't going to let me deal with it alone. He stayed with me the whole night. Looked out for me. Made sure I got home safely and carried my drunk ass up the stairs. He held my hair back when I got sick."

Tears shined in her eyes. "Sweetheart…"

"And then do you know what he did?" I asked. "He took care of me. He got me water and tucked me into bed and didn't make a single move on me. The next morning, he got breakfast, and we talked. He wanted to know what had me down, so I told him. And Mom, he understood. Do you want to know why?"

"Why?"

"Because *he'd* felt like Brennan did." My voice broke. "He was depressed like Brennan was. That's what brought him here to Nashville. He's getting help. We understand each other in a way other people don't."

She opened her mouth as though she was going to say something but then closed it again.

"What?" I asked.

She hesitated a moment. "Honey, I can tell he means a lot to you, but…"

"But?"

"It seems like he might be dealing with a lot right now," she answered, her voice gentle. "And I worry that could bring up a lot of difficult memories for you. I also know how much responsibility you felt for what happened with Brennan. I just don't want you to get in a situation where you take on the weight of things you have no control over."

My gaze fell to my feet. Kia had brought up something similar weeks before. I'd shoved those thoughts aside then but hearing them echoed by my mom caused a wave of anxiety to wash over me, plunging me into shadowy waters.

"It's not like that," I insisted, clinging to my attachment to Luca like a life raft. "I think we found each other for a reason."

My mother closed the distance between us, taking me in her arms. She smoothed her hands over my hair.

"It sounds like maybe you did," she said, swiping the tears from my eyes with her thumbs. "I'm sorry. I didn't mean to misjudge him."

I nodded. "It's okay. I just...I think he's been dealt a lot of shit, and people don't know the full story."

"And you feel protective of him," she said. "I get it. And I'm sorry. It's just...I'm protective of you. You're my whole life, McKenzie. I want to keep you safe."

"He does too. I really believe that." Letting anyone in was a risk—one I didn't take often because I knew all too well how it could end. But Luca walked straight through the walls I had up, rendering them useless against him. So, instead of using them to keep him out, I'd begun to see them as a way of bringing him in and locking him inside my heart.

"Okay. I believe you." She pulled back and squeezed my shoulders. "When can I meet him?"

"I don't know," I answered. "We're not quite there yet."

"How serious is it?"

"We've been spending time together these last few weeks but only just started dating," I said. "I do want you to meet him. Just not yet."

She gave me a reassuring smile. "Okay. Well, whenever you're ready, so am I."

I hugged her again. "Thanks, Mom."

"But tell Katie if she ever gets tired of that Dallas, I'll take him off her hands," she joked, lightening the mood.

I grinned and gave her a gentle punch in the arm. "That's it. I'm disowning you."

"LUCA, THESE SONGS ARE...INCREDIBLE," GRACE SAID. It was Sunday at the hobbit house. I'd stayed over the night before, and Grace had arrived around noon bearing coffee and a binder filled with ideas to discuss with Luca.

"That's what I've been telling him," I said, poking Luca's leg.

He grinned at me before turning to Grace. "So, you think this could be something?"

"I think it could be something huge." She sighed and sank deeper into the armchair across from us, Emilia curled in a ball on her lap. "Trends are moving toward solo artists, and we're seeing albums that are a lot more stripped down, less produced. I know Midnight in Dallas wasn't heavy on the production, but it's even less now than what you probably remember. I think that would lend itself really well to what you've got here."

Luca nodded, a smile spreading over his face.

"But I do think there's something else we need to consider," Grace continued, stroking Emilia's head as she slept, her brows furrowed together.

"What do you mean?" Luca asked, and I folded one leg under the other as I listened.

"Well," she began, "you already have a built-in fan base that'll be clamoring for anything new from a member of their favorite band since Jax is the only one still in the spotlight."

I tilted my head. "That's a good thing, right?"

"It could be," Grace answered. "But with more attention comes more scrutiny. The media hasn't always been kind to Luca."

Luca released a heavy sigh. "You think they won't even give me a chance."

Grace hesitated. "I didn't say that."

My heart dropped as I pictured the articles my mom had shown me just days before. And those were just the tip of the iceberg. I'd gone down my own Google rabbit holes in the past and found plenty more where that came from.

"But you think it," I said, filling in the blanks.

She twisted her lips to the corner of her mouth as she considered what she wanted to say.

"This could go one of two ways," Grace said. "The press might latch onto this music as kind of a comeback. A rebirth of the Luca Sterling they knew."

Luca blew out a breath. "Or they'll be harder on me than ever and shoot this project down before it ever grows wings."

"Exactly." Grace gave him a sad smile. "That's why I want to make sure you're ready for this. Because once we put the wheels in motion—once your music gets out there— there's nothing we can do to stop the train."

"What do you suggest?" Luca asked her. "I'm sure you and Cash talked about it before you came here. What do *you* believe I should do?"

"Well, I certainly didn't come here for an engagement present." Grace gave him a pointed stare that had her mother Ella written all over it.

Luca winced. "Grace, I'm sorry I didn't call. Congratulations. Truly. I'm happy for you and Sam."

She laughed. "I'm messing with you. But seriously, I

wouldn't be here if I didn't think this was something worth pursuing." She paused and leaned forward, running her fingers down Emilia's back, her gaze fixed on Luca. "I wouldn't be here if I didn't have faith in you."

A faint smile tugged at the corners of his mouth, his gaze falling to his lap.

"Thank you," he said.

"But as my client, and more importantly, as my friend," Grace said, "I have to prepare you for every possible outcome."

Luca inhaled deeply before turning to me. "What do you think I should do?"

"Oh, um, I…" I trailed off for a moment. "Luca, I don't know this business."

"That may be true, but you know *me*," he said softly, his hand squeezing my knee. "And I care what you think."

I swallowed hard as I considered his question. I didn't know a lot about the music business or the media, but the look on my mom's face Thursday night when she pulled up those articles about Luca was burned into my mind. She'd come around once I'd explained the truth, but most people weren't like that. We lived in a world full of clickbait headlines—one where people weren't afforded the ability to fuck up, least of all in the public eye. People made assumptions first and asked questions later, if they asked questions at all.

But Luca's music, his story, deserved to be heard. And once people heard his songs, there'd be no way they could see him as anything less than the amazing man I'd come to know.

"McKenzie?" he said, his eyes searching mine.

"I believe in you," I finally answered, reaching for his hand. "And I believe in your beautiful songs. So, do I think you should do it? Yes. But more importantly, I think you *want* to do it. Ever since the idea became a possibility, there's been this…*light* in your eyes. You want this, and it's okay to want it."

He chewed his lip. "I do. I want this."

I squeezed his fingers and turned to Grace. "What can we do to prevent the media from being dicks? How do we get them to give him a fair shake?"

"We'll do a crash course in media training, and we'll start small," Grace replied.

Luca spoke up. "Cash mentioned the idea of me playing The Bluebird. I wouldn't call that small."

"As far as venues go, it is," Grace said. "But it's also prestigious. It shows the world you're coming out swinging. That you're a force to be reckoned with."

I gave him an encouraging smile. "And you are."

He studied my face for a moment and nodded.

Grace opened her binder and pulled out a few sheets of paper. "I have a management agreement right here. It's pretty much identical to the one you signed with Cash back when you were in the band. There's absolutely no pressure on my end. I can leave it here for you to look over and—"

"That won't be necessary," Luca said. "I'm ready to sign."

Grace beamed and let out a high-pitched squeal. "Really? Are you sure?"

"Yeah," he answered, looking over at me. "I've never been more sure of anything in my life."

He held my gaze, and for a moment, it seemed like he was talking about more than just his career decisions.

"Me either," I said, releasing a contented sigh. "Me either."

TWENTY-TWO

Luca

GRACE GOT ME INTO THE RECORDING STUDIO EARLY THE NEXT week to start laying down tracks. McKenzie came when she could, and I started to wonder how I'd ever made music without her. She wasn't afraid to tell me when something wasn't working, but she was also generous with her praise. For the entire month of November, what time wasn't spent in the recording studio was spent with her. We spent part of Thanksgiving with one another too. She came to Dallas and Katie's after having dinner with her mom, and it was perfect. That evening, she came back to the hobbit house with me, and I played her a few more songs I'd been working on.

What was supposed to be an EP ended up becoming a full-length album; once I gave voice to the thoughts in my head, they all demanded to be heard. I had more material than I knew what to do with, so I tucked some of it away in my notebook to save for later after Grace said she felt confident there would be a second one.

By the time afternoon rolled around the second Thursday in December, the album was already half recorded. We decided to stop for the day, and Grace and I stepped outside into the cold air.

"Come on," I said, leading her to my car. "We're going to lunch."

"You're buying." She beamed up at me with her signature smile, and years flashed before my eyes. When I first met Grace, she was just a teenager backstage with her mom and Liv, Ella's best friend, at one of our meet and greets. And now, here she was, a grown woman—Cash's protégé and stepdaughter—managing my career. I could never have anticipated how that single moment in time, one that could've easily been as ordinary as the rest, would set in motion a series of events that would change the rest of our lives.

I grinned over at her as I unlocked the door, opening it for her.

"Look at you being a gentleman," Grace teased as she climbed in. "McKenzie's been good for you."

I smirked as I moved around to the other side and slid behind the wheel.

"I'll have you know it's not *all* McKenzie's doing," I said. "Though she's definitely helped."

She laughed, gazing out the window as I pulled out of the studio parking lot. "I know. I'm just teasing you."

We made the short drive down the street to The Loving Pie Company and parked out front. She fell in step beside me as we walked inside, and the owner, whom I recognized from being there countless times over the years, seated us in the back by the window.

"You are different, though," Grace said once we were left to browse our menus.

"How so?" I asked, not looking up.

"You're softer," she answered. "Kinder. To yourself and

everyone else. Not that you haven't always had a certain softness lurking beneath all your attitude and crude remarks."

My eyes flicked up to hers.

"You thought I didn't notice?" She raised her brows. "I may have been a teenager when I met you, but I still saw things over the years. You've always had a gentle side. It comes out when you think people aren't looking and maybe most people aren't paying attention. But I saw it. And even though you were a jerk sometimes, you've always been pretty great to me."

I tilted my head. Katie had said something similar to me several months back. I'd thought this softer side had only appeared once I'd begun to chip away at the armor that had kept my emotions locked away for so long. But maybe there had always been cracks in the foundation I'd spent most of my life constructing.

"I don't feel like I've been great to anyone," I confessed. "I spent a lot of time shutting people out. It was easier to push everyone away than it was to admit I fucking cared."

"We still knew," she said softly.

"That doesn't mean I shouldn't have said it. I'm sorry, Grace." I shook my head. "I wasn't there to celebrate you when you got engaged. Or to support you and your mom when your grandmother passed away. I wasn't there, and I should've been."

"You're here now," she said as though it was just that simple.

I attempted to swallow down the lump in my throat. "That doesn't feel like enough."

"But it is," she insisted. "When you love someone, that *is* enough."

My blurred gaze fell to the folded menu in front of me,

and I cleared my throat. Telling people I love them wasn't something I did often before I finally hit rock bottom, before I'd started therapy. I still wasn't entirely comfortable with these displays of affection or feeling my emotions, but I was getting better. It was becoming easier.

I blinked back the moisture glossing over my eyes. "I do love you guys. Even if I haven't always done the best job of showing it."

"We still knew," she said again.

"And while I'm admitting things, I want you to know, I'm glad you're here. That it's you helping me with this project." I folded my arms, leaning them on the table. "It feels right. I'm glad Cash is involved too, of course. But having you in the driver's seat…It feels like a new beginning. The start of something big for both of us."

"I'm happy I'm here too."

A server came and took our orders, bringing us glasses of water while we waited on our coffees. Once we were alone, I spoke again.

I pushed my hand through my hair. "Can I ask you something?"

"Of course," she replied.

"It's going to seem weird coming from me."

"Now I'm even more intrigued. What's up?"

I blew out a breath. "How did you know you loved Sam? I mean, you're young. So many people my age and older never find love or maybe they do and aren't smart enough to recognize it."

Her eyes went wide. "Wow, I didn't have you coming to me for relationship advice on my bingo card," she said with a laugh. "Why do you ask? Is it because of McKenzie?" She flashed me a big cheesy grin.

I narrowed my eyes at her. "Maybe."

"Really?" she squeaked out.

"Maybe I shouldn't have asked you for relationship advice." I smirked and crossed my arms over my chest.

"Oh *stop*." She swatted the air with her hand. "I'm allowed to get excited for you. She's worth getting excited about."

"What was it about Sam?" I pressed on. "How did you know it was beyond simply caring about him? How did you know it was love?"

She sighed and sat back in her chair as the server dropped our coffees off. "It wasn't really an epiphany for me. It wasn't like that moment in the movies when the female lead is suddenly struck with the realization she can't live without this guy. It wasn't one big moment. It was a million little ones."

I nodded. "Explain."

She twirled a piece of her long golden hair around her finger. "When I have a rough day, he knows exactly how to make me feel better. He brings me donuts and holds me on his lap while I tell him about it. He doesn't try to fix it. He just listens." She pauses a moment, a smile spreading across her face. "If we're in the car and 'Cruel Summer' comes on the radio, he turns it up and scream-sings it with me. And when something big happens, no matter if it's good or bad, he's the first person I want to tell. What he thinks matters to me. If I'm considering something, whether it's an opportunity or if I wake up one morning and want to chop off all my hair, he's who I'm going to talk to about it because he gets me. He understands me in a way no one else does. He'll support me no matter what I decide, but he also reminds me how strong I am when I forget."

Her words kicked me in the chest, knocking the wind right

out of me as McKenzie's face consumed my mind in a beautiful mosaic of the moments we shared together over the past couple of months.

"That's…that's incredible," I managed through the tightness in my throat before I gave her a sincere smile. "I'm happy you found that, Grace. You deserve it."

She leaned forward, her eyes turning soft. "You deserve that too, you know?"

I wanted to believe it was true, that it was possible for me. But there was still a small part of my brain that questioned if I was worthy of someone so precious. Did my previous transgressions and wrongdoings cancel out my right to happiness?

"You wanna know what it feels like to love someone?" Grace asked, steepling her fingers. "It's like coming home. It's that sigh of relief when you walk through the door and know you're somewhere you don't have to pretend to be anything other than what you are. It's where you can be the worst version of yourself and know those four walls will protect you and keep you all the same. Does that make sense?"

"It does."

McKenzie was all of those things to me and more. The fear of whether or not I deserved her paled in comparison to how much I needed her. She was my safety, my refuge, my sanctuary.

She felt like coming home.

***

I couldn't get to my notebook fast enough after my lunch with Grace. The words flew from my pen as though they were trying to escape before I could change my mind. In the span of an evening, I'd written an entire song.

When I arrived at the recording studio the next morning, Grace was already waiting inside with two coffees.

She raised one to me when I entered the room. "Brandon, the engineer guy, stepped out for a minute, but he'll be right back. I got you a—"

"I've got to play something for you," I said, already pulling my guitar from its case and sitting on the couch inside the booth.

She laughed. "Good morning to you too."

I dug a pick out of my pocket. "I couldn't stop thinking about what you said yesterday, and well, I wrote a song about it."

Grace took a sip of her coffee and perched on the arm of the sofa, placing the extra cup on the end table beside her. "I'm intrigued."

"It's called 'Coming Home.'"

My eyes closed as I strummed the opening chords and began to sing. I pictured McKenzie that night at The Basement East and her wildflower ways as she danced. I remembered the way she fearlessly fought that drunk asshole at the tavern the night I signed the lease on the hobbit house and felt the warmth of her lips on mine after Dallas and Katie's wedding. Even though I hadn't realized it at the time, each moment had become a brick in the home she'd built for me.

I'd fallen in love with McKenzie one cup, one brick at a time.

Each look, the sound of her laughter, her smile, every word she said had laid the foundation. Her arms had become the safest place I'd ever known. She didn't care how I showed up, only that I did. McKenzie accepted me exactly as I was.

When I finished the song, it was the sound of Grace's sniffles that brought me back to the moment.

I pressed my lips together as I set the guitar aside. "Was it that bad or that good?"

She laughed through her tears. "Are you kidding me? That has to go on the album, Luca. In fact, I think it's your title track."

My eyes grew wide. "You really think so?"

She nodded. "I do. This album…this feels like *you* coming home to the person you were always meant to be. The person I think you've always been at your core."

I dropped my gaze, leaning forward on my elbows with my hands clasped. She was right. Maybe this version of me had always existed, but it took McKenzie giving me her hand to lead me out of the darkness and into the light.

"You have to tell her," Grace said as though she had somehow heard my thoughts.

"What?"

She pinned me with a knowing stare. "McKenzie. You have to tell her."

"What do you mean?" I asked, not meeting her gaze.

Her words were soft when she spoke again. "Come on, Luca. You may have written that song after our conversation yesterday, but you can't tell me every word wasn't for her. You love her."

I swiped my tongue over my teeth and squeezed my eyes shut. She was right again.

The cushion shifted as Grace moved to sit beside me. "I know it's scary. It's terrifying to tell someone how you feel. It's like jumping out of a plane without knowing if your parachute will go off. Without knowing if you even *have* a parachute."

I swallowed hard as I met her eyes. "What if I fall to my fucking death?"

She placed her hand on my arm. "What if you fly?"

"Shit," I muttered through a shaky breath. McKenzie wasn't even in the room, but she might as well have been. I felt her everywhere.

"Play her the song," Grace said. "Tell her how you feel."

My foot tapped nervously as I considered what she said. "Okay. I'll tell her."

"But first, we're going to lay down this track," she said as Brandon entered the room.

I laughed, picking up my guitar. "You got it, boss."

"You guys ready?" Brandon asked, looping his headphones around his neck as he took his seat behind the soundboard.

"Yep." I grabbed my coffee off the table and entered the booth, setting it on the ground beside me.

Grace gave me a nod of approval as I sat on the stool, propping my guitar on my lap.

"Let's roll," Brandon said into the booth.

I nailed it in one take.

We wrapped the day around seven, and I drove straight to McKenzie's. She hadn't even made it home from work yet, so I waited in her driveway for nearly forty-five minutes.

When I saw the headlights of her truck pull in behind me, I got out of the car.

"Hey, you," she said as she started toward me. "What are

you doing here? I didn't think I'd be seeing you till tomorrow."

"Yeah, I know." I slid my arms around her waist and pulled her close, kissing her forehead. "I couldn't wait."

She narrowed her eyes up at me. "Everything okay?"

I pushed my hand through my hair and rubbed my hand across the back of my neck.

"Yeah. I just…I wrote a new song, and I want to play it for you."

"Oh really?" Her face lit up, turning on all the lights inside my heart. "Well, I can't wait to hear it. Come on up."

She started toward the stairs, and I grabbed my guitar from the back seat, blowing out a breath. I followed her inside and set my case down by the couch as the cats came slinking out of the bedroom to say hello. Binx meowed and circled my legs where I sat.

"Hey, guys." I leaned down and gave them scratches on the head before picking up Earl Grey, holding him like the giant baby he was.

McKenzie set her bag on the counter and joined me. "You and that cat." She laughed.

"What?" I asked. "He's my buddy."

"I know, and it's adorable," she said, folding her legs beneath her. "Okay, I'm dying to hear this song."

I placed Earl Grey on the back of the couch and got my guitar out of the case, positioning it on my knee.

"We actually laid this one down at the studio today." I fumbled for my pick with trembling fingers and dropped it. "Fuck," I muttered, grabbing for it.

"Are you all right?" McKenzie furrowed her brows. "You seem nervous."

My throat was dry as though I'd eaten an entire sleeve of crackers without a single sip of water.

"Yeah," I lied. "I'm fine."

"Are you sure?" she asked while Binx hopped on the back of the couch to join Earl Grey. "You know you can tell me if something's bothering you, right?"

"I know." My voice was barely above a whisper as I reached for her hand, giving it a squeeze. "I just…I need you to listen to this song."

She nodded. "Okay."

I released a shaky breath, centering myself before I closed my eyes and began to play the soft, tender melody. Then, I began to sing.

"Don't have to wipe my feet on the mat
You don't care where I've been
You let me track in all my dirt
Leaving my sins all over your den
Never one for empty platitudes
No 'take it on the chin'
You're the warmth in my cup of coffee
Even when I burn like your shot of gin

You make me feel like coming home
The only one I've ever known
Where I can heal my broken bones
And lay down all the stones they've thrown
You feel like coming home

Your eyes are my safe house, my refuge
Your voice is my favorite song
Singing my soul softly to sleep

In your arms I always belong
You turned on the lights in all my rooms
And painted my gray skies blue
You make me wanna be the air you breathe
I wanna be the ink in your tattoo

Come what may, come whatever
It'll only get better
My sun will always rise and set for you
Even when I wanna quit
You're what makes it worth it
My sun will always rise and set for you

You make me feel like coming home
The only one I've ever known
Where I can heal my broken bones
And lay down all the stones they've thrown
You feel like coming home
I wanna make you feel like coming home
The one your heart's always known
Let me heal your broken bones
And take on all the stones they've thrown
Let my arms be your home"

I played the last chord progression and finally opened my eyes. When I did, I saw McKenzie looking at me, her gorgeous face streaked with tears.

My chest was tight as I returned her gaze. There was more to say, but I didn't know how.

"That was…" She sniffled, wiping away the dampness with her fingers. "Oh wow. That was beautiful, Luca. I think that's my new favorite song."

I swallowed the lump that threatened to form in my throat.

"You're my favorite song," I whispered.

She blinked, sending fresh tears rolling down her cheeks. "Wh-what are you saying?"

I set my guitar aside and took her hands in mine. "I'm saying I wrote that for you."

She released a soft exhale.

"I wrote it *about* you," I added.

"You did?"

I nodded. "McKenzie, you've changed my life. You made me believe in something I didn't think was possible for me. Something I didn't know could exist for me."

She smiled through her tears and climbed onto my lap, taking my face in her hands. "You feel like coming home too."

I gazed into her eyes, and I could see my whole damn future inside them. This woman had single-handedly altered the course of my life. She'd given me something worth sticking around for.

"What?" she asked.

"You're beautiful." I answered, my voice low and husky. "And…"

"And what?"

My heart felt like it might hammer a hole right through my chest.

"McKenzie, I love you," I confessed.

She brought her hands to her mouth for a moment, then cupped my face.

"I love you too." Her words were thick with emotion. "I love you so fucking much."

"But I've got to be honest, it scares the shit out of me. I've never done this before. I've never had something like this. I don't want to fuck it up. I don't want to hurt you."

She pressed a gentle kiss to my jaw. "You won't."

I pulled back to look into her eyes. "But what if I do?"

"Then we work through it," she said softly. "Look, we're gonna do things that hurt or piss each other off if we stick this out long enough. But we don't bail when things get hard. We stay."

"We stay," I echoed, taking a strand of her hair between my fingers. "I want to piss you off for years to come. I'm all in on this thing with you."

"This thing, huh?" she asked, lifting her brows. "What is this *thing* you speak of?"

"You know…You and me."

She looked at me as though I'd just spoken pig latin. "I think there's actually a word for that."

The corners of my mouth curved upward. "Do you need me to say it?"

She held up her hands in mock surrender. "I just want to know if you can."

"I can say it," I insisted.

"Go ahead, then."

"But you said you don't need me to."

"Oh, I don't," she said with a laugh. "But now I kinda want you to."

I shook my head and grinned, raking my teeth over my bottom lip.

She tapped a finger to her chin. "I believe it starts with an *R*."

"Hmm…'Radioactive'?" I teased.

"No, I think it's *reee*-something."

"Ah, I believe the word you're looking for is 'relentless.'"

She punched me in the shoulder. "I'll show you *relentless*."

"Ow." I covered the spot her fist had hit. "Okay, okay. *Relationship*. There. Are you happy?"

She giggled and rubbed her hands together. "Did it hurt when you said it? Did it feel like razor blades crawling out of your throat?"

"Not even a little," I answered. "Not when it means I get to be your boyfriend."

Her nose scrunched as though she'd smelled something foul. "Ew. No. What am I? Twelve?"

"Oh, so I'm *not* your boyfriend?"

"That just sounds so…" She cringed and wiggled her entire body. "Bleh."

"Man friend?"

She mimed a gag.

I chuckled. "Then what would you like to call me?"

"Your name."

"You're not getting out of this," I said, tightening my grip on her. "If I had to say 'relationship,' you have to come up with an appropriate relationship term for me that doesn't make you want to hurl."

"Fine." She rolled her eyes. "You're my…'b-word.'"

I snorted a laugh. "Did you just call me your bitch?"

"No, but that could be arranged." She waggled her brows and flashed me a sultry grin.

"'B-word' it is, then." I gripped her thighs that were straddling me and pulled her closer, capturing her lips in a tender kiss. She deepened it, her tongue moving with mine like an old dance partner. Intimate and familiar. Her hands grazed down my chest, her fingers exploring me slowly. She slipped them beneath my shirt, the feel of her skin on mine like dropping a lit match to a trail of gasoline.

"Do you even know what you do to me?" I asked.

Her hips pressed into mine, and I couldn't contain the groan that escaped me.

"I don't think I do," she said with a devilish grin. "Why don't you show me?"

"Gladly," I said, rising to my feet with her in my arms. She wrapped her legs around me as I carried her to the bedroom and laid her down.

I kicked off my shoes before climbing over her, hovering close enough that our breath mingled.

"You're mine, McKenzie," I whispered, gliding my hand beneath her sweater, leaving a trail of goosebumps behind.

"I'm yours," she replied between shuddering breaths that made my dick strain against my jeans.

I rose on my knees and slipped my jacket off, quickly ripping my shirt over my head.

She licked her lips as she took me in.

"I've never wanted anyone the way I want you." She sat up and pulled her sweater off.

I wrapped my fingers gently around her neck, tilting her face to meet mine in a searing kiss.

"I've never *needed* anyone like I need you." It was equal parts admission and revelation. I'd *wanted* girls before, but what I felt for McKenzie was far beyond a primal desire. She was like oxygen—vital for my existence.

Her fingers traced invisible lines down my chest while I reached behind her, unhooking her bra. I slowly slid the straps down her arms like I was removing the bow from a perfectly wrapped present. One of those gifts that's almost too pretty to open.

"Jesus." I released a shaky breath as I drank her in, guiding her back against the mattress. I leaned over her with my weight on one arm while one hand moved down her body, committing every dip, every curve, and every valley to memory.

She placed her palm against my cock, applying enough pressure to make me want to lose my fucking mind.

"So greedy for me," I said, my eyes darkening. "I love it."

"You have no idea."

"I think I do." I unbuttoned her jeans, sliding them down her legs, my fingertips kissing her thighs as I did. I tossed them aside and hovered over her as she gripped me through my pants.

"Two can play that game." I touched her clit through the thin fabric of her panties, moving my thumb in slow circles.

Her breath caught in her throat.

"Do you like that?" I asked, continuing to caress her.

"Yes," she answered, raising her hips to meet my hand.

I slipped my fingers beneath the cotton, skimming over her most sensitive spot.

She whimpered as I pressed one finger inside her tight heat.

"Goddamn," I groaned. Feeling how wet she was made me impossibly hard. I could have pounded nails through a fucking cinder block with my dick.

Her hand found mine and guided it down, taking her panties with it. I pulled them the rest of the way off and pushed them aside.

"Is this what you want?" I knelt between her thighs, my gaze heavy with desire as I licked her slit, not taking my eyes off her.

"Fuck," she cried out, fisting my hair.

I flicked my tongue over her bud in light strokes. The tensing of her thighs and each gasp from her lips drove me wild. I throbbed in my pants, dying to be enveloped by her velvety warmth.

"Luca, please," she murmured.

"Please what?" I asked, the vibrations of my words against her causing her to shudder.

"I…need you…inside me," she said between pants. "Please."

"Since you asked so nicely." I kissed her folds one more time before rising to unfasten my pants, shoving them down, along with my briefs.

She reached for me, taking my length in her hand.

My eyes nearly rolled back in my head as she worked me from base to tip.

Her eyes were hazy as she looked at me. "How do you want me?"

"Get on all fours," I growled.

Her body trembled as she rolled over, obeying my command. She backed her sweet little ass up to me, and I couldn't resist smacking it, reveling in the way it shook.

"You're so fucking hot," I whispered.

She lowered her forearms to the bed and spread her legs, giving me a delicious view.

"Are you aching for me yet?" I asked, sliding my fingers over her sensitive flesh again.

She moaned her answer, and I lined myself up with her entrance, touching her only with my tip at first.

I bit down hard on my lip. "You're so fucking wet for me."

She pressed back against me, her body begging for mine.

"I'm right here, sweetheart." One hand dug into her hip while I used the other to guide myself into her depths.

She gasped as I filled her, and my eyes closed from the overwhelming pleasure of having her wrapped around my cock.

"How does that feel?" I asked, moving against her.

"So good," she said, dropping her head against the pillow for a moment.

I reached one hand around her, finding her clit, tracing slow circles over it while my other hand threaded through her hair.

She bounced her ass against me, meeting my every thrust.

"You fit me like a glove," I rasped. "So tight. So perfect."

Her muscles clenched around me, and the sensation would have brought me to my knees if I wasn't there already.

"Because I was made for you," she said.

"Come here." I carefully pulled her up against me so as not to break our connection and took her breast in one hand. She arched against me, matching every move as I kissed her neck, continuing to tease her clit.

I drove into her again and again, my pleasure mounting. Her pants turned ragged, and I cupped her face, tilting it back to mine, crushing my lips to hers.

Her mouth went slack and her breaths became shallow, her entire body tensing.

"That's it," I purred in her ear. "I want to feel you fall apart."

Another thrust and she shattered around me, her walls pulsing against my dick. I bit down on her shoulder as I slammed into her, trying not to come undone as she rode out her aftershocks. It wasn't until I heard her breaths begin to slow that I allowed myself to fall apart too. I stilled, pressing her as close to me as I could get her. She snaked her hand into my hair and covered my mouth with hers, swallowing my moans.

I held her tight and laid kisses along her shoulders, unable to form words for a couple of moments.

"You're incredible," I whispered when I was finally able to speak again. I slipped out of her and collapsed against the mattress, pulling her down with me. She curled into me, resting her head on my chest.

"I didn't know sex could be like this," she said, still trying to catch her breath. "Is this normal? Has everyone but me just been out there having phenomenal sex?"

I laughed and pressed a kiss to her forehead. "I don't know, but I haven't. Not till you."

She grinned and shook her head. "Liar."

"No, I mean it," I admitted. "Yeah, I've had a lot of sex. I'm not gonna pretend I haven't. But none of it ever came close to this. I didn't know it could feel like this."

Her eyes softened. "You mean that?"

I nodded. "I do. It's different because it's you."

She nestled into me, and my heart felt like it might take flight.

Everything was different because of McKenzie. Because I loved her.

I remembered hearing love songs and thinking how fucking ridiculous they all sounded. Like the stories old fishermen told about that elusive fifteen-pound bass they'd once caught but had no proof of.

But McKenzie caught me, and what we'd created was rare. There weren't colors bright enough to paint her portrait, no words strong enough to describe how magical this love was. But I'd spend my days trying to find them.

TWENTY-THREE

McKenzie

"Theres nothing to be nervous about," I said, touching Luca's arm as we started up the path to my mother's house about a week before Christmas. "My mom's easygoing. You'll love her, I promise."

"Yeah, but she's *your mom*," he insisted. "I'm almost forty years old, and I've never met anyone's parents before. Because I've never been in a *relationship* before."

"Ah, that's right." I gave him an exaggerated wince. "Yeah, you're screwed."

He stopped me from reaching for the doorknob, grabbing my shoulder with one hand, the holiday-colored bouquet he'd picked out for my mom in the other.

"I don't want to mess this up." His throat bobbed as it worked to swallow. "She's the most important person in your life. I want her to like me. What can I do to make her like me?"

The sincerity in his words made my heart melt into a puddle.

"Luca," I said, gripping his arms. "She's going to like you. Just be yourself."

"Have you met me?" he asked, narrowing his eyes. "That's terrible advice."

"My mom is like me, but with more back pain and orthopedic shoes. She's going to love you," I repeated with a laugh.

"Like you, huh?" he asked, raising his brows. "So, she's hot?"

"I hate you." I rolled my eyes and reached for the handle again, but he stopped me, sliding his hand around my neck and turning me toward him for a kiss.

"You love me," he whispered.

"I do," I said with a mischievous grin. "By the way, my mom is more of a Dallas girl."

"Wait, what?" he asked as I flung open the door and stepped inside, calling out to my mother. "Mom, we're here."

"In the kitchen," she shouted back, but I already knew that from the scent of garlic and homemade marinara wafting through the air. She'd made her lasagna, which was my favorite.

I reached for Luca's hand and gave it an encouraging squeeze as I led him toward the source of the aroma. There, in her pink "Just Fucking Eat It" apron, was my mother with her hair twisted into a claw clip.

"Hi, sweetie," she greeted me, wiping her hands on the apron as she smiled up at Luca.

He held out the flowers to her. "These are for you."

"Well, aren't you a doll?" she replied, taking them and burying her nose in the blooms.

"They're so pretty. Thank you."

"Here, Mom," I said, reaching for the bouquet. "Let me put those in a vase for you."

She kissed my cheek. "Thank you, Kenz. I want to get a look at your man candy here."

I snorted. "Oh my God, Mom. If you keep that up, he's gonna break up with me on the spot."

Luca chuckled. "Nah, I've been called worse."

"I've heard so much about you, Luca," she said, pulling him into a hug. "Between McKenzie and your Midnight in Dallas music, I feel like I know you already."

"I told him you're a Dallas fan," I teased as I pulled a vase from the cupboard beside the fridge and moved to the sink to fill it.

"My condolences," Luca joked.

"Not anymore," she said. "He's my second favorite."

"Since when?" I asked, unwrapping the flowers to place them in water.

She gestured toward Luca with her thumb. "Since this one came along and made my daughter so happy."

I cleared my throat, my cheeks burning.

She folded her arms over her chest, inspecting Luca through squinted eyes. "Plus, he looks like he could be one of those *Twilight* vampire guys if they'd lived a little longer before they were bitten."

Luca burst into laughter. "The apple doesn't fall far from the tree, does it, Ms. James? Wait…is it James?" His eyes went wide with panic.

My mom cringed. "It is, but please call me Laurel. Ms. James makes me feel like I'm one bad trip away from a Life Alert bracelet, and I'm nowhere near that."

Luca grinned. "Well, then. I like your apron, *Laurel*."

"Thank you," she said, grabbing her hand-knitted potholders and taking the lasagna out of the oven. "It's only a suggestion, but please be advised that if you don't at least pretend to love my cooking, I will guilt-trip you about it for the foreseeable future."

"It's true," I sang, fiddling with the blooms in the vase. "But you're in luck because she's actually a pretty good cook. Unless she tries to make Julia Child's boeuf bourguignon, in which case, run."

"Hey! It wasn't *that* bad." She plopped the lasagna on some hot pads, then pulled out the garlic bread and nudged the stove closed with her hip.

"Maybe if you had the jaw of a werewolf or wolverine," I said, placing the flowers at the center of the already set table in the connecting dining room. "Let's just say it was *very* well done."

"Kenz definitely didn't get her cooking skills from me, but I'm not half bad." She plunked the garlic rolls in the bread basket waiting on the counter. "And what I can't make, this prodigy daughter of mine can figure out."

"How *did* you get started cooking, anyway?" Luca asked me.

"That was all Brennan," my mom answered, leaning against the counter.

I nodded. "He used to cook a lot. He made dinner most nights when we were younger."

"I was a single mom, and I have fibromyalgia, which is a chronic pain condition. Being on your own with two kids is already a job in and of itself, but then you factor in something like that…It was a lot. But I always wanted my children to have home-cooked meals." My mom gave him a wistful smile. "Brennan saw how tired I was and wanted to help, so he took it upon himself to learn how to cook."

I couldn't help but laugh as I thought about his early kitchen experiments.

"Surprisingly, we only had to call the fire department once," I said. "He got pretty good. By the time he was ten, he'd started making things like meatloaf and beef Stroganoff."

"Then he started teaching McKenzie, and it became a team effort," my mom added. "I'd find the two of them joking around in the kitchen while they made supper. Coming home to a meal was a treat, but nothing compared to hearing their laughter when I walked through the door."

Her eyes turned misty as she held my gaze, and a lump formed in my throat before Luca's arm curled around my shoulders.

"I'd love to hear more about Brennan," he said softly. "About him and McKenzie both as kids."

My mother beamed as though Luca had just presented her a million dollars and an all-expenses-paid trip to the Bahamas.

"I'll go get the photo albums," she said, removing her apron and placing it on the hook inside the pantry.

Luca was about to get a front row seat to every single awkward moment of my life from birth, but after seeing how happy it made my mom, I couldn't bring myself to mind.

"Thank you," I whispered.

"What for?" he asked.

Before I could answer, my mother returned with a stack of five albums.

"This only covers through elementary school," she said, plunking them on the dining table. "But we've got to start somewhere."

She served up the lasagna, and we all sat at the table together as my mom opened one of the oversized albums. I watched as she pointed at pictures and recounted stories I'd heard dozens of times before, while Luca listened with rapt attention. He didn't mind the tangents she went on that spiderwebbed out into tales woven together by the threads of our lives. Including one that was cut impossibly short. He encouraged her to keep talking and sharing.

That was something most didn't do. In the early days after Brennan's passing, people were happy to hear about him. The first few days were an acceptable time to grieve. But after the first few *months*, people tended to get weird about it. It was like they thought death was contagious. Like chicken pox or the flu. Or maybe it just forced them to confront their own mortality and acknowledge that one day, they too would become memories that would make people uncomfortable, until one day people stopped talking about them at all.

Luca didn't realize the magnitude of what he did that night —the gift he gave us both. The freedom to reminisce and remember minus the risk of making someone uncomfortable. Not once did he give us a pitying stare. He sat with us in our love and grief for my brother without empty platitudes or forced positivity. For one evening, it was as though Brennan was seated at the table alongside the three of us. And to me... that was everything.

"The Fainting Goat Coffee Shop." My mom read the name printed on the gray shirt to Luca and me in the nearly empty aisles of The Thrift Stop the last Thursday of January. Luca had started joining us on some of our weekly thrift store outings since I'd introduced them. We'd had dinner together a few times too, listening to records and playing games. After Mom opened up to him about Brennan, he'd begun to feel safe sharing pieces of his own life, his troubled upbringing, and the future he now held hope for.

"That can't be a real place, right?" Luca asked, inspecting the illustrated goats.

"It says Spring Hill, Tennessee," she replied, tossing it in our cart. "Sounds like we need to check it out."

I wasn't sure what warmed my heart more—how much my mother adored Luca or the way he took to her. Over the last month, I'd witnessed the man I loved get to become a boy again. He hadn't had parents that loved him the way they should have, but my mother did. She welcomed him with open arms, and there was something healing about their relationship—a void they filled for each other. He was the son she didn't get to see grow up, and she became the mother he'd always deserved.

"So, how are you feeling about your show at The Bluebird?" my mom asked as we continued to peruse the shirts. "Are you getting excited?"

He blew out a breath. "I'm actually nervous as hell."

"You're going to be great." I gave his arm an encouraging squeeze. "The world won't know what hit 'em."

"You're biased," he said, hooking his arm over my shoulder and kissing the top of my head.

I grinned up at him. "Maybe, but it also happens to be true."

They had finished the album the week before, and the first thing he'd done was play it for me and my mom in its entirety. She wept through multiple songs like "Death Row" and the title track "Coming Home." When she found out he wrote it for me, she cried even harder.

"What if my stuff is too different for Midnight in Dallas fans?" he asked.

"Then you'll find new ones," Mom answered with unshakable confidence as she continued to sift through the shirts. "Your music is going to mean so much to so many, Luca. I just think about all the people out there like you, like Brennan. People who need to know they're not alone, and you're going to tell them that."

"She's right, you know," I agreed. "You're going to bring hope to a lot of people. Not only with your music but with your *life*. Look how much you've overcome...the work you've done to get where you are now."

My mom nodded. "You're going to show everyone it's never too late to start over. That it's okay to ask for help."

"I feel like I'm the last person anyone should be looking up to," he admitted, sliding a hanger along the rack.

"That's not true," I insisted, but my mother touched my arm as if to say *I've got this*.

She gripped his shoulders and turned him to face her.

"I want you to listen to me," she said, her voice soft and sincere. "You don't even realize how special you are, Luca Sterling. What a miracle it is that you're still here. I know what you've fought through—what you're *still* fighting through—hasn't been easy, but you're here, in spite of it all. There are so many who aren't. Every day we lose more and more people...people who don't stay because they can't ask for help. Because they think they're beyond help."

Tears filled her eyes and mine. I knew she was picturing my brother—one of the beautiful souls who hadn't been able to stay. Not because he wasn't strong enough. Not because his life mattered less. We just didn't know how to spot the signs that he needed extra support, and he didn't have people, especially men, he could look to for guidance. Mental health was still stigmatized, but it was far worse when Brennan and I were growing up. Back then, it was even more frowned upon for men to show any signs of softness or emotion.

"You are *exactly* the person others should be looking up to," she continued. "Because you can show them vulnerability isn't a flaw. You've taken yours and created something beautiful with it. And I'm not just talking about your music. I'm talking about your life."

He chewed the inside of his cheek, emotion misting his eyes.

"Look at this beautiful life you're making for yourself, sweetheart." She cupped his face in her hands. "You got knocked down, time and time again, but baby, you're still swinging. And you're gonna show others they can keep swinging too."

He wrapped her small frame into a bear hug, nearly swallowing her whole, then he drew me in too. The three of us stood there, holding each other in the aisle. There was no one around to see, but I wouldn't have cared if there was.

"You're still coming, right, Mama Laurel?" he asked, using the nickname he'd affectionately given her as he pulled away.

"I wouldn't miss it for the world," she answered with a proud smile as she returned to browsing.

We continued our treasure hunt until my mother squealed with delight.

"Look at this!" She wrenched a black shirt from the metal rack and held it out for us to inspect. The message "Hope is Defiant" was printed across the front.

A square on the side held the logo "To Write Love on Her Arms."

"I've heard of them," I said, checking the label to see what size it was. "They're a nonprofit that connects people with resources to help with things like addiction and depression.

I've read some pieces on their blog before. Their platform is all about finding hope."

"And so is yours," my mom said, pointing the hanger in Luca's direction. "I'm getting it for you."

He laughed. "You don't have to do that. I can get it."

"Nonsense," she declared in a way that let him know this wasn't up for debate. "I'm getting it because I want it to serve as a reminder of how much I believe in you."

He gave her a soft smile. "Thank you."

"You just get on that stage next Friday and sing your ass off," she said. "That's all the thanks I need."

His gaze fell slightly as my mother turned her focus back to the shirts lining the wall, and I knew he was still feeling insecure about the show. But I hoped once he got up there it would feel like riding a bike. That he'd remember all the reasons he'd loved performing to begin with.

"It's going to be amazing," I whispered, looping my arm around his waist.

I was so proud of him for all he'd accomplished, and I'd put together a surprise to show him just how much. With Jo's help, I'd managed to secure the attendance of a couple of important people from Luca's past. He'd been so busy with the album and rehearsals, he hadn't even noticed the extra time I'd spent on my phone concocting my plan, making sure everything was set.

This was going to be a big moment for him, and I wanted the place to be packed with people who believed in him, both past and present.

TWENTY-FOUR

Luca

Hi Luca,

Hope you're doing well! I wanted to touch base because I noticed you rescheduled your past two sessions. I know things were going better the last time we spoke, but I want to make sure we check in soon. Even if we need to decrease it to once or twice a month, I think it's a good idea we keep going for a while to keep you on the right path. When can we get you on the books next?

Lacey

It was the following Friday evening, and I was getting ready for my show at The Bluebird. I'd already showered and started to get dressed, pausing to check my email for any last-minute details from Cash or Grace to find a message from Lacey.

I hadn't intended to miss those sessions, but life kept getting in the way. Between preparing the album for release, getting ready for the show, and spending as much time with McKenzie as I possibly could, making space for those appointments just wasn't a priority. I'd get back to them as soon as I could, as soon as things slowed down. Besides, I *was* feeling better. For the first time since I could remember, I felt truly happy. Sure, healing was a journey, but it felt like I'd arrived at my destination.

My phone pinged from my back pocket with a text, and I reached for it, smiling when I saw McKenzie's name.

Okay don't freak out, but I got here to pick up my mom and she definitely made a T-shirt to wear to the show tonight. I can spill something on it and make her change if you want me to. Just say the word.

Attached was a photo of Laurel with a big smile on her face and the words "Luca Sterling's #1 Fan" emblazoned across her shirt.

I laughed and shook my head before tapping out my response.

Don't you dare. It's perfect.

Bubbles popped up to let me know she was typing.

We'll see you soon. 🩶

I pulled on the shirt Mama Laurel bought me at the thrift store and shrugged on my leather jacket, pushing my hands through my hair until it looked decent enough. With my guitar case in hand, I was out the door. I tapped my fingers against the steering wheel in a haphazard rhythm the whole way to The Bluebird, my nerves taking up so much space in my brain they were practically passengers in the car.

As I drove by the lot to get to the rear of the building, I was stunned to find a line of people outside the door in the cold just waiting to get in. Grace had told me it was a sold-out crowd, though most shows there were. But the venue said it had happened in less than ten seconds and that hundreds of people had called, trying to get on a wait list.

McKenzie had texted to let me know she and her mom

were already waiting with Grace and the rest of my friends who were able to make it. I'd received good luck calls from Cash, Ella, and Antoni earlier in the day, and I knew Grace would be filming it for them. All that was left to do was head inside.

"Hi, Mr. Sterling, I'm Lena," a petite blonde woman welcomed me through the back entrance, my guitar in tow. "I'm the stage manager here at The Bluebird, and I'll be helping you out this evening."

"Hi, Lena," I said, shaking her hand. "It's just Luca but thank you."

"Well, Luca," she continued, "you've got a few friends from your guest list here in the listening room already, so I can take you there to see them and do a quick sound check. Then I'll show you to the dressing room where you'll hang out till showtime. So, if you'll follow me."

"Of course." I fell into step behind her as she led me into the main room where I spotted everyone.

"Let me take your case for you and put it on stage so you can meet your fan club," Lena said with a wink, reaching for my guitar.

McKenzie, Mama Laurel, Grace, Dallas, Katie, Liv, Jax, Jo, and Derek were already seated alongside two other people I didn't immediately recognize. One was a balding man who looked to be in his fifties, and the other was an elderly woman with dyed black hair who had to have been at least eighty. She wore a blue pantsuit and a jacket with beaded fringe dangling from the back.

"Hey," Dallas boomed when he noticed me. "There he is!"

The entire group cheered as I approached, everyone taking their turn to greet me with hugs and fist bumps, but my eyes kept coming back to the oddly familiar faces sitting at

McKenzie's table with Mama Laurel, who beamed in her homemade shirt.

McKenzie had been first to jump up to kiss me hello, and she stayed by my side until the only folks I hadn't talked to were the ones I didn't know.

McKenzie gestured toward them. "There were a couple of special people who wanted to be here to help celebrate your big day."

The man helped the lady to her feet, her fringe shaking as she moved toward me.

"Well, honeybun," she said with a smoky rasp. "It's sure been long enough, ain't it?"

"Aunt Gladys?" I asked, her voice instantly transporting me back to my high school years, watching her play "Stairway to Heaven" every bit as well as Jimmy Page.

I looked from her to McKenzie, then to the man at Aunt Gladys' side.

"Mr. Fink?" My eyes widened, and my breath caught in my throat.

"Hey, bud," he said in that same warm tenor I remembered. "It's good to see you."

"Oh my God." My hand covered my mouth for a second before I pulled them each into an embrace. "What? How? I can't believe you're here."

"Your girl McKenzie hunted me down on the Facebook," Aunt Gladys explained.

"Well, it wasn't quite that simple," McKenzie added with a small laugh. "I enlisted Jo's investigative journalism skills to help track them down."

"It was not an easy feat, darlin'," Aunt Gladys said. "I've been through more than a couple name changes in my day.

Mr. Hibbert died, probably about five years after I saw you last, God rest his soul."

Mr. Fink rolled his lips inward and gave me a knowing glance like he'd heard her spiel a million times before.

"Then I met a man named Wallace a year later, married his dumb ass, and took his name," she continued. "Let's just say that was never gonna last. I have lived too long and worked too hard to put up with bullshit from any man. You know what I mean? Changed my name back to Fink for a while before I met my Larry three years ago. Anyway, listen to me rambling on like an old coot." She placed her hands on my arms and looked me over, a smile spreading across her mouth. "Look at ya. Tall as a goddamn palm tree. Handsome. Talented. I always knew you were gonna go places, kid. I always said it, didn't I, Kenneth?"

Mr. Fink nodded. "She did."

"I've been following your career, and I can't tell you how proud I am of everything you've accomplished, sweetheart," Aunt Gladys said. "I hate that we lost touch, but now that McKenzie has brought us back together, I'm gonna be worse than a seven-year itch."

"She's not joking," Mr. Fink deadpanned, and I laughed.

"I mean it," Aunt Gladys went on, ignoring her nephew. "We're gonna exchange numbers and talk all the time. We've got a lot of years to catch up on. Are you on the Instagram?"

"You know it's just Instagram, right?" Mr. Fink asked.

"When you're eighty-three years old, it's whatever the fuck you want it to be," she countered, folding her arms over her chest.

"I've missed you, Aunt Gladys," I said, pulling her into another hug. "I'm glad you're here."

"Me too, darlin'." She took my face in her hands and

kissed my cheek, wiping at the lipstick smudge she left behind with her thumb. "Me too."

"Luca, I'm sorry to interrupt," Lena said as she approached, "but we need to get your sound check done so we can open the doors."

"You go on, doll." Gladys shooed me away with her hands. "We'll have plenty of time to chat later. We're staying in town for a couple of days. You break a leg."

McKenzie wrapped her arms around me, and I leaned down to kiss her softly.

"Thank you," I whispered in her ear.

She nodded and touched the sides of my face. "You're welcome."

I climbed on stage to hoots and hollers from my loved ones and did a quick sound check before Lena ushered me to the back to await showtime.

Having McKenzie and all my friends—my family—there in my corner helped to ease my nerves. At the end of the day, seeing the pride on their faces because of something I'd accomplished made everything worth it.

My phone pinged from my jacket pocket, and I pulled it out to find a text from McKenzie.

Full house!!!

Next came a photo she'd taken of the bustling room filled to the brim with fans.

My heart leapt into my throat as I wrote out my response.

This wouldn't have been possible without you.

What part? she asked almost immediately.

"All right," Lena said, poking her head inside the cracked door. "You ready?"

"Just one second," I answered, smiling as I typed out my reply.

Every part.

"THIS NEXT ONE IS THE FIRST SONG I WROTE ON MY OWN," I said into the mic, my guitar resting on my knee. My gaze returned to McKenzie who was seated directly in my line of sight. As the evening progressed, I continued to seek out her face, blurring out every other person in the room. Performing at The Bluebird wasn't like anything I'd done before. There were no other band members to bounce off, no one else to relieve any of the pressure. It was just me, my guitar, my songs, and my stories.

I cleared my throat. "I'd been given an assignment from my therapist to begin putting some of my feelings down on paper, and like most assignments I'd been given before, I had no intention of actually doing it."

The crowd laughed softly as though we were all just friends, gathered around a campfire, having a private conversation. It wasn't like the Midnight in Dallas shows I was used to. There was no screaming or shouting to cover up a sour note. The audience was so quiet, you could hear when someone so much as placed their pint glass on the table.

I looked at McKenzie. "But then, someone much smarter than I am told me I was looking at it all wrong. That I needed to think about it as though I was crafting a song. And that's when it clicked for me. Once the words started coming, they didn't stop. They still haven't."

"I always enjoyed performing when I was with Midnight in Dallas, and I was part of the writing process, but until I worked on this record, I didn't feel like there were any songs that belonged to me. I never contributed much in the way of my own lived experiences when we wrote as a band. And that's probably because, up until this past fall, I kept everyone in my life at arm's length." I gave a subtle nod toward where Jax, Dallas, and Derek were seated. "I didn't share much about what I dealt with because I was…ashamed. I didn't tell people what I went through because I didn't want them to know."

"Writing the songs for this album felt like…a reclamation. Of music and the life I led that brought me here. It's become the way I process my emotions. Each song on this album reflects my healing journey, but this next one is special to me because it was the one that made me realize maybe I had something to say," I continued. "I think a lot of people do, but they're afraid. Of being perceived, judged, or being told there's something wrong with them because they're not like everyone else. Then eventually, you become prisoner to this echo chamber of thoughts that say you're broken—that you're not good enough."

"You stuff yourself into the boxes other people make for you, tripping over yourself to meet their expectations, just trying to make something fit," I said, my focus returning to McKenzie. "But all you really want is someone who sees you. This one's called 'Death Row.'" I closed my eyes and played the haunting opening notes before beginning to sing.

"Locked inside the confines of my own mind
A cage built by my own hands is still a prison
How long must I cry alone in the dark
Until shame becomes my true religion
Knees down at the altar
Jump then falter
I wish I were someone else

The prison guards became my priests
They took my confessions through the iron bars
Writing them down word for word
They used them to fill their memoirs
Knees down in the dirt
Pray to end the hurt
Can I be someone else"

My lids squeezed shut, and I lost myself in the words, in the images that flashed through my mind like a grainy home movie. There were nights locked inside my empty apartment or in a hotel room in whatever state we were in. Even when there was some nameless person lying beside me, I was still alone.

I pictured gossip rag headlines and Google searches filled with stories about me. Some were true, but even when they weren't, I never tried to fight it or say they were wrong. For so long, I'd allowed myself to believe their narratives. They'd picked apart my bones to build their campfires, and I'd been handing them marshmallows to roast.

"Fed my last meal and swallowed my last rites
The judge said there'd be no stay of execution
So I prayed for death to snuff me out
And bury me in the walls of this institution
Knees down on shards of glass
What if this too shall never pass
And I can't be someone else

I hand off my belongings to the friends I never made
A death row inmate sentenced to a life of freedom
Where he'll spend his days longing to mean something

To a world who refuses to see him
Knees bruised and broken
Crushed by the weight of words unspoken
Can this rusted vessel ever be golden
Will my heart ever be open
To someone else"

I strummed the last note, letting it fade. The room was silent for a moment before it erupted into applause and cheers. When I finally opened my eyes, I found many people, my friends included, dabbing at their eyes with napkins.

My chest constricted, my heart bursting with something that felt a lot like happiness. These people heard my story and didn't reject me. Judging from the looks on some of their faces, they might've even recognized parts of themselves within my lyrics. It felt like acceptance after a lifetime of being rejected or merely tolerated. It felt like redemption.

McKenzie beamed up at me as tears streaked down her cheeks, radiating love and pride. I took a moment to soak it all in, to revel in the roads I'd traveled to get here. At nearly forty years old, I felt like I finally made it.

"Thank you," I said as the clapping slowed. "I've got one more song to play for you all tonight. I wrote it for someone who means the world to me. She showed me what it is to love someone. For the first time in my life, I have somewhere I belong. It's called 'Coming Home.' McKenzie, this one's for you."

TWENTY-FIVE

McKenzie

AFTER THE SHOW, LUCA TOOK A FEW PHOTOS WITH FANS before the venue began pushing people to leave. He worked the room with quiet confidence before thanking each of his friends for being there. We lingered for a bit while Luca spent time catching up with Aunt Gladys and Mr. Fink. He didn't stop smiling once.

Dallas and Katie offered to give my mom a ride home so I could stay with Luca. She was all too happy to take them up on that, but I did jokingly warn Katie that my mother might try to steal her man. Luca followed me home when we left The Bluebird, and I laughed when he picked up Earl Grey, spinning him around in pure unadulterated joy, while Binx hid beneath the sofa.

We recounted the evening curled up on the couch, sharing our favorite moments before falling into bed together where I celebrated his performance with one of my own.

The next morning, we were roused from our slumber by the muffled sound of a phone ringing.

He groaned, the soft light spilling around the blinds, casting shadows over his face.

I pried one eye open to find my phone on the nightstand. The time read 10:37 a.m.

"It's yours," I mumbled, my voice thick with sleep.

He pulled me closer.

"They'll call back," he murmured.

And they did. Immediately.

"Goddamn it." He grunted and slid out of bed, taking the warmth of his body with him. The floors creaked beneath his weight as he rifled through his discarded clothes. "Shit."

The ringing stopped only to start up again.

"What on earth is going on?" I asked through a yawn.

Finally, he retrieved the device from the pocket of his leather jacket before dropping it back on top of the heap of fabric.

"It's Grace," he grumbled.

"I hope everything's okay," I said as he swiped his finger across the screen and placed it on speaker. He climbed in bed beside me, leaning back against the headboard.

"Hey Grace," he answered. "What's going—"

"Everyone on the internet is talking about you," she blurted out. "Some videos from the show got posted on Instagram, and now you're all over the place."

My eyes widened, and Luca's jaw fell open.

"Page Six, the New York Post, and hell, even CNN posted about you," she continued, her voice a full octave higher than normal. "They even talked about you on *Good Morning America*!"

"What?" I half-asked, half-shrieked as Luca gripped my arm.

She squealed. "But that's not even the best part. Jacob

Waterton from *Rolling Stone* shared a clip of you singing 'Death Row' on Twitter or X, or whatever the hell it's called, and it already has 1.3 million views. He said, 'I'm calling it now: this new record is gonna be the renaissance of Luca Sterling.'"

I gasped. "Oh my God."

"Are you serious?" Luca raked his hands down his face, his eyes never leaving mine.

"My inbox is already flooded with interview requests," she said. "Jimmy Fallon, Kimmel, Seth Meyers...you name 'em, they wanna talk to you."

I screeched with excitement as I shot up, clutching the sheets around me.

"I...I can't believe it." Luca cupped my face in his hands, gazing up at me with disbelief.

"Believe it," Grace said with a laugh. "This thing hasn't even dropped yet, and people are already throwing the G-word around."

"G-word?" I asked. "Wait, as in the Grammys?"

"Yup," she answered.

Tears pricked at the corners of my eyes as I placed a kiss on Luca's forehead. "You did it."

"*We* did," he corrected, taking a strand of my hair between his fingers.

"Luca, I think you're about to blow up," Grace said, and I could practically hear her smile through the phone. "Cash does too. I sent him the video from last night, and he predicted this before the internet started losing its mind over you. I hope you're ready for the storm that's coming because I'd be willing to bet that by the end of next week, you won't be able to go online or heck, *anywhere*, without seeing your name."

He cleared his throat. "So, what's next? What do we need to do?"

"*We* don't need to do anything," she replied. "You take the weekend to enjoy this. I'll start compiling a list of everyone who wants to chat with you, and we can meet Monday and take it from there."

"Are you sure?" Luca asked. "I thought you were heading back to LA to see Sam for a few days?"

"I'm pushing my trip back a couple weeks," she said. "I want to hang around a little longer while we plan our next steps. I think it may be time we start thinking about a tour. Hope you haven't gotten too used to being in one place because that's all about to change, my friend."

I gulped. A tour? It wasn't like I hadn't known that was part of the deal, but I didn't think it would happen so soon. I thought we'd have more time to solidify our relationship before he left for weeks or months at a time.

Luca chuckled, turning his attention to the phone. "The road is basically home for me, so I'm ready. You just say the word."

I thought *I* was his home? I mentally kicked myself for allowing my mind to even go there. This wasn't about me. This was about Luca. He'd worked hard for this, and it wasn't like I didn't want him to have it. But I'd been so caught up in the journey that I hadn't let myself consider what would happen when we reached the destination.

Grace said her goodbyes, and Luca folded me in his arms.

"Can you fucking believe it?" he asked as we fell back against the mattress.

"I know," I said, burying my face in his neck so he wouldn't see the emotions warring inside me.

I was happy for Luca and what this meant for him, but I couldn't shake the dread over what it might mean for us.

It was barely 8 a.m. on Friday, and I was about to lose my shit. It had been two weeks since the show, and work was hell. Katie's MS was flaring up, so she'd been out for several days, which meant Dallas had been scarce too. I was always happy to take over when Katie couldn't be there, but it became challenging when the other employees weren't there to help. Car trouble, illness, family emergencies, even jury duty had everyone calling out left and right for the past week.

It was the day before a catering gig—one that was especially important to me. Kia's boutique was having a twentieth anniversary party, and I was in charge of the event. Which wouldn't have been an issue if I didn't have to also run the restaurant.

"Hey, McKenzie." Bella, one of our new hires, poked her head in the kitchen looking like a mouse standing in front of a boa constrictor.

"Yeah?" I asked, continuing to swirl icing over the cupcakes in front of me.

"Sydney just called out," she answered softly, as though the volume of her statement would be the thing to set me off.

My blood turned to ice. "What?"

Bella swallowed hard. "She has the flu."

"Fuck," I said through gritted teeth. I couldn't say I hadn't seen it coming, since she and Grant had started dating, and *he'd* called in with it two days before. "She was supposed to be running the kitchen today. Grant and Jacob are out, and I'm swamped. I'm behind on what I need to prep for the party tomorrow night, and I can't run the entire kitchen and get it done."

"I know. I'm sorry. What can I do?" The poor thing looked so terrified that if I'd made any sudden movements, I'm fairly sure she would've screamed.

I dropped the pastry bag on the counter and pressed my wrists to my skull in a vague attempt to relieve the pressure mounting behind my eyes.

What could I do? Call Dallas and tell him I had a DEFCON 1 level emergency on my hands and beg him to come in? I hated the idea of him leaving Katie when she wasn't well, though I knew she'd likely insist on it. Maybe I could call the two new hires who hadn't started yet and plead with them to come in a couple days earlier than planned. They hadn't gone through orientation yet, but they at least had some kitchen experience, whereas Bella had none. Or perhaps I could just disappear like Homer Simpson backing into the bush, flee the country, and change my name. That option was looking better and better.

"How many servers do we have up front today?" I asked.

"Just Abbey and Tiffany."

I scrubbed my hands over my face. Abbey had some kitchen experience, but I couldn't leave Tiffany on the floor alone. She'd started at the same time as Bella and was still learning the ropes.

"Okay," I said. "Here's what we're gonna do. Call Tyler and Fallon and see if they'd be willing to come in. They're not supposed to start till Monday, but it's worth a shot."

She nodded. "You got it. Do you want me to call Dallas?"

"No." I shook my head. "That's a last resort. I think I can manage. Are you going to be able to handle the counter and the coffee bar on your own?"

Her wide-eyed expression told me I had a better chance of winning the lottery.

"I'll ask Abbey for help if I need it," she said.

I released a slow exhale. "Okay." I gestured toward the tray of freshly iced chocolate raspberry cupcakes in front of me. "Take these up front and put them in the case, will you?"

She stepped closer, slowly reaching her hands out to take the tray. My intrusive thoughts begged me to yell *BOO*, but I couldn't afford to be down another staff member. With the cupcakes in hand, she scurried toward the door.

"Let me know what Tyler and Fallon say," I called after her.

"I will," she said as she disappeared to the front of the restaurant.

This was fine. Worst-case scenario, I'd have to pull an all-nighter to prep for Kia's party and work through the day tomorrow. Sleep was for the weak. Or for the people not freaking out about their boyfriend going on tour in a few months.

I wasn't a freaking out kind of woman. I'd spent the entirety of my adult life not getting attached to people because I hated the idea of allowing myself to depend on someone only for them to leave. But that was exactly what I was doing.

Luca had been so wrapped up in press opportunities the last several days that he hadn't even caught on that I was struggling—with work or with what our new normal would soon become: extended time away from each other...opposing schedules...lives that were growing apart instead of together. I felt myself beginning to withdraw. He hadn't noticed, and I definitely hadn't told him. The last thing I wanted to be was a needy girlfriend.

He'd gone to New York for a couple of days earlier that

week for back-to-back interviews about his musical come-back, while I fell asleep every night on the couch in my work clothes. Part of me was dying to talk to him, to tell him how much these changes were affecting me. That's what grown-ups did in grown-up relationships. But I also knew I had to figure out how to deal with it on my own. I'd become comfortable having him to myself, but my world was about to be turned upside down. I couldn't just call him anytime I wanted while he was on the road when I had a bad day or felt insecure. What was he going to do? Answer his phone in the middle of a show and say *Sorry guys, I gotta take this*?

I shook my head, desperate to scatter the anxious thoughts threatening to take control of my brain as I moved to the other side of the kitchen where I kept the files for our catering events. Kia's was right on top, so I opened it and scanned the list I'd already made of everything that needed to be done. I just needed to focus. This was my job. I was a professional, damn it.

And an expert at avoiding anything that might hurt me.

TWENTY-SIX

Luca

THE LAST TWO WEEKS HAD BEEN A WHIRLWIND. AFTER MY show at The Bluebird, the world suddenly became interested in Luca Sterling again. But for once it wasn't for being the wild card of Midnight in Dallas. It wasn't because I'd done anything wrong—it was because I'd finally done something right.

Grace was overwhelmed with interview requests from outlets that wanted to talk with me, especially once we released the news that the new album would drop at the end of April with a tour following over the summer.

I quickly learned I wouldn't be able to fly under the radar anymore when I was out in public after I got bombarded at LaGuardia, then again when Grace and I stopped for a coffee after my chat with *Good Morning America*. People kept coming up to me, sharing stories about their own struggles. And I had to admit...I liked it. For the first time, I felt like I was doing something meaningful with my life.

By the time Saturday evening rolled around, I was back at the hobbit house enjoying a little downtime while McKenzie catered a party at her friend Kia's boutique. I'd hardly seen her since I'd gotten back from New York. There'd been some staffing issues at the restaurant, so she'd been working crazy hours to prepare for the event while also keeping the business afloat. She'd even opted to stay at her place Friday night because she had to work so late. I offered to drive to her because I still wanted to see her, but she insisted she was tired and needed to crash.

It was a little before nine, and I was lying on the couch, absentmindedly scrolling on my phone while a movie played in the background. I toggled over to the Instagram app and swiped through my newsfeed until I was staring at a picture taken of me at The Bluebird with *Is Luca Sterling Faking Depression for Likes?* printed over it in bold lettering. The caption below urged readers to check out the full story on the blog.

What the fuck? My throat went dry, and my blood turned cold. I checked the account that posted it, and it was a Nashville-based gossip column with over 200,000 followers called *The Party Buzz.* In comparison to a lot of media organizations, that wasn't a lot, but if they put something like this out, anyone could get a hold of it.

I released a slow breath. It was probably some internet troll who didn't take mental health seriously. I almost didn't look. In the past, I wouldn't have, because back then, I told myself I didn't care. But my trembling fingers moved over the screen almost of their own accord, unable to simply let it go.

The post was easy to find. It was right there on the landing page of the website.

Is Luca Sterling capitalizing on fans' empathy to hype up his new album? Local singer/songwriter, Tate McCreedy, thinks so. McCreedy sent The Party Buzz *a video that depicts Sterling up to his old antics, shoving him into a wall. "He was clearly drunk. I asked to take a photo with him, and he could have just said no, but he pushed me. Honestly, I was scared. He was belligerent, and he's not a small guy. It just sucked because he's my idol, you know? I'm his biggest fan, or at least I was," McCreedy told us. "The girl that was with him looked scared too. You just never know what's going on behind closed doors."*

While the video captured by McCreedy's friend did not show the conversation they had, Sterling's aggression was abundantly clear. You then see the A-lister storm out with his female companion by his side. McCreedy says the entire incident was a blessing in disguise because it inspired him to write his new track "Not Who I Thought You Were," which is out now on Spotify. Click below to watch the altercation, then sound off in the comments to let us know what you think. Is Luca Sterling using his mental health as a sales gimmick?

My stomach sank as I hit play, watching the short clip. Out of context, it looked pretty damning. Of course, there was no proof to show I'd been perfectly nice to the asshole and that *he'd* been the drunk one. He hadn't wanted to accept no for an answer when I told him I didn't want to take a photo, and when McKenzie intervened, he acted like *he* was going to get violent with *her*. But the post painted him a victim and even brought McKenzie into it as though she'd been afraid of me.

There were already over a hundred comments, but I stopped reading after the first three.

I fucking knew it. #CancelLucaSterling

What kind of a lowlife do you have to be to use mental health as a marketing scheme?

Did you guys see that the local news picked it up? They're running the story at nine.

I checked the time and quickly found the one Nashville news channel that ran their broadcast at 9 p.m. and turned it on. My heart slammed against my chest as the anchor read out the evening's top headlines. About fifteen minutes in, I started to think the commenter had been wrong. Maybe that garbage gossip column wouldn't catch fire. But then a picture of my face appeared in the right-hand corner of the television.

"In entertainment news tonight, we're covering a story breaking right here in Nashville. Luca Sterling, the former guitarist of acclaimed rock band, Midnight in Dallas, made headlines recently when he unveiled a new solo project at The Bluebird, telling fans about his struggles with depression. Once known for his drunken and sometimes troublesome antics, interviews conducted since that performance had Sterling claiming he'd turned over a new leaf. But a video leaked by local gossip column, *The Party Buzz*, paints a different picture."

The grainy cell phone footage I'd seen moments before appeared on the screen, and I pressed the heels of my palms into my eye sockets, willing the image to go away.

"No. No, no, no, no," I whispered to absolutely fucking no one. "That's not how it happened." But even as I said the words, I started to question my own sense of reality and the chain of events that occurred on that night. I knew I hadn't been drunk, but maybe I *had* been unnecessarily rude to the guy.

I looked back up to find a camera on Tate McCreedy, standing outside the very tavern we'd met in.

"It was completely unprovoked," he said. "I knew the guy had a troubled past, but I never dreamed he would attack me. It's just hard because he was the person I looked up to, but now…"

"Do you believe Luca Sterling is using mental health as a means of gaining fans and trying to seem relatable?" someone off camera asked.

Tate's mouth turned down into an exaggerated frown as he dropped his gaze, running his hand over the back of his neck.

"You hate to make assumptions, you know? But it seems like that," Tate answered. "All these interviews he's doing make it sound like he's this changed guy, that he's done all this work on himself. But what he did to me…does that sound different to you?"

"Fuck!" I slammed my clenched fists against my knees.

The camera shifted its focus to the clean-cut reporter with close-cropped blond hair.

"It turns out Tate McCreedy isn't alone in his thoughts about Sterling's motives," the man said, his tone serious as though he were reporting about a bomb threat. "Earlier today, we also spoke with Brandi Sewell, a former romantic interest of Sterling's who said she saw this coming from a mile away."

"Who the fuck…" I trailed off as Brandi's vaguely familiar face filled the screen. She was young and pretty with platinum hair and thick lashes. Out of context, I could have easily passed her on the street and not recognized her.

"He took me to a family dinner once," she said in an almost bird-like voice. "He couldn't even remember my name. He kept calling me Mandy, Candy, everything but my name. It's not that hard. It's Brandi. With an *i*. But I wanted him to like me, so I didn't correct him. I just played dumb about it."

"How did that make you feel?" the reporter asked.

"Like crap," Brandi answered. "Like I was being used. I mean, he took me into the bathroom at his family's house and we…you know…" She raised her brows. "I mean, I *wanted* to. It wasn't like that. It wasn't my proudest moment though, but I just wanted him to like me. I don't know. He didn't seem to care about anyone. I'm not sure he, like, *can*."

The reporter nodded, his eyes filled with concern. "So, you're saying you don't think he's capable of caring about others?"

Brandi shook her head. "No, I don't."

"And you don't believe he's changed?"

Brandi answered his question with one of her own. "Do people ever really change?"

The evening anchor reappeared on the screen with the same photo of me from the beginning of the segment.

"And according to numerous reports online, Tate McCreedy and Brandi Sewell are not alone. Numerous people are sharing their own encounters with Sterling, and fans and strangers alike are chiming in with their thoughts about the infamous rock star. Many are asking him to take accountability for his actions, while others are calling for the A-lister to be canceled. Luca Sterling's album *Coming Home* is slated for release this spring. Next up, we have Brian Storm with the forecast."

The walls felt like they were closing in. The sound from the television melted away into a low mumble, and a high-pitched ring pierced my ears. I grabbed my phone, barely able to see through the film that clouded my vision as I opened Google and typed in my name.

I knew it was a mistake before the first article had even loaded, but I had to know. I had to see it for myself.

The entire first page was filled with think pieces about what was wrong with me and blog posts written by people who wished I'd faded into obscurity. TMZ, Page Six, CNN, *Rolling Stone*, and *The New York Times* had already picked up the story, which meant by morning, the entire world would know and begin to form their opinions of me. Then there were the social media apps where I was trending. There were a few hashtags bearing my name, but one in particular stood out.

#LucaSterlingIsOver

My hands shook as I dropped the phone to the sofa. It bounced off the cushion and slid to the floor with a loud thud. The bomb had detonated, turning everything I'd worked so hard for into rubble. My life had been shattered into millions of pieces, some so small I'd never be able to find them, let alone glue them back together. There was no search and rescue that could fix this—fix *me*. Maybe Tate McCreedy's account of our brief meeting wasn't entirely accurate, but had there been a kernel of truth? And Brandi Sewell, whose name would now be etched in my memory forever...everything she'd said was correct. It had been years since it happened, but I'd done everything she said and more. I was exactly who she'd said I was.

Do people ever really change? Her words reverberated through my brain, causing the debris to settle a little more. I never should have left Kentucky. I should've allowed the darkness to swallow me whole while I had the chance. What had I been thinking, coming to Nashville and starting a solo career like I was somehow reformed? I paraded myself around like I was a beacon of hope and perseverance instead of what I actually was—a cautionary tale.

The dam holding back my tears broke, and I buried my head in my hands, my entire body shuddering beneath the weight of my emotions. I was a fuckup.

Useless.

Broken.

Worthless.

I clawed at the floor and grabbed my phone. Through blurry eyes, I opened my email, sending a single sentence to Grace.

The album and tour are off.

Then I dialed the number of the only person who understood me—the one person whose voice I needed to hear.

TWENTY-SEVEN

McKenzie

My phone buzzed from my back pocket as I loaded more sliders onto a serving platter Saturday night around 9:30 p.m., topping off more of the appetizers and desserts. It was the third time it had gone off in the last ten minutes, but I didn't have time to check it. My week from hell had stretched through to the weekend. I'd only managed to get about four hours of sleep the night before, and because we'd been short-staffed at work, I was also short-staffed at the party.

About fifty people were sandwiched into Kia's boutique, including Jen and Ravi, who'd just gotten drink refills from Abbey, the one person who'd been able to join me when I was supposed to have two more sets of hands on deck, before ambling over to me.

"McKenzie, you killed it," Ravi said, piling his plate with sliders, blueberry mac and cheese, and a few more of the dessert offerings. "These mini pie bites are insane."

"The blackberry bourbon is my fave," Jen garbled around a pie bite. "The crust is so flaky."

"Thanks, guys." I barely looked up from the confections I

was placing on one of the tables, decorated in shades of pink. My phone buzzed again, and I gritted my teeth, finally plucking it out of my pocket. It was Luca.

Can you talk?

Call me please.

Something was up. This wasn't like him, and he knew how important this party was to me. Or maybe he didn't. He hadn't seemed much aware of anything that wasn't directly related to him and his new album, his upcoming tour, or the interviews he'd been doing.

I chided myself. That wasn't entirely fair for me to say. He may not have been aware, but I also wasn't exactly going out of my way to make him aware either.

I tapped out a quick text and hit send.

Working. Call u in a bit.

I shoved my phone back in my pocket.

"Hey, is everything okay?" Jen asked, her brows knitted together.

"Oh yeah. I'm fine," I said, waving her off. "Just busy."

She narrowed her eyes as though she wasn't sure she believed me, but she let it go.

"Okay. We're going to mingle, but if you need anything, let me know," Jen said.

"Hey, Abbey, can you keep an eye out?" I asked as Jen and Ravi disappeared into the sea of people. "I need to mix up some more punch."

"Sure," she answered, and I weaved my way through the crowd to the break room. My phone vibrated as patrons stopped me to rave over the food and hummed again when I finally made it to the back to throw together more punch. I released a frustrated groan as I brought out the pitcher to Abbey to load into the dispenser, my backside buzzing.

"I need to go to the restroom real quick," I whispered to her. "Can you handle things for a couple more minutes?"

"Yeah," she said, pouring someone else another glass of the fizzy blush-colored liquid. "Just hurry back."

I nodded, then quickly moved toward the back again and into the break room, pulling out my cell. Before I could call him, his name showed up on the screen. I swiped to answer the call, pressing the phone to one ear, while I plugged the other with my finger to drown out the noise filtering in from the party down the hall.

"Hey, babe," I said. "I'm kind of swamped here. What's going on?"

"I know." His voice came out choked, ragged. "I'm sorry."

My tone softened. "Luca, what's wrong? What happened?"

"I have to kill the album, the tour," he blurted out. "Everything…it's over."

"What do you mean?" I asked, pressing the phone closer to my ear.

"There's this story going around about me. A lot of stories, actually," he said, his words cracked with emotion. "It's all over the fucking internet. TMZ. Page Six. It was even on the local news. I'm fucking over. Done. And it's all my fault."

"Wait. What are you talking about? What stories?"

"That guy from the tavern," he said, his words strangled. "The one you almost got in a fight with. Some girl I was with years ago. It's like everyone has come out of the woodwork to tell the world what a piece of shit I am."

"I know I'm not famous or anything, but isn't this kinda how it works?" I sat at one of the dinette tables. "People hate when someone finds success, so they shit on it. It'll blow over. People will forget all about it in a day or two."

"No," he insisted. "I know what you mean, and this…is not that. This is worse. I never should have come here. I should have stayed in my apartment alone, where I fucking belong."

He started speaking again, but I couldn't hear him because Abbey poked her head into the break room.

"I need you," she said, her face frantic.

"Shit," I muttered, covering the mouthpiece. "I'm coming."

"McKenzie, can you hear me?" Luca asked.

"Listen, I've got to go," I said into the phone. "Things are nuts out there, and it's just me and Abbey."

"I know this is terrible timing, but I need you. I can't do this."

"Luca, I know this press stuff is important to you, and I get it. Really, I do," I said, trying my best to keep the stress and frustration out of my voice. "But I have a life and a job too. One that has been kicking my ass lately, and I can't just drop everything because someone said something mean about you on the internet."

"I can't handle this without you, McKenzie," he pleaded.

"And you don't have to, but I can't deal with this right now, okay? I'll come over as soon as I'm done here, but right now I have to go."

"Please. I—"

"I can't just leave," I snapped. "What are you gonna do when something happens and you're on the road? I'm not going to ditch my job and follow you all over the country or take off in the middle of the night because someone says something that hurts your feelings. I won't be there to hold your hand through everything."

I knew I was being harsh, but I couldn't seem to stop the words rolling off my tongue.

"Look, call Grace or Dallas or something," I continued. "I'll be over later, and we can talk about it then, but I have to go."

My stomach dropped as I ended the call, not giving him a chance to say another word, and headed back out to the party where half of the food I'd just put out was already gone, and Abbey had a line for drinks eight people deep. My eyes burned, but I refused to be the girl that cried at work, especially not at my friend's party.

Though cold as it might have been, what I'd told him was true. I still didn't know exactly what the stories he was so upset about entailed, but I did know he was going to have to find a way to cope. He couldn't put his entire emotional well-being in my hands, especially not with him going on tour in the near future. The more his career took off, the less we'd be together. He couldn't depend on me for everything, just like I couldn't depend on him.

But my guilt was eating away at me. Even if what I'd said was true, I didn't have to say it the way I did. I reached for my phone and sent him a text.

I'm sorry. Are you okay?

I stuffed the device back in my pocket and waited for the inevitable buzz, but it never came. A few minutes passed, and I sent another message.

Luca, please answer me.

About forty-five minutes and no response from Luca later, the party was winding down, and Kia made her way over to me with a big grin on her face. "I have at least six customers who want to get your information for their weddings or corporate events. You've been quite the hit."

"Really?" I asked, not even bothering to smile. "That's great."

She fixed her gaze on me. "What's the matter?"

"Nothing," I replied, clearing away some of the discarded plates.

"Doesn't look like nothing," she said, arching her brow. "You look like you want to cry."

I swallowed hard, tears stinging my eyes.

She stepped behind the table and grabbed my hands. "McKenzie, what is it?"

"It's Luca. He kept calling and texting me earlier. I finally answered, and he was upset. Something about some bad press. He said he needed me. He was begging me to go to him right then, and I kinda lost my cool. I didn't mean to, but I was stressed and—"

"Hey, you don't owe me an explanation," she said. "I know you've been busting your ass all night. Did you try to call or text him back?"

I shoved my fingers through my hair. "I sent him a couple messages and nothing."

Just then, Jen and Ravi appeared, concern etched into their faces.

"Oh God, you saw it, didn't you?" Jen asked.

I shook my head. "Saw what?"

"The stuff about Luca," Jen answered, but it came out almost like a question. "When we saw you over here upset, we figured it must be because you heard about it."

My throat went dry. "Is it bad?"

Ravi's throat bobbed, and I could tell by the look on his face that it was, in fact, worse than bad.

I released a shaky breath. "What have I done?"

"Listen to me," Kia said, taking me gently by the shoulders. "Go to the back and try to call him. I'm going to get everyone out of here, and we'll get this sorted out, okay?"

I nodded. "Okay."

Jen was on my heels as I sprinted down the hall. Kia's words to her guests were drowned out by the sound of my own blood whooshing in my ears. I was already dialing his number when Jen clicked the door to the break room shut, leaving only the sound of my heartbeat.

The call went straight to voicemail. I tried three more times with the same result.

This was all my fault. Luca needed me, and I drove him away, all because I was too fucking wrapped up in myself to just hear him out. I burst into tears, and Jen pulled me into her arms.

"It's gonna be all right," she said. "We'll find him, okay? Just breathe."

THE DOOR TO THE BREAK ROOM OPENED AND KIA APPEARED with Ravi close behind.

"Your coworker is out there packing up. I told her you're not feeling well," Kia said as she stepped inside and squeezed my arm. "Did you reach him?"

"No," I cried, wiping my hands down my damp face. "It goes straight to voicemail every time."

While I tried to call Luca, Jen gave me the abridged version of what was happening in the press. I knew her well enough to know she was choosing her words carefully because my mental state was already hanging on by a thread.

But even as she tiptoed around the harsh reality of the situation, I knew it was far worse than I'd imagined. It was no wonder Luca was so distraught. People weren't just coming for his reputation or his integrity. They were coming for blood.

"I didn't even tell him I loved him," I muttered. "When I got off the phone, I didn't even tell him I—"

I choked back a sob. I was supposed to love him, protect him. And when he came to me, troubled and shattered, looking for support, I turned him away.

My mind went to Brennan and the days leading up to his death, replaying every moment on fast-forward. Had I pushed him away too? Had I really learned nothing after all these years?

"What if he…" I trailed off, unable to finish the question, yet it hung in the air like gunpowder after a shot rang out. I was standing in a room filled with people who'd lost the ones they loved most the same way I lost Brennan. "I have to go. I have to go now."

"You're not going alone," Kia said. "I'm taking you."

"But—"

"This isn't up for discussion." She placed her hands on either side of my face. "You are in no condition to be driving."

And if anything bad *had* happened, she didn't want me to be alone. The thought sent an icy chill shooting through me.

I sniffed, wiping my fingers beneath my lashes. "You shouldn't be worrying about me. This was your big night, and I messed it all up."

Kia shook her head. "Stop. You didn't mess up anything. This is what friends do, McKenzie. It's not all sunshine and rainbows. We sit with each other in the shit. We've all done it for each other. Now just happens to be your turn."

"Thank you," I whispered.

Kia dug in her pocket and pulled out a key, handing it to Jen. "Will you two stay and lock up? Make sure McKenzie's friend doesn't need any help cleaning up?"

"Of course," Ravi said as he and Jen both pulled me into a hug.

Jen kissed the top of my head. "Let us know as soon as you hear something."

I nodded as Kia reached for my hand.

"We will," she answered for me before grabbing both our purses from the cabinet beside the door and leading me out the back to her car.

In a matter of seconds, we were on the road.

"Do you have a key to his place?" she asked, keeping her voice even. "In case we can't get him to answer the door?"

"Yeah," I rasped, my eyes glued to the blur of the street lights as they passed by.

The forty-minute drive to Leipers Fork from East Nashville was quiet, except for the hammering of my heartbeat and the directions I gave Kia.

We finally pulled in the mostly darkened driveway, and my heart sank when we found it empty.I jumped out of the car before Kia had fully put it into park, fumbling for the key.

"Wait a minute," Kia called after me, but I'd already jammed the key into the lock and flung the door open.

"Luca," I yelled into the darkness, slapping my hand against the wall as I felt for the light switch.

The stillness shouted back at me, the only noise coming from the ticking of the old grandfather clock in the living room.

Kia was right behind me as I tore through the house, turning on every light, searching through every room. Even though I already knew he wasn't outside, I still checked the garden. I frantically called his name as though he might materialize out of thin air and ask what all the fuss was about. But Luca was nowhere to be found.

I walked back into the kitchen, and that was when my heart nearly stopped. There at the corner of the table sat Randy McNutt. I stepped closer, my bottom lip quivering as I realized Luca's house key was right beside him.

Tears blurred my vision. Why would he have left his key here?

Unless he didn't plan on coming back.

"Oh my God." My chest felt heavy, like I'd been lifting hundred-pound weights without a spotter, and they'd come crashing down on me. My breaths ripped through me in sharp gasps.

"McKenzie, talk to me," Kia said, putting a hand on my arm.

"His…key." I barely managed to get the words out before the room started to spin. A cold sweat seeped through my skin as my knees buckled.

Kia caught my arm and eased me to the floor, crouching beside me.

"Have…to find him…" I wheezed. I reached for the table in an attempt to pull myself up, but my trembling arms fell limp at my sides. "He…needs help."

"You're not going anywhere right now." Kia's voice was gentle but firm.

Each breath was like a knife twisting in my chest, white-hot pain burning my lungs. There was a high-pitched scream in my ears. Was *I* screaming? Were my ears ringing? Was I having a heart attack?

"It's a panic attack," Kia said as though she could hear my thoughts, or maybe I'd said it out loud. Her voice sounded far away, like I was in the deep end of the pool, and she was shouting at me from dry land.

Kia reached for my phone, holding it in front of my face to unlock it. She dialed someone, and I tried hard to focus on her words.

"Katie, this is McKenzie's friend Kia," she said. "I need your help."

***

"HERE," MY MOM SAID, HANDING ME A STEAMING MUG OF chamomile tea. Kia and I sat on my couch, and she sank into the armchair beside me. "Drink this."

I nodded, still feeling somewhat shell-shocked as I took it into my hands. After my panic attack, Kia had folded me into her Honda and called my mother to meet us at my apartment. She'd already let herself in with my spare key by the time we arrived.

It was after midnight, and Binx was curled up on my lap, his constant soft purr a balm to my soul. Kia stroked the top of Earl Grey's head from where he was perched on top of the sofa.

"How are you feeling?" Kia asked, her watchful gaze fixed on me as though I might fall apart if she looked away.

"Like this is all my fault," I admitted, my voice a hoarse whisper. "Luca left because of me."

Both Kia and my mom shook their heads.

"No, baby," my mom said, leaning forward to place her

hand on my knee. "Luca's struggling right now. None of this is your fault."

"But I should have been there for him," I whispered.

"You are," she insisted. "You have been. But there are some things we can't fix for other people."

"Your mom's right," Kia said. "The only person responsible for Luca's healing is Luca. All you can do is love and encourage him."

"But I didn't," I choked out.

"Because you didn't drop everything and run to him?" Kia asked. "McKenzie, that's too much weight for one person to carry."

My mom nodded in agreement. "You can't be his entire support system."

"I don't know Luca, but I *do* know you," Kia said. "You don't love easily, but when you do, you love hard. It's just that…when someone's struggling the way Luca is, sometimes even love isn't enough to reach their darkest places."

My mom gave me a wistful smile. "If only it were that simple. If love were enough, Brennan would still be here. It's just so much more complex than that."

"But what if it could be that simple?" I dropped my gaze to the mug in my lap. "What if I could—"

"No." Kia held up her hands as though she could stop the thoughts before they formed in my mind. "You can't. And I know how much it sucks to hear that. It hurts even more to accept it. But you don't have that kind of power. Nobody does."

"Have you heard from Katie yet?" I asked Kia, though I already knew the answer. If she'd heard anything, she would have told me.

"Not yet," she answered. "But she told me she'd text me

as soon as they got to Luca's place in Kentucky." Dallas and Katie had told Kia that was where they believed he'd taken off to, and when I'd come out of my panic attack enough to form words, I remembered he'd said something about how he should have stayed in his apartment.

I sighed. "I should try to call him again."

"It's still going to voicemail," my mom said gently. "I tried."

I swallowed hard. "I could leave another message."

"I think the best thing you can do for Luca right now is take care of yourself." Kia reached over and touched my arm.

"I am," I argued.

Kia shot me a look. "I beg to differ."

"It's just work stress," I said. "What I have going on is nothing compared to what Luca's dealing with."

"It's not just 'work stress,'" Kia countered. "I think you still have a lot of unresolved feelings surrounding Brennan's death."

"He's gone," I said with a wry laugh. "You can't get much more resolved than that."

"But you're still blaming yourself for what happened," my mom said. "And I think you've carried that into your relationship with Luca. You can't save him, sweetheart."

I felt my defenses rising. "I wasn't trying to *save* Luca." Even as I said it, I knew it was a lie. I'd wanted to prevent him from ever feeling the way my brother did, and I'd failed.

Kia kept her tone calm and steady. "I think you were. And you thought if you could save him, you could somehow save part of Brennan too."

"That's not true," I protested, but the words came out weak, even to my own ears.

"McKenzie, you can't save other people. The only person

you can ever save is yourself," Kia continued. "And as your friend, I'm telling you that you need to seek help or you're going to end up in a dark place. I know because I've been right where you're sitting."

I lifted my watery eyes up to hers.

"How do you think I recognized you were having a panic attack?" she asked with a sad smile. "Because I've had them myself. I think the milestone anniversary of your brother's death last year unearthed a lot of stuff for you. Mine started on my fortieth birthday. I felt like I was moving into a new stage of life, and I guess my brain finally caught up and realized my husband wasn't coming with me—that we weren't gonna grow old together. It was a tough pill to swallow." She took a deep breath and cleared her throat. "The grief I felt was so all-encompassing I thought it would drown me. And it might've if I hadn't gone back into therapy."

"I started back recently too," my mom confessed.

I shifted my focus to her. "What? When?"

"After the New Year," she answered. "Having Luca around…He reminds me a lot of Brennan and the man I think he might've become. And that's a beautiful thing. But it's also a hard thing."

"Why didn't you tell me?" I asked.

"Because the last thing I wanted was for you to feel like you needed to save me too," she said. "Kia's right. You need to take care of yourself. And if you really want your relationship with Luca to work, you're going to have to prioritize your own mental health. It's like when you're on a plane, and they tell you to put on your own oxygen mask first in the event of a crash. You can't help someone else when you're gasping for air."

"I'm just so worried about him," I choked out.

"We know you are," my mom said. "And nobody is saying you shouldn't talk to him. But right now, you need to let some of the other people in his circle step in."

"And let us take care of you," Kia added.

I wanted to argue. I wanted to tell them nobody could help him the way I could, but I had no fight left in me. My body was weak, my brain foggy and exhausted.

"Okay," I agreed. But no matter what Kia or my mother told me, all I really wanted to do was to save him. To save *us*.

If there was an us left to save.

TWENTY-EIGHT

Luca

___

When McKenzie disconnected our call, the last thread tying me to the earth snapped. I started to call someone else—maybe Dallas or Cash—but I didn't deserve their words of comfort. I wasn't worthy of the excuses they'd inevitably make to help me feel better about the person I was. The piece of shit I knew I'd always be at my core. There was no righting the amount of wrongs I'd caused in my life. It was best for everyone if I just disappeared quietly into the night.

The walls of the hobbit house were closing in on me, squeezing the air from my lungs. I packed what shit I had there, which wasn't much more than some clothes and my guitar. The squirrel McKenzie had given to me was the last thing I grabbed, but in the end, I left him along with my key. The last thing I needed was another reminder of the ways I'd failed the woman I loved.

I turned the lock and shut the door, leaving behind every hope and counterfeit dream that place had held. But even as I walked away, that suffocating feeling followed me into the car. My old demon friends had returned...or maybe they'd never left. Either way, they were unwilling to let me cast them aside.

There wasn't a lot of traffic on my drive back to Kentucky, but my mind was filled with noise. An endless assault of thoughts and questions shot through my brain, hitting me with punch after punch.

Why did I ever think I could amount to anything more than a fuckup? I wasn't a changed man. I hadn't healed. All I'd managed to do was slap bandages over gaping wounds. Except I wasn't the one being injured. I was the cause of the damage, and the longer I stuck around, the more I risked those I loved bleeding out.

It started with canceling me, but the aftermath would be felt by McKenzie, Laurel, Grace, and anyone else connected to me. Because people would wonder why they stood by me. I couldn't ask them to stake their reputations on mine. I *wouldn't*. But more than that, I didn't want to stick around long enough for them to begin to question why they were still putting up with me. At least if I left on my own, I could still maintain some illusion of control instead of the devastation I'd feel if—*when*—they finally had enough and walked away.

I'd been looking at my musical comeback as a second chance, but that couldn't have been further from the truth. I'd squandered hundreds of chances and spit on every opportunity I'd been handed for years. Having everything I could have hoped for dangled in front of me, only to have it slip through my fingers, felt like a penance for every ounce of potential I'd thrown away. It was nowhere near the punishment I deserved, but it was a start.

Even though music blared through the speakers, the monsters had taken control of the playlist inside my mind, blasting McKenzie's words on a loop. No matter how loud I turned up the volume on the radio, I couldn't drown them out.

I won't be there to hold your hand through everything.

She was right, of course. I'd been so wrapped up in the prospect of a tour, of having my own music career, that I hadn't stopped to consider what that meant for *us*. What would happen if I went on the road or if one album became two or three or five? I'd assumed she'd be there beside me. I hadn't even considered the possibility of her *not* being there because what kind of relationship would that have been? Dozens of missed phone calls and *sorry-I-missed-you*'s. Birthdays, anniversaries, and holidays celebrated apart. More time spent away from each other than together. I'd been too caught up in my own selfish desires to ask what she wanted. And she deserved more than that. She deserved more than *me*.

She needed someone who'd put her first, who wouldn't drag her down, who understood how to love someone self-lessly. McKenzie knew how to do that. She lifted me up and cheered me on from the very beginning. But I'd been so caught up in how good it felt to be wanted, respected, and loved that I'd failed the one person I felt those things for. I took her for granted. Just as I'd done with every other good thing in my life.

She was better off without me. Everyone was. She deserved an explanation or at least a goodbye, but I'd just have to add that to the long list of things I wasn't capable of giving her.

It was nearly 2 a.m. by the time I made it back to my place in Kentucky and climbed out of my car. The bitter cold would have been enough to freeze me to my bones if I wasn't made of ice already. I gathered my things and stepped inside, not bothering to turn the lights on. I left my bags by the front door and dropped onto the sofa, lying on my side. The cushions enveloped me in a musty greeting of dust and stale air.

Even in the absence of light, I sensed the shadows creeping closer. I felt their breath, hot against my skin, as they crawled back inside me where they belonged. My eyes drifted closed, and I sighed with relief as the darkness welcomed me home.

A LOUD THUDDING ECHOED IN MY EARS, JOLTING ME AWAKE. It was like someone was banging their fist against the walls of my skull.

Jesus. I can't even get peace in my sleep. I grabbed a throw pillow and crushed it to my face as I squeezed my eyes shut again

"Luca, open up," a deep, muffled voice called.

"We know you're in there," another added, this one soft and sweet.

I bolted upright. *Dallas and Katie?*

Boom, boom, boom. The pounding wasn't coming from inside my head—it was coming from my front door.

"Come on, man," Dallas said. "Let us in. We want to help."

The events of the hours before washed over me in an endless pour, as if every moment I wished I could take back was waterboarding me. I had no idea what time it was, but the darkness inside said it was still nighttime.

"Dude, don't think I won't rip this door off its hinges," Dallas bellowed again.

I trudged over to the door and opened it, finding my

friends' worried faces staring back at me, Emilia clutched in Katie's arms. She wagged her tail when she saw me.

"What are you doing here?" I asked, blinking in disbelief.

"I believe we could ask you the same thing," Katie answered. "Can we come in?"

I nodded and stepped aside, allowing them to cross over the threshold.

Seconds later, the living room was bathed in light with Katie's hand hovering over the switch.

I squinted as my vision adjusted and pushed my fingers through my hair.

"What time is it?" I asked.

"Almost four in the morning," Dallas replied, moving over to the sofa and sitting down. "We came as soon as McKenzie's friend called Katie. What happened, man?"

"Wait. McKenzie's friend?" I shook my head and looked from Dallas to Katie. "Why would her friend call you?"

Katie shot Dallas a glare and swallowed hard before gesturing toward the couch.

"Come sit down." She placed a hand on my arm, guiding me across the room as she set Emilia on the floor.

"Why did McKenzie's friend call you?" I asked again, taking a seat between them.

"We'll get to that," Dallas said. "But right now, we want to know what's going on with you."

"Just google my name." I folded my arms over my chest. "That'll tell you everything."

Dallas nodded. "We saw. But…why did you leave like that? You didn't tell anyone. McKenzie showed up at your house and you weren't there. Grace got a single-sentence email from you, calling off the album and the tour. We all tried your cell, but it went to voicemail every time."

I released a slow exhale. "I shut it off."

"We were worried sick," Katie said, touching my shoulder. "Why didn't you call one of us? We would have been there."

"I know." I stared straight ahead at an invisible spot on the wall. "But I didn't want you to be."

"Why not?" Katie asked.

"Because I don't fucking deserve it, all right?" I said, rising to my feet. "Everything they're saying about me online? It's all true. Every bit of it."

Dallas leaned forward, his elbows on his knees. "I really don't think that's the case. Maybe there's a few kernels of truth, but a couple crappy stories don't tell everything there is to know about you."

"What about Brandi?" I asked, throwing up my hands. "I don't remember much about that night because I was so shitfaced, but what I do know is, I was enough of an asshole to cause Ella to throw her water on me. I wasn't a good guy, Dallas. I'm still not a good guy."

"You're wrong," Katie insisted, her eyes glossy with unshed tears. "Remember the night of Jo's big event for Project NENA when I was so sick and she didn't want to leave me alone? *You* were the one that came and stayed with me. You didn't just keep me company, either—you took care of me."

"You were there when we took Katie to the hospital," Dallas added. "You didn't have to go, and you certainly didn't have to stay, but you did."

"Those were two incidents over the course of *years*," I argued.

"But there are more where that came from," Dallas said. "So, you've made some bad choices in the past. Done or said shit you regret. Who hasn't? Have you forgotten what a dick I was back when Derek wanted to leave the band? Or the fact that I blamed Jo for it all because I didn't want to see the truth?"

"That's different," I said, pacing the floor.

"Only because it's not out there on the damn internet for everyone to see," he said. "Luca, we *all* fuck up. We say or do things we wish we could take back. But most people don't have to do it in front of the whole goddamn world. You need to give yourself a break."

"This is exactly why I didn't call you. I knew you'd do this—make excuses for me," I shouted, my fists clenched at my sides. "Don't you get it? There's no fucking excuse. For every bad story out there about me right now, there's ten more that are worse that nobody will ever know about. But *I* know."

"You're holding yourself to impossible standards." Katie's voice was soft. "Your mistakes don't define you. They're not who you are."

"The fuck they're not," I yelled, whirling to face them. "That's all I am. A mistake. My own parents knew it, I know it, and I think deep down you all know it too. I'm not *good*."

Tears spilled down Katie's cheeks as she jumped to her feet and gripped my arms.

"You are not a mistake." She punctuated every word. "Do you hear me? And anyone who thinks that doesn't know what they're talking about."

Tears blurred my vision. "*I* think that."

"Then you need to take some time to get to know the man I have the honor of calling one of my best friends." Her voice broke. "If you could see what I see…what we *all* see. You are magic, Luca Sterling. Your thorns are part of what makes you so magnificent. Because even in spite of them, you bloomed."

I blinked, sending tracks of salt water down my cheeks.

"She's right, you know." Dallas rose to join us. "We love you, brother."

"Damn right, we do," Katie said as they enveloped me, my body shaking with emotion as I clung to them. I felt like I was free-falling, and they were my emergency parachute—deployed just in the nick of time.

"No more running," Dallas said, squeezing me tighter. "Let us help you."

"Please," Katie whispered. "We can't lose you."

I wept so hard I could hardly breathe. Once again, I'd proven myself unworthy, but they didn't care. They wanted me around, even with my flaws and glaring imperfections. Despite the years of hurt and disappointment I'd caused. They saw something that warranted saving. And if they weren't willing to give up on me, maybe I could hang on a little longer.

One cup at a time.

"Okay," I choked out.

"Listen, you need to get some rest," Dallas said. "Let's crash, and we'll talk more in the morning."

I pulled back, using the neck of my shirt to wipe my face. "You guys don't have to stay. I'm not a flight risk. Not anymore. You need to get Emilia home."

"We packed an overnight bag." Katie squeezed my arm. "We're not going anywhere."

"I'll go grab our stuff," Dallas said, heading toward the door.

"Then you two take my bed. Down the hall, first door on the left," I insisted as Dallas stepped outside. "I'll stay out here. I'd offer you the guest room, but the only things in there are a few boxes and an old dresser. I never got around to furnishing it because…well, because I never really wanted anyone to visit."

"But you don't have to give up your—" Katie started to argue, but I cut her off.

"With your MS, you need a bed. I'm taking the couch."

She nodded her agreement as she knelt to scoop up Emilia. "All right."

Seconds later, Dallas returned with a duffel slung over his shoulder.

He clapped me on the back. "We'll be in the bedroom if you need anything."

"Wait a second," I said. "You never answered me before. Why did McKenzie's friend call you?"

Katie's gaze dropped to the floor.

My stomach tied itself in knots. "What is it?"

"McKenzie had a panic attack when she realized you were gone," Katie replied. "That's why her friend Kia called."

The realization of what I'd done collided with me head-on. Of course, she'd panicked. After what she'd been through with Brennan, she was probably terrified.

"Fuck," I muttered, my hand covering my mouth.

"She's all right," Katie interjected before I had the chance to spiral any further. "She's shaken up, but she's okay. I talked to Kia again on the way here. Her mom is staying with her."

"Thank God," I said, immediately searching my pockets for my phone. "I should call her. I need to tell her I'm sorry."

Dallas held out a hand to stop me. "There'll be plenty of time for that. Right now, you need to take care of yourself."

"And I think she may need a little time. This brought up a lot for her. Give her a day or two to process," Katie added. "Kia said she'd touch base with me later. I'll tell her to let McKenzie know you're thinking about her."

I swallowed hard and nodded, reaching out to scruff the top of Emilia's ears.

"Do you mind if she stays with me?" I asked. "The company might be nice."

"Of course." Katie gave me a faint smile as she passed her to me. "I think she'd like that."

"Hey there, Princess Piss-a-lot," I said as she settled into my arms.

"Good night." Katie's eyes lingered on me a moment before she and Dallas started toward my room.

"Night," I called after them.

I moved to the sofa, then set Emilia on the cushion before shrugging off my jacket and tossing it aside. When I laid back, the little dog wagged her tail before climbing onto my chest to give me a gentle lick on the nose.

"Thanks, girl," I said, stroking her ear as she curled herself into a ball on my stomach.

There was something comforting about her presence. She was no stranger to rejection, either. She'd been abandoned by the person who was supposed to love her the most. It was a feeling I understood on a cellular level. I hadn't been in a place to give the dog the home she needed, but I knew Dallas and Katie could. And though I tried to pretend I didn't, I cared about her. I just knew I couldn't be everything she needed— everything she *deserved*.

I looked at Emilia where she lay on me: safe, happy, and most of all, loved. Dallas and Katie were her people, but she also had a family that extended beyond them in me, McKenzie, and all of our friends. Maybe it wouldn't make up for the neglect she'd suffered, but despite the odds, she was thriving.

And maybe one day, I could too.

"I'm glad you're here." Lacey settled into her armchair while I sat on the couch in her office late Sunday afternoon. I'd kept my phone off other than the three minutes it took me to send Lacey an email asking for her first available session and leaving Katie's number as my contact. She was also giving me updates on McKenzie. I didn't want to be tempted to open social media or Google until I was in a better headspace, so I avoided it altogether. Lacey called soon after I sent the message and told me to meet her at 5 p.m.

"You didn't have to come in on your day off," I said, staring straight ahead at one of the colorful paintings on her wall. It was a field of wildflowers, but one stood bigger and brighter than the rest. My mind immediately recalled an image of McKenzie the night we danced together at the My Chemical Romance cover band show. The night that I'd later found out was the anniversary of Brennan's passing.

Guilt crawled over me like a spider. It felt like a small tickle at first, a harmless itch begging to be scratched, only for me to look down and find a black widow ready to strike and fill my blood with poison.

"I was already planning to come in and do some charting." She reached for the bottle of water on the table beside her, and the sleeve of her sweater inched up, revealing her semicolon tattoo.

"McKenzie has one of those." I gestured toward her exposed ink. "Behind her ear. She...told me what it means. She got it after she thought about ending her life, when she realized she wanted to keep living and that her story wasn't finished yet."

She nodded and gave me a sad smile.

"You know what it's like, don't you?" I asked. "To feel like this. You've been there."

She didn't speak, and her face gave nothing away.

"And if I had to guess, I'd say you weren't actually coming in to do charting. You came in because you've been the one sitting where I am."

"I had charting to do," she said with a shrug. "Now, let's talk about why you're here."

I lifted my brows. "Because you were already coming in today to do some charting. *Allegedly.*"

She narrowed her eyes and took a sip of her water before placing it back on the table.

"You're really not going to tell me, are you?" I asked.

She placed her notepad on her lap and a pen in her hand.

"Why are you here today, Luca?" she asked softly.

I sighed and dropped my head back against the cushion. "If you've been online or turned on your television in the past twenty-four hours, then you probably already know the answer to that question. You've seen what everyone's saying about me."

Once again, her face gave nothing away.

Geez, she should take up poker.

"I'm familiar with what people are saying online." Lacey crossed one leg over the other. "But I'm more interested in what *you* have to say."

I picked at a frayed thread on my jeans, not meeting her gaze.

"I'm getting what I deserve," I answered, my voice barely above a whisper. "It feels like retribution for the shitty person I've been."

"Is that really what you think?" she asked.

"A lot of the things coming out about me are true," I

admitted. "Like that Brandi girl whose name I couldn't even remember. She was right. I didn't care about her. Hell, I barely cared about myself. For a long time, there was nothing but a revolving door of nameless, faceless women and an endless supply of liquor and whatever else I could get my hands on. Anything to numb the pain. And then I had the nerve to put myself out there like I was some role model for mental health and not the train wreck I actually am. I'm a fucking fraud. I don't deserve for people to look up to me, let alone love me."

"Did you put yourself out there as a role model, or did other people give you that title and you felt you had to live up to it?" she asked.

"What difference does it make?"

"It's hard enough to manage our own expectations of ourselves, but trying to live up to everyone else's at the same time?" She paused, allowing her words to settle over me. "That sounds pretty impossible, don't you think?"

I blinked. "Okay. Maybe I didn't *claim* to be anything, but when I started sharing my personal experiences, I became one —whether I wanted to be or not."

She steepled her fingers in her lap. "And you think that means you can no longer mess up? Not only that, but you also can't have messed up *ever* in your life because…what? Because people who make mistakes don't deserve anything good?"

I pushed my tongue onto the roof of my mouth. *Well, when you put it like that.*

"You're dealing in absolutes. Black or white. Either or," she continued. "And when you try to place human beings in these finite categories, you'll be disappointed every single time. People are nothing if not the gray areas in between. We are living proof that multiple things can be true at the same time. You can make mistakes *and* be a good person. You can feel better *and* still not be healed."

I barked out a dry laugh. "I know I'm nowhere near healed. I'm not sure I'd even say I'm better."

"You're not giving yourself enough credit. You've made a lot of progress, but you did what many people do when that fog starts to lift. You stopped devoting that time to yourself and fell into old habits when things got difficult. And for you, that means distancing yourself from those you love."

"I tried to call McKenzie first," I confessed. "When I saw that shit online…I panicked. I called her and begged her to come to me. I felt like the walls were closing in, and she was the only person who could take that away."

"And what did she say? Did she come to you?"

I shook my head. "She was working, and I knew it, but I still selfishly asked her to ditch what she was doing for me. She was frustrated because she was dealing with stress of her own, and she asked me what I would do if something like this happens while I'm on the road."

"That's a fair question, but you weren't selfish to reach out and ask for help," Lacey said. "Just as it wasn't selfish of her to not be in a place to hold space for you at that moment. Again, two things can be true at once. Did you ask anyone else for help?"

"No. I freaked out. When she turned me away, even though I didn't blame her for it…it triggered something inside me. I…I was afraid."

She leaned forward, her elbows on her knees. "What were you afraid of?"

"Being abandoned," I answered. "I was scared everyone would leave me because I…I'm not good enough. Because

I'm not worth the fucking trouble. But…my friends came looking for me. I wasn't in Kentucky long before they showed up."

"I thought you said you didn't call anyone else. How did they know to come to you?"

"McKenzie called them," I answered. "Actually, it was her friend. McKenzie showed up at my place in Tennessee looking for me, and when she saw I was gone, she had a panic attack. Which was my fault."

"You can't blame yourself. You were doing what you needed to do at that moment to survive," she said. "The situation might have stirred up a lot of emotions for her, but she also has her own previous trauma that formed her response."

"That may be, but it doesn't make me feel any better."

She gave me a faint smile. "See? Two things can be true."

"I'm afraid I ruined our relationship," I said, my voice breaking. "I was so terrified she'd leave me that I let it become this self-fulfilling prophecy. And I guess when I think about it, that's what I've always done. I walk away before anyone has the chance to walk away from me."

"It's not uncommon for people to do the very thing they're afraid of others doing to them. It's a defense mechanism. But you being able to recognize the pattern? That's growth."

"But how do I stop an instinct that comes to me as easily as breathing?"

"It may never stop. At least not fully," she answered. "It takes time and building up your arsenal of tools to cope. The only person you can rely on to aid your healing is you. Yes, you need a support system. Having loved ones you can count on is vital, but if you're constantly seeking validation and comfort from outside sources, you'll never be truly satisfied. Your contentment can't come from others. It has to come from you, because you're the only one who will always be there."

"I don't know if I can ever be happy with myself."

"You spent years collecting reasons to believe you're not worthy of love. Those don't go away overnight," she said. "You have to take it one step at a time."

One cup at a time.

"Why don't we start by coming up with three things you can work on over the next week to improve your relationship with yourself?" she suggested. "Things you can do to increase your self-trust."

"Like what?"

"What if you start by committing to weekly sessions for the next month and following up with your psychiatrist? Does that sound doable?"

I nodded. "Yeah, but I think I need something…I don't know…bigger?"

She tapped the tip of her pen to her notebook. "Well, you seem to be carrying around a lot of guilt and shame about some of your previous actions. Is there anyone you feel you owe an apology? I tend to think accountability is where self-awareness and self-compassion intersect. Taking ownership of our actions is an important part of our internal growth. You're holding on to so much blame. It might help you to find forgiveness."

My stomach clenched like a fist. "And if they can't forgive me?"

"Maybe you could try forgiving yourself," she replied.

I tried to swallow, but my throat felt dry. "I guess I can try."

"That's two things," she said. "What else could you do to better your relationship with yourself?"

I pressed my palms together in front of my lips as I pondered the question. The task felt almost inconceivable. How could I ever—

The wheels of my mind clicked into place. The answer had been in front of me all along, but I hadn't believed in myself enough to really try. I'd been so afraid of rejection, of being left, that I'd always kept one foot out the door, ready to run at any moment. But without an escape hatch at my disposal, I'd have to start trusting not only myself but those I loved. Selling my place in Kentucky was the ultimate trust fall.

I didn't even know if I'd have McKenzie to return to, and that scared me. But it was all the more reason to take the leap. I couldn't let my fears keep holding me back from the good things in life. The people I loved. A second chance at a career in music. Finding peace.

"You look like you've thought of something," Lacey said, her gaze piqued with curiosity.

I nodded. "Yeah, I did."

"What is it?"

My words came out shaky, belying the conviction I felt. "I'm moving to Nashville."

TWENTY-NINE

McKenzie

From the moment I sat on Dr. Florene Zott's sofa in her office that rainy Monday morning, I felt like a ball of anxiety that might simply bounce from the room. But even if I did, I wouldn't have made it far. My mom had come with me for moral support and was waiting in the lobby.

I'd squirmed through the entire intake process, my stomach knotting like a dainty necklace. Even the slightest movement would've had it tangled beyond recognition.

Dr. Zott tapped a few more notes into her laptop before looking at me through her thick cat-eye glasses.

"Let's talk a little about this panic attack you experienced Saturday night," she said, tucking a strand of her black bob behind her ear.

I tucked my hands under my legs in a vague attempt to stop my fidgeting. "What do you want to know?"

"What happened leading up to it?" she asked. "Were you under more stress than usual?"

I nodded, then told her about the pressure I'd been under

at the restaurant all week and how our staffing issues had bled over into Kia's party.

"Mmm," she murmured. "I imagine your sleep schedule was disrupted too because you were under so much pressure."

"Yeah. It was." I swallowed hard. "Things hadn't been so great with my boyfriend, either."

She tugged the sleeves of her cardigan down. "Tell me about that. Were the two of you fighting?"

"No," I replied. "It was nothing like that." I filled her in on how my relationship with Luca began and how things had started to pivot over the last two weeks. "Our lives had been on this parallel path since the fall, then all of a sudden, it was like we were going in two different directions."

I picked at my cuticle while I continued to explain the events that occurred Saturday night, including Luca's texts and frantic phone call. "He'd gotten some bad press—not just a little, either. A *lot*. It was like the gates of internet hell opened up and swallowed him whole."

"I imagine it was hard for you to give him the assurance he was probably seeking from you at that moment," she said. "Because you already had a lot on your plate."

"Not only did I not give it to him, but I essentially told him to just deal with it himself." I scrubbed my hands over my face. "It was partly because I was stressed out, but there was some resentment there too. I'd been feeling this sense of impending...*loss* because he would be going out on the road soon, and he wasn't affected at all. Or at least he didn't seem to be."

"Did you ever ask him?" Dr. Zott questioned.

I shook my head. "No, and I know that's my own fault. But there was a part of me that was afraid to say anything."

"Why?"

My gaze fell to my hands. Why *had* I been so scared? I didn't have a lot of experience with relationships, but I couldn't entirely blame my behavior on my lack of expertise in matters of the heart. There was something much deeper at play.

"Luca has a history of depression...of self-harming thoughts. Like my brother did." The words squeezed out of me like the last dredges of toothpaste from a nearly empty tube. "Brennan...he took his own life fifteen years ago this past October."

"I see," she said, pushing her glasses up the bridge of her narrow nose. "So you were worried that saying something might upset Luca and potentially send him down a rocky path?"

"I guess so," I said with a shrug. "It seemed like he was finally happy, you know? I didn't want to ruin that for him by being selfish. But when he called me like he did...something in me kind of snapped. Like, had he not stopped to consider what life would be like once he started touring? I can't just drop everything and be there all the time."

"Is it possible he thought you'd be going with him? That perhaps he took for granted that you'd always be there?"

"Maybe." I hadn't even considered that. It wasn't something we'd discussed, but then again, our communication had broken down. And even if he had thought that, I didn't *want* to go. My life was in Nashville.

She nodded and tilted her head. "I want to go back to your panic attack. Did it happen after your conversation with Luca?"

"No. Not right after," I answered. I relived the entire night, telling her every detail: my unanswered texts and calls, Kia driving me to the hobbit house, and the devastation I felt when we went inside and saw all of his stuff was missing. "He was just…*gone*. That's when I had the panic attack."

Just thinking about it made my palms begin to sweat and my stomach churn. I told her about Kia calling Dallas and Katie and how they found him in his apartment in Kentucky.

"Discovering Luca's place was empty must have been painful for you, given what happened with your brother." Dr. Zott's tone was gentle and compassionate.

"It was like finding out Brennan was gone all over again," I admitted, my eyes filling with tears. "And it was all my fault."

"You didn't make Luca leave," she said. "That was his choice."

"But I could have stopped him." I didn't know whether I was talking about Luca or Brennan anymore, but it didn't really matter. It was true for them both.

"I know it's easier to think that than to accept there's nothing you could have done, but I need you to understand that you're not responsible for Luca's actions," she said. "And the same is true for your brother."

"But if I'd just been there," I managed with a sniffle. "Maybe I could have changed things."

Dr. Zott clicked her laptop shut and set it aside, leaning forward.

"What do you think might have changed?" she asked.

"I don't know—maybe they wouldn't have left me," I choked out, a sob ripping through me. "Maybe I could have been enough to make them want to stay."

Her face softened. "Their choices had nothing to do with you and everything to do with them. There's no amount of *enoughness* that would have changed that."

"How can you know that?" I cried, hours…days…*years*

worth of pent-up anguish pouring out of me. "If I'd done more, if I'd loved them better, maybe I could have eased their pain."

"This is a hard truth, but it's one you need to hear," she said, her voice kind but firm. "Love is something—a very important something. But it's not everything, and contrary to what every platitude would have you believe, we need more than that—a lot more—to survive."

I wiped my face with the sleeve of my sweater.

"McKenzie, the shame you're feeling is just control with nowhere to go," she continued. "As humans, we want to believe we have the ability to turn the tides. It's easier to blame ourselves than it is to believe we are but a small ripple in the ocean, and it's going to keep moving with or without us."

"But how am I supposed to accept that?" I asked. "That there's nothing I can do."

"Whether you accept it or not doesn't change that it's true," she answered. "So, you're left with two choices. You can keep swimming against the current, knowing you'll exhaust yourself and the waves will pull you under, or you can let go."

I reached for a tissue from the glass coffee table and blew my nose. "Those are terrible choices."

"The first one is," she agreed. "But I think there's a certain amount of comfort in letting go of what we can't change."

"Comfort?" I echoed. "How is that comforting in any way?"

"Because when we finally acknowledge the things we can't control, we can release some of the burdens we carry. We can lighten our load and set our focus on the one thing we *do* have control over: ourselves."

Her words crashed over me as I blew out a breath and tried to imagine what it would feel like to let go of the blame and expectations I'd set on myself. One word came to mind. *Free.*

She went on. "That kind of change doesn't occur all at once, but with time, I think we can get you there."

"Do you think I'll continue having panic attacks?" My voice came out in a rasp that was barely above a whisper.

She twisted her lips to the corner of her mouth. "It's possible, but I think we can lessen the chances if we get a handle on what's triggering them."

"We have to," I said. "I don't want to feel like this anymore."

She nodded. "All right. If you're up for it, I'd like to start with biweekly sessions where we focus on mindfulness and shifting your perspective around the events of your past. In doing that, we'll also effectively help you change your narrative for the future. All I ask is that you stick with me. If something doesn't work, that's okay. There are a lot of things we can try, but we just need to take it one step at a time."

I sighed. It wasn't a guarantee, but it was better than the alternative. I didn't want to live my life being slowly consumed by shame. I'd been holding onto the guilt I felt over my brother's death, because in a strange way, it was all I had left of him. However, there was no amount of remorse, no sum of love that would ever bring him back, no matter how much I wanted it to.

The same was true of Luca. I didn't know what lie ahead for us or if there even *was* an us anymore. But I did know that I deserved to find healing. To be the best version of myself for him, my mom, my friends, and anyone else who might come along. Above all else, I deserved it for me.

I turned my gaze to Dr. Zott. "Let's do it."

———

"How do you feel after your first therapy session?" my mom asked once the server took our breakfast orders at Biscuit Love after my appointment. Katie said she was feeling a lot better and insisted I take the day off. She'd driven back to Nashville early that morning so she could be at the restaurant, leaving Dallas with Luca.

"A little drained," I answered. "I feel like I could sleep for a week."

She nodded. "That's understandable. These past couple of days have been hard."

"I wish I'd realized sooner how much I still needed help," I admitted, taking a sip of my water. "But I can't go back and change it, and I'm trying this new thing where I don't let myself worry about things that are out of my control."

She raised her brows, a mixture of surprise and amusement on her face.

I laughed. "Don't look at me like that. I said it's a *new* thing."

"No, I think that's great," she assured me. "It sounds like this therapist might be a good fit. I'm proud of you for taking that first step. I know it wasn't easy."

"Thanks," I said, "but I can't take all the credit. I don't know if I would've gone had it not been for you and Kia giving me the push I needed."

"It doesn't matter how you got there. What matters is that you did it." She glanced down, scanning her menu. "Have you gotten any updates on Luca?"

I took in a breath. "Actually, he texted me as I was

walking into my appointment." It was the first time I'd heard from him since Saturday night.

"What did he say?"

I recited the message I already knew by heart. *I'm sorry. For everything. Can I see you?*

"Katie told me earlier that Luca saw his therapist yesterday," I said, clearing my throat. "She said he and Dallas were heading back to Nashville later this afternoon."

"Did you text him back?"

"Not yet."

"You think he's going back to the hobbit house?" she asked.

I shook my head. "I doubt it. He'll probably go back to Dallas and Katie's. I mean, he left his key, so I'm taking it that chapter is over."

She lifted her gaze to me. "I think it would be good for you to see him. Clear the air."

"I want to," I said, running a hand along my arm, my leg bouncing beneath the table with such force that I caused it to vibrate.

Her forehead creased. "I feel like there's a *but* coming."

"I love Luca," I said with a sigh. "But I guess I don't know where we stand."

"Do you still want to be with him?"

"I do," I answered quickly. "It's just that I'm also feeling a little…gun-shy. Even if I understand *why* he left, it doesn't change the fact that he did so without a single word. How can I be sure he won't run again?"

"I don't think you *can* be," she said. "I know you want a guarantee it won't happen again, but there's no way to know for certain. You just need to have faith and hope for the best."

"Maybe you haven't noticed this about me, Mom, but I'm not exactly a risk-taking faith-haver."

She chuckled. "Some things are worth the risk, though. Some people are too."

"So, you're saying you think we should stay together." It was a statement, not a question.

"I didn't say that."

"You didn't *not* say that."

"When you two were together, you seemed…*happy*. Not content, not just going through the motions, but happy for the first time since before Brennan died." She gave me a wistful smile. "And I want that for you, you know? That's the kind of love and joy you deserve."

"I'm just afraid of losing him, and I guess this whole situation reminded me how real of a possibility that is."

"That's true of any relationship," she said.

We understood that more than most. It was the reason I'd worked so hard to keep people at a safe distance since Brennan's death. People couldn't leave if I never opened the door for them to begin with.

"If you were to walk away now, you'd still be losing him, just in a different way. Whether you stay or go, it won't be easy. But this is where you've got to pick your hard. Only you can decide if that means pushing him away or letting him in." She reached for my hand across the table. "Kenz, all we can do is love people as much as we can while we can. There are no guarantees."

I squeezed her fingers. "I know."

And despite the risks, I knew exactly what my heart wanted. I longed to run into Luca's arms and never look back. But there was still a nagging question lingering in the back of my mind. Even if he was what I wanted…even if we loved each other deeply…would the fear that one day I'd lose him ever really go away?

AFTER MY MOM WENT HOME THAT AFTERNOON, I CURLED UP on the couch with Earl Grey and Binx, my phone staring holes in my head from beside me on the cushion. I needed to call Luca, but every time I reached for the device, my hand hovered over it before retreating back to my lap.

I groaned to myself. "Get it together, McKenzie."

Just the thought of talking to him made my palms start to sweat. My heart raced as I imagined the last time I'd heard his voice and what transpired afterward—the devastation I felt when I went inside the hobbit house only to find he was already gone.

"You can do this," I said to myself.

Binx regarded me through squinted eyes as though he was saying 'you sure about that?'.

I wasn't. Not even a little bit.

I scooped up the device, illuminating the screen. I swallowed hard as I swiped my finger over it and found his contact. Before I could stop myself, I pressed the call button.

He answered on the second ring. "McKenzie?"

My mouth opened but no sound came out.

"Are you there?"

"Yeah," I managed. "I'm here. Sorry."

"God, I miss you."

My chest ached. "I miss you too."

"How are you feeling?" His voice was thick with emotion, heavy with the weight of his question.

"I…I don't really know," I admitted. "I had my first

therapy appointment this morning. It was…good. I think it'll help."

His shaky breath traveled through the cell towers. "I'm sorry, McKenzie. I'm so fucking sorry."

"It's okay." Was it, though?

"No," he said, answering for me. "It isn't. After everything you've been through…I should have handled things differently. I wasn't thinking."

"I know," I whispered. "And I'm sorry too."

"You have nothing to apologize for."

"I didn't exactly handle things so well, either," I said. "I was stressed out and—"

He cut me off. "And I should've known that. But I was so wrapped up in my own shit that I stopped paying attention."

"What I don't understand is why you didn't call someone else. Why you didn't wait for me. *Something*." Tears stung the corners of my eyes. "Anything besides leaving."

"Because that's all I know how to do."

My heart sank. Would there ever come a time when that wasn't his first instinct?

"But I want that to change," he continued, as though he were reading my mind. "I went back to therapy yesterday. I never should've stopped. I let myself get lured into this false sense of security, thinking I was all well and good, but I wasn't. I've got to keep doing the work even when I'm not falling apart because that's what's going to hold me together when the chips are down."

I pressed my tongue onto the roof of my mouth, trying to keep from crying.

"Yeah. I guess I kind of realized the same thing," I said. "But God, it sucks. It sucks so much."

"Yeah, it does," he rasped. A silent beat passed between us

before he spoke again. "Dallas and I are coming back to Nashville this afternoon. I was wondering if…Can I see you?"

I wanted to say yes. I didn't want to hurt him, but I couldn't make the words come out.

My hands trembled, and I dug my fingers into the cushion. "I want to see you, Luca…but I…"

"Do you…not want to be with me anymore?" he asked, the words painted with sorrow.

"No, it's not that," I answered. "I just…I think I need a little more time. To catch my breath."

I longed to hold him, to be held by him, but I couldn't. Not yet. Not while I was still so jumbled up inside.

"All right," he said, and I detected the slightest break in his voice. "Take as much time as you need. I'm not going anywhere."

I'm not going anywhere.

The words sent a warning flare shooting up from my heart. That was exactly what I was worried about.

I released a slow exhale. "Okay."

Another pause stretched between us with only the soft sounds of our breathing on the line. It took every ounce of self-control I had not to tell him I changed my mind—that I had to see him right away because having him in front of me was the only surefire way to keep him with me, to keep him safe. But I kept my mouth clamped shut. If I ever hoped to truly let go of things I couldn't control, I had to start somewhere.

"I love you, McKenzie," he said.

I pressed the phone tighter against my ear as though that would bring him closer.

"I love you too." The tears I'd been fighting spilled onto my cheeks. I loved him more than anything in the world, but I had to figure out how to love me too. And that meant taking some time apart. "I'll talk to you soon."

"Soon," he echoed before the line went dead.

I squeezed my eyes shut and didn't move a single muscle, desperate to hang on to him a little longer.

THIRTY

Luca

"You're really gonna sell this place?" Dallas asked Monday afternoon as I finished packing my bags to head back to Nashville with him and Emilia. "I never thought I'd see the day."

"It's time," I answered.

"What did McKenzie say when you told her you're gonna move?" he asked, petting Emilia where she sat beside him on the foot of the bed.

I stuffed another T-shirt in my suitcase. "I didn't tell her yet."

"Why not?"

"I didn't want her to feel pressured. Our relationship is on shaky ground right now, and I don't want her to think she's the only reason I'm moving."

"She's not?"

I shook my head. "No. I'd be lying if I said she wasn't a big part of it, but there's a lot more to it. I need to be near my people—my family."

Dallas splayed his hand over his chest in mock surprise. "Do my ears deceive me, or did you just admit that you need us?"

I tossed a wadded up sock at him.

"I hope that was clean," he said when it bounced off his head.

"It wasn't."

He laughed and threw it back at me. "Seriously, man, I think this is a big step."

"It feels like one," I admitted. "Even though the gang has started going their separate ways, Nashville is still home base for everyone. I'm tired of living on an island. I want to be nearby."

"I'm glad." He gave me a faint smile. "That way I can be just a few minutes away the next time I need to come beat down your door."

"Well, I appreciate it," I said, closing the large suitcase and zipping it. "But you won't need to do that again."

He arched a brow at me.

"I'm gonna make sure you and Katie have a key. Derek and Jo too," I explained. "I've kept myself locked away for years and look where it got me. I think it's time I keep some doors open for a change."

He put a hand on my arm and gave it a squeeze. "I'm proud of you, brother."

"Is it weird if I say that I'm proud of myself too?" I asked with a laugh.

"Nah," he replied with a grin. "I think that's called *growth*."

I chuckled. "What a concept."

"So, do you think Darcey Dubois, the realtor extraordinaire, will be able to convince the owner of the hobbit house to sell?" he asked.

My chest constricted when he referred to the place by the nickname McKenzie had given it.

"I hope so. I pretty much told her I could pay whatever they wanted in cash," I said. "But if not, that's okay. I'll find something else. At any rate, I have the rental till the end of next month. That gives me some time to figure it out."

"I know that place is special to you."

I shrugged. "It is, but it's special because of the memories. I'll take those with me wherever I go. Speaking of going, are you ready to get out of here? We need to get on the road so I can meet Darcey to pick up that extra key."

"You bet," he said, rising to his feet, tucking Emilia under his arm. "You got everything?"

"Everything I care about," I said. "The movers can get the rest when the time comes."

"You don't think you'll come back?" he asked as we padded into the living room where my other two bags and guitar were waiting to be loaded into the car.

"I know I won't. I'm dropping my key off with a realtor Darcey knows in the area on the way out of town so they can get it on the market."

I took a breath and glanced around.

"Do you want me to give you a minute?" he asked.

"No," I answered. "I think me and this place have done all we can for each other. All that's left to do is go."

"Then let's do it," he said, gripping the handle of one of my suitcases and rolling it toward the door.

I dug my keys out of my jacket pocket and followed behind, grabbing the rest of my stuff. Once I'd moved everything to the front stoop, I pulled the door closed and turned my key in the lock one last time. It was the place that held me when I thought I had nowhere else to go. But I didn't need it anymore.

Dallas clapped his hand over my shoulder. "Ready to go home?"

Home.

My heart swelled as I shut the door. It took nearly half my life, but I finally had somewhere I belonged.

It didn't matter if it was the hobbit house or if I ended up having to find someplace else. While I loved that little cottage in Leipers Fork, it wasn't the building that made it home. It was the people—my people. And I'd carry them with me for the rest of my life, no matter where I ended up.

GRACE ARRIVED AT THE HOBBIT HOUSE LATE TUESDAY afternoon with her binder clutched in her hands. The second I opened the door, she flung her arms around me, squeezing me like she thought she might never get the chance to hug me again.

"It's good to see you," she said when she finally pulled away.

"I'm sorry I scared you like that." I stepped aside, allowing her to enter.

"What matters is that you're here now."

I led her to the living room where my guitar was still propped against the sofa. Randy McNutt was perched on the coffee table beside my open notebook, where he'd kept me company while I'd put my feelings to music earlier that day.

"So, how are you doing?" Grace took a seat in the armchair across from where I sat on the couch.

"It's a day to day thing," I answered. "Minute to minute, really. I've avoided looking at social media, the internet, anything that could send me backward right now."

"That's good," she said. "You've got to protect your peace somehow. I've been keeping track of what's coming out, and I'll only tell you what you need to know."

"How bad has it been?" I asked, crossing one leg over the other.

She shrugged. "Mostly people sharing the same stories over and over again. Like the one about that Tate McCreedy asshat. There's not been a lot of new stuff coming out. You kept a low profile for a while. Nobody was able to photograph you for months, so most of what's out there is old news. That's gonna be in your favor with the press when you decide to move forward. *If* you decide to move forward."

"That's actually what I wanted to talk to you about," I said.

"I figured that's why I'm here." She leaned forward, her elbows on her knees. "How are you feeling about everything? Do you know what you want to do?"

I gave a wry chuckle. "It depends on the time of day. Part of me wants to shelve the record altogether and disappear from the limelight for good."

"I don't blame you one bit, and I don't think there's a wrong choice here. There's certainly not an easy one."

"No, there isn't," I said. "But I think what I want to do and what I *need* to do are two different things."

"How so?" she asked.

"My gut instinct is to run." I leaned back, propping my arm across the back of the cushion. "To kill the album, the tour, my public image. To let people think what they want, while I fade away into the news cycle until people eventually forget my name. But I'm tired of running, Grace. That's all I've ever done."

"Does that mean you're considering putting the record out?"

"Yeah. I guess I am." I ran my hand along the back of my neck. "I'm scared out of my mind, and I might live to regret it. But I *know* I'll regret it if I don't take this chance on myself. I'll always wonder what I could have done if I'd been brave enough to try."

She smiled. "Well, you know I'll be by your side every step of the way. What can I do to help?"

I chewed the inside of my cheek. "I want to know what you think I should do, what our next move should be."

"What if we find a way to get your side of things out there? Give people the chance to get to know you."

"How?"

"An in-depth interview," she replied.

"Hmm," I said, my finger rubbing along my jaw. "Where? Something like *Rolling Stone*?"

She shook her head. "I'm thinking more like television."

"Maybe Jo would be willing to do it?" I suggested. She was our television connection, not to mention, her father was a legend in journalism.

"I don't know." She twisted her lips to the corner of her mouth. "I think it needs to be someone you don't know. Someone who can't be accused of tossing you softball questions."

I sucked in a shaky breath. "Well, I guess if I'm already dipping my toe outside my comfort zone, I might as well dive into the deep end."

"You don't have to do this if you don't want to. It's just an idea."

"No, I think you're right," I said, picking at a thread on my jeans. "There's a lot of me I've kept hidden over the years, and if I want people to trust me, I need to give them a reason to."

"You don't owe anyone anything."

"I do," I said. "I owe it to myself. If people hear what I have to say and they still don't like me, fine. But I have to like me."

"Okay," she agreed. "I'll put out some feelers for an interview. Maybe Jo will have some ideas."

Grace's phone chimed from her purse, and she reached for it. Her eyes scanned across the screen before she grinned and placed it back inside her bag.

"We can talk more about this later," she said, rising to her feet. "But right now we have to go."

I furrowed my brow. "What? I thought we were having a meeting."

"We are. Were. Meeting's adjourned. We gotta leave."

"And where exactly are we going?"

"It's a surprise."

"I don't know if I'm up for surprises at the moment, Grace."

"This is a surprise you're gonna love." She stepped closer and extended her hand to help me up. "I just need you to trust me."

I narrowed my eyes at her, and she shoved her hand closer. "Who was it that texted you?"

"Trust me," she insisted. "And you'll find out soon enough."

Finally, I took her hand but not before giving her a suspicious side-eye.

"All right. Let's go."

"I STILL CAN'T BELIEVE YOU GUYS ARE HERE." I'D BEEN AT Jax and Liv's dining table for the last hour, surrounded by all of my friends for the first time in over a year. Ella, Cash, Antoni, and his husband Nate had all come into town so we could get the whole gang back together. Derek, Jo, Katie, and Dallas were there too, along with all the kids, who had since retreated to the playroom with Jax and Liv's sitter to give the adults some time together.

It was almost perfect. The only thing I was missing was having McKenzie by my side.

"I told you this was a surprise you'd love," Grace said, poking me in the arm from where she sat beside me.

I held up my hands like two white flags. "As usual, you were right."

"She gets that from me, you know," Ella quipped. "I have a one hundred percent success rate."

Cash tapped a finger to his chin. "Is that so?"

Antoni snorted, pinning Ella with a playful stare. "Math's never been your strong suit, has it?"

"Who needs math when you have an iPhone calculator and a dazzling personality like mine?" Ella teased before turning her attention to me. "Okay, listen, I've been dying to talk to you about your new music. 'Death Row' is masterful. I mean…wow. I just…I had no idea you could write like that."

My cheeks burned. "Honestly? Neither did I."

"There's a reason for all the early Grammy buzz," Derek said. "It's an amazing record, Luca. You should be proud."

"God knows we are," Dallas added with a smile.

"How are you feeling about…things?" Cash asked, tiptoeing around the enormous media-frenzied elephant in the room. "You're still planning to release it, aren't you?"

"You have to," Jo insisted. "It's incredible."

I released a slow exhale. "Yeah, I am. I'm terrified, but this is something I have to do, even if just to prove to myself that I can."

"Hell yes, you can." Antoni pointed a slender finger at me. "You're Luca fucking Sterling. You can do any damn thing you want."

I chuckled. "I don't know about that."

"Well, we do," Katie said. "We all believe in you."

Jax met my eyes across the table. "Damn right, we do."

"Is there anything we can do to help?" Cash asked.

Grace spoke up. "Actually, there is. We were talking earlier about what we can do to shift the narrative surrounding Luca right now, and I was thinking an exclusive televised interview might be a good idea. It would give him the opportunity to address some of these stories floating around and let people get to know the real him."

"Jo could do it," Derek suggested, but she shook her head.

"As much as I'd love to," Jo said, "I think I'm too close."

"Exactly," Grace agreed. "We need someone who's more of a neutral party. But I was thinking you might have some connections for someone who *could* do it."

Jo twirled a piece of her auburn hair around her finger. "Definitely. How soon are you thinking?"

"As soon as possible," I answered. "This week. I don't want to let this go on too long without addressing it."

"I have some people in mind," Jo replied. "I'll make some calls first thing tomorrow."

"I don't want to discourage you from doing it if it's important to you," Liv said, taking a sip of her wine. "But what do you hope to gain from doing this interview? I worry about what happens if it isn't received the way you're hoping."

I understood Liv's hesitancy. Not long after Jax and Liv made their relationship public, she'd been the target of a lot of online hate.

"People are fickle," she continued. "When they love you, they're all about you. But they can also turn on a dime. I just don't want to see you get hurt if this goes south."

"That's a valid point," I said. "And it's something I'm still kind of working through. Ultimately, I think I have to distance myself from the noise—the bad *and* the good, because both get inside my head. The bad makes me feel like I'm a fuckup, and the good makes me feel like I can *never* fuck up. Either way, I'm left with a mile-long list of unreasonable expectations and a mountain of pressure."

Ella tilted her head, her brows drawn together. "But the internet is a cesspool of half-baked hot takes and lies. How do you tune that shit out altogether?"

"I don't know that I can," I answered. "At least not completely, but I can start by giving Grace access to all my social media. She can be my eyes and ears and keep me informed of anything important."

Grace gave an emphatic nod. "Nobody gets to you without going through me first."

"Look at your cute little guard dog," Ella joked, wrinkling her nose at her daughter.

"I think that's smart," Jo said. "People will always find something to hate on. One day last week, after I did my segment on the *Today* show, I got at least a hundred emails about how hideous my dress was. It happens all the time. Seriously, it's bananas."

"What?" Katie asked.

Jo nodded. "Yep. It happened when I was on the news in smaller markets too. People suck everywhere."

Ella grimaced. "Well, that's comforting."

I shifted my gaze to Jo. "How do you cope with it?"

"It takes practice," she answered. "I think you also have to consider where the feedback is coming from and how much information they have when they're giving it. Do these people know you? Do they love you or care about you? Our loudest criticisms usually come from those trying to poison the soil where we're planted just to keep us from growing."

Nate snapped his fingers repeatedly like he was at a poetry reading in a coffeehouse.

"Hot damn, yes ma'am," Antoni said, clapping his hands together.

"Jo hit the nail on the head." Cash leaned forward with his elbows on the table. "I think an interview is the right move. There will still be those you can't please, but they're not your people."

"Your story is important, Luca," Dallas said. "It deserves to be told."

"I think it does too," Liv added. "I just want to make sure you're okay. Your well-being is what's important."

"I think I need to do this *for* my well-being." I paused and blew out a breath. "The interviews I did over the last couple of weeks barely scratched the surface of what led me to this point in my life. I don't think I owe people every piece of me. There are some things I'll keep for myself, but I feel like I'm finally ready to…let people know me."

"Anyone that gets to know you is lucky," Katie said. "You're a pretty awesome guy."

Dallas shrugged. "I guess he's all right."

"If you're comfortable putting yourself out there, I think it's a solid choice," Jax said. "People have a bad habit of just filling in the blanks for us. There's power in owning your story."

His words echoed through my mind. For a long time, I didn't want people to know my history. The patchwork of my past was sewn with shame, guilt, and resentment. That's why I kept it hidden away, stuffed under boxes of things I'd rather forget in the dingy attic of my mind. But when I finally brought it down the rickety stairs and carried it into the sun, I realized there was so much more to it than I remembered. There were golden threads of strength and endurance and unbreakable strings that connected me to those I loved.

There was disgrace and glory. Pain and beauty. Darkness and light. The fabric of my life was woven in dualities, each one a vital part of what made me.

I slid my fingers through my hair. "You're right, Jax. I hadn't thought about it like that before, but that's exactly what I need to do: take ownership of my story. I can't control how other people receive it. All I can do is be honest and tell it."

Jo nodded. "Yep. Other people's opinions of you are none of your business. What really counts is what *you* think."

"And what we think, of course," Ella said with a grin. "But we're gonna support you no matter what."

I returned her smile. "Thanks, Ella."

The prospect of doing an in-depth interview still terrified me, but knowing I had my friends on my side made it easier, somehow. Regardless of what happened, I could turn off my phone and television screen. Once I put my story out there, it was up to others to interpret it how they wanted, to take it how they choose. At the end of the day, it didn't matter what they thought—good or bad, whether they cared or were completely indifferent.

What mattered most were the faces right in front of me and the one who wasn't there, but who was always at the fore-front of my mind.

THIRTY-ONE

McKenzie

Tuesday went by in a series of well-rehearsed motions at work. It felt good to let my brain shift into autopilot and stop thinking for a few hours. Katie and Dallas had been in and were excited about a surprise family dinner they'd planned to lift Luca's spirits. Ella and Cash had dropped by the restaurant for lunch and to say hi. It made me smile to imagine Luca's face when he saw all of his friends gathered together. Part of me wished I could be there with him, but knowing they were there holding space for him gave me the chance to relax a little and think about what I needed.

I stopped by The Piccadilly Deli on the way home for a to-go burger and was on my couch in my pajamas by 7:30 p.m. Binx and Earl Grey snoozed beside me, seemingly exhausted from their day of doing absolutely nothing, while I flipped through the offerings of every streaming service imaginable. But nothing caught my eye or sounded remotely interesting.

"What should we watch, guys?" I asked the cats. "Give me something to work with here."

Binx opened his eyes to a slit, glaring at me as though saying *I'm attempting to watch the backs of my eyelids, peasant, but you won't shut your trap.*

To further prove they would be of no help, Earl Grey stretched his stout body out long, looking like a fluffy loaf of bread.

"You guys need to get jobs."

I clicked the television off and opted for some music instead, playing My Chemical Romance on my phone while I finished dinner. Once I was finished and discarded my trash, I piddled around the kitchen, wiping down the already clean surfaces.

As the music played softly in the background, I thought of Luca and wondered how his dinner was going. I imagined how good it probably felt for him to see the friends he'd been missing, and I was hit with a pang of envy. Not because I wasn't there, but because I couldn't just call up or visit the person I missed most.

I'd have given anything to talk to Brennan…to hear his voice. I tapped my fingers along the counter, desperate for a place to channel some of my anxious energy.

The worn composition notebook I used to write out to-do lists and what I needed from the grocery store stared up at me from its place beside my old stand mixer. It reminded me of the notebooks my friends and I would pass back and forth to each other in middle school, only those had been decorated with stickers, while this one was adorned with coffee rings.

Letters.

It had been years since I'd written one.

I could write one to Brennan.

Sure, I could just talk to him out loud, but something

about that always felt a little too *Ghost Whisperer* to me. But a letter…that was something I could do.

I dug a pen from the junk drawer, carrying it and the notebook back to the couch. Binx gave me the stink eye for disturbing him as I sat on the floor with my back against the sofa and the composition book open on the coffee table. I leafed through until I found the next blank page.

Should I write the date in the corner? Does that matter? God, McKenzie, it's not like Brennan is actually gonna read this, and even if he could, he wouldn't give two shits about what date it is.

I tapped my pen against the paper for a moment, then silenced the music playing on my phone until the only sound left was that of the thoughts bouncing through my brain. What was I so worried about? It wasn't like Brennan was going to be looking over my shoulder, reading every word, replying to my unanswerable questions or feeling like he had to comfort me as I told him how much I missed him. But maybe that was exactly what had my stomach twisted in knots. What if I wrote the letter and didn't feel his presence at all?

I blew out a breath and poised my pen over the notebook one more time, attempting to quiet my mind.

You can do this. It's not the next great American novel. It's just a letter. Write something.

I closed my eyes for a moment and pictured Brennan the way I remembered him—tall and lanky, no longer a boy but not quite a man, with dark hair and green eyes that matched my own. I imagined him leaning against the doorway of my childhood bedroom the way he used to do when he'd ask how my day was, pretending he cared about my friends' latest drama because he knew it mattered to me.

Finally, I began to write.

Dear Brennan,

I hate everything about this. That the only way I can speak to you is through letters you'll never get to read. But that's where we are.

Time is weird. Because the longer you're gone, somehow the years feel shorter, and the time that stretches between when you were here and when you left almost seems to shrink. I guess it's because time slips by faster the older I get. Do you remember those lazy summer nights when we were kids? We'd spend hours catching lightning bugs, scooping them into mason jars before setting them free. Or Sunday evenings watching America's Funniest Home Videos together while we drank homemade milkshakes. I swear time stood still back then. Minutes felt like hours.

Everything we wanted to do felt so far off. At first, we wished for our birthdays, for Christmas, for spring break. Then we started wishing to be grown-ups, to be independent, to be on our own. I just never thought that I'd truly be on my own—that you wouldn't be here, doing life with me. I wouldn't have wished so much time away if I'd known how little I had left with you.

We had so many plans, Brennan. You were gonna play in a band while I worked in a bakery, and together we'd scrounge up enough cash to spend a summer traveling the country with nothing but a couple backpacks, sacks filled with enough candy to rot our teeth out, and My Chem blasting through the speakers. We'd get tattoos, and Mom would pretend to be horrified, but she'd secretly love them. You wanted to be a dad one day, to be the father we never had growing up. You would've been the best dad, and we both know I would've been the best aunt ever. But that's not how it happened, and some days I'm still angry at you for it.

It doesn't make me feel good to admit that, but there you go. You abandoned our plans for one of your own. But more than that, you abandoned me. I know you didn't mean to, but that's how it felt. How it still feels sometimes.

You've missed out on so much of my life, and I might be able to get past that if losing you hadn't caused me to miss out on it too. Do you know how hard it's been for me to let people in? I live in constant fear of a phone call, a single sentence, taking away the people I care about. And that's why I never allowed myself the luxury of loving someone. But then I met Luca, and I didn't have a choice. And even if I did, I think I still would have chosen him because he makes me feel things I never thought I'd feel. He gets me in a way no one else does.

I love him so much it terrifies me. Because what if I lose him like I lost you?

You were my best friend. I know Dad leaving affected you more than it did me because you were older at the time, but still you did everything you could to soften the blow. You played with me as much as I wanted, even when I got on your last nerve. You never turned me away. I guess it hurts so much because you were my safe place. You weren't supposed to leave. We were supposed to always have each other.

Maybe you didn't tell me what you were going through because you wanted to shield me from your pain. You always tried to protect me. But the one thing you couldn't protect me from was losing you.

If I could go back to those endless summer nights, even knowing how it would all end, I'd go willingly. I'd lose you all over again if I got to love you a moment longer. Maybe there's a lesson somewhere in all this. Because if I knew then that I was going to lose you, if I knew there was an expiration date, I wouldn't love you less or distance myself. If anything, I'd love you more. I'd stay up later on those summer nights, collecting little glimmers of your laughter and your smile. I'd watch you glow in the darkness all over again, even knowing that one day I'd have to set you free.

I've beaten myself black and blue thinking I could have done something differently. That I could have saved you. But I'm not that powerful. Or maybe power has nothing to do with control. Maybe it's the ability to enjoy the light while it shines and then let it go.

All I know for sure is that I can't keep carrying this around anymore because it's suffocating me. There's so much light I'm missing because this weight on my chest keeps pushing the air from my lungs and blowing it out. So, it's time for me to forgive us both. I want to remember the fireflies and the way they shimmered. I want to remember the way they rose toward the sky once they broke free from the confines of the jar we kept them in.

And I'll remember you that way too, Brennan.

I love you.

Tears fell from my eyes, blurring the ink as I signed my name. I sucked in a breath and I tore the pages from the binding, folding them into thirds. Maybe I'd take the letter to his gravesite and tuck it into the vase that sat atop his marker. Perhaps I'd hold onto it and revisit the words when I needed to. Or maybe this would be the first of many letters to Brennan, where I'd write down glimmers from my own life for him.

Maybe these letters to my brother would become therapeutic like a journal or the songs Luca wrote. Putting pen to paper seemed to help him—maybe it could help me too. If nothing else, it would serve as a record of all the lights in my life. When Brennan and I finally saw each other on the other side, we'd have years to catch up on. I wanted to make sure I didn't leave anything out.

THIRTY-TWO

Luca

It was around 10 p.m. the night of our family dinner. Everyone else had already left Jax and Liv's for the evening except Ella and Cash. We were all sitting around talking, making sure to keep our volume low so as not to disturb the children sleeping upstairs. Mama, Liv's sassy tuxedo cat, was curled up in Jax's lap.

"This is wild," I said, glancing at the faces surrounding me. "It seems like yesterday when Jax met Liv, and we all became friends."

Cash nodded. "Back before kids and weddings and whole new careers."

"I miss living here," Ella admitted, leaning against the arm of the sofa and laying her feet across Cash's lap. "Being close to everyone."

"Do you think you guys might ever move back?" I asked.

"We'd love to, but it'll be a while," Cash answered. "The label is growing in LA, so that's where I'll need to be for the next few years. We'll still visit often in the meantime, though. More often the older Betty gets."

"Yeah, airplanes are stressful enough without wondering if your child is going to require an in-flight exorcism." Ella blew out a breath. "But since Grace has decided to abandon me, the woman who gave her life, our visits will be more frequent."

Grace chuckled. "By abandon, she means get married and move here so I can run the Nashville branch of Carrie On Records."

I nudged her arm. "What? That's amazing. Congratulations, Grace."

"How is this possible?" Jax asked, shaking his head in disbelief. "I swear, you were only seventeen two weeks ago, and now you're all grown up."

"I can't wait till you're living here." Liv smiled at Grace, who may as well have been her niece. "I'll get to see you all the time."

"Reveling in my pain, I see," Ella teased Liv.

"Have you set a date for the wedding?" I asked Grace.

"Next October," she said. "So, we've got about a year and a half to plan it."

"Are you sure you don't want to be a spinster?" Ella asked.

"I think I'll pass," Grace replied. "Actually, Luca, I was thinking I'd love to get married at the hobbit house if you end up keeping it."

"I'd love that." I said. "I'm hoping to hear something by the end of the week."

"I really hope you get it. I know how much that place means to you." Grace beamed before stifling a yawn.

I glanced over at her sleepy eyes. "It's getting late."

"Yeah," Ella agreed, as everyone rose to stand. "It's about an hour and a half past my bedtime. But man, tonight was fun. I needed this."

"Me too," I said as we all exchanged hugs.

Cash clapped me on the back. "You know we'll do anything we can to help you prepare for that interview."

"We all will," Jax added. "We're here for you, man."

Liv placed a hand on my shoulder. "Always. We love you."

"I love you guys too," I said, amazed at how much more easily the words came.

Ella stepped in front of me, and I embraced her.

"Can I talk to you for a minute before we go?" I asked her.

She pulled back so she could look into my eyes, her brow furrowed with concern.

"Cash, do you mind getting Betty while I talk to Luca?" she asked.

"Of course," he said. "Take all the time you need."

"Let's go to the kitchen," she said, guiding me from the room. Once we were away from everyone, she spoke again. "What's up? Is everything okay?"

"Yeah." I swallowed hard. "I just...I want to apologize....for not being there when your mom passed away."

"Hey, it's okay—" she began before I cut her off.

"No," I said. "It isn't. I care about you, Ella. I should've been there."

"I understand why you couldn't be." She placed her hands on my arms. "But you're here now, and that means everything."

"How've you been holding up?" I asked, leaning against the counter.

She gave me a sad smile. "I'm okay. It's been hard. With her Alzheimer's, it felt like I lost her so many times before the end. I miss her, but there's also a sense of peace in knowing she's not suffering anymore."

I nodded. "I'm so sorry."

"I'm sorry too. I wasn't there for you the way I wish I had been," she said, her voice soft. "We should have tried harder to reach you…to find you."

"It wouldn't have mattered," I assured her. "I wasn't ready to be found. But I am now."

"I'm glad. Our little group…our family…it's not the same without you. And I'm sorry we ever let you forget that."

"You didn't let me forget," I said. "I just…I guess I couldn't allow myself to believe it. Because that meant I belonged somewhere, and I had something to lose."

"Don't you worry. We're not going anywhere," she promised. "You're stuck with us whether you like it or not."

"You know, I think I'm actually okay with that."

"You better be." She grinned, moving to stand beside me. "So, you and McKenzie, huh?"

I chuckled. "I'm amazed it took you this long to ask."

"To be clear, it was killing me."

"Yeah, me and McKenzie." Thinking of her made my chest ache. God, I missed her so much. "We're giving each other a little space right now, but I think we're gonna make it through." The words came out with more conviction than I felt. "I hope so, at least."

"I hope you do too. Grace told me how happy you are with her." She put an arm around me and gave me a squeeze. "You deserve that. You deserve to be loved."

I felt like it might be true. Maybe I could show up exactly as I was, imperfections and all, and be worthy of love anyway. My friends had shown me that I was still loved even when I felt unlovable. They'd still be there when I wasn't the best version of myself or if I tried to push them away. If they could love me then, maybe I could find a way to love me too.

Grace appeared in the doorway, yawning.

"You about ready to go?"

I nodded and gave Ella one more hug.

"Thanks again," I whispered. "For being here."

"Always," she said.

Grace and I headed to the car, and we started back toward the hobbit house. She sang along to the radio, but my thoughts were on the McKenzie-sized hole in my heart.

I wished I hadn't left the way I did the other night because even though I hadn't intended to, I'd hurt her. But I'd come to realize that having depression was like waiting for a storm. It wasn't a matter of *if* one would roll in but *when*. And I was so waterlogged Saturday that I hadn't realized McKenzie was stuck in a deluge of her own. I'd been looking to her to hold the umbrella when I should've been holding her while we waited for the rain to stop. Now all I could do was hope that this storm would eventually pass and we'd weather anything else life threw at us together.

***

BY WEDNESDAY AFTERNOON, GRACE AND JO HAD MANAGED to secure an interview for Friday evening. Apparently, the noise surrounding me was enough to warrant a prime-time spot with Warren Wright, the host of one of the most popular prime time news shows. The network had been so excited to secure an exclusive live interview that they bumped whatever had been on their schedule in favor of "Live and Uncut with Luca Sterling." I still wasn't turning on the television, but Grace let me know that the first promo came out the day they booked the spot. By Thursday morning, *everyone* knew it was happening.

I did everything I could to take my mind off what was coming. I had therapy with Lacey, I channeled my nervous energy into a song I was working on, and I even decided on a whim to go get my first tattoo.

As I lay in bed Friday morning, my finger swiped over the small semicolon printed on the inside of my left wrist. It could easily be covered by a shirtsleeve, a watch, or a bracelet. Nobody even had to know it was there, but *I* would know. It would be my silent reminder that I had a story worth telling—worthy of continuing.

I grabbed my phone off the nightstand and checked the time. It was a little after 9 a.m. I needed to get up and get myself together before the television crew arrived, taking over the hobbit house. Everyone I cared about would be here for moral support, letting me know they loved me and believed in me no matter how things shook out. Well, almost everyone.

McKenzie still hadn't reached out, and the more time that passed, the more I worried we might not survive this after all —that the fear I'd caused her had been too much after what she'd been through, and though I didn't blame her, it still hurt. Part of me wanted to call her. Because despite everything that happened, I knew she'd show up for me if I asked her to. But I wanted it to be her choice. I had to find it in myself to be okay, with or without her.

I swung my legs over the edge of the bed and stretched. What was the appropriate way to greet the day that had the potential to change my life for better or worse? Before I could consider the answer, my phone rang. My heart leapt into my throat, and I said a silent prayer that it was McKenzie. But my hopes were squashed when I saw my realtor's name flashing across the screen.

"Hey, Darcey," I answered.

"Luca," she drawled. "Sorry to bug ya this mornin'. But I heard back from the homeowners, so I wanted to call you right away."

"You did?" I asked, holding my breath.

"I've got good news, hon. They want to take your offer."

"Oh my God," I said. "Are you serious?"

"As a heart attack," she replied. "And since you're paying cash, we can get this show on the road pretty much whenever you're ready."

"Right. Yes. Okay. So, how does this work since I'm staying here and their stuff is still in the house? Do I have to leave until we close on it?"

"Actually, no. The owner said they weren't attached to anything in the house. It was mostly stuff they bought used to furnish it as a rental property. They said you could keep everything, or they'd have it hauled off to Goodwill."

"No," I answered. "I'll keep it." The quirky treasures hidden within the walls of the hobbit house were part of its charm. It made me think of McKenzie and her penchant for loving thrifted items because of the stories they held.

"Well, they'll be pleased as punch to hear it, I'm sure," she said in her syrupy southern accent. "Listen, I know you've got a big day ahead of you. Everybody's talking about the interview."

My stomach lurched. Knowing it was news was one thing, but hearing it put so plainly was sobering.

"How about you touch base with me Monday and we'll set a date?" she suggested.

"Yeah, of course. That's a good idea," I said. "Thanks, Darcey. I appreciate it."

"And sugar, for what it's worth, I don't believe you've been given a fair shake. Not that what I think amounts to a hill of beans, but everybody has a past. We've all done things we're not proud of." She snickered, then dropped her voice low. "Heavens to Betsy, don't you dare ask me about the Miss Tennessee Iris pageant of '91. I definitely said some things about Miss Hickman County that I regret. Oh, and let's not forget the Ex-Lax I *accidentally* let slip into Putnam County's Diet Coke."

I stifled a laugh as she continued.

"Now, let me tell you, the good Lord humbled me real quick. I didn't even place in the top three," she said. "What I did ate me up inside for months, but my mama, God rest her soul, she told me something that stuck with me. First, she told me to quit my cryin' because I was gonna give myself premature wrinkles. But then she told me this gem. She said, 'Darcey, every day you wake up is the chance to be someone else. Someone yester-you would be proud of. So you can sit here bellyaching about what you wish you could change, or you can go out there and change it.'"

The corners of my mouth tugged into a smile. "I like that."

"I don't know how much of this nonsense is real, and if you ask me, that Tate McCreedy fellow looks like a clout chaser if I ever saw one," she said. "But even if every bit of it is true, honey, you can start over. You ain't gotta be who you were yesterday."

My throat tightened. "Thank you, Darcey."

"You're welcome, hon. I'm gonna go on, but I'll get with you Monday so we can buy you this house."

"Thanks again," I said, ending the call. My throat tightened, a surprising wave of emotion crashing over me. I was in the bedroom of my new home. The hobbit house was going to officially be mine.

Darcey's call and her words of wisdom, though unexpected and a little strange, felt like a sign that no matter how the day ended, I'd been given a chance at a new beginning. And I was going to take it.

"HOW ARE YOU HOLDING UP?" GRACE ASKED AS A WOMAN with a nose ring fluttered around where I sat on the couch, using some sort of device to check the lighting in my living room. The camera crew had rearranged the furniture so it faced away from the fireplace, turning the space into something reminiscent of a late-night talk show set. There were giant lights set up everywhere and a dozen people I didn't know buzzing around the place. It was completely unnerving.

"Um, honestly?" I answered. "I'm kinda freaking out."

"You're gonna be great," she assured me as the tech pretended she wasn't listening to every word of our conversation.

Grace grabbed my tattooed wrist and turned it so the ink faced me. She'd noticed it earlier in the day and asked me about it.

"Remember, your story deserves to be told," she said.

I nodded and swallowed hard as I looked up to see all of my friends enter the room. Antoni had come bearing a couple of shopping bags, having taken it upon himself to find me something suitable to wear for the interview.

Cash stood at my side and squeezed my shoulder. "You ready for this?"

"As ready as I'm gonna be," I muttered.

"I know it's gotta be weird having all these people in your house," Derek said.

"You're gonna be great," Jo assured me. "I don't know

Warren well, but he's got a pretty solid reputation in the industry."

"Wait, what? Warren?" Antoni wrinkled his nose. "As in, Warren Wright? Isn't he the one that all but buried that quarterback from New York?"

My eyes widened, and my stomach sank. "What?"

"Antoni," Liv said through gritted teeth as Jax scrubbed his hand over his face.

"Not helping, man," Dallas mumbled.

"Yes," Jo said, shooting eye daggers at Antoni before turning back to me. "But that guy had also been throwing games and gambling on them to the tune of millions. He did everything he was accused of and then some."

That didn't make me feel any better. I hadn't exactly been the golden boy of the music industry.

"Why don't we give Luca a moment to breathe," Ella suggested, noticing the panicked look on my face.

"I think that's a good idea," Katie added. "Y'all come into the kitchen and help me set up the food we brought."

Grace reached for the bags in Antoni's hands. "How about you give those to me?"

"Sorry," he whispered through gritted teeth before Nate steered him from the room.

"Oooh, you're in trouble," Ella said, filing out behind Antoni. "Grace is gonna eat you alive."

Once everyone was gone, Grace turned to the tech who was still lingering.

"Do you have what you need?" Grace asked, tapping her foot impatiently.

"Oh yes," she answered. "Sorry."

"Great." Grace grabbed my arm and pulled me down the hall toward the guest room that would be my makeshift dressing room. She closed the door behind us and placed the bags on the bed.

"Don't let any of that get in your head," she said. "What Antoni was talking about…that isn't the same thing. It's nowhere close."

I sank down onto the foot of the mattress and pushed my hands through my hair.

"But what if this ends just as badly?" I asked.

"I don't think it—"

"But what if it does?" I blurted, my palms starting to sweat.

"Breathe," she said, moving to sit beside me.

I released a long exhale, then she continued.

"It's not going to end like that, but even if it doesn't go the way we want it to, so what? At the end of the day, those who matter are going to love and support you, regardless. Remember, people can say whatever they want about you, but only you get to decide what's true."

I swallowed around the lump that formed in my throat.

"Listen," she said, "we can call this whole thing off right now if you don't want to do it."

"No. I'm gonna do it," I said with a determination I didn't quite feel. "I have to. I guess I just needed to panic a little first."

"I'm gonna step out so you can get dressed." She gave me a faint smile as she rose to her feet, sliding the closet doors open. "I hope you don't mind, but while you were busy talking to the associate producer earlier, I took the liberty of pulling a couple of alternate options in case you don't like what Antoni brought."

She stepped aside, and hanging there was the "To Write

Love on Her Arms" shirt McKenzie's mom had bought me at the thrift store, my leather jacket, and a pair of gray jeans.

I chuckled and shook my head. "You know me too well."

She shrugged. "I just know that if you want to show the world who you really are, you should feel like yourself."

She was right. I didn't even have to open the bags to know exactly what I'd be wearing.

"Thanks, Grace."

"I'll see you out there." She exited the room, leaving me alone with my thoughts.

I pulled the clothes Grace had collected from the closet and laid them across the bed, the message printed across the T-shirt staring back at me.

"Hope is Defiant."

If hope could defy the odds, maybe I could too.

THIRTY-THREE

McKenzie

It was a quarter to eight Friday night, and I was on my couch, surrounded by my mom, Kia, Jen, and Ravi. They'd come over to watch Luca's interview with me for moral support. Everyone had brought food and drinks to share, but the mood was decidedly somber. I'd been on edge all day. My thoughts had me wound up like one of those creepy jack-in-the-box toys, ready to strike at any moment. There were a few too many people around, so the cats had made themselves scarce.

"You need to eat something, sweetheart," my mom said, placing her hand on my leg. "How about I make you a plate?"

I shook my head. "I can't. Not now."

She nodded, but she couldn't hide the concern on her face. "How are you feeling?"

"Not great." I sighed. I'd done little besides go through the motions at work in the days since I'd talked to Luca. The letter I'd written to my brother earlier in the week had lifted a weight off my chest and given me a sense of clarity around his death that I hadn't had in…well, *ever*. But I still missed Luca.

I was already thinking about him before I saw the commercial for "Live and Uncut with Luca Sterling" while channel surfing Wednesday evening, but since then I'd been going out of my mind with worry. An interview this big could be a turning point in his career, but it also had the potential to go south. The only thing people loved more than a comeback was a total takedown. And if the worst *did* happen, would that send him running again?

"I just want him to be okay, Mom," I whispered, my voice choked with emotion.

"I know you do, Kenz." She pulled me close and kissed the top of my head. "I do too."

Another promo for the interview played on the TV screen, and my stomach clenched.

"Have you reached out to him at all?" Kia asked as she sat at my other side.

I shook my head, then buried it in my hands. "No. I've just been so fucking scared. I want to be with him, but I can't stop wondering if I'll lose him."

"Hey, that's perfectly understandable," Kia said. "After the kind of losses we've suffered, it's something we have to at least pause to consider. When Luca disappeared on you the way he did, it triggered something deeply painful for you. That's not to say his response to that kind of stress was irrational. He was in survival mode, but it still shook you up."

Ravi shifted in his chair nearby, and Jen propped herself against the armrest.

"After we lost our son, we struggled a lot with how to sit in our own grief while also holding space for each other," Jen said.

"And we'd been together for *years*," Ravi added. "It's not easy to be a support person when you're hurting too."

Jen nodded. "There was a point about a year after Carson died when I thought we might not make it. But we did therapy, separately and together. We learned to communicate better and realized we didn't have to *fix* things for each other. That we couldn't."

"Yep," Ravi agreed. "We were both putting a lot of pressure on the other to be everything—our comfort, our happiness. That's too much responsibility for one person. So our therapist encouraged us to work on strengthening our bonds with our family and friends."

"And that doesn't mean we don't love and support each other," Ravi said. "If anything, we're able to do it so much better because we're not carrying the load alone."

I stared ahead at the screen, not really seeing what was on it. There was still a part of me that felt like I had to be everything for Luca, but that wasn't true. Over the past week, he'd been able to lean on his friends. Though I didn't know the details of how he was doing, I knew he wouldn't have agreed to the interview if he didn't feel like he had the support he needed.

"I think the important part of any relationship is that you can't be two halves of a whole. You have to be whole all on your own," Jen said. "Of course, that doesn't sound as romantic."

My mom spoke up. "You know, I think I have to disagree with that last part. I think there's something really beautiful about not needing someone else to feel complete. It says you can survive without them, but you choose to spend your life together anyway because you love them so much."

Jen beamed and gazed down at Ravi, her eyes filled with love. "Aw, babe. Look. We *are* romantic."

"Your mom is right," Kia said. "Honestly, that's one of the

reasons I haven't gotten into another relationship. I haven't met anyone I want to choose."

Ravi held up a finger. "Not yet, anyway."

Kia shrugged. "Maybe I will, maybe I won't. But either way, I'm gonna be okay." She reached for my hand. "And so are you."

Our moment was interrupted by the intro music to the *Tonight with Warren Wright* show as images from the terrible press about Luca flashed across the screen. I couldn't even hear the voice-over through the sound of my heart thumping in my ears.

Kia squeezed my fingers, and my mom put an arm around me.

I held my breath as Warren's solemn face appeared, and I realized he was in the living room of the hobbit house.

"Welcome to *Tonight with Warren Wright*," he said. "We have a special version of our program for you this evening as I chat live with the performing artist everyone's talking about, Luca Sterling, right here in his own home. In this exclusive hour-long show, we're going to be taking a look at the rumors surrounding his musical comeback since his days as lead guitarist of the acclaimed rock band, Midnight in Dallas."

"Breathe," my mother whispered, rubbing my shoulder.

"We'll be talking about the Tate McCreedy controversy and accusations that Sterling is using mental health as a marketing ploy to engage new listeners." The camera widened to show Luca sitting on the couch. "We'll be diving deep into the rocker's past as music's resident wild child, and we'll even have a surprise message from someone in the superstar's past that will have everyone talking."

The rest of Warren's words faded away as I saw the expression on Luca's face. His eyes widened slightly, and his jaw tightened. Whatever this *surprise* was, he definitely didn't know about it.

"What kind of surprise?" my mom mumbled.

"I don't know." My mind whirled with the possibilities of who it could be. I doubted it was someone like Mr. Fink or Aunt Gladys, because I felt sure they'd have told Luca if it was them or someone they knew. Anyone even remotely close to him knew a surprise like that could throw him off his game.

I pulled my phone out of my pocket and texted Grace.

Any idea who this surprise person is?

Her reply came only seconds later.

No clue, but Luca looks scared. 😢 *Jo's trying to see if she can find out something.*

"Shit," I muttered. "Grace said they don't know what this is about either."

I shoved my fingers through my hair and took in a shaky breath as the program went to commercial.

"I should've been there," I said, my voice a hoarse whisper. "I didn't even send him a text to let him know I was thinking about him, that I was in his corner."

"Well, what are you waiting for?" Kia asked.

"I can't text him now," I cried. "He's on national television."

"No, you can't text him." Kia rose to her feet and held out a hand to me. "But it's not too late to show up. If we leave now, we can be there by the middle of the interview. And whatever this surprise is, you know they're gonna save it for the end."

I took her hand and jumped up. "You're right."

My mom, Jen, and Ravi all stood.

"You guys don't have to go with me," I said.

"We're going," Kia insisted. "We want to be there for you."

"And Luca's important to you, which means he's important to us," Jen added.

My mom nodded. "If that Warren Wright has some sort of tricks up his sleeve, I'll take him down myself. Give that jerk a real story to report on."

"Come on," Ravi said, starting for the door. "I'll drive."

We quickly made our way outside, filing into Ravi and Jen's SUV. My mom placed her hand on my knee as Ravi turned onto the street.

I reached for my phone and typed out a text to Grace.

I'm on my way.

THIRTY-FOUR

Luca

BEADS OF SWEAT FORMED ALONG THE BACK OF MY NECK AS Warren Wright continued his line of questioning. It started off simple enough with him asking how I was feeling and how I'd been handling the onslaught of press. But with every response, my mind wandered back to the promise of the surprise message from my past. Nobody who actually knew me would agree to something like that without giving me a heads-up because they'd know how important an interview like this was.

That meant it was someone who didn't know me at all, which could cause this entire thing to go up in flames.

"I want to talk to you a little about your past," Warren said, crossing one leg over the other. He was a tall and imposing figure with his salt-and-pepper hair and his tailored blue suit. "During your time with Midnight in Dallas you were known for being a bit...wild."

I nodded. "Yeah. I was."

"You were often photographed drinking alcohol, which on its own isn't necessarily a bad thing," he began. "But those pictures appeared alongside tales of drunken brawls and unruly behavior. It's often been speculated that you may have a substance abuse problem. Would you say that's a fair assessment?"

Between the heat from Warren's interrogation and the burn of the set lights, I would've given my left nut for a glass of water.

"It was," I admitted. "There was a long period of time when I drank heavily. Nearly every night. I used to pop pills like they were candy and chase them down with tequila. But I haven't had a drink or taken anything that wasn't prescribed by a doctor in over two years. I stopped because I saw myself going down a path that scared me. My thoughts were dark enough without the shadows cast by the alcohol and drugs."

"Hmm," Warren said. "But there were still some pictures taken of you within that two-year period where you were spotted with a flask in hand."

I shifted in my seat and cleared my throat. "Yes, there were. But that flask didn't have any alcohol in it."

"What was in it, then?"

"Water. Sometimes soda."

"I think people are going to find that hard to believe." Warren leaned closer, his brows drawn. "If you didn't want people to think you had a problem with alcohol, why carry a flask out in public?"

"At the time, I didn't care what people thought of me," I said. "Or at least that's what I told myself. Look, it didn't matter if I carried around a bottle of water or a Starbucks cup —people were going to say what they wanted. There was this preconceived idea of who and what I was, and I didn't feel like fighting it. I let people think what they liked."

"Do you have regrets about that?" he asked.

"Yeah, I do."

Warren folded his hands together in his lap. "You were also known for the seemingly revolving door of beautiful women you kept on your arm. In fact, it was a running joke in the tabloids. They called you 'One Strike Sterling.' Did you know that?"

I shook my head. "I didn't know about the nickname, but I was aware of my...reputation."

"In the past couple of weeks, a few stories have come out from various women who've said they had encounters with you over the years. They're saying you didn't bother to learn their names, that you never attempted to get to know them." He paused, his eyes narrowed. "Is there any truth in that?"

"Yes," I confessed.

"How many of these types of encounters would you say you've had over the years?"

What the fuck kind of question is that?! Is he really asking for my body count on national television?

"Honestly? I don't know." I ran my thumb along the edge of my jaw. "I didn't respect myself, let alone anyone else. That's not an excuse for my behavior, but I didn't have the emotional capacity to give more to anyone."

"Did these women know that?"

"I can't speak to what they did or didn't know, but I was always very clear about what my expectations were for these encounters."

"Sex," he said, filling in the blank.

My answer came out almost inaudibly. "Yes."

"Now, I do want to be clear for our viewers that there have been no allegations of sexual misconduct. But I think some of these women had hopes that their experiences with you might lead to something more." His eyes bore into mine like a laser.

"Do you have any regrets over how you handled those situations?"

"Yeah," I said. "I mean, being in a band, these kinds of things happen, but I took it to an extreme. Just like I did with the booze, I was always looking to numb my feelings."

"And what were you feeling, exactly?"

I pressed my tongue onto the roof of my mouth. "Lonely. Sad."

"Many would argue that you were at the peak of success, surrounded by fans who worshipped you and you had no reason to feel lonely."

"Being worshipped isn't the same as being known. Being understood." I swallowed hard. "Being loved."

Warren nodded. "I think that's a poignant perspective on the parasocial relationships people develop with their favorite celebrities and influencers these days."

"Yes," I agreed. "There's so much more to me than what people see in the tabloids or on social media…or even when they have a two-minute interaction with me at the airport."

"Do you feel people have misjudged you?"

"I do. Some of that is my own fault. In not caring what people thought about me, I perpetuated an image that was no longer an accurate representation of who I am." I dug my fingers into the rip on the thigh of my jeans. "I can't deny that version of me existed. I did a lot of stuff I regret. I wasn't a person I was proud of. But people can change."

"And you believe you've changed?"

"I know I have."

Warren studied me for a beat. "I want to talk to you about the breakup of Midnight in Dallas. You were a part of that band for most of your adult life. I imagine that split was hard on you."

I scratched my neck. "It was."

"What happened after that?"

"After we called it quits, everyone started going their separate ways. It hit me hard because the guys from the band are like my family, and I felt like I was losing them. That's when I started to withdraw."

"Several months passed last year with no photos taken of you," Warren began. "We scoured the internet and couldn't find a single one. Why is that?"

"Because I didn't leave my apartment."

"At all?"

"At all," I echoed.

"Why not?"

I swallowed hard. "Because I felt like the world would be better off if I disappeared."

"Did anyone come looking for you?"

"No," I answered. "I told everyone I was traveling, so they had no idea where I was."

"Did you ever have thoughts of harming yourself?"

"It was more that I just wanted the pain to stop."

"What was the turning point that made you realize you were in serious trouble and needed to get help?" he asked, his voice sincere.

The corners of my eyes burned. "I hadn't been answering my phone. In fact, I'd let the thing die. Then one night at the end of September, out of nowhere, it powered on. I still don't know how or why, but it did. And when it did, I found a bunch of voicemails from my friends, and I started listening to them. That was when I realized they missed me. I'd assumed they'd forgotten about me because *I* wanted to forget about me, but they hadn't. They wanted me around."

"What did you do then?" he questioned.

"I started leaving messages for therapists, and I went to see the first one who called me back. She's still my therapist today," I said. "She's the one who encouraged me to come back to Nashville to be close to my friends. She referred me to a psychiatrist who prescribed medication for my depression. I started channeling my feelings into writing songs, and" —I took in a breath— "I fell in love."

"Wow," he said. "That's big. Had you ever been in love before?"

"No. Not till her."

"Who is she?" he asked.

"I won't answer that," I said. "She's not in the public eye, and I'm not going to subject her to that kind of scrutiny."

Warren chuckled. "Fair enough. What can you tell me about her?"

A series of mental snapshots I'd taken of McKenzie during our time together flashed through my mind. Dancing with her at Basement East. When she'd given me Randy McNutt. The way she'd looked walking down the aisle at Dallas and Katie's wedding.

"She's the best thing that ever happened to me," I replied with a faint smile.

Warren nodded, then turned to the camera. "We'll have more with Luca Sterling when we come back."

THIRTY-FIVE

McKenzie

"Come on in. The break's almost over," Grace whispered, leading us into the foyer of the hobbit house. Even though I still had my key, I'd texted, letting her know we'd arrived so we could come in without disturbing the show.

"What did I miss?" I asked once we were inside.

She looked weary. "Let's just say nobody will be accusing Warren Wright of going easy on him."

My chest squeezed. "How's he doing?"

"He's been handling it well," Grace answered as we made our way closer to the living room. "But I can tell he's rattled."

"They still won't tell you who this surprise person is?" my mom asked.

Grace shook her head. "Production won't crack, so it must be someone big."

"Thirty seconds," someone called.

"You go," Kia said. "We'll hang out here so we're not in the way."

Jen squeezed my arm. "You know where we are if you need backup."

Grace grabbed my hand, guiding me past Katie, Dallas, and the rest of Luca's friends, standing me right in Luca's line of sight just as the booming voice began counting down from ten.

His eyes found mine, and a million unsaid words passed silently between us. His face relaxed slightly as I gave him an encouraging nod, letting him know he had this and I was right there in his corner.

"I love you," I mouthed as Warren Wright began to speak.

"And we're back, live and uncut with Luca Sterling," he said. "I want to shift gears to this incident with Nashville singer/songwriter Tate McCreedy. There's been a video circulating that was taken by a witness to an altercation the two of you had a few months ago. We're going to show the viewers at home this clip, and then I want to get your take on what happened."

There was a beat of silence, and even though there was no video playing for me, I remembered the night vividly. I'd seen the clip and knew how much that loser had altered the story, leaving out the part where I'd punched him for harassing Luca and he'd nearly hit me.

"Watching this, it seems like you and Mr. McCreedy had words before you pushed him into a wall," Warren said. "Is that how it happened?"

"No," Luca answered. "There's a lot you don't get to see on that video."

Warren nodded. "Walk me through what happened that night."

Luca began describing the events and how they'd *actually* unfolded, including the insults Tate had hurled at him, my reaction, and the way Tate had raised his fist at me which led to the clip everyone had seen.

Warren nodded again. "Wow, that's quite a different picture than the one Mr. McCreedy has painted. Why didn't you attempt to set the record straight before now?"

"Part of it was because I fell back into that thought pattern where I felt like nobody would believe my side of the story because they'd already decided who I was," he replied. "But there was also a part of me that started to wonder if I somehow deserved what was happening."

"How so?" Warren asked.

"I thought that even if I didn't do what he said, maybe I'd not been as nice as I should have been," Luca said. "When you've lived your life letting people tell you who you are, you eventually start to believe them. As all this stuff started coming out, it sent me spiraling backward."

Warren steepled his fingers. "How are you coping now?"

"Um." Luca exhaled slowly. "One day at a time. I've finally realized I'll likely always have depression. I'll probably always struggle with my sense of self-worth. This isn't something that goes away so much as something I have to learn how to manage and live with."

"And I imagine there's a certain amount of *un*learning you have to do too," Warren said.

"Absolutely," Luca began. "There are so many false narratives we start to believe about ourselves. Maybe they come from society, or sometimes, they come from people in our lives. A lot of my issues stem from the rejection I felt as a kid."

Luca's eyes became misty as he continued. "My mother was an alcoholic who couldn't be bothered to take care of me, and my dad was in prison. He never tried to have any sort of relationship with me. Neither of them were capable of being the parents I needed, and instead of seeing that for what it was, I internalized it. I felt like if I'd just been a better kid, they would have tried harder—that maybe they would have loved me."

Warren paused for dramatic effect, allowing Luca's words to hang in the air like a dense fog.

"Do you wish things could've been different with your family?" Warren finally asked.

"Of course, I do," Luca replied. "But they're not, and it doesn't do me any good to think about what might have been."

"Luca, I know we've been teasing a surprise message for you from someone in your past," Warren said. His face was unreadable, and I held my breath. "When we started promoting this show, our production team received an email from your father."

What???

The color drained from Luca's face, and I could see his throat working to swallow.

"He's out on parole now, and I had the chance to speak with him via telephone earlier today," Warren went on. "I asked him if he had anything he'd like to say to you, and we're going to play that audio for you and our viewers now."

Grace reached for my hand, and we exchanged a worried glance as a man's voice filled our ears.

"Luca, son, it's your father," he said, his southern lilt slurring slightly. "God, kiddo, you're a grown man now. I know things were tough back when you were young. You were always causing trouble, and I guess you got that from me. I shoulda had more patience with ya. I didn't try the way I should've back then, but I'd like to now that I'm out, you know? But I just…I need a little help getting on track. It's hard to get a job when you're as old as me and been in and out of jail as much as I have. I ain't getting any younger, son, and I'd like to see you. It's been too long."

The audio ended, and Luca's eyes were glossy with unshed tears, his pale face frozen in shock. My blood turned to ice.

"How does that make you feel?" Warren asked, his voice laced with innocence as though he hadn't single-handedly reopened a traumatic wound in front of the entire country.

I wanted to throttle this asshole.

Luca's mouth opened but no words came out, and a moment passed before he finally spoke.

"I, uh, I'm stunned," he said. "That's the first time I've even heard my dad's voice since I was seven years old. This is…it's a lot."

"You said earlier you wished things could have been different with your family," Warren began. "And now they can be. It sounds like your father wants a chance to start over."

Even from where I stood, I could see Luca's hands tremble, and it filled me with anger.

"That's not…that's not how that works," Luca choked out.

Warren pinned him with a challenging stare. "You said yourself that people can change. It seems like you want people to give you grace, but shouldn't you be willing to do the same? Don't you want to at least meet with him? See what he has to say?"

A tear slipped down Luca's cheek, sending me over the edge. How *dare* this guy use Luca's own words to gaslight him. Before I could stop myself, I stormed onto the set and sat beside him, taking his hand in mine.

"Are you okay?" I whispered.

Luca's jaw clenched, and I knew he was just trying to hold it together. I squeezed his fingers.

"Excuse me," Warren snipped. "Who are you?"

I whipped my head around to face him. "You've got some nerve ambushing him with something like that on live television. What was the goal here? Did you think you were gonna facilitate some happy family reunion?" I tilted my head and tapped a finger to my chin. "Or were you hoping Luca would decline his dad's half-baked offer that's *clearly* a cash grab so you could still paint him out to be some hypocritical villain?"

Warren's eyes darted from side to side, and he tried to speak, but I cut him off, unable to stop the words from pouring out.

"I'm not done," I spat. "Your first clue this guy hasn't changed a bit should've been that he reached out to a TV show to pull this stunt instead of trying to make amends with his son personally. His beautiful, resilient, loving son that he is worse for not knowing. Frankly, even if his dad has changed, that doesn't negate the years of trauma he caused, and that's not something that can be overcome in the span of a twenty-second voice message."

"Cut," someone yelled off camera. "We need to go to commercial *now*."

"I…what…" Warren's cheeks turned red. "Who the hell *is* this girl?"

I was ready to tell him exactly who I was, but Luca spoke first, his voice thick with emotion.

"She's the love of my life." He gave me a soft smile before shifting his focus to Warren. "And you need to get the fuck out of my house before I run out of grace and kick your ass."

THE PRODUCTION CREW AND WARREN WRIGHT PACKED UP with lightning speed, but not before Jo ripped them a new one. A few minutes later, everyone was chatting in the kitchen of the hobbit house like old friends. It felt good, seeing both our worlds collide.

"Hey," Luca said, reaching for my hand. "Can we talk for a second?"

"Of course." I smiled up at him and let him lead me out to the garden.

Once we were outside, our breath appeared in front of us like tiny clouds in the cold night air. I shivered and he pulled me close, sliding my arms beneath his jacket.

He kissed the top of my head. "Thank you. For being here."

"I'm sorry I didn't come sooner, I—"

"You did nothing wrong," he said. "What matters is that we're together now. And I promise you, I'm not running anymore. I know I've got a long road ahead of me, but I want to walk it with you by my side."

"I want that too," I whispered. "This whole thing made me realize how much unresolved grief I have for Brennan. The guilt I've been carrying around, this desire to be able to fix everything, has been eating me alive. I have a lot of work to do, but I want to do it all with you."

"I'm gonna be right here next to you, McKenzie. For as long as you'll let me," he promised, rubbing his hands in slow circles over my back.

The laughter of our friends filtered outside, and we stood there in each other's arms for a moment, soaking it all in.

Every person in that house had shown up for us, and I knew beyond a shadow of a doubt, they always would.

"You know, we're pretty lucky," he said. "And we've got some pretty great friends. I'm glad I finally got to meet Kia, Jen, and Ravi."

I nodded. "They're the best."

"I was thinking maybe I could have a Sunday dinner here in the new house before everyone has to go back home." He gazed down at me. "You think they'd want to come?"

My eyes widened. "Wait. What? The new house?"

"Yep." A grin spread over his mouth. "I'm buying the hobbit house."

I squealed. "Are you serious?"

"And you know what the best part is?"

My mind was reeling. Luca was going to be living here.

"What?" I asked, the corners of my mouth curling upward.

"I get to keep everything in it," he said. "I would have hated for Randy McNutt to feel out of place with all his stuff gone."

"You're really moving here?"

He pressed his lips to my forehead. "I told you. No more running."

"I love you," I whispered, holding him closer.

He tucked a piece of hair behind my ear. "I love you too."

The back door creaked open, and Grace poked her head out.

"There you are," she said, her voice chipper and excited. "The internet is blowing up over you guys. Do you want to hear what they're saying?"

Luca shook his head. "You know what? I think I'm good."

THIRTY-SIX

Luca

A year and a half later…

"IF THIS WHOLE MUSIC THING DOESN'T WORK OUT, WE COULD always turn the house into a wedding venue," McKenzie joked as she helped me with my tie. Earl Grey and Binx watched with a mixture of amusement and annoyance from the bed. They were unenthusiastic about the amount of people running around their home for Grace's wedding and had decided to take cover in our bedroom.

"I'm not so sure the kids would be on board with that," I said, gesturing toward the cats curled up on the comforter. The windows were open, beckoning the cool October breeze inside.

"Well, they have to grow up and get jobs eventually," she joked. "We might as well make it a family business."

"There." She finished with my tie, straightening it one last time.

I caught her left hand in mine and brought it to my lips, ghosting a kiss over the vintage black sapphire ring on her finger. I'd found it tucked away inside one of the cases in a little antique jewelry store while I was on tour last summer and knew she had to have it. I gave it to her after I won my first Grammy earlier this year. It was rare and beautiful just like her.

"So, what do you think?" she asked, twirling so I could fully admire her in the navy bridesmaid dress she wore. McKenzie had been thrilled when Grace asked her to be in the wedding. They'd become close since I started working with Grace. There were many times when we were on the road that I got booted off phone calls with my own girlfriend so the two could chat, but I didn't mind.

"Gorgeous," I answered.

She smiled and turned so her back was facing me, her hair gathered to one side.

"You mind zipping me up?" she asked.

I obliged, then pressed my lips into the crook of her neck and began to slowly work my way up to her ear.

She spun on her heels and jabbed a finger into my chest. "I said to zip the dress, not make me want to take it back off."

"So you're saying you don't want to take it back off?"

"I'm *saying* Jo is already on the warpath because the DJ was half an hour late. She won't think too kindly if we are as well, especially since we live here," she said. "And since she's seventeen months pregnant, I'd really like to not piss her off."

"How did Jo become the resident wedding planner, anyway?" I asked, sitting on the edge of the bed to slide on my socks and shoes.

"I don't know," she answered, slipping her feet into a pair of heels. "I know she wanted to do it for Katie, but this time, I think she's just doing it to torture herself."

Derek and Jo had gotten engaged late last spring and were

planning for a summer wedding the following year, but when they'd discovered they were expecting, they decided to push their nuptials out another year.

"We better get out there," she said. "It'll be starting soon."

But I didn't budge, smiling as I took her in. She was so fucking beautiful. And it wasn't just because of how stunning she looked. It was something more, something deeper. She had a glow about her these days. She was happy.

"What's that look for?" she asked.

I shook my head. "Just enjoying the view."

"Come on," she said, reaching for my hands to pull me to my feet. "Let's go."

We exited the bedroom to a flurry of activity.

"Jonathan, Chloe," Liv called. "No running in the house."

Jax was at the end of the hall, waiting to intercept them as we headed toward the back door.

"Has anyone seen Cash?" Jo asked, her eyes frantic.

"Um, Jo?" Cash said from behind her with a wave. "I'm right here."

"I'd lose my head if it wasn't attached," Jo muttered, turning around. "Grace is ready for you."

Cash took in a deep breath and blew it out, his eyes already misty. "I guess this is it."

"All right." Jo clapped her hands together. "Everyone who isn't a part of the wedding party needs to be outside. She scurried off, her heels clicking against the floor.

"That means you better scoot," McKenzie said, smoothing her hands over her dress. "I gotta go grab the flower girl basket for Betty."

"I'll see you out there," I said, kissing McKenzie's cheek before heading outside behind Jax and the kids.

A string quartet played over the sound of hushed voices

as the autumn sun cast a soft golden veil over everything it touched. The scene was so perfect, it almost didn't look real.

I took a seat beside Derek where he sat with his and Jo's daughter, Addison.

"I think Jo missed her calling as an event planner," I said to him as I took in the way she'd transformed my garden, making the already magical space feel like something plucked straight out of a fairytale.

Derek chuckled. "I'm not sure any of us would survive that."

I laughed as I glanced around at the faces surrounding me. There were a few I didn't recognize beyond knowing they were some of Grace's clients and childhood friends. But then there were the ones I did know. The ones I loved.

Jax and the kids sat in the row in front of me, beside Antoni and his husband Nate, who was holding the six-month-old baby they'd adopted. Dallas and Katie were on their other side, oohing and aahing over the little boy.

Grace's soon-to-be husband, Sam, stood beneath the archway in front of us, flanked by the officiant and his groomsmen. Sam had been around long enough to know what he was getting into, officially joining our crazy little family. But I hoped he also knew just how lucky he was.

The quartet began to play their own rendition of my song "Coming Home" as the bridal party started down the aisle. I'd been touched when Grace told me she wanted it to be a part of her big day. In the time she'd been working with me, we'd grown closer. She'd become like a little sister to me, but more than that, she was my friend.

Betty scattered her petals to a chorus of *awws* as she made her way toward the front, hand in hand with Ella, who was already crying. Liv followed, dabbing at the corners of her eyes with a tissue.

Then came McKenzie. Her eyes locked on mine as she made her way down the aisle, and she smiled. My focus was drawn to her as the rest of the wedding party filed in. God, she took my breath away. Everything about her—every look, every laugh—made life better. I'd struggled with my share of dark moments over the last year and a half. We both had. But with the support of our friends, our family, and each other, we'd made it through.

The bridal march began to play, and we all stood as Grace and Cash emerged from the house. I clasped my hands together, my thumb grazing over the inside of my wrist where the semicolon tattoo was hidden beneath my jacket. It was something I'd done a lot since I'd gotten it. The tiny symbol reminded me of the pages in my story I'd overcome and the hard-won chapters that gave way to this amazing life I now called mine. And when things inevitably became hard again, it would be there to remind me that sometimes there is pain before beauty, and that both things can, and often do, coexist. But above all else, it was a reminder that my story deserved to be continued.

Epilogue

GRACE

Five and a half years later…

"How you feeling, mama?" Jo asked from across the table, sipping her punch.

I scrunched my nose. "Like I hope this baby doesn't come before the Grammys next weekend." Luca was nominated for his seventh award, and his record, *To Be Continued*, was up for album of the year.

It was the last weekend of January, and I was less than a month away from my due date. We hadn't intended to push my baby shower out *quite* this far, but life had been more than a little chaotic for all of us. Liv and Jax had been on the road for their farewell tour, while Katie's Kitchen had opened its second location in November with McKenzie James as owner. Then, of course, Sam and I had been all over the place. I'd been traveling with Luca and a few of my other clients, and

Sam had been on the European leg of his own tour. When all of us ladies realized we had this *one* weekend collectively free, we pounced on it.

McKenzie had offered to host the event at her restaurant, and with Jo's help, they'd decorated the place beautifully.

"I've got a good seamstress if you need an emergency alteration," Liv said.

My mom returned to her seat, placing a plate of appetizers in front of me with a fresh glass of punch, as my little sister's small hands massaged my shoulders.

I chuckled. "You guys are spoiling me."

Another exciting thing that had happened over the past few months was my mom, Cash, and Betty had moved back to Nashville. Cash still made frequent trips to LA, but the second he and Mom found out they were going to be grandparents, they'd started packing and bought a place near our family home where Sam and I still lived and would raise Maeve.

My heart swelled as I thought about my daughter. It still seemed surreal that in a few short weeks, Sam and I would have a child of our own, and she would get to grow up with a whole extended family that already loved her beyond measure.

"So, *Grandma*." McKenzie elbowed my mom. "How are you feeling about all this?"

My mom laughed. "I *know* you're not talking to me. Because I will only be answering to Gigi."

"That's not what the sweatshirt I got you says." McKenzie lifted her brows and crossed her arms. "In fact, I'm pretty sure it says 'World's Best Grandma'."

"And that sweatshirt is buried in the bottom of my closet where it belongs," Mom said with mock disapproval.

"You wore it yesterday," Betty said with a giggle, and we all laughed.

Mom's mouth fell open. "Betty!"

"I don't even have kids, and I live like a grandma," Katie joked. "*The Golden Girls* marathons, knitting Christmas stockings, in bed by nine. It's actually pretty great."

"So, wait, how is everyone here connected?" my friend, Reah, asked. Reah was the assistant I'd hired six months earlier who'd be filling in for me while I was on maternity leave. We worked closely together and were around the same age, so we'd become fast friends.

"You guys are all related, right?" she continued, trying to connect the dots.

I nodded. "Not by blood, but we're definitely a family."

Reah smiled, tucking a dark curl behind her ear. "How did y'all meet?"

"It's a long story," I said, tracing circles over my round belly before my mom chimed in.

"It all started with a Midnight in Dallas meet and greet for this one's birthday," she said, touching my arm.

The next thing I knew, everyone was jumping in, picking up where the others left off, telling Reah the story of our family. As I listened, it hit me just how deeply intertwined we all were. It was crazy to think that this life wouldn't exist, and none of us would be here if Liv, my mom, and I hadn't gone to that one single event—one night that began the chain linking us all together.

I'd like to think we would've found each other, anyway— that these souls were always meant to become my home, my safe harbor. But I'm not sure. Perhaps it was part of some predestined plan or maybe it was all just a coincidence. As I gazed around at the faces surrounding me, I knew we'd all ended up exactly where we were supposed to be. It didn't matter where life took us or how busy we got because this… these people…would always be home.

Learn more about To Write Love on Her Arms by visiting
www.twloha.com.

Acknowledgments

There are so many pieces of me buried within these pages. It's the most personal book I've written to date. But this story and mine wouldn't exist if someone hadn't stepped up during my darkest hour. Thank you, P. In the words of Taylor Swift, *there wouldn't be this if there hadn't been you.*

This book—this series—would be nothing without the love, support, and wisdom of my critique partner and one of my dearest friends, author Jen Davis. She's been there since page one, and I hope we'll still be writing together a hundred years from now. Love you times a million shrimp emojis, Jen!

Kate, my treasured alpha reader and friend, I couldn't do this without you.

Reah, I always wanted to live right down the road from my best friend, and now I do. I'm always grateful for your thoughtful feedback, but I'm even more thankful for the wine nights, the reality TV binges, memes, and coffee dates. Love you so much!

Nicole, my SSMATBMDFFAATE. I don't know if I would have ever picked up writing again if it hadn't been for you. Thank you for always dreaming bigger for me than I did for myself.

Brooke with Nashville Center for Trauma and Psychotherapy for sensitivity reading Luca and McKenzie's story.

Allie B and Kayla, you both have been instrumental to this process, and I'm so grateful for your insight and your friendship.

Elle Maxwell, as always, you knocked it out of the park. Thank you for making the Midnight in Dallas series shine.

Chris, my editor for this project, for not firing me when I fall off the face of the earth.

Stacey Graham, my agent, for always responding to my unhinged emails.

Sydney and Lauren, team MID forever!

Mrs. Ross, the first person who encouraged me to use my voice.

Love and hugs to my book club ladies. And special thanks to Kia, Ali, Brooke, Erin, Jena, Sammi Jo, Danielle, Kerry, Abby J, Sophie, Eve, Sam, Abbey, Tiffany, Christana, Leigh Ann, Kaley, Lauren. And to my amazing street team, y'all are the best.

Shout-out to Steamy Lit Con, Romance Con, and Midwest Bookish Fest for letting me crash your parties.

Mom and Dad, thank you for the many library and book-store trips. Love you both.

To my fur babies for being the best writing partners in the world.

To my husband, thank you for putting up with my late-night rants and worry sessions, for always being willing to answer the weirdest questions possible with no context, and for supporting this little dream of mine and making it ours. You're still my favorite love story.

And to my readers, thank you for making it possible for me to do what I love. Not a day goes by that I don't think about how grateful I am to each and every one of you. We've been through a lot together, and with any luck, this is just the beginning.

Melissa Grace is the author of the *Midnight in Dallas* romcom series, and her freelance work has been featured in publications like *Medium, Thought Catalog,* and *The Mighty*. She resides just outside of Nashville, Tennessee with her husband and many fur children. When she's not writing, she can often be found reading or curled up in her bed with snacks like a trash panda, avoiding simple tasks because of her anxiety.

Find Melissa online @heymelissagrace on all social media platforms.